JILL SORENSON

FREEFALL

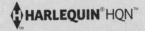

HARLEQUIN® HQN™

Recycling programs
for this product may
not exist in your area.

ISBN-13: 978-0-373-77795-2

FREEFALL

Printed in U.S.A.

Praise for

JILL SORENSON

"Sorenson fuels this fast-paced romantic thriller
with nonstop adrenaline.... This twisty rollercoaster ride
keeps the pages turning."
—*Publishers Weekly* on *Aftershock* (Starred Review)

"Sorenson makes her characters realistic,
flawed, and appealing. Deftly handled violent action
and red herrings rush this thriller to a believable ending."
—*Publishers Weekly* on *The Edge of Night*

"Taut with emotion, suspense and danger. Sorenson expertly
weaves the two stories into a heart-wrenching conclusion."
—*RT Book Reviews* on *The Edge of Night*

"One of the best books of the year...
nonstop, heart-pounding excitement."
—*RT Book Reviews* on *Stranded with Her Ex*,
Top Pick! 4.5 stars

"It was definitely hot. Sooo hot. Jill Sorenson is
my new favorite romantic-suspense author!"
—*USA TODAY* bestselling author Victoria Dahl
on *Crash into Me*

**Also available from Jill Sorenson
and Harlequin HQN**

AFTERSHOCK

For Ruthie

FREEFALL

CHAPTER ONE

H<small>OPE SMILED AT</small> her sister in the passenger seat as she started the Jeep's engine. "This is going to be so much fun."

Faith groaned, glancing out the window. The sparkly insignia on her D&G sunglasses glinted in the morning light. She wasn't an early riser or a nature lover, so she didn't share Hope's enthusiasm.

"You can't bring those sunglasses on the raft," Hope said.

Faith removed them with an exaggerated sigh. Her eyes were brown, like Hope's. When they were younger, strangers used to ask if they were twins. They'd shared the same heart-shaped face and chocolate-colored curls. Although Hope kept her hair natural, Faith's was straight and blond, courtesy of the upscale salon where she worked.

Faith checked her appearance in the mirror. "I look hideous in your clothes."

"You look adorable."

Hope had let Faith borrow the shorts, tank top and hiking boots. None of her sister's chic L.A. outfits were appropriate for a whitewater adventure. Faith had spruced up the ensemble with pigtail braids, and she wore her own skimpy bikini underneath. She'd balked at the idea of donning one of Hope's demure swimsuits.

Faith flipped up the visor and stashed her sunglasses in the glove compartment. "Remind me why I agreed to this."

"Because you planned our vacation last year."

"And it was fabulous. There's nothing wrong with relaxing on the beach."

Hope drove down the bumpy dirt road toward the Kaweah River, humming along with the song on the radio. She spent a week with her sister every summer, and she always looked forward to it. Whether they were lounging in the sun or hiking through the Sierras, Hope enjoyed Faith's company.

"This weather is perfect for rafting," Hope said. The heat wave that had struck several days ago showed no signs of letting up.

"If there aren't any cute guys in our group, I'm jumping overboard."

Hope smirked at the threat. Faith had broken up with her boyfriend several months ago, and she'd seemed melancholy ever since. Her sister tended to treat men like passing fashions, easily discarded. But she'd been different with Tom, more committed. More upset when things didn't work out.

"I've met our guide, and he's gorgeous," she said. He was also gay, but that didn't matter. Faith would flirt with him anyway. "Three of the rafters are college guys, probably jocks. You have to be strong to handle a Class Five run."

Faith's eyes narrowed. "Class Five?"

"Don't worry. The rest of us are experienced paddlers."

"Hope! You know I hate exercise."

"You hate sweat."

"Exactly."

"Not much chance of that, with water splashing you all day."

Faith made a noise of protest. "This reminds me of the time you made me hike up that huge mountain. I almost died."

"You did not," Hope said. "Physical activity is better for you than dieting. You'll get a tan and look great in your bikini."

"I don't like jocks."

"You liked Tom."

"College guys are immature."

"Not always. They could be…grad students."

Faith wrinkled her nose.

"You're not usually this choosy."

"What's *that* supposed to mean?"

"Nothing."

"Are you calling me a slut?"

"No! You're just…free-spirited." If anything, Hope was jealous of Faith's casual attitude about sex. Her flashy self-confidence attracted men in droves. "I admire that."

"You should go out more."

"I know," she said, sighing. Hope was only eighteen months older than Faith, and they'd always been close, but their personalities were nothing alike. Faith didn't have a shy bone in her body. Hope was quiet and reserved. Although she wanted to meet someone special, she worked around the clock and rarely socialized.

This winter, Faith had begged her to join an online dating service. Instead, she'd gone to the local watering hole and bolstered her courage with white wine. She'd engaged in her first one-night stand—what a disaster.

"I'm still recovering from my last attempt."

"That guy was a jerk," Faith said.

"Yes."

"Where does he live?"

"In Long Pine," Hope said, naming the closest town. "Why?"

"Let's toilet-paper his house."

With a low laugh, Hope pulled into the Kaweah Campsite on the east side of the park. "That wouldn't be environmentally responsible."

"You're such a buzz kill."

"We could use biodegradable toilet paper," she said.

"How about flowers?"

Hope laughed again, turning off the engine. Their parents owned an organic plant nursery, and one of their mother's favorite sayings was "give your enemy a flower." The sisters had rebelled against her peacenik philosophies in different ways. Faith, by valuing material things. Hope, by becoming a gun-toting park ranger. She wished she could carry a bouquet of daisies to fight crime, but some situations required brute force.

Hope couldn't wait for the three-day rafting trip to start. She hadn't enjoyed a full weekend off in months. Even as they waited in the shade for the whitewater guide, her work radio trilled with an emergency message.

"All rangers please respond for SAR."

Hope had been a ranger at Sierra National Park for five years. Her job was part law enforcement, part nature guide, and she loved it. Although she was supposed to be on vacation for the next week, she couldn't ignore a call for a search-and-rescue operation. In an area with huge cliffs, swift-moving rivers and sprawling forests, accidents happened. Rock climbers fell. Hikers got lost in the woods. Children became drowning victims.

"Don't you dare answer that," Faith warned.

"I have to," she said. As a district ranger, she was required to stay in radio contact and respond to emergencies. She picked up the receiver to speak with the dispatch office. "This is Ranger Banning."

"Hope, we have word of a single-engine plane down at Angel Wings."

Her stomach clenched with unease. "Any survivors?"

"There's been no radio communication from the craft. A climber saw the crash a few hours ago and came into the station to report it."

"Which station?"

"Mineral King."

Hope swore under her breath. Mineral King was her station, and she was more familiar with Angel Wings than the other rangers. She also had experience with high-angle rescue, which this operation might require. "I'll be right there."

"You can't be serious," Faith said.

She wavered, torn between loyalties. Both her sister and her job were extremely important to her.

"Why can't someone else go?"

"I don't know if anyone else is available. The guy covering my station isn't qualified to organize a search-and-rescue."

The busy season didn't officially start until July, and it was the first week of June. They only had twelve year-round staff members with law enforcement badges. During an emergency situation, all rangers in the area were ordered to check in. Hope had to step up to this responsibility or take the heat for it.

"I'm sorry," she said.

"I told you not to answer the call," Faith wailed. "Five minutes later and we'd have been on the water."

Hope hurried out of the Jeep Liberty and grabbed Faith's backpack before approaching the passenger side. "Best-case scenario, another ranger will handle it and I'll be back by launch time. I can also rent a kayak to catch up with the group."

"Are you high? I'm not going without you."

"Come on, Faith. They might have to cancel the whole trip if we both don't show. They need a certain number of people in the raft."

She crossed her arms over her chest. "So?"

"It's bad for park business."

"Park business," Faith muttered, climbing out of the vehicle. "That's all you care about."

Hope's heart twisted in her chest. She knew she worked too much. During last summer's vacation, she'd returned to the park two days early to fill in for an injured employee. Faith and Hope had argued about her dedication to her job before. "No, it's not."

"Next year we're going to Las Vegas for an indoor vacation. We'll buy cocktails instead of trail mix." Faith's mouth thinned as she pointed a slender finger at her. "And I'll make you wear *my* clothes."

"Done."

"If I drown, I'll never forgive you."

"You won't drown," Hope said, hugging her tight. "I love you."

"I love you, too."

She let go of her sister with regret and climbed behind the wheel once again, waving as she drove away. Faith looked disappointed, even forlorn, and Hope felt awful. If she missed the entire trip, their vacation would be ruined.

Hands tightening around the steering wheel, she turned down the winding forest service road toward Mineral King.

Although she tried to stay upbeat, it wasn't easy. She worked a lot of solitary hours as a park ranger. During her time off, she enjoyed quiet individual pursuits like hiking and photographing wildlife. She'd been anticipating her sister's visit for months. Faith was right—she needed to interact with people more.

The Mineral King Station was in a remote section of the park, popular with backpackers and rock climbers. Families with small children often just drove through, and day hikers flocked to more accessible places like Giant Forest and Crescent Meadow. Because of its distance from the main tourist attractions, Mineral King had the hushed, pristine quality of true wilderness. Bear sightings were common.

She parked outside the station house, next to a forest service vehicle. Owen Jackson, a park attendant, had been appointed to take her place this morning. He sat behind the front desk, across from Sam Rutherford.

Sam was a local rock climbing celebrity, a recluse and the last person on earth Hope wanted to see.

Her mood plummeted further. Sam must have reported the plane crash. She'd been hoping for an unreliable witness, maybe a hippie backpacker who'd taken some psychedelic drugs and confused a shooting star for a horrific accident.

Sam glanced over his shoulder at her, his dark gaze skimming her body. Recognition and unease registered in his eyes, but he didn't flinch or tense his muscles. Instead, he returned his focus to Owen, as if waiting for an introduction.

How dare he pretend not to know her?

The two men appeared comfortable with each other, which didn't surprise her. Sam had recommended Owen for an entry-level position last summer. He donated fat checks to the park every year, so his suggestions were greeted with polite consideration. Hope had interviewed Owen herself and found little fault with him, other than a felony record. He'd worked on a prison forestry crew, so he had wildfire experience.

"Ranger Banning," Owen said, rising to his feet. He was a lean, cagey young man with close-cropped blond hair and haunting blue eyes. There was a thin red mark on his neck, and a larger, thicker welt on his hand. When she'd inquired about the scars, he told her that he'd had some tattoos removed.

Since his start date, Owen had been a model employee. He had a quick mind and a strong back. Unlike some of the young male park attendants, he didn't hit on tourists or drink too much. Hope had come to like him.

She wondered, and not for the first time, what connected a former inmate to a former Olympian. According to a rumor spread by women who'd struck out with one or the other, they were lovers.

Hope had personal evidence to the contrary.

"This is Sam Rutherford," he said.

"We've met."

"He reported the incident."

Sam stood to greet her with insulting belatedness. "Nice to see you again...Ranger Banning."

She realized that he was fishing for her first name. Indignation filled her, suffusing her cheeks with heat. "It's Hope."

"Hope. Right."

Judging by his expression, he remembered what she looked like naked, if nothing else. She took a deep breath, counting on her tanned complexion to mask her embarrassment. "When was the crash?"

"Around 3:00 a.m."

"What were you doing at 3:00 a.m.?"

He hesitated for a second. "Climbing."

Night climbing was unusual, but not unheard of, in summer months. Visitors took advantage of the cooler temperatures and available moonlight. Illegal activities like BASE jumping were often done under the cloak of darkness, as well.

"What did you see?"

"Just lights. I think it was a single-engine plane, flying too low. It hit the top of Angel Wings and burst into flames."

"Where were you?"

"On Valhalla. Near the summit."

Valhalla was a steep rock face directly across from Angel Wings. She checked her watch, noting that it was eight-twenty. "You got from there to here in five hours?"

"Yes."

"How?"

"I ran."

Upon closer study, his shirt was damp with perspiration. The lightweight fabric clung to his broad shoulders and flat stomach. Maybe he'd been slow to stand because he was tired, not out of disrespect, but he didn't appear fatigued. Despite the sweat, he was an endurance athlete and it showed. From the soles of his well-worn shoes to the top of his dark-haired head, he radiated strength and vitality.

She remembered how he looked naked, too: good. Very good.

"Have a seat," she said, clearing her throat. She turned to Owen. "You've relayed this information to Dispatch?"

"Yes, ma'am."

She excused herself and stepped outside. Her mind raced with worst-case scenarios as she picked up her radio. The dispatcher answered her a few seconds later. "What can you tell me about the craft?"

"There's been no emergency transmission or distress calls from the area. No flight plan was recorded."

In uncontrolled airspace, a pilot could use visual flight rules, but it wasn't recommended. The weather over the Sierras could be dangerous in the daytime. Flying close to the mountains at night without instruments looked suspicious.

This search-and-rescue might turn into a drug-smuggling bust. "Where's Dixon?" she asked, naming the park manager.

"I haven't been able to reach him."

"What about Mark?"

"He's at Moro Rock with the SAR team. Two hikers fell. One is unconscious and the other has a broken leg."

Hope swore under her breath, rubbing a hand down her face. This was her worst nightmare. Of the twelve park rangers with law enforcement badges, only Hope and Mark Griffon were accomplished climbers. Mark wasn't available. The SAR team wasn't available. Her supervisor wasn't available.

Heart racing, she weighed her options. The clock was already ticking. If she didn't reach the crash site before sundown, she couldn't call for a helicopter. Night rescues were too dangerous to attempt at a place like Angel Wings, where extreme wind conditions were common. And when the temperature dropped, crash victims often died of exposure.

Hope had responded to a similar call a few years ago. Before she became a permanent employee at Sierra National Park, she'd worked winters in Joshua Tree, one of Southern California's desert parks. A family of four had gone down in a twin-engine plane near Jumbo Rocks. Two of the wounded were children, and there was nothing anyone on the SAR team could do to save them. Hope had been training for her EMT certificate at the time. The scene was so horrific she almost quit the next day.

She didn't want to face another tragedy like that, especially on her own, but she couldn't afford to wait for a backup team. Her window of opportunity was too narrow. She had to get to the crash site and assess the situation as quickly as possible. If she left now, she'd arrive in time to request air transport.

The fastest route to the top of Angel Wings was

straight up the rock face. Hiking from the Kaweah trailhead on the east side of the mountain was easier, but it would take twice as long. The only problem with a direct ascent was that she couldn't do it alone. She'd never solo-climbed Angel Wings. It was an expert-only wall, rated 5.10+ in difficulty. She needed to find a suitable partner. There were several skilled climbers in the area who volunteered for high-angle search-and-rescue.

Sam Rutherford was one of them.

At least, he used to be. These days he avoided crowds, and most people, but he'd worked more rescues than Hope. A few years ago he'd been part of the elite SAR site team at Yosemite National Park. The man also knew Angel Wings like the back of his hand, and he'd witnessed the crash. He might be able to pinpoint its exact location.

"Just a minute," she said, signing off.

Hope clipped the radio to her waistband and went back inside the station, her blood pumping with adrenaline. Instead of scrambling for another volunteer, she faced her nemesis. "Can you take me to the crash site?"

His brows shot up. "Is there anyone else?"

She'd forgotten that he had run ten miles to get here. "Yes, of course. You must be exhausted."

"No, I'm fine," he said, shaking his head. "I mean… is there anyone besides you?"

"Besides me?"

"That I can climb with."

Hope gaped at him in disbelief. She didn't know if he assumed she couldn't keep up with him because she was a woman, or if he objected to her company because they'd slept together. Both reasons offended her.

"I'll go," Owen offered.

"You're not a ranger," she said.

"Neither am I," Sam pointed out.

"One of us has to be for this kind of mission. I'm the only qualified law enforcement ranger in the area, and I need a rescue climber to go with me. You're a convenient choice, but I can find a replacement."

He knew as well as she did that they had to start hiking now to reach the site before dark. "No. I'll do it."

Although his reluctance rankled, she told herself he was wise to be cautious. "I should warn you that this aircraft might have been flying at night to escape detection. There's no recorded flight plan or distress call."

This information didn't seem to faze him. He skimmed her casual clothes. "Do you carry a firearm?"

She had a handgun in her vehicle. "I'll get it."

"I'm ready when you are."

Owen seemed fascinated by their exchange. He leaned against the counter, studying Sam as if he'd grown two heads.

Hope didn't have time to second-guess her decision. Dragging a hand through her hair, she walked out to her Jeep. Her service weapon was in the lockbox. Normally she wore it on a utility belt, but she didn't have one with her. She shoved the gun into her day pack, along with extra clothes and some snacks.

Sam and Owen accompanied her to the SAR cache, where they housed rescue supplies.

"I need Dispatch to arrange for a helicopter and a backup rescue team on standby," she said to Owen.

"Can they fly over the crash site to check it out?" Sam asked.

Hope shook her head. "I'm not supposed to call for a helicopter unless there are confirmed life-threatening injuries. Angel Wings is in a dangerous flight zone and the cost of an air rescue is astronomical."

He made a noise of understanding. Ordering an expensive flyover when there might be no survivors wasn't an efficient use of tax dollars. Budget cuts, otherwise known as "service adjustments," had hit national parks, like everywhere else.

She didn't want to bring the same items as Sam, so she glanced around for his gear. "Where's your rack?"

"I don't have it."

Her eyes flew back to his, startled. "You were free-soloing at night?"

"There's a full moon," he said, as if that made it reasonable.

Hope sorted through the rescue supplies with a frown. Free-soloing was an extreme style of climbing without ropes or harnesses. The practice was outrageously risky in broad daylight. She'd never heard of anyone doing it at night. He was a maniac. And she had to depend on him to keep *her* safe?

Trying not to panic, she added the necessary equipment to a second pack. She didn't know what was worse—climbing with a lunatic or spending time with a man who'd thrown her out of his bed.

CHAPTER TWO

SAM TOOK THE path toward the High Sierra Trail, feeling like a fool.

He hadn't known Hope was a park ranger. The night they'd slept together, he'd assumed she was a slope bunny on vacation. In hindsight, he'd been careless. Seducing a woman he didn't intend to see again only worked if they didn't see each other again. He should have made sure she wasn't local.

A quick glance behind him revealed that she wasn't having any trouble matching his longer strides. It figured. She'd been an energetic bed partner, too. He remembered her strong, slender thighs, gripping him like a vise.

Giving himself a mental shake, he pushed aside the memory and picked up speed, setting a relentless pace. He'd never been able to outrun his problems, but physical exertion soothed him in a way nothing else could. The day was already warm, the sun peeking over the tall treetops. After twenty minutes, he was sweating.

Hope used her radio to call the whitewater rafting guide. "Go ahead without me," she said, signing off.

"You're missing a rafting trip?" he asked over his shoulder.

"Yes. We were planning to spend three days on the Kaweah."

"We?"

"My sister and I."

"Does she live around here?"

"No. She's from L.A."

He heard the telltale inflection in her tone. Los Angeles was a dirty word in the Sierras. How could he have mistaken her for a tourist? He'd really been thinking with his dick that night. "Where are you from?"

"Ojai."

Now that he thought about it, he remembered her sharing that detail at the bar. Ojai, pronounced Oh-hi, was a sleepy town near the coast. They'd laughed together over its hippie nickname, Get-high.

No wonder he hadn't realized she was local. Maybe she'd kept him in the dark on purpose. It wasn't a secret that he didn't date climbing groupies or park residents. He didn't date at all, since Melissa.

Sam couldn't fault Hope for the miscommunication. Even if she'd lied to him, which he doubted, it didn't matter. They'd had anonymous sex. Honesty wasn't required. He hadn't exactly given her a full disclosure, either.

Concentrating on the climb, he adjusted his gait along a steep incline. His legs moved forward at a steady clip, step after step. Hope didn't slow down or complain, so he continued to push hard. When he was in the zone, his thoughts drifted away, leaving nothing but the moment. They were making good time.

Two hours later, at midmorning, the sun was blazing, and his shirt was damp with sweat. She stumbled behind him, her breathing labored.

He stopped under the next shady tree to rest. "We

should eat lunch," he said. "You don't want to get light-headed on the climb."

She agreed, reaching into her pack for two protein bars and two apples. He accepted her offering without complaint. His dehydrated meals weren't half as tasty. The crisp apple awakened his senses.

Although he tried not to stare, he couldn't avoid glancing at her. She was even lovelier than he remembered.

The night they met, he hadn't been able to take his eyes off her. The moment she walked into the bar, his pulse had kicked up and his throat had gone dry. After more than a year of his feeling next to nothing at the most challenging, dangerous summits, this flood of sensation left him breathless.

She'd been wearing a dark blue thermal with a cute snowflake pattern. It was about as sexy as a reindeer sweater, not revealing in the least, but he'd ignored the good-girl giveaway and focused on the body underneath. He'd been mesmerized by her bright smile, smooth skin and shiny dark hair.

Why hadn't he left her alone? She'd looked disgustingly sweet, innocent and healthy. Easy pickings.

They'd both been drinking. She sipped white wine like a teetotaler while he knocked back shots. He'd waited until she was tipsy to make his move. At that point, he'd been drunk enough to go through with it, but not too drunk to perform.

He knew Hope wasn't a no-strings type, and he hadn't cared. He hadn't cared about her name, or her profession, or her feelings.

And the way he'd acted afterward—Jesus. He couldn't get rid of her fast enough.

Since then, he'd tried not to think about her. He'd convinced himself that she wasn't special; any woman would feel fantastic after a long stint of abstinence. She wasn't beautiful; he'd had beer goggles on.

He'd really been kidding himself.

Out of the corner of his eye, he watched her bite into the apple. Her white teeth pierced the fruit's ruddy skin. She was flushed from the hike, dewy with perspiration, her tank top plastered to her chest. No, he didn't need alcohol to find her attractive.

"How do you know Owen?" she asked.

"Owen?"

"Owen Jackson."

He blinked a few times to dispel the sexual voodoo. "We met in San Diego during the earthquake."

She arched a curious brow, crunching on another bite of apple. He hadn't spoken to the media about the incident, but it was widely reported that he'd almost died in a freeway collapse. "You were in a coma."

"Most of the time," he agreed. "A group of us were trapped in the rubble. Owen used my climbing equipment to get out and find help."

"Really?"

"Yes."

"And now you're friends?"

Sam wouldn't go that far. Even his close friends didn't talk to him anymore, and he avoided his family. He'd alienated everyone who loved him. "We're friendly enough," he said. "Why do you ask?"

"I was just wondering."

"Has he given you any trouble?"

"No. He works hard."

"He seems like a good kid," he said, shrugging. "I owed him one, and I thought he deserved a second chance."

She nodded, finishing her lunch.

It occurred to him that she might be interested in Owen as a man. The "kid" was in his early twenties, but prison had matured him beyond his years. Although he had some issues, he wasn't half as screwed up as Sam.

"How old are you?" he asked, suspicious.

"Twenty-eight."

He let out the breath he'd been holding. Most park rangers were college graduates, and she was hardly jail-bait. "You look younger."

"How old are you?"

"Thirty-two."

"You look older."

He acknowledged this truth with a wry smile. Even before grief and illness ravaged him, the sun had stripped any hint of youth from his skin. "I owe you an apology," he said, surprising them both.

She almost choked on a mouthful of water. "For what?"

"I…wasn't myself that night."

"Who were you?"

"I don't know."

Hope didn't seem impressed by this nonexplanation.

"The way I reacted was rude," he said, feeling lousy. "I'm sorry. I could have handled it better."

She still looked skeptical, and he couldn't blame her. There was no polite way to tell the woman you just had sex with to get out of your house. He shouldn't have brought it up; his behavior was inexcusable.

"Let's just forget about it," she said, forcing a smile.

Sam wasn't relieved that she'd let him off the hook. On the contrary, her words plucked a painful chord inside him. He'd never forget anything on purpose. Every memory he'd been able to retain was precious to him.

She rose to her feet and brushed off the seat of her pants.

"Do you want me to carry your pack?"

"No, I'm okay."

As they continued toward Angel Wings, the silence became increasingly uncomfortable. His apology, though sincere, hadn't cleared the air. If anything, it made the situation worse. Tension swirled between them, thicker than ever.

The last two miles of the path were the most challenging. He didn't want to exhaust her before the climb, so he let her walk in front of him. This way she could set her own pace, rather than struggle to keep up.

Her other physical attributes were just as fine as her face. She had an athletic build, taut and toned, but not skinny. She was curvy in all the right places. Her cropped jogging pants clung to her slender thighs and cute ass. She had long, graceful arms. If she climbed with as much gusto as she did everything else, they'd have no problems reaching the summit.

Sam wasn't looking forward to the ascent. He didn't partner anymore. Not with men at his skill level, not with women at any level. The idea gave him hives. He didn't want to hold Hope's life in his hands.

Angel Wings rose in the distance, a massive wall of

pale gray granite. This angel had dirty wings, feathering high into the sky. Mighty Valhalla stood directly across from her. Both monoliths had smooth faces, ribbed with cracks and handholds, etched by ancient glaciers. It was the stuff of climbers' dreams.

Hope stopped and flashed a smile, more genuine than the one she'd offered earlier. "Which route did you take up Valhalla?"

He fell into step beside her, following her gaze to the wall. There were five or six charted routes with fixed pitons. Climbers could follow a trail that had already been blazed, or strike out on their own. "North Arete."

The smile fell off her face. "You free-soloed North Arete?"

"Yes."

"That's impossible."

He didn't argue. It was the most difficult route on Valhalla, and a challenging free solo, but hardly impossible.

"It hasn't been done. Not even in the daytime."

"I did it."

She squinted into the distance. "How?"

He rotated the elastic band on his wrist, uncomfortable. A climbing feat didn't exist without a witness, so there was nothing to brag about. Glory and record-breaking no longer appealed to him. "Never mind."

But clearly, she did mind. "You free-soloed a 5.12 route in the middle of the night? Are you crazy?"

"Maybe." Probably. Yes.

"Next you'll tell me you BASE-jumped off the top."

He smiled at her horrified expression. "That's illegal."

"So is backcountry hiking without a permit," she said, her dark eyes flashing.

"I don't free-BASE," he said. Some young dare-devils were combining free-solo climbing with BASE jumping. Sam wasn't tempted. He liked the freedom of climbing without gear; the sensation of falling just made him nauseated.

"I'd arrest you in a heartbeat if you did."

Oddly, this conversation thrilled him more than the risky climb. He pushed the limits because he felt dead inside. Although he still had some capacity for fear, he'd lost his sense of self-preservation.

What he'd retained, in overabundant amounts, was concern for others. He couldn't belay a partner without anticipating a fall. His intense anxiety interfered with his love for the sport. He didn't want to be responsible for another climber. Often, he didn't trust the gear. Solo-climbing had become his only solace.

Partnering with Hope would be excruciating.

"Why did you report the accident, instead of checking it out?" she asked.

"What do you mean?"

"You could have climbed up to investigate the crash."

"Before contacting park authorities? That's against rescue protocol."

"You're a rule-breaker. We've already established that."

He scowled, guilty as charged. "I was afraid of what I'd find."

"Survivors?"

"Corpses."

She tilted her head to one side, deliberating. "I suppose you saw a lot of those in San Diego."

He didn't want to talk about it. "Have you ever done a 5.11?"

"Yes," she said, moving her attention from him to the wall. "I've climbed this one."

"Which section?"

"South Ridge."

"With a partner?"

She nodded.

"Okay. I know that route, too."

They checked and rechecked the gear. He gave her a pop quiz on ropes and knots, pleased to find her proficient. Most of the prep was second nature to him. He could tie an eight in his sleep.

At noon, they were ready. It was the hottest part of the day, near ninety degrees on the rock face, but a pleasant breeze drifted through the canyon. Sam did the lead climbing and Hope followed, steady as it goes. Although she was a natural athlete and a fair climber, he couldn't relax while she was in motion. Every time she reached for a new handhold, he held his breath. Disaster seemed imminent. Images of her plummeting to her death swarmed his vision. He saw frayed ropes, broken harnesses...cracked skulls.

Melissa's ashes.

Sam knew better than anyone else that climbing was mental. The sport required intense concentration, a quiet mind and a positive outlook. Fear would literally kill you on the rock face. If he didn't rein it in, he might endanger Hope.

Luckily, he was experienced enough to know the

difference between foreboding and phobia. Climbers were a superstitious lot. They followed their instincts, weighing risks in a fraction of a second. Only a fool ignored his internal warning system. But Sam's reaction was based on psychological trauma, not the situation at hand.

Hope could do this.

Besides, abandoning the effort would have grave consequences. She'd have to find another partner, maybe even wait until morning. While any possible survivors battled the elements on top of the mountain after the temperature plummeted.

Sam tried to tamp down his fear, but it wasn't easy. He didn't get scared that often, and he wasn't accustomed to dealing with it. He'd become soft, in a way. Apathetic. Caring about life or death required effort.

Oblivious of his struggle, Hope continued to climb. She was confident, but cautious, spending too much time thinking about every move. Time dragged out into an eternity. He had to bite his tongue to keep from criticizing the flaws in her technique. She wasn't an expert and it showed.

A few years ago, Sam had been an easygoing partner who enjoyed initiating newcomers to the sport. Now he was quickly frustrated, his body humming with impatience. The type of climber he used to loathe.

To her credit, Hope stayed positive and kept a smile on her face. He began to suspect that she was doing it just to annoy him. When she made a minor misstep and almost lost her grip, he swore up at the sky.

His negative attitude made an impact on her near the top. She came to a wide gap about ten feet away from her last placement. A fall from this distance could be dangerous, whether the gear held or not. Even during short drops, climbers could get tangled in ropes, crack their heads against the rock and break bones.

If the gear failed, death was certain.

Her footing looked off as she stretched out her arm. He muttered another curse, and she must have heard it, because she spooked. Instead of committing to the reach, she second-guessed herself and faltered. Her questing fingertips found no purchase, and her foot-hold crumbled.

With a sharp cry, she tumbled backward, her arms and legs flailing. Her harness caught and held, jerking her body roughly.

Sam braced himself against the rock and listened for the sound of gear popping, his blood thundering in his ears. To his intense relief, the protection bore her weight as she dangled in midair, a thousand feet from the ground. He held the safety rope, her last lifeline, clenched in his trembling hands.

She grasped the rope that attached them, staring up at him with frantic eyes. He let out a slow breath, his heart hammering against his ribs. They'd get through this a lot easier if she didn't look down.

"Are you okay?" he asked.

She moistened her lips. "I'm okay."

"Reach out to the wall."

Her gear was keeping her safe, not his gaze, but she seemed reluctant to look away.

"I've got you."

After a short hesitation, she straightened, focusing on the rock face. She let go of the rope with one hand

and touched the wall with the other. The tip of her shoe found an overhang, and her fingertips gripped a small fissure. She flattened her belly against the sun-drenched surface and paused there, as if soaking up its spirit.

After a moment of communing with the climbing gods, she made her way up. The final push went by in a blur. Before he knew it, they were at the summit. With Sam's help, she scrambled over the edge.

He studied their surroundings, breathing hard. The top of Angel Wings was jagged, with dips and crags, like the surface of a tooth. He couldn't see the remains of a plane, but there were hints of its trajectory. Burned-up bits of fuselage marred the landscape.

Sam pulled up their haul bag while she rested, her shoulders trembling from fatigue. The elation he usually felt after a climb was tempered by worry. They had a new obstacle to meet: searching for survivors.

"That was close," he said.

"I'm sorry."

"My fault."

"You're a difficult partner."

"Does that surprise you?"

"Yes."

He searched her face, wondering why she'd overestimated him. Then he realized that she was judging him by his performance in bed, which had been a hell of a lot more generous. Until he threw her out.

A flush crept up his neck at the backhanded compliment. He drank water from his pack, flattered and confused. The fact that he'd given her pleasure didn't excuse his behavior, but she seemed determined not to demonize him. Maybe she saw the good in everyone. Or maybe she just expected poor treatment from men.

The thought depressed him. He didn't like the idea of being one of a long string of jerks. He wanted better for her—and himself.

Hope took her gun out of her pack.

"What are you doing?" he asked, startled.

She shoved the weapon into her waistband, against the small of her back. "I have to check out the crash site. Stay here."

"No way."

"You can't come."

"Why not?"

"Because you're a civilian, and this is a potential crime scene. It's risky to fly at night without GPS or a flight plan. The plane might have been carrying illegal cargo."

"Not every risk-taker is a criminal."

"True," she said. "Some are just idiots."

He winced, knowing which category she placed him in.

"The crash victims could be smugglers, protecting their stash."

"Don't you need backup?"

"I won't try to arrest a group of thugs by myself. I'll just survey the scene and collect information."

"I'm coming with you."

She deliberated for a moment, her mouth pursed. "You have to take my lead, be quiet and stay back when I tell you to."

"Okay," he said, swallowing hard. He might be an adrenaline junkie, crazy as fuck, but the situation scared him. He didn't like guns and he wasn't keen on getting shot. There was a difference between free-solo climbing, in which he trusted his abilities, and assisting an armed park ranger he hardly knew.

He also worried that they'd find a dead body. His aversion to corpses was stronger than his fear of guns or drug smugglers.

But he had to accompany her. *Had* to. Because his biggest fear was that Hope would be hurt or killed on his watch. The last woman he'd climbed with was dead. He couldn't handle another blow like that.

Sam was already broken, hanging on to sanity by a thread. At the slightest provocation, he'd fall apart.

As Hope walked across the uneven, pebble-strewn surface of the crag, he followed close behind, his heart racing. It was ten degrees cooler at this altitude. Wind rippled through his microfiber shirt, evaporating the sweat from his body. Although he'd just slaked his thirst, his throat was dry.

When the wreckage came into view, she paused. It appeared that the plane had clipped the southwest corner of the mountain and broken up across the surface. The majority of the fuselage was still intact, perched very close to the edge of the opposite cliff. A figure was slumped over in the pilot's seat.

Sam's stomach clenched with unease.

Although the pilot appeared to be dead, she approached with caution. "We're with search-and-rescue for Sierra National Park," she called out, shading the sun from her eyes. "Do you need help?"

No response.

She glanced at Sam, her face tense. Motioning for

Sam to stay there, she crept forward. He ignored the gesture and stuck by her.

The plane's front windshield was broken. Inside the cockpit, the pilot was motionless, his head resting on the dash, gray hair fluttering in the breeze.

"Can you hear me?"

Nothing.

It didn't appear that any bodies had been thrown from the plane. When she was at an arm's length from the broken windshield, she leaned over to peer inside. The wreckage was so close to the cliff's edge, he pictured it toppling over with one touch. He bit back a warning as she craned her neck for a better view. A black crow flew out of the cockpit with a shrill screech, wings flapping.

Sam almost had a heart attack.

Hope screamed at the top of her lungs and leaped backward, bumping into him. He stumbled sideways.

"I told you to stay over there," she scolded.

Sam didn't answer. He couldn't take his gaze off the pilot. The lower half of the man's face was obliterated, and he had a second wound in the center of his chest. Blood spatter coated the interior.

This wasn't just a crash site. It was a murder scene.

CHAPTER THREE

Javier Del Norte reached the campsite at the edge of the river sometime after dawn.

He was thirsty, and hungry, and tired. His shirt had stains and his slacks were ruined. His feet were bleeding inside his Ferragamo loafers, he just knew it.

Luckily for him, Americans on vacation were a trustworthy lot. They left all sorts of clothing and supplies out in the open while camping. He didn't understand why successful people with luxury vehicles would choose to sleep on dirt or torture themselves physically in their free time, but their masochism wasn't his problem. California culture was ineffable. He'd accepted that and moved on long ago.

His main concern was getting out of this wilderness without detection. And hopefully without having to kill anyone else.

Shoving the items he'd scalped into a stolen backpack, he headed toward the public restrooms to change. Near the men's entrance, he noticed a door for a utility closet. Unlocked, of course. Because tree huggers didn't steal toilet paper. He reached inside, helping himself to bleach, hydrogen peroxide and Band-Aids.

In the men's room, he studied his reflection. His once-white shirt was dotted with blood and bits of gore. Teeth fragments, perhaps. Removing it with a grimace, he tossed the garment into the sink and uncapped the hydrogen peroxide.

With heavy regret, for his jet-black hair was striking, he leaned forward and poured the bottle over his head. The liquid burned his nostrils and dripped down his chin, but he gave himself a good dousing, keeping his eyes shut tight. When he couldn't stand the sting anymore, he rinsed his hair and studied the effect.

Awful.

The rusty bronze color didn't look natural, or attractive, but it was different. With sunglasses on, he might be unrecognizable. Satisfied, he took off his pants, socks and shoes, piling them in the sink. He added bleach. While he was standing there in his boxer briefs, soaking his bloodstained clothes, another man came in to use the facilities. He was young and spot-faced, his eyes puffy. Mumbling hello, he disappeared into the first stall.

Retching sounds emanated from the confined space.

Javier shook his head in disgust. He fantasized about shooting the sick camper to put him out of his misery. There wasn't a shower at this imbecilic place, so he washed with cold tap water and patted himself dry with rough paper towels. It was impossible to eliminate every spec of evidence, so he didn't bother trying. After rinsing his wet clothes, he stuffed them in the trash can.

The pack he'd stolen contained several stray clothing items. He donned a gray V-neck T-shirt and low-slung plaid shorts, lamenting the owner's bad taste. The shirt was too snug and the shorts too loose, but at least they were clean. He sat down on a wooden bench to bandage the blisters on his feet.

Two more young men walked into the restroom, glancing in his direction. He froze, hoping they weren't the campers he'd just robbed.

Dismissing Javier, the first guy banged on the bathroom stall. "Dude, pull it together. We're going to be late for the trip."

The sick man vomited again.

His friends laughed at the noise, goofing around and punching each other.

"Just leave without me."

"No way, dickhead! I can't get a refund if you cancel."

"I'll pay you back," he groaned.

"Stop being such a pussy. We're all hungover."

"It's the altitude."

"You'll feel better on the raft."

The man started dry-heaving, and his friends continued to ridicule him.

Javier almost felt sorry for the poor bastard. There was nothing more emasculating than puking your guts out in a public toilet. He'd done it himself, several years ago, after drowning his sorrows at Hector Gonzales's bachelor party. The next day Hector had married the woman Javier loved.

Wincing at the memory, he put on a pair of sturdy athletic socks and black canvas tennis shoes that were only half a size too large. The backpack also boasted a hat. A beanie, he believed it was called. Tugging it over his wet hair, he walked outside, bypassing the foolish young men. An area map was posted on an information board next to the restrooms. Warnings about bears and safety instructions appeared in several languages.

He studied the map, which indicated that he was at the Kaweah Campsite in Sierra National Park. Only one road led in and out of the park. Both the entrance and the exit were more than thirty miles away.

That was a problem.

Hitchhiking was common in Venezuela, where he was born, and in many of the other countries he'd visited. Here in the U.S., it was rare enough to attract the attention of the authorities. He needed another mode of transportation. He could continue walking, pay for a ride or steal a car. But what if the park exits were being monitored? Law enforcement officials might know about the crash already. His boss would definitely be looking for him.

A man in Javier's profession couldn't leave behind a million dollars' worth of drugs—and a dead pilot—without consequences.

On the right side of the map, there was an advertisement for Kaweah Whitewater Adventures. A blue line marked Kaweah Campsite as the launch point. The tour stretched past the borders of the park, ending at Moraine Lake.

The river was another exit.

While he considered his options, the hecklers walked out of the men's room. They hadn't convinced their friend to come along. Javier gave them another quick once-over, recognizing the type. After leaving Venezuela, he'd honed his English in Costa Rica, which was popular with surfers and potheads.

"You guys going on the whitewater trip?" Javier asked.

"Yep."

"I've always wanted to try that," he said, falling into step beside them. One of the guys had short, spiky blond hair. The other had long brown hair like Jesus. Both appeared strong, probably from athletic pursuits, rather than hard labor. "How do I sign up?"

"You have to reserve in advance."

"Oh."

The longhair exchanged a shrewd glance with his buddy. "We could bring you along if you have enough cash."

"How much?"

"Four hundred. It's a three-day trip."

Javier had enough money, but he didn't want to appear overeager. He also suspected them of trying to hustle him. Who would pay so much money to get abused by a river? "I've got two fifty," he said, lowering his voice. "And an ounce of weed."

That perked them up. "What kind?"

"Chronic."

The guys smiled at each other. "Let's see it."

Javier glanced around to make sure they were alone before showing his stash. Neither the pot nor the cash belonged to him, so it was no loss. The deal suited his acquaintances just fine. They became very friendly all of a sudden.

"I'm Caleb," the long-haired guy said. "This is Ted."

Javier shook their hands. "Jay Norton."

Caleb and Ted debated over smoking a bowl right then and there, but decided against it because they were already late. Javier breathed a sigh of relief. He needed to stay alert, not get stoned with a couple of *pendejos*.

The rafting group was supposed to meet in the camp

parking lot at eight. They hurried down the dirt road as a dark green sport utility van with Kaweah Adventures printed on the side was about to pull away.

"Hey," Caleb yelled, waving his arms. "Wait up!"

The three of them jogged to the vehicle. "You just made it," the driver said. "Hop in."

Javier took off his backpack and climbed inside. The backseat was occupied by two short-haired women in their forties. A cute blonde sat in the middle. There was space available beside her, or next to the driver.

"Hello," he said, choosing the blonde. "I'm Jay."

She fluttered her lashes. "Faith."

"Pleasure to meet you," he said, shaking her hand.

Although he wanted to keep staring at her, because she was beautiful, he introduced himself to the women in back and nodded hello to the driver. When infiltrating a group, it was important to adopt their customs. Outdoor lovers were gregarious. They liked to hug strangers and bond with nature. He couldn't be standoffish.

Caleb and Ted struck up a lively conversation, using a lot of terms Javier didn't understand. Class Five, portage, PFDs.

He turned to the girl beside him, studying her with interest. She was wearing long shorts, a tank top and hiking boots. Her platinum-streaked hair was braided into two sections. She had a demure, fresh-scrubbed look, but she wasn't a teenager. Her brown eyes twinkled with a sexy sort of mischief.

While he sized her up, she did the same to him.

Coño de la madre. If all female campers were this

young and hot, he'd been missing out. "Faith," he said, liking her name. "Where are you from?"

"L.A."

City of angels. "You're together?" he asked, indicating the women in back.

"No, I'm alone. My sister was supposed to come along, but she got called into work."

"Sorry to hear it."

She arched a brow. "You don't look sorry."

He wiped the grin off his face. "Is this your first time rafting?"

"Yes."

"Mine, too."

"Really? I thought this route was for experts."

"Is it?" He glanced behind him for confirmation. "Are you ladies experts?"

"We've been around a few rivers," the redhead said. Her name was Paula.

"Don't worry," Caleb said. "Ted and I have done some sixes and lived to tell the tale." He launched into a boastful account of their accomplishments. Javier wasn't impressed, but he believed that the guys knew how to paddle. Whether they stayed sober enough to do so safely was another question.

Faith didn't seem as enthusiastic about rafting as the others. Maybe she was nervous. Javier wanted to promise he'd look out for her, which was strange. If anything, his presence in the group put everyone at risk.

And the less he said the better. He'd impersonated an American before and it wasn't as easy as it seemed. His English was almost perfect, and he could mimic a Californian accent. He knew U.S. history. But there were gaps in his education. TV shows he hadn't watched, rock stars he didn't know, movies he'd never heard of.

Cultural references would trip him up every time.

They drove down a bumpy dirt road to an area called the put-in. As he climbed out of the van with Faith, he drew in a deep breath, amazed by the size of the river. At the campsite, the Kaweah had been a bubbling brook. This monster was immense, full of jagged rocks, with angry froth churning down the center.

Faith made a noise of distress at the sight.

"Don't worry," he blurted.

"Why not?"

"I'll take care of you."

She lifted her gaze from the water. "How?"

"I'm an excellent swimmer." He'd given surf lessons to tourists in Costa Rica. That had been a sweet gig. He should have stayed.

"You look strong," she said, her eyes trailing down his body.

Well, yeah. Being physically intimidating was part of his job. Also, beating the hell out of people.

They spent the next hour going over safety rules and rafting techniques. Javier paid close attention, memorizing much of the information. Caleb and Ted invited him for a smoke break, which he declined. He didn't want to leave Faith's side. His presence seemed to comfort her. She listened to the guide carefully, partnering with Javier to practice paddling. He did his best to look like a guileless outdoorsman. Every few minutes, he glanced up at the sky, searching for Gonzales's helicopter.

Soon they'd be coming for him.

He hadn't expected there to be women on this trip,

and he felt conflicted about staying. On the one hand, traveling coed was a good cover. He enjoyed female company and he'd gone too long without it. On the other hand, he was running for his life. He'd waited months for an opportunity to break free. He'd shot and killed the last man who tried to stop him. If he had to do the same to Caleb or Ted, he wouldn't hesitate.

Hurting women didn't sit well with him, though.

That was why he'd never go back with Gonzales. He was going to escape or die trying. God help anyone who got in his way.

"You smell like peroxide," Faith said, interrupting his thoughts.

Another problem with women: they were intuitive and observant. He shouldn't have been standing so close to her. By gazing at her appreciatively and acting flirtatious, he'd invited her to ask him personal questions.

Denying the obvious was no use, so he tugged the beanie off his head and braced himself. "How bad is it?"

"Pretty bad."

Stupidly, he regretted the dye job. He wanted her to think him handsome.

"Did you lose a bet?"

"Yeah. Sort of."

She reached up to touch his hair, rubbing a few strands between her fingertips. He could see down the front of her tank top, which was disconcerting. "I could fix it," she said, dropping her hand. "I'm a hairdresser."

"Really?"

"Yes. Color's my specialty. I do mine."

He evaluated her pretty brown eyes and honeyed skin tone. "You're not a natural blonde?"

She laughed, swatting him on the shoulder. "That's for me to know."

The guide presented a pair of life jackets, dispelling the mood. Any clothes they wanted to stay dry had to be placed in waterproof sacks. Javier removed his T-shirt, watching Faith pull her tank top over her head.

Coño.

Before she put on her life jacket, he got an eyeful of her breasts, covered by little scraps of fabric. They looked real. He wasn't the type of man who cared either way, but he'd seen so many strippers lately that her subtle curves seemed exotic in comparison.

Tearing his gaze away, he shoved his T-shirt into his backpack and placed it in the plastic. His shorts weren't for swimming, but they'd have to suffice. She stared at his bare chest, her lips curving into a smile.

Bring on the cold water. He needed it.

WHEN SAM PUT his arm around her, Hope buried her face in his shirt, shuddering.

He was a jerk, but his strength felt reassuring. She'd almost peed her pants a second ago. His heartbeat thumped against her cheek, *alive, alive, alive.*

"Any chance this was self-inflicted?"

She forced herself to move away from him and take a better look inside the cockpit. There was a handgun on the seat next to the pilot, and shells from two different weapons. It looked like a close-range gunfight. "No."

Sam turned his back on the wreckage with a grimace, keeping his distance while she photographed the scene. Or maybe he was keeping watch. She noticed his eyes scanning the mountains and trees nearby.

There were few clues inside the fuselage. She didn't see any illegal cargo or formal identification. From what she could surmise, the 9 mm next to the pilot wasn't responsible for his death. He'd returned fire with his killer. She took pictures of the weapon and a pair of bullet holes on the opposite side of the fuselage.

She was about to report to headquarters when static buzzed over the plane's radio. Her heart seized at the sound of a man's voice. "Del Norte, come in. *Ya, contesta.*"

Hope rushed forward to pick up the receiver. Swallowing hard, she pressed the button to speak. "This is Ranger Banning of Sierra National Park. I need some information about this aircraft and pilot, over."

The man ended the communication.

She replaced the receiver, her mouth dry. Careful not to touch anything else, she exited the fuselage.

"What was that?" Sam asked.

"Someone called on the plane's radio. When I answered, they hung up."

"You answered?"

"Yes."

He thrust a hand through his short hair. "Fuck!"

"What?"

"I don't like this. Let's get the hell out of here."

She wasn't a big fan of the situation, either. There had never been a murder at Angel Wings. It could be days before a thorough investigation was organized. The logistics of processing a crime scene on a remote mountaintop were dizzying.

They also had a killer to find. He must have left the area on foot.

She walked away from the plane, examining their surroundings. A hiking trail led down the backside of the mountain and ended at the Kaweah River Campsite. Where she'd dropped off Faith this morning.

"I have to go after him."

He gaped at her in disbelief. "You can't be serious."

"I'm dead serious," she said.

"You're not a homicide detective."

"No, but I have to protect the park's visitors, and it's my job to investigate any crimes committed here."

"Alone?"

She frowned at his incredulous tone. Tracking a single assailant by herself wasn't against procedure. Park rangers often worked solo, especially in the backcountry. But it was unorthodox, and perhaps unwise, to hunt down a murderer without help. "He's got to be headed for the Kaweah. Faith is there."

"Who's Faith?"

"My sister."

Hope would do anything for Faith. She loved her with the fierce protectiveness of an older sibling and the deep loyalty of a best friend. Faith had always meant the world to her, but their connection had become even stronger after a heartbreaking incident in her past. Hope had lost someone precious to her, and she'd vowed never to let it happen again.

Sam swore under his breath. There was no way he could talk Hope out of pursuing the suspect. "You can't make it to the river before dark. Let's rappel down, go back to Mineral King and call for help."

She shook her head, stubborn. "I have three more

hours of daylight. I won't waste it by traveling backward."

"You can drive to the Kaweah camp faster!"

That was true, but Faith wasn't at the campsite. She was rafting down a river that intersected the killer's path. "I might not be able to pick up his trail from there. I know I can track it from here."

"You should wait for backup."

She didn't have time to argue, so she radioed Dispatch and relayed the details. "Send a couple of rangers to look for any suspicious activity at Kaweah. We need to contact the sheriff's department, monitor the exits and put all park employees on alert."

The dispatcher repeated her instructions and signed off. Although the ground was too dry and rocky for footprints, Hope noticed signs of a disturbance. "Drag marks," she said to Sam, following them down the trail. They led to a pair of boulders about a hundred feet away. There was a crack between them large enough to hide another body.

While Sam watched her, his face taut as a bowstring, she removed her gun from the waistband of her pants.

In her five years as a ranger, she'd drawn her weapon only a handful of times. She'd aimed it once, last summer. A drunken idiot was shooting at marmots near the Giant Forest Campsite. When she'd shouted a warning for him to put down the gun, he'd swung around to face her, pointing his .38 at her chest. She'd damn near fired on reflex.

Incidents like that were rare, however. Most of the park's visitors were law-abiding, nature-loving people.

Guns were allowed inside park boundaries, but discharging a firearm was strictly prohibited.

That didn't mean her job wasn't dangerous. Hope was more likely to be assaulted in the line of duty than an FBI agent. Rangers stationed at the parks along the Mexican border were targeted by drug cartels, but the Sierras had their share of narcotics-related crime, as well. Secret marijuana fields, guarded by armed men, had become increasingly common. These brazen growers used federal land for their crops.

"This is Ranger Banning of Sierra National Park," she called out, holding her weapon at her side. "Anyone there?"

Wind skimmed across the mountain. The sun was still bright, but the temperature had dropped and the air felt cooler. Hope shivered in her damp tank top. Gesturing for Sam to stay back, she crept forward, pointing her gun at the rocks. A jumble of dark shapes came into view. Her eyes struggled to identify a human form and failed.

Duffel bags. She was looking at a pile of duffel bags.

Hope lowered her weapon, releasing a slow breath. She made sure the safety was on and replaced it in her waistband. When she stepped close enough to reach between the boulders, Sam was right there beside her.

The duffel bag she removed was large and heavy. She unzipped it, revealing what appeared to be high-grade marijuana. It was in loose brick form, lightly compressed and wrapped in plastic to disguise the skunky odor.

Sam let out a low whistle.

Hope looked in another bag and found the exact same

contents. Ten bags, each weighing about forty pounds, equaled…a whole lot of drugs. It was probably local. Sierra's finest had a street value of about five thousand dollars per pound. She estimated the pot's worth at over a million dollars.

"Someone will be looking for this," he said.

"Yes."

"All the more reason to go back to Mineral King."

Hope agreed that the illegal cargo escalated the danger. Protecting park visitors—Faith included—was imperative. If she didn't go after the suspect and someone got hurt, she'd be devastated.

Saying nothing, she photographed the evidence and replaced it. When she was finished, she updated Dispatch and requested a radio communication with Ron Laramie, the rafting guide. He wouldn't be answering calls while on the river, but he was supposed to check in after the group stopped to camp.

She prayed for good news.

"I'm going to Kaweah," she said to Sam, shrugging out of her pack. "You can head back to Mineral King. Just give me the overnight gear before you leave."

He frowned at the trail that led down the mountain. How different he seemed from the man she'd met at Long Pine Lodge. That night, he'd been relaxed and charming. She'd known he was Sam Rutherford, reclusive Olympic champion, but he hadn't acted arrogant or self-important. They'd laughed together and spoken of inconsequential things. She'd been fascinated by him. And wildly attracted.

But Jekyll had turned into Hyde after he'd gotten what he wanted. She still remembered waiting outside in the snow for a cab. Big, fat snowflakes melting in her hair. Hot tears sliding down her face.

And when she'd offered to forget about it, he'd flinched as if the suggestion pained *him*. What was his problem?

Other than making the foolish decision to go home with a man she didn't know well, she'd done nothing wrong. She wasn't in the habit of sleeping with strangers. It was a week before the holidays; she'd been tipsy and lonely.

Today, he was more Hyde than Jekyll. She understood that he considered their one-night stand a mistake, and that he didn't want to be reminded of his boorish behavior. He felt so uneasy around her that it threw off his climbing rhythm. He'd appeared anxious on an ascent he could have done blindfolded.

Or at night. Without ropes.

To be fair, his current duress was probably related to the crime scene, not her. He couldn't wait to get out of here.

"No," he said flatly.

"No?"

"I'm not giving you the gear. Let's go."

"I'm going that way." She pointed at the footpath.

"You'll freeze tonight."

"I have a jacket and a safety blanket in my pack."

He made a skeptical sound. Even in the summer, temperatures at the higher altitudes often dropped below thirty degrees, and the weather could change at a moment's notice. If a storm blew in, she'd be screwed.

"As long as I keep walking, I'll be fine."

"You can't track in the dark."

Her temper flared. Tamping it down, she forced a smile. "Then I'll build a shelter and make a fire. I don't need the extra gear."

A muscle in his jaw flexed.

"I'm leaving either way, so you might as well give it to me."

"No."

She realized that he wasn't going to budge. Annoyed with his attempt to deter her, she put on her backpack and started walking. He was lucky she didn't commandeer the tent and sleeping bag at gunpoint. Bastard.

"Goddamn it," he said, following her down the mountain.

She whirled to face him. "What are you doing?"

"What does it look like? I'm coming with you."

CHAPTER FOUR

FAITH WAS HAVING more fun than she'd anticipated.

The rapids were scary, and she didn't like the way the boat bobbed up and down on the surface of the water, threatening to dump its inhabitants, but a foot brace prevented her from falling overboard. Although the required helmet was dorky, and a boxy life jacket covered her cute new bikini top, both would protect her in a spill.

She didn't really have to exert herself, either. The guide, who called himself "Captain Ron," did the bulk of the paddling, shouting directions for assistance every so often. With Ron behind her, Caleb in front and Jay at her side, she felt insulated from danger. They probably didn't need her help, but she paddled just to be a good sport.

The best part of the trip, by far, was Jay. Her heart skipped a beat every time he gave her a reassuring smile. He was distractingly hot, even with quirky clothes and dye-scorched hair. Before they disembarked, he'd donned a pair of hideous square-framed sunglasses that reminded her of Napoleon Dynamite. It was almost as if he was trying to hide his handsomeness under a nerd disguise.

He couldn't hide the body, though. His torso was lean and strong, his arms well defined and his stomach rippled with muscle. When he dipped his paddle into the water, biceps flexing, her throat went dry and her thoughts scattered.

The day flew by. After lunch, they hit a long, easy stretch that didn't demand much maneuvering. Caleb waxed stoner-poetic on everything from the sun sparkling on the water to the immense height of the surrounding trees. Although Faith wasn't a nature lover, she thought peaceful quiet would better suit the atmosphere. When he launched into another implausible rafting tale, Ron rolled his eyes in Faith's direction. Jay caught sight of the expression and laughed, glancing away.

"What's so funny?" Caleb asked him.

"Nothing," Jay said.

"He thinks you're full of shit," Ted supplied.

Caleb looked over his shoulder at Faith. Maybe his boasting was meant to impress her, but she couldn't suppress a giggle at his expense. He returned his attention to Jay, squinting with antagonism. "Oh yeah?"

Although Jay didn't look intimidated, Captain Ron came to the rescue. "I tried to run a six-plus on the American River once."

"What happened?" Paula asked.

"I got dumped."

Everyone laughed except Caleb, and the conversation moved on to less contentious topics. Jay didn't say a word but managed to monopolize her complete attention. Whenever she snuck a peek at him, he was watching her.

The last run of the day was a monster. It churned fast and furious between jagged chunks of granite, eager to chew them up and spit them out.

"This is Devil's Drop," Ron shouted. "Get ready to paddle!"

Faith froze with terror as they approached. She'd never seen water like this before. Falling out of the boat here would be like getting thrown from a car on the freeway. She imagined herself sailing through the air, her bones snapping on sharp rocks.

"I'm going to die," she blurted.

The rest of the group chuckled and Caleb let out a war whoop. She was on a trip with a bunch of crazy people!

"You'll be fine," Ron said, his brow furrowed in concentration.

For once, Jay focused on paddling instead of her. But he spared her a quick nod to remind her of his promise. They'd been instructed *not* to enter the water to rescue another swimmer. It was dangerous, and not usually an effective lifesaving technique in these conditions. Despite the warning, he'd vowed to come in after her if she tumbled overboard.

She felt comforted by the thought. Taking a deep breath, she clutched her paddle and hung on for dear life. The rapids hit in a dizzying rush, tossing the front of the boat up in the air and slamming it down again. Icy water surged over the edge, soaking her to the skin. She gritted her teeth against the cold shock.

Although she paddled when called upon, her main concern was staying inside the boat. She noticed that most of the other passengers looked happy, rather than terrified. Only Jay appeared grim and determined.

Like her, he was enduring this, not enjoying it.

Then they were free from the rapids' grip, and his

tension disappeared so quickly she wondered if she'd imagined it. Everyone in the group was smiling and exuberant, Faith included. She couldn't believe they hadn't capsized.

What a wild ride.

After the slippery section passed, the sun sank lower in the horizon and a chill settled over the air. By the time they reached the takeout, where they would camp for the night, Faith was shivering.

"Everyone lends a hand in pitching the tents," Ron said as they exited the boat.

"I pitch an excellent tent," Caleb said with a grin, elbowing Faith. "You can sleep with me and Ted."

"Dream on," she said, laughing.

Ron tied off the raft and started tossing out supplies. "Girls' tent goes over there," he said, pointing toward the trees. "Guys over here." He removed one more tent bag, which looked smaller than the others.

"Whose is that?" Jay asked.

"Mine," Captain Ron said, walking away. "It's a single."

Caleb smirked at Jay. "Disappointed?"

Not bothering to respond, he picked up the tent and headed the opposite direction. Bunking with him wasn't an option, so she joined the other women. Faith stood clear while Paula and Meg put up the tent. Inside, she changed into warmer clothes. The fleece jacket and water-resistant pants were her sister's usual style, function over fashion, but she didn't mind. It was almost dark. No one cared how she looked.

Ron spoke to Hope on the radio while they were making camp. Faith couldn't hear the entire conversation, but she gathered that Ranger Banning wouldn't be joining them. Typical Hope. Always on duty.

Faith needed to have a serious talk with her sister. Hope worked more and dated less every year. She wasn't equipped for one-night stands, like Faith. The last jerk she'd slept with had reduced her to tears. Hope rarely let her guard down with men, so she was slow to recover from disappointments.

Faith knew why Hope shied away from relationships. Ten years ago, her sister had made a mistake she couldn't forgive herself for. Other than that one slipup, she was the perfect daughter, the responsible student, the valiant rescuer. "Great White Hope," Faith called her when she was feeling peevish. Hope was saving the world with her park ranger job. Their flower-power parents were so proud.

Faith was the black sheep of the Banning family. She liked big cities, throngs of people, expensive things. Where Hope had substance, Faith was all flash. She had no interest in saving anything, least of all money. She was an unrepentant pleasure seeker, coasting through life on a useless art history degree.

She'd never *be* as good as Hope. The best she could do was *look* good.

Despite their differences, Faith didn't resent her sister. She adored her. It broke Faith's heart to hear the loneliness in Hope's voice. She wanted to help her sister come out of her shell. Hope needed to stop hiding in the woods and start living.

After the radio call, Ron started a fire. Faith sat down on a log and stretched out her hands, trying to thaw by the flames. Jay took the space next to her. He'd donned his beanie, along with a long-sleeved T-shirt and vintage Levi's jeans.

"Cold?" he asked.

She nodded.

He put his arm around her. Not asking permission, but moving slowly enough that she could say no if she wanted to.

She didn't.

His body felt warm and hard where it pressed against hers. He was like a side of beef, with no give. His hand cupped the curve of her waist as if it had been molded for that purpose. She was comforted and thrilled in equal measures.

He kept his gaze on the fire, probably because looking into her eyes at this distance would be weird. But he was still attuned to her. When she exhaled a ragged breath, he smiled and squeezed her waist. She snuggled closer, enjoying the contact.

Faith hadn't been held by a man in over six months. Since her breakup with Tom, casual hookups had lost their appeal. She wasn't as adventurous or carefree as she used to be, and that worried her. If she stayed abstinent much longer, she'd become a born-again virgin like Hope. Maybe it was time to knock the dust off her vagina.

Jay was a perfect candidate for a fling. He didn't match her mental picture of an avid outdoorsman, however. His jaw was shadowed by stubble, and his clothes were on the thrifty side, but he didn't appear dirty or unkempt. He had good skin, straight teeth and nice hands. This was no hippie backpacker or scruffy wildlife hunter.

His hair had felt thick and luxuriant, and it was expertly cut. He looked more like a lawyer than a lumberjack.

"What do you do?" she asked, fluttering her lashes.

"I'm in shipping."

"Shipping?"

He nodded. "I work for a company in Las Vegas."

Las Vegas. Close enough for a friendly visit, but too far for anything serious. That suited Faith just fine.

The others gathered around the fire a moment later. Jay eased his arm away as smoothly as he'd introduced it, giving her an apologetic glance. Maybe he didn't want to invite comments about how cozy they were getting.

Ron boiled water for freeze-dried meals and served them in the bag with plastic forks. The beef stew tasted awful to Faith, but Jay ate it like a starving man. She offered him her portion and shared a handful of trail mix with Paula, who was a vegetarian. Hot cocoa was the highlight of the evening.

There were no roasted marshmallows or campfire sing-alongs. Faith felt certain that someone would request a round of "Kumbayah," but no. Ron and the other women went to bed early. Caleb brandished a flask and a smile. He unscrewed the cap and held it out to Faith, who accepted with enthusiasm. After tossing back a shot, she coughed and grimaced. The men laughed at her girlish reaction.

Jay also took a drink, swallowing easily. They passed around the flask until it was empty. By the time Ted rolled a joint, Faith was already buzzed.

"This is good shit," Caleb said, holding in the smoke.

"Tastes local," Ted agreed.

Faith declined a toke. The liquor was strong enough, and she hardly knew these guys. Getting wasted out of her mind wasn't a smart idea. Jay didn't hit the joint, either, which seemed to surprise them.

"You don't want any?"

He shook his head.

Caleb and Ted continued to share the pot. Soon they were in la-la land by themselves, debating on the other side of the campfire about how ancient civilizations had been influenced by space aliens.

Faith giggled at Caleb's wild gestures and turned her attention back to Jay. He was studying her again. Although her face felt naked without makeup, she reminded herself that firelight was flattering.

"Warmer now?" he asked.

"Yes," she said, with some regret. The combination of alcohol and masculine attention made her cheeks hot. If she wanted another excuse to cuddle with him, she'd have to move away from the fire.

First things first.

She met his eyes. "Do you have a girlfriend?"

"No," he said, seeming amused. "What about you?"

"No girlfriend," she said coyly, twirling the end of her braid. "I tried that once in college but it didn't work out."

His mouth went slack at the implication.

"No boyfriend, either."

He shook his head, as if to clear it. "Why not?"

"I haven't felt like dating anyone since my last breakup."

"What happened?"

"I guess we didn't have anything in common. He was a total jock, and…"

"You don't like sports?"

She hesitated, not wanting to admit it. She knew that men appreciated women who rooted for the home team, drank beer and ate hot dogs. But Faith hated hot dogs. Besides, her sister was the sporty type, and being so hadn't improved *her* love life.

Maybe Faith should have made a better effort with Tom. She'd rarely attended his events or watched games with him. He hadn't taken an interest in her social activities, either. They'd never been able to compromise.

"I like some sports," she said.

"Which ones?"

She thought hard. "Dirty dancing."

He laughed at her answer.

"Are you a sports fan?" she asked, hopeful.

"Yes."

Her spirits sank. "What's your favorite?"

"Boxing."

Tom hadn't been into boxing. He'd followed most of the popular sports, so he'd been glued to the television every night. "That's it?"

"Pretty much."

"No football or baseball?"

"I like soccer, but I don't understand football, and baseball is boring to watch. Not physical enough."

She wasn't sure what he meant, but she shivered in response to the word *physical*. He had a unique way of speaking, a brevity that appealed to her. Everything about him was spare and lean, from his taut body to his clipped sentences.

Leaning toward him, she whispered in his ear, "I have to pee."

He rose to his feet, eager to assist. She took his proffered hand and stood up, swaying a little. Caleb and Ted were too busy arguing about the space-time continuum to notice their departure.

Although Faith was afraid of bears, she could have squatted behind a bush without help. Jay stood guard at a nearby tree while she tinkled in the moonlight. She prayed that the leaves near her backside weren't poison oak.

When she was finished, she fastened her pants and returned to his side. She tripped on the last step by design, stumbling into his arms.

Oh my.

His biceps were very firm beneath her palms, and his chest felt like a warm, hard cocoon. She clung to him, not caring if her pratfall was convincing.

"Are you all right?"

"Mmm-hmm."

He placed a hand at the small of her back, holding her steady. The action also brought her lower body flush against his. They were much closer than polite distance allowed, and he was making no move to extract himself.

She twined her arms around his neck, encouraged.

Not only did he take the hint; he took control, turning her toward the tree and slanting his mouth over hers. She parted her lips on a gasp as her shoulders met the rough bark. Groaning, he dipped his tongue inside.

He tasted smooth and hot, like campfire whiskey. She hadn't kissed a man since Tom and it was nice to cleanse her palate.

Jay did a thorough job, exploring her mouth with silky strokes. He wasn't pushy or overeager. This was a man who could wait for the main event. His lips were deliciously firm. In her experience, sloppy kissers were sloppy lovers, and anyone who rushed first base didn't deserve to get waved on to second.

She moaned and sucked on his tongue, appreciative.

He must have enjoyed that, because he made a sound in the back of his throat and slid his hands lower, cupping her bottom. Faith approved of the maneuver, and of the desire she felt swelling between them. She pressed her breasts against his chest. Her skin tingled with awareness and heat blossomed between her legs.

As if reading her mind, he lifted her higher, fitting his erection into the notch of her thighs.

Unh.

That was good.

Still kissing her, he rubbed his hard denim button fly against her cleft, stimulating a riot of sensations.

She dug her fingernails into his shoulders and swooned, dizzy from arousal. He was going to make her come with her clothes on! She shouldn't have gone so long without sex. This was embarrassing.

It wasn't his fault that she was teetering on the edge of orgasm, and if they had a private place to retreat to, her extreme horniness wouldn't be a problem. But there was no way she'd let him screw her against a tree twenty feet from the campsite. Faith was adventurous, but she wasn't *that* adventurous.

She tore her mouth from his, panting.

He didn't remove his hands from her ass, but he stopped grinding against her, which helped her think.

She braced her palms on his chest and gave him a light push. He released her at once, stepping back.

Her brain wasn't functioning on all cylinders yet. He was damned near irresistible, standing there in the moonlight, an erection straining the front of his jeans, his dark eyes locked on her mouth.

"That was hot," she said.

"Yes."

"I have to go to bed now."

"Okay."

He walked her to the girls' tent, not seeming displeased or frustrated in the least. She liked that. Some guys thought every make-out led to sex, and wouldn't take no for an answer. After a traumatic experience with an aggressive date, Faith had vowed never to let a man overpower her again.

When they arrived at the entrance, she stood up on tiptoe and brushed her lips over his. She wanted to smooth her palm down his body to test his size, but she restrained herself. Teasing him would be cruel.

"See you tomorrow," she said, sinking to her knees to unzip the tent.

He murmured something under his breath that sounded oddly like a foreign language. Then he said good-night and disappeared into the dark.

HOPE AND SAM hiked until sunset.

Her legs were shaky from overexertion, and she felt light-headed, but she soldiered on, determined to keep moving. Although she was accustomed to strenuous exercise, twelve hours of it tested her physical limits.

When she stumbled and almost fell down a ravine,

Sam suggested a break. She sat down on a flat rock, her thigh muscles quivering. While he disappeared into the trees to relieve himself, she radioed Dispatch, getting a detailed update. Then she checked in with Ron Laramie. To her relief, the rafting group was fine.

Sam didn't say anything when he got back. His body language was closed, his mouth set in a hard line.

She took a sip of water to ease her parched throat before sharing the latest news. "The attendant at Kaweah hasn't seen any suspicious characters, but one of the campers reported a stolen backpack, and a sheriff's deputy found a strange set of clothes in the men's room trash can."

"Strange how?"

"Business attire, soaked in bleach. They cordoned off the bathroom in hopes that evidence can be collected." Tomorrow, investigators would retrieve the illegal cargo, process the crash site and launch a park-wide manhunt.

"You think he's still in the area?"

She shrugged. They hadn't seen any sign of him. He might have reentered the wilderness to hide, but there was no way he could have caught up with Faith's rafting group on foot. She breathed a little easier, knowing that.

"What about his friends?"

"They'll be looking for the cargo. They might not know where it is, or even where the plane crashed."

"They'll know if he tells them."

Hope wasn't sure he would. There'd obviously been a conflict between the suspect and the pilot. It was possible that he wasn't on good terms with the rest of his crew. Someone had been trying to contact him on the plane's radio. He must have fled the scene in haste, without relaying any information.

"Let's make camp under that tree, away from the trail," he said, pointing to a more secure location.

"If we push, we could reach Kaweah by midnight."

"You're exhausted."

She couldn't deny it. "I'll be fine."

"You'll be *unconscious* in another mile."

"Okay, He-Man," she shot back. "Clearly you never get tired, so you can go on ahead without me if my company offends you so much. I'll catch up tomorrow." As soon as the words left her mouth, she regretted them. The stress and muscle strain had really done a number on her. All of the hurt she'd bottled up inside had risen to the surface.

She was usually more upbeat.

"I'm tired," he said, walking away from the trail and removing the tent from his backpack. He didn't bother to deny that he found her company offensive. She followed him, finding another rock to sit on. With a heavy sigh, she stared into the distance, determined to enjoy the play of light in the clouds as the sun dipped below the horizon.

The next thing she knew, it was full dark, and he was shoving a tin cup into her hands. She must have dozed off.

"Drink," he said.

It was chicken noodle soup from a freeze-dried packet. He molded his hands over hers as she took a tentative sip. The liquid was hot and tasty, reviving her senses. She drank half the cup before he moved away, trusting her to finish it herself.

"Thank you," she said.

He grunted a dismissal and made another cup of soup. While she was sleeping, he'd set up the tent under a tree and built a small fire.

"How long was I out?"

"Ten minutes."

She drained her cup, suddenly ravenous.

"You should drink some water, too."

Hope did as she was told, because dehydration was no joke, and she was showing signs of serious fatigue. When she'd stopped moving, her body had shut down. Her core temperature had also dropped considerably. She was cold.

They shared several packets of soup, a powdered drink that tasted like hot Tang and a bag of roasted almonds.

Once her hunger was satisfied, she became very sleepy again. She yawned behind her hand, catching his watchful gaze from across the campfire. He looked ready to point to the tent and order her to go to bed, like a dog.

"Are you going to stay out here all night?" she asked.

He poked a stick at the fire, contemplative. "No."

"I only brought one sleeping bag."

"You can have it."

"I'll use my blanket."

He didn't argue, so she took that as an agreement. She removed her shoes and crawled inside the tent, bringing the space blanket with her. It was a shallow, narrow space, designed to hold in heat. Once he joined her, they'd be like two sardines in a can. She zipped up the door and scooted to one side, leaving room for him.

Then she wrapped her body in the crinkly, aluminum-sided blanket, rested her head on the crook of her arm and closed her eyes.

Sleep was elusive because her mind wouldn't rest. She couldn't stop second-guessing her interactions with Sam. She'd replayed their night together a thousand times, wondering what had gone wrong. He didn't seem like the type of man to discard a woman after one use. Well, three uses, but who was counting?

He seemed even less like that type now. He was irritable and short-tempered, not deliberately cruel. A man without a heart wouldn't follow her down the mountain or feel responsible for her safety. She knew why her presence made him uncomfortable: guilt. She reminded him of his worst behavior.

She rolled onto her side, frustrated. He hadn't planned to throw her out. She'd bet her Patagonia backpack on it. The action was too bizarre, too abrupt.

Another ugly suspicion reared its head. Obviously, he liked her looks, or he wouldn't have taken her home with him. Her personality wasn't a major consideration—they hadn't done much talking. And she'd never been more responsive or uninhibited, so he couldn't fault her sexual performance.

What did that leave? Her body.

Hope had a nice enough figure. She was strong, but naturally slender, with curvy hips and small breasts. Although she hadn't stripped in front of a man in years, she'd felt no attacks of shyness that night. He certainly hadn't voiced any complaints. She'd been tipsy, and he'd been downright drunk. His eyes had darkened with appreciation when he saw her naked. If she remembered correctly, he'd kissed her all over.

But maybe, during that final session of foreplay, when he'd gotten up close and personal with her private parts, he'd noticed the marks on her lower abdomen.

Her biggest flaw. Her darkest secret.

This was why she never slept with strangers. She didn't want to explain the telltale signs of pregnancy. The story was too painful to share with a casual acquaintance. Sometimes it was too heavy for a steady boyfriend.

Sam hadn't said anything, so she didn't know if the sight had triggered him.

Hope smoothed a hand over her flat stomach and blinked back the tears of remorse, pressing her lips together tightly.

She didn't want him to hear her cry.

CHAPTER FIVE

HOPE AWOKE WITH a start.

She'd been dreaming about falling. It was a repeat of yesterday's close call on Angel Wings. Only this time, her harness hadn't held. The nylon had snapped, sending her hurtling toward the ground, her arms and legs flailing.

The nightmare faded and she let out a slow breath, trying to orient herself. She was in a single-man tent. With Sam.

He hadn't kept his distance; it was impossible in the cramped space. He also hadn't kept his sleeping bag to himself. The thick, down-filled fabric covered them both, so he must have unzipped it to share with her. Underneath that layer, she had the safety blanket, which wasn't big enough for two.

She felt cozy, insulated from the chilly morning air. And a little guilty, because he'd put her comfort above his own.

They'd been sleeping spoon-style, with her back to his front. Her head was pillowed on the crook of his right arm. His left was locked around her waist in a manner that could only be called possessive.

He stirred behind her, mumbling something in his sleep. His lips brushed against the nape of her neck.

She'd always melted when a man kissed her there.

Sam had paid special attention to this erogenous zone during round two on that ill-fated night. He'd dragged his open mouth all the way down her tingling spine.

Hope forced the memory aside and tried to ignore the feathery sensation, to no avail. Her skin prickled with awareness and her nipples tightened in the cups of her sports top. She had to extricate herself from this predicament ASAP. When she touched his arm, attempting to remove it from her person, his muscles tensed. He tightened his grip on her waist and brought her closer, aligning her bottom with his lap.

Oh no. Was he awake?

She couldn't tell for sure, but the quickening of breath, along with an obvious erection, indicated some level of awareness.

The best strategy at this point would be to say something and move away from him. But she stayed right where she was, her mouth closed and her body humming with arousal. He rewarded this choice by lifting a hand to her breast, brushing his thumb over her nipple. When she didn't protest, he buried his face in her hair.

She gasped as he nuzzled the sensitive spot behind her ear. His heartbeat thumped against her back and his erection prodded her buttocks.

"Melissa," he groaned, smoothing his hand down her belly. He traced the cleft of her sex with his fingertips.

And then the name registered.

She shoved his arm away and scrambled upright. "Melissa?"

He blinked at her in confusion. His eyes were bloodshot, dark with desire, and there were sleep lines on his lean cheek.

"You just called me Melissa," she prompted.

"You're...Hope."

She couldn't believe he had to *reach* for the information, as if they hadn't spent the past twenty-four hours together. As if he didn't know her. "Are you sure? Because you thought I was someone else a second ago."

He stretched out on his back and looked up at the ceiling of the tent, raking a hand through his hair. The sweatband he always wore on his right wrist was pushed up over his palm, revealing a piece of tattooed script. They both noticed it at the same time. As he read the insignia, his eyes filled with anguish and his throat worked in agitation.

She grasped his forearm, holding it still.

R.I.P., Melissa.

"Who is she?"

He tried to speak, but the words were strangled. Shaking his head in apology, he covered his face with one hand and rolled onto his side, shutting her out.

Hope couldn't bear to watch him cry. It seemed like a foreign level of emotion for a controlled risk taker who never even flinched. He clearly didn't want her to witness this breakdown, or to offer him comfort in any way. So, instead of staying with him, she unzipped the tent and walked away.

It was a chilly, misty morning. Her muscles groaned in protest as she sat down to put on her boots, so she did some yoga stretches.

Hope didn't feel good about leaving him alone. He'd taken care of her and kept her warm last night. On the other hand, he'd thrown her out of his bed after their first encounter, and added injury to insult by forgetting her name—again.

She owed him nothing.

When he emerged from the tent a few moments later, his eyes were red-rimmed, but clear, and his mouth was set in a tight line. He laced up his hiking boots in silence. "I'm sorry," he said finally. "I didn't mean to touch you."

A hint of indignation seeped back in. "Did you mean to touch me that night you took me home from the lodge?"

He flashed a sardonic smile. "Yes."

Apparently she wasn't worth a repeat performance. He didn't offer any further explanation, and she couldn't bring herself to ask.

She'd done a Google search on him the morning after their one-night stand, struck by the awful suspicion that he was married or in a serious relationship. The internet search had brought up articles about his business endeavors, his climbing feats and his entrapment in San Diego. He'd been linked to various women, including an Italian supermodel, but she hadn't found any information about wives or current girlfriends. Not even on Facebook.

She'd closed her laptop, resolving to forget about him. Faith was the only person she'd mentioned his name to. The female rangers she worked with were friendly, but asking them about Sam's love life would only provide gossip fodder. Rumors that he was gay, or unable to perform since the coma he'd suffered during the San Diego earthquake, were baseless. She just wanted to put the humiliating experience behind her.

Sam broke down camp while Hope ate her last granola bar, her thoughts churning. Together, they set off toward Kaweah.

Her stiff muscles loosened up and her resentment faded. He'd lost a woman he loved. If he wasn't over her, he shouldn't have taken Hope to bed, but whatever. He'd been drunk. He'd made a mistake.

She knew how hard it was to let go. Better than anyone.

By the time they reached the base of the mountain, she'd brushed off her hurt feelings. She wasn't the type to hold a grudge, and his apology seemed genuine. She suspected that he was struggling with severe depression. Anyone who free-soloed at night had one foot in the grave.

Hope had worked a number of suicide scenes. Sierra National Park was a popular place for cliff jumpers. It was wide open, with few witnesses and many high points to leap from. Often the bodies were unidentifiable, and it was difficult to distinguish between a purposeful death and a falling accident.

The thought of finding Sam's body at the base of a cliff, his internal organs obliterated and bones crushed, chilled Hope to the core.

At midmorning, the sun was burning through a haze of clouds and the air felt heavy. They might be in for rain, another complication she didn't need. Instead of moping about it, she put a spring in her step, following her mantra to stay positive.

Kaweah was bustling with activity. As they arrived, a team of investigators headed up the path to Angel Wings.

She stopped to speak with Deputy Phillip Meeks, the leader. He was a young man, former military, kind of a hotshot. A more experienced deputy wouldn't be amiss, but at least Meeks was strong and fit. She showed him the pictures on her camera, pointing out the exact location of the drug stash.

"You'll want to take East Slope, the trail on the left. It's faster."

"Ten-four," he said, wearing the ghost of a smirk.

Meeks had been at the bar the night she'd gone home with Sam. He might have seen them leave together, but he hadn't run his mouth about it, as far as she knew. Long Pine was a small community, and members of local law enforcement were a tight-knit group. If Meeks had talked, she'd have heard.

She said goodbye to the team and continued to the ranger station with Sam. Ranger Cordova, who usually worked at another region of the park, was in the back office. She offered them a seat and cold sodas.

"Thanks," Hope said, cracking hers open. "Where's Kruger?"

"He called in sick today."

Bill Kruger was the head ranger at Kaweah. He'd gotten the job through a family connection with the park manager, and he shirked his duties on a regular basis. She was glad he wasn't here to screw anything up.

Bernice Cordova had a great attitude and lots of energy, like most rookie rangers. She was a cute little thing with brown eyes and a pixie cut. Her girlfriend was a park attendant at Giant Forest. They were "out" as a couple, which drew some attention from the male staff. Although she didn't play for his team, Cordova seemed mesmerized by Sam.

"This is Sam Rutherford," Hope supplied.

"I know," Cordova said. "I'm a big fan of yours. I started kayaking when I was ten, after I watched you on TV."

Sam had earned two gold medals in whitewater slalom twelve years ago, but he was better known for his daredevil ascents. The Olympics had made him a local hero; extreme rock climbing had made him famous. Not to mention rich, through lucrative endorsement deals and sports-related business ventures.

He took a drink of his soda, seeming embarrassed by the praise.

"What have we got?" Hope asked.

Cordova pulled her gaze away from Sam. "Deputy Meeks dusted for fingerprints in the men's room, but he didn't find a good set. Too much traffic in there."

"Where are the clothes?"

"Bagged and taken to the crime lab. Here's the information from the labels." She handed Hope a printout.

"Ferragamo loafers, size twelve," she read, glancing at Sam. "Are those expensive?"

"Yes."

"What about…Bugatchi Uomo?"

He leaned over to read the name on the paper. "Never heard of it."

"The shirt is a large and the pants are thirty-two/thirty-two." She studied the length of Sam's legs. "What size are you?"

"Thirty-two/thirty-four."

"You're bigger than he is?"

"I'm taller."

Ranger Cordova gave her another printout. "I also have a description of the stolen backpack and a list of the items inside."

"Excellent," Hope said, scanning it. "Do you know if any single men left the campsite yesterday morning?"

"Just one, according to Morgenstern. A young guy in a red truck. He bowed out of the rafting trip at the last minute, complaining of stomach problems."

Hope frowned at this news. Alan Morgenstern was a VIP, or volunteer-in-park. He actually did most of Kruger's work around the campsite for a small stipend. "Did Ron check in this morning?"

"Yes."

"How many in his group?"

She consulted the computer. "Seven, including him."

"That's strange."

"Why?"

"I was supposed to be on that trip, in a group of eight. If two rafters are missing, there should be six left."

Cordova found the original list and confirmed the numbers. "You're right."

"Maybe that guy in the truck was our suspect," she said, her heart racing. "Where's Morgenstern?"

"In his trailer."

Hope leaped to her feet. She wanted to talk to him in person.

"Should I come?" Cordova asked.

"No need," she said, waving her hand in the air. Morgenstern hated rookies, especially females. He probably hated lesbians, too. To be fair, he also hated Bill Kruger, and pretty much every employee on staff. He was an equal opportunity asshole.

Cordova smiled at Sam, eager to chat with him one-on-one. He stood and followed Hope out of the office.

"You didn't want to be alone with Cordova?" she teased.

He shrugged, rubbing the back of his neck.

"Aren't you interested in adoring women?"

"Not remotely."

"I think you're safe. She has a girlfriend."

His brows rose. "Now I'm interested."

She laughed, knowing he didn't mean it. He had a dry sense of humor that she found very appealing. He'd joked around a lot that night at the bar. Paired with his rugged good looks and ridiculously hot body, he was hard to resist.

He also seemed surprised by her amusement. That was another attractive quality. He didn't expect compliments or laughter, like most celebrated people. His gaze lowered to her lips and lingered there. If Sam was interested in anyone, it was Hope. He stared at her with a mixture of longing and confusion.

Clearing his throat, he glanced away. "Melissa was my fiancée," he said, answering the question she'd posed earlier. "She died in a climbing accident in Greece."

"I'm sorry," she said, stricken. "I didn't know."

"It wasn't a big news story. Only our families and close friends knew we were dating. She was a professional climber, and she wanted to be judged on her abilities, not mine."

Hope felt terrible for him. It was speculated that head trauma during the San Diego earthquake had knocked the sense out of him. In reality, another tragedy had inspired his current, reckless free-soloing habits.

"When I woke up this morning—"

"You don't have to explain," she said, touching his arm.

His mouth twisted at the contact. "I'm not going to forget about it."

After a moment, she realized he was referencing her offer from yesterday. He didn't want to forget their night together, or his unwitting advances from this morning? She searched his dark eyes, curious. His triceps tensed beneath her fingertips. He had lean muscles, like most rock climbers, but she'd never felt such raw power.

"Okay," she said, dropping her hand. She wouldn't forget, either.

Morgenstern's trailer was at the campground entrance. Once a ranger, he'd been forced into early retirement after a knee injury. His wife, also a NPS employee, had died of cancer. He'd given the best years of his life to the park in exchange for an aluminum shelter and permanent squatting rights.

She didn't blame him for being bitter.

"Have you met Morgenstern?" she asked Sam.

"No."

"He won't be as fawning as Cordova."

"Good."

She rapped on the door.

Morgenstern opened it with a glare. His eyebrows were bushy, his hair coarse and wild. He reminded her of the mad scientist character from *Back to the Future*. "What?" he barked, his mouth half-full of bologna.

"Sorry to bother you," she said. "I wanted to ask about the sick camper who left yesterday."

"What about him?"

"Did he look suspicious?"

"No, he looked sick," he said with disdain. "He was a zit-nosed kid, not a damned Mexican drug smuggler."

She didn't bother to tell Morgenstern that they didn't know the ethnicity of the suspect. He was a cranky old coot, but he did his job, which was more than she could say of Bill Kruger. If he carried some extra resentment toward Hope, it was because she'd taken over his position at Mineral King. He was also from a different generation of rangers. A lot of throwbacks like him didn't believe women should be wearing the Smokey the Bear Stetson.

At least Morgenstern was up-front about his prejudice. She'd take bald sexism over the subtle, insidious bullshit any day.

Morgenstern took another bite of his sandwich and set it down next to a cell phone. He eyeballed Sam, still chewing.

Hope considered the possibilities. If the guy in the red truck wasn't her suspect, who was the seventh person in Ron's group? "Oh my God," she said, an icy hand trailing down her spine. "He's on the rafting trip."

"Who?"

"The killer!"

Morgenstern harrumphed in disbelief. "Ron wouldn't add a random stranger on a whim. Reservations are made months in advance."

"Did you see them depart?"

"Yes. Three men almost missed the van."

"Can you describe them?"

He thought about it, squinting. "Two college-kid river rats, one tall, one short. They were with a medium-sized guy in a gray hat."

Hope referred to the list of items in the stolen backpack. Gray beanie was number four. "That's him."

"He might have been Mexican."

She thanked Morgenstern for his trouble and walked away from the trailer with Sam. Heart racing with distress, she picked up her radio to call Dispatch. "I need to talk to Ron. It's an emergency."

"I'll try to reach him, but he isn't due to check in again until evening."

"Get Dixon."

The dispatcher asked her to wait a moment. It felt like an eternity. Sam stood beside her, close and silent. "He's on three," she said when she returned.

Hope switched to channel three, which was used exclusively for communications with the park manager.

"Banning?"

Although she was on a first-name basis with Doug Dixon, he didn't show familiarity during work hours. She told him about her suspicions in a rush. "I need a helicopter team to take me downriver."

"Hold on," he said. "We don't know it's him."

"There were three men scheduled for the rafting trip. One went home."

"Maybe the other two called a friend."

Her gut said otherwise. "I have to go after them."

"Negative."

"My sister is in that group!"

"Which is exactly why you should take a step back.

I'll talk to Ron and assemble a whitewater team. Or a helicopter crew, if it comes to that. I don't want you involved. You've made too many rash decisions."

"What do you mean?"

"You left base without a team yesterday."

"Only because SAR was busy and I couldn't reach you."

"Continuing to Kaweah was also ill-advised."

She clenched the radio in her sweaty grip. He'd never reprimanded her before, and it didn't feel good.

"Take a break, Hope. You've covered a lot of ground in twenty-four hours."

"I'm fine."

"Go home and get some rest. We'll do everything we can to catch this guy."

Hope stared at Sam, swallowing hard. She couldn't believe Dixon had ordered her to stand down. This wasn't just unfair, it was humiliating. Was he cutting her out of the action because she was too emotionally involved, or because he didn't want her to get hurt? She was the only female law enforcement ranger in the park. Maybe her boss wasn't much different from Morgenstern after all.

"Is that clear, Banning?"

"Yes, sir."

She clipped the radio to her waist with shaking hands. Ron might not check in until dark. His group would be thirty miles downriver by then. The Kaweah ran along the east side of Angel Wings, through the most remote area of the park. It was pristine wilderness, totally undeveloped. There were no roads, only a few hiking trails. The only way to reach the rafters quickly was by helicopter.

Or kayak.

If she left now, and paddled hard, she could catch up with the group by nightfall. She'd planned to do that anyway. Dixon wouldn't be pleased with her insubordination, but she doubted he'd fire her. She had some pretty good dirt on him.

Hope hurried toward the ranger station, where the rescue kayaks were housed.

"What are you doing?" Sam asked.

"Taking my vacation."

CHAPTER SIX

RANGER CORDOVA UNLOCKED the storage shed at Hope's request.

She removed the necessary supplies from her pack and shoved them into a dry sack, along with her service weapon. Then she slammed a helmet on her head and wrestled into a life jacket.

"What are you doing?" Sam asked.

"I'm borrowing a kayak. For recreational purposes."

"Recreational purposes, my ass!"

As she reached for the kayak on the middle shelf, she gave him a sidelong glance, surprised by his vehemence. He was standing in the doorway, blocking her exit. His chest rose up and down with agitation. She wasn't sure why she had such a strong effect on him. The night she'd slept with him, he'd responded to the barest touch, a whisper of breath. Whatever had drawn them together still hummed beneath the surface, ready to ignite.

"Dixon told you to go home."

She unstrapped the hull, her pulse racing.

Sam turned to Ranger Cordova, who was watching with wide eyes. "Are you really going to let her do this?"

"She's my superior, Mr. Rutherford."

"Then call her superior!"

"Don't you dare," she said, pointing her finger at Cordova.

"I'll call him," Sam threatened.

"Go right ahead. Get on the phone with your crony and throw some more money at him. I'll be ten miles downriver by then."

"You're really prepared to attempt Class Five whitewater on your own?"

"I'm an experienced kayaker."

"Those rapids are brutal."

She removed the kayak from the rack. "You free-solo a thousand feet above the ground, so spare me the safety lecture."

"They have more than a day's head start," he said through clenched teeth. "If, by some miracle, you don't get slammed in the slickies, you'd have to paddle like hell on the slow sections. Only an expert could catch up with them."

"You're familiar with this river?"

Cordova made a coughing noise. She knew something Hope didn't.

"I used to be a guide here," he said.

He'd grown up in nearby Tulare, so it made sense. He must have honed his Olympic skills on the three local rivers as a teenager. "Great," she said, unzipping the kayak cover. Now she understood why he was so agitated. He felt obligated to come with her—again. "I don't need your assistance this time, Sam."

"You need a partner."

"I'll go," Cordova said, her expression eager.

Hope didn't want to get Cordova in trouble. She was a seasonal employee with high aspirations. "I'll be fine," she said, hitching the kayak over her shoulder. If he tried to stop her, she'd javelin him with the pointed end.

He stepped aside, muttering a string of curses as she exited the shed. She scrambled to the river's edge, worried that he was going to follow through on his threat to contact Dixon. Placing the kayak on the bank, she sat down to remove her hiking shoes.

He joined her a moment later, carrying the second kayak.

"You can't come," she said. "This isn't a search-and-rescue."

"Are you willing to wait for someone else?"

She slipped her shoes into the dry sack, annoyed. There were a few rangers on staff who could run this river, Cordova included, but she couldn't bring them on an unauthorized mission. Besides, she had to leave now. Her chances of catching up with the group by evening were already dwindling.

"You might be putting your sister in more danger by getting involved," he said. "Have you thought about that?"

Hope cleared her throat, swallowing back tears. "She's not due to arrive at Moraine Lake until late tomorrow. If something happens to her between now and then, I'll never forgive myself."

With a dark scowl, he glanced away. She could tell that he knew how she felt. They'd both lost loved ones. Hope had given hers up by choice, but that didn't make her heart ache any less at night.

"What's your plan?"

She took a deep breath. "Yesterday morning, I told Faith I'd try to catch up with the raft. So that's what

I'll say I'm doing. I won't challenge the suspect. He's probably still armed. I'll just keep an eye on him until we reach Moraine."

He deliberated for a moment. "What will you do with your kayak?"

"I'll leave it at the campsite."

"Have you run this river before?"

"Yes. I did it twice last month."

"Okay," he said, sighing heavily. "You lead, I'll follow."

"If we don't scout the tricky sections or take any breaks, we can probably make it to Mist Falls by sundown."

"Is that where they'll camp?"

"Most likely."

"We're stopping for lunch. That's nonnegotiable."

She agreed and they started off, cutting through the shallows that snaked through the campsite. Her leg muscles needed a rest, but her arms were still strong. By the end of the day, her whole body would be sore. For now, it felt good to be in motion, her blood pumping, the sun shining on her bare shoulders.

Dixon would castigate her again, and Sam didn't approve, but she refused to turn back. Faith was her baby sister. Hope had always been the responsible one, the protective one. She enjoyed taking care of others and especially loved rescue work. These attributes had served her well as a park ranger. It felt rewarding to keep the peace.

She knew she had an unhealthy zest for maintaining order. The more unsettled her personal life, the more she attempted to control her environment. When a situation slipped out of her grasp, she felt helpless. Like a teenage girl in a hospital bed, stretching out her empty arms. Tears streaming down her face.

She'd do anything—*anything*—to avoid that feeling. Knowing that Faith was in danger caused an unbearable panic within her. Her only recourse was to take action. To keep moving forward and never give up.

Hope couldn't rest, physically or mentally, until Faith was safe.

FAITH WAS TOTALLY over camping.

She'd had a great time snuggling by the fire and making out with Jay, but sleeping on the hard ground sucked. Screeching birds woke her at the crack of dawn. She sat up and glanced around, shivering from the cold.

She was alone in the tent. Rubbing her eyes, she reached into her pack for a compact. When she saw her reflection, she gasped in dismay.

There was a bug bite—on her cheek! Some creepy, crawly little bastard had disfigured her while she was sleeping.

She hadn't brought any concealer, so she couldn't hide the red bump. She snapped the compact shut with a groan. After putting on her boots, she emerged from the tent. The other women were already awake and looking chipper. She mumbled hello and ducked into the bushes, checking the ground for snakes. Peeing outdoors was hazardous.

After washing her face, brushing her teeth and fixing her hair, she felt human again. Hungry, actually.

She joined the others around the campfire. Ron was serving cinnamon oatmeal. Accepting a bowl, she took a seat by Jay, careful to give him the good side of her face. Mornings-after could be awkward. Some guys acted evasive or avoided eye contact. Others lingered too long or talked too much.

Jay didn't talk at all. Nor did he avoid eye contact. He stared at her openly, as if enthralled by her presence.

"Did you sleep well?" she asked, smiling a little.

"No."

"Why not?"

"Caleb snores."

Laughing, she tested a spoonful of oatmeal. She'd hardly eaten yesterday, and she was starving.

"How about you?"

"I miss my bed," she said.

Faith didn't understand why Hope liked roughing it so much. Maybe her sister was a masochist. For the past ten years, she'd been punishing herself.

Faith dealt with loss in a different way. She was more of a hedonist. Hope wallowed in martyrdom; Faith chose to carpe diem. She wanted to forget her troubles and be carefree. While Hope tried to rule the wilderness and save everyone within a hundred-mile radius, Faith stayed on top of her appearance and any men in her vicinity.

It wasn't that she didn't have deep feelings. She just preferred to skim over the surface and keep things light.

A helicopter rose over a nearby mountaintop, flying so close that the sound of the whipping blade drowned out conversation. Jay went still beside her, frowning at the intrusion. The stubble on his jaw was black as pitch, which made his dyed hair appear even more incongruent.

The helicopter disappeared, but a strange tension remained. As they broke down camp and loaded the raft,
Jay continued to glance up at the sky.

"Friends of yours?" she asked him.

He took the question seriously. "No."

"It was a joke."

"Oh." Picking up her bag, he carried it to the raft for
her. "I enjoyed your company last night."

"I could tell."

The corner of his mouth tipped up. She liked the
way he responded to her, and not just in the physical
sense. Men had found her cute and funny before, but
his attention felt different. He seemed surprised by her.

She vowed to catch him off guard again, to delight
him with her daring. "Are you going to take care of me
out on the water today?"

"Of course," he said.

"Then maybe I'll take care of you later."

His eyes darkened at the suggestion. Smiling, she
joined the other rafters. He watched her strip down to
her bikini top and shorts, looking as if he wanted to
toss her over his shoulder and carry her into the woods,
caveman-style.

She'd forgotten how much fun it was to flirt with
a hot guy.

Rafting, however, dampened her enthusiasm. It
was still chilly when they headed downriver, and her
scrawny arm muscles were sore from paddling. She'd
much rather be lounging poolside with a cocktail in Las
Vegas. Maybe next summer, when she brought her sister
there on vacation, she could squeeze in a visit with Jay.

Faith rejected the idea as soon as it popped into her

head. She had nothing against booty calls, but scheduling one a year in advance, with a guy she'd just met, wasn't her style. Pleasuring him in the woods was as far as her plans needed to go.

She moistened her lips in anticipation.

An hour later, Faith was clinging to the raft for dear life, her steamy fantasy doused by ice-cold rapids. They entered the first stretch of a section Ron called "the slickies." Underwater whirlpools, which appeared deceptively flat and slick, lurked at frequent intervals, ready to spin the boat backward.

The dips and drops were worse. The front of the boat caught air, only to slam down with an epic splash.

After they made it to a relatively calm area, Ron pulled over to "scout ahead." He jumped out of the raft and scrambled up a tall rock, studying the next bend of the river. While he was busy, his radio chirped twice.

"How does it look?" Paula asked.

"Hairy," Ron replied, giving the boat a push and hopping in.

Caleb howled like a coyote, splashing Ted with his paddle.

Faith exchanged a glance with Jay. He looked worried.

"Your radio beeped," Paula said.

"Yeah, they've been paging me all morning. Must be something important. I'll answer it when we stop for lunch."

Faith was looking forward to lunch. She might never get back in the raft. As they approached a huge drop between two boulders, her worst nightmare materialized. The left side of the raft lifted high in the air and she went with it. Screaming, she tumbled over the edge, gripping the wet guard rope in her clenched fist.

Ron had both hands full paddling, so he couldn't assist her.

Jay lunged across the space, grabbing the front of her life jacket and hauling her inside. Her eyes locked with his. "Okay now?" he asked.

When she nodded, he let go.

He'd risked his own safety by standing to help her. As he returned to his side of the raft, they hit another huge wave.

Jay toppled overboard, just like that.

Faith screamed again, throwing herself across the raft. She searched for him in the whitewater, her arms outstretched.

This time, it was Ron who hauled her backward. "You can't help him," he shouted. "Stay on your side and paddle!"

They still had a treacherous run to complete. Faith paddled as well as she could, sobbing in dismay. She scanned the rapids as they rushed by, praying for a glimpse of Jay's red helmet or a flash of his yellow life jacket.

She couldn't see him anywhere.

"We've got a swimmer," Ron said, alerting the other paddlers. They redoubled their efforts to reach an eddy behind a boulder. From there, they combed the water in all directions. "Look for him!"

There was no sign of Jay.

"I'm going in," Caleb said. He was the strongest swimmer, besides Ron, and they needed the guide to stay in the boat.

Before he jumped overboard, Paula pointed to a blur of color by the shore. "There!"

Faith could have wept with relief. Jay was clinging to a group of wet rocks near the opposite bank. Ron ordered them to paddle that direction. As they got closer, it became clear that he was injured. He was waist-deep in the water, his helmet askew, left arm hanging at an awkward angle.

Ron tied down the raft and leaped out. He got a grip on Jay's life jacket and dragged him toward the shore, his face contorted from the effort. Faith and Caleb came with him, sloshing through the icy shallows.

"Where are you hurt?" Ron asked.

"My shoulder," Jay said, wincing. "It's dislocated."

Faith stared at his left arm in horror. It looked detached from his body, like a limb on a scarecrow.

"Damn," Caleb said. "I've done that before. Hurts like a bitch."

"I'll call Dispatch," Ron said. "Emergency services has a helicopter—"

"I don't need a fucking helicopter," Jay interrupted. He took off his helmet and tossed it on the muddy bank. "I can walk."

"It's at least twenty miles, either direction."

"I'll live."

Caleb nodded, as if this sounded reasonable. "You can walk, but you can't carry gear. Someone will have to come with you."

He scowled at the suggestion, but Faith perked up. "I can do it."

"No," Ron said. "Your sister will have my ass."

"Your sister?" Jay asked.

"She's a park ranger," Faith said, waving away Ron's concern. "Don't worry about her. It's my fault he fell overboard, so the least I can do is help him. I'm also the weakest paddler. You need the others on the raft."

"She just wants to jump his bones," Caleb said with a smirk.

"Shut up," Faith said. "I'm not going to jump his bones."

Jay shuddered. "Please. Stop talking about bones."

Ron couldn't think of a solution that didn't involve emergency transport. Jay refused his repeated offers for a helicopter on the grounds that his injury wasn't serious. He also didn't have health insurance. Finally Ron relented, gathering a backpack of food and supplies for Faith. Together, they helped Jay out of his safety vest and into a sling.

"Good luck, bro," Caleb said.

"Thanks," Jay said gruffly, seeming surprised by his magnanimity.

"Follow the path downriver, to Moraine Lake," Ron said.

"Shouldn't we go back to the Kaweah Campsite?" Jay asked.

"It's a steeper hike," Ron said, his eyes sliding to Faith. "And...your sister said there's a murder suspect on the loose in that area."

Faith was taken aback by the news. "You're kidding."

"No. She was tracking him all day yesterday."

A chill traveled up her spine. Faith knew her sister's job was dangerous, but she hadn't been confronted with the cold, hard reality before. The idea of Hope tangling with a murderer disturbed her on many levels. Her sister was a self-sacrificing nutcase. She'd probably take a bullet for a squirrel.

"Who did he kill?"

"I don't know. She said something about a plane crash and drug smugglers."

"You should stay with the group," Jay said.

She shook her head, adamant. "No way. There's a psycho in the woods, and you can't even move your arm. You won't be able to unbutton your pants by yourself, let alone carry a backpack or set up a tent."

Ron and Jay exchanged an uncomfortable look.

"She's right," Ron said. "The only other option is to hike as a group."

Jay wouldn't consider it. "I don't want to ruin the trip for everyone. It's a dislocated shoulder, not a broken leg. I'll be fine."

"Okay," Ron said. "I'll notify Dispatch of the situation when I check in. They'll send a wilderness medic, but they probably won't reach you until tomorrow morning."

Although Jay insisted that he didn't need a medic, or Faith to accompany him, Ron wouldn't listen.

Faith waved goodbye to the group before they left. Then they were off, rafting down the sun-dappled river. She wasn't sorry to see the back of the boat, but she knew that hiking twenty miles wouldn't be a picnic. She'd never been strong or selfless, like Hope. Helping strangers wasn't her style. On the other hand, she liked Jay. There were worse ways to pass the time than playing nurse to a handsome patient.

As soon as the raft was out of sight, Jay tore the sling off his arm and wrenched it backward. She actually heard it pop. The effect was so disturbing that she retreated a step, almost losing her footing on the slippery rock.

His forehead was dotted with sweat, his breathing labored. But the pain in his face faded quickly. He rotated his shoulder, testing the socket.

"Wh-what did you do?" she asked.

"I popped it back into place."

"Have you done that before?"

"Yes, years ago. I didn't think of it until just now."

"Does it feel better?"

"Much."

Faith's stomach twisted with unease. Something wasn't right. This was Jay, the same man she'd kissed last night. The man who'd saved her from falling overboard a few minutes ago. But his entire demeanor had changed. He looked like a stranger. Maybe it was the ruthless, semirobotic way he'd put his arm back together.

He scared her.

CHAPTER SEVEN

SAM COULDN'T WALK away from Hope.

He should have made good on his threat to call Doug Dixon. Hell, he should have demanded that Doug fire her. Sam had donated over a hundred thousand dollars to Sierra National Park in the past two years. The park manager was in his back pocket.

He hadn't done it because of *guilt.* It was the same reason he'd climbed with her, and stayed with her last night. He'd been racked by guilt for years. It had prevented him from moving on after Melissa's death. It mocked him on a daily basis. He'd survived epic disasters and taken insane risks. Why was he even alive? There were many more deserving people who could have been spared.

When he heard Hope crying in the tent, the sound had brought him low. He hadn't wanted to sleep next to her, to listen to her soft breathing or smell her hair. Before lying down, he'd moved his wristband away from his tattoo and clutched it in his palm. He'd squeezed his eyes shut and tried to remember Melissa.

The memories he had were faded. The ones he couldn't access were locked away, out of reach, like a blind crux on a first ascent.

This morning had been like every other. He woke up in a panic, looking for Melissa. Some days it took him minutes or even hours to find the tattoo and accept her death. Usually he processed the information in seconds.

Today, for the first time, he wasn't alone. In the predawn light, he'd mistaken Hope for Melissa. They were both slender and dark-haired. Instead of feeling anxious, he'd been comforted by her presence. He was aroused, aching for female touch. And intensely disturbed, once the fantasy was torn away.

He would *never* fall asleep beside a brunette again.

Gritting his teeth, he continued to cut through the water with smooth strokes, keeping up with Hope's pace easily. She was a good kayaker, long-armed and graceful. More patient than Melissa had been.

His mind rejected the comparison. Melissa had been an intense competitor, like him. Hope couldn't match her raw athleticism, but she was a natural on the river. She paddled with the currents, her motions fluid.

By noon, the air felt heavy with moisture. Sam glanced up at the cloudy sky, anticipating rain by nightfall.

They pushed on to Devil's Drop, a difficult stretch of rapids. Hope executed a duck roll with confidence, proving she could hold her own on a Class Five. But she also showed a desperate urgency, refusing to slow down when she needed rest. He shouted at her three times before she pulled over.

Mouth pursed with annoyance, she banked her kayak and removed some items from the dry sack. After she took a quick drink of water and a bite of an energy bar, she radioed Dispatch, still chewing.

"Where are you?"

"Just past Devil's Drop."

"I have bad news."

"What is it?"

"Ron checked in at noon with an injury report."

Her eyes flew to Sam's. "Who?"

"A guy named Jay Norton. He's not on the passenger list. Apparently he paid another rafter cash to join the group."

"That's our suspect," she said.

"He fell overboard in the slickies and dislocated his shoulder. Ron offered to call in a helicopter, but he opted to hike to Moraine Lake instead. The rafting group left some supplies with him and continued downriver."

She took another bite of energy bar, considering.

"Your sister stayed behind with Norton."

Her face paled. "Why?"

"Faith volunteered to hike out with him."

"She would never do that."

"According to Ron, the two of them were…friendly."

Hope gripped the radio until her knuckles turned white. "Connect me with Ron," she said through clenched teeth.

Sam heard the barely restrained fury in her voice. She was going to rip Ron a new one.

"I'll try, but he's in the process of packing up the rafting equipment and hiking the remaining passengers back to Moraine Lake."

"I thought they were continuing downriver."

"That was the plan until a few minutes ago. The guys who accepted the cash from Norton decided to go after him on foot. They said they felt responsible for the trouble because they brought him along. Ron couldn't stop them." He paused for a moment. "Their names are Caleb Renfro and Ted Harvey."

Hope demanded descriptions of all three men.

After the dispatcher supplied this information, he added, "It's raining on Angel Wings, so Deputy Meeks turned his team around."

"They didn't process the scene?"

"No."

"Why can't they camp?"

"I think someone forgot to pack the tent. They're on their way back to Kaweah. We have rangers there and at Moraine Lake, waiting to see what the weather does. Looks like a storm is coming your way."

She studied the dark clouds overhead.

"Ron also reported seeing a low-flying helicopter in that area. Another craft without a flight plan."

"Shit," Hope muttered. "They're searching for the cargo."

"Dixon wants you to head back. Or else."

She let the arm holding the radio drop into her lap, defeated. It was too dangerous to kayak during heavy rain or lightning. They didn't have any overnight gear. The rafting group they were chasing had split up.

And there were more drug smugglers nearby.

Hope brought the receiver back to her mouth, pressing the button. "I'll check in later," she said, and signed off.

While he gaped at her, incredulous, she finished her lunch and rose to her feet, walking toward the bushes.

"What are you doing?" he called after her.

She didn't answer.

He powered down his own energy bar and stepped into the trees to relieve himself, worried that she might leave without him. Sure enough, she hitched up her pants and put her helmet back on, preparing to depart.

Sam hurried to follow. "Is this worth losing your job over?"

"I'm not going to lose my job."

"What about your life?"

"My sister is the one in danger," she said, lifting her chin. "This guy probably feels cornered. I think he's trying to avoid the authorities *and* his crew. That makes the situation more unpredictable."

"I predict rain."

"It won't start for an hour or two. If I can get to the slickies before the storm hits, I'll be able to pick up their trail."

He stared after her, his blood pumping with adrenaline. The urge to reach out and detain her was difficult to resist. He wanted to wrestle her to the ground, to lock his hands around her slender wrists.

The feeling unsettled him greatly. He'd always been attracted to strong women, and never felt the need to overpower them. Melissa had challenged him on a regular basis, but their arguments hadn't turned physical. One of the models he'd dated had slapped him for an imagined insult. He hadn't even been tempted to respond in kind.

Hope brought out the beast in him. And…he enjoyed it, on some level. Maybe because dark, ugly emotions were better than none. Maybe because she represented the only bright spot in his stark existence, his only real pleasure since the accident. He didn't know if he wanted to tackle her or bang her or both.

"Thanks for coming this far," she said, climbing

aboard the kayak. She shoved her dry bag inside and attached the spray skirt. "I appreciate it."

"I'm not staying behind, Hope."

"Suit yourself."

Sam gritted his teeth, thinking of all the friends and family members who'd tried to convince him not to free-solo. He hadn't listened to any of them. He knew his climbing practices were unsafe and he didn't care.

Right now Hope was in the same place. She'd disregarded the danger as unimportant. Nothing he said would change her mind.

It was intensely frustrating to be on this side of the coin.

Cursing under his breath, he crammed himself into the cockpit and maneuvered his kayak away from the shore. For the first few miles, they encountered nothing hairier than a few lazy rapids. Then it started to drizzle, and visibility became an issue. Although her paddling skills were impressive, he imagined disaster around every corner.

Cold sweat broke out on his forehead, sliding down his spine.

An hour later, the skies broke open with a crack of thunder, dumping buckets of rain. During bad weather, fallen logs and other dangerous objects were more likely to come loose. They were already cold and wet. If the strainers didn't get them, hypothermia would. Sam paddled harder, shouting at Hope to bank her kayak.

She ignored him.

Hail peppered the surface of the river like buckshot, pelting the top of his helmet. Hope showed no sign of letting up. Her paddle cut through the water with swift, powerful strokes. The slickies were only a hundred feet downriver.

She was trying to lose him!

Sam went into overdrive, paddling as hard as he'd ever done in Olympic competitions. His heart felt as if it might burst from anxiety. He pictured her getting caught in a deadly spin, held under by a powerful current.

He pulled his kayak alongside hers and executed a tight turn, driving her into the riverbank. They crashed into the shore, hulls scraping over wet rocks. Hailstones the size of marbles perforated the surface of the water as lightning bisected the darkening sky.

Hope scrambled out of her kayak and upended it, using the hard fiberglass as a shield. He did the same. After a few moments, the hail subsided, melting into slush. A hard, heavy rain continued to fall.

She stared at the roiling river, her breath coming in short pants. He suspected that she was contemplating another reentry, but a strike of lightning—very close by—seemed to snap her out of the stubborn haze.

"We have to find a better shelter," he said.

She nodded glumly. Any trail her sister and the suspect might have left was long gone.

They left their kayaks on higher ground and pulled jackets from the dry sacks. "There's a cave system near here," she said, pointing west.

They trudged for several miles to the mouth of a gaping cave. It was shrouded with hanging moss, and damp inside. He dropped his dry sack on the pebble-strewn ground, shoving down the hood of his jacket.

The interior of the cavern was spacious, opening up

to a network of smaller rooms and passageways. Sam knew better than to leave the relative safety of the entrance. This was bear country, and he didn't want to walk into a den.

"That was some fucking stunt," he growled, facing Hope.

She tossed her dry sack next to his, her jaw tense. Rain droplets clung to her skin. In the dim light, with mist creating a halo effect behind her, she appeared ethereal and luminous, like a wood nymph.

"Were you trying to get yourself killed?"

She squinted at him in annoyance. "Is that what you were trying to do on Valhalla?"

"No," he said, insulted. "It's not the same."

"Why, because you're a man?"

He scowled, raking a hand through his wet hair. If he'd subscribed to that sexist bullshit, he'd never have dated Melissa. "I know my limits."

"And I don't know mine?"

"Only an idiot would run a Class Five during a hailstorm."

"Don't confuse me with yourself, Sam."

"What's that supposed to mean?"

She crossed her arms over her chest. "I don't take risks for cheap thrills," she said, her voice wavering. "I'm worried about my sister!"

He could have kicked himself for opening this can of worms. Especially when her face crumpled and she turned her back on him. She made him feel things he didn't want to feel. Like passion, and fear, and anger.

And sympathy.

He looked up at the ceiling of the cave, wishing it

would fall down on him. "I'm not after cheap thrills, either," he said softly.

She wiped the tears from her cheeks, hazarding a glance over her shoulder. "Then why do you do it?"

His condition wasn't easy to put into words, and he'd never been a great communicator. But he felt compelled to explain this to her. He wanted to ease the sting of his rejection. "Since the accident, I don't experience fear like I used to. I can still feel it. I meant what I said about corpses. And you...you terrify me."

"Me?" she asked, whirling around again.

"I'm not afraid for myself," he explained. "I'm numb, as far as personal safety and self-preservation go. But I feel fear for others. Too much fear. When you were climbing the wall, I was paralyzed."

A crease formed between her brows.

"I can't stand seeing you in danger, Hope. This is why I don't partner-climb anymore. I'm convinced that everyone around me is going to die."

"Is that what happened in the freeway collapse? You saw a lot of people die?"

"Maybe."

"You don't remember?"

"No. I have no memory of the earthquake, or several months prior."

"Several *months?*"

Sam nodded, avoiding her gaze. He hadn't lost any ordinary stretch of weeks, either. He'd wiped out an entire period of mourning. His last moments with Melissa had been obliterated.

How could he move on? In his fractured mind, she was still alive.

Hope glanced down at the band on his wrist, but she didn't ask about his tattoo. Maybe she didn't want to trigger another humiliating breakdown, or remind him of the awkward mistake he'd made this morning.

The two women didn't look alike, not really. Not even from the back. Hope's hair was softer, curlier, more lustrous. She had a curvier figure. Melissa had been tall and slim-hipped, her hair pencil-straight.

He had a hard time remembering how good it had been with Melissa, but he could recall the silky clasp of Hope's body with ease.

Damn her.

"You have amnesia," she said.

"I prefer the term 'brain damage.'"

"Will you get your memory back?"

He shrugged. His doctors didn't even know if the problem was neurological or psychological. They couldn't predict his recovery.

"And you feel nothing when you're solo-climbing?"

"I feel…a little less dead inside."

Her eyes darkened with understanding. And that was when he knew why he'd taken her home from the bar. It wasn't because of her pretty face, although he'd noticed that first. He hadn't been unable to resist her sexy figure or sweet-looking mouth. If their attraction was based on physical appearance only, he could have walked away.

It wasn't.

He saw something in her, a quiet pain that mirrored his own. He'd gotten drunk enough to quash the feeling that night, but it was still there. It was the reason he'd pursued her, and one of the reasons he'd enjoyed her so much. She responded like a woman who hadn't indulged herself in a long, long time.

This morning, she'd melted in his arms once more.

Sam clenched his hands into fists, awash with memories of her pleasure. He didn't want to want her. He didn't want to know what had happened to her, or why she'd isolated herself in the Sierras. Using her for sex was out of the question, and he sure as hell couldn't have a relationship with her. He was mentally unstable. Emotionally challenged. Given half a chance, he'd hurt her again.

"I'm sorry," she said.

"So am I."

She shivered, examining the damp interior of the cave. Although her jacket was waterproof, she was soaked to the skin underneath it. When the storm let up, he might be able to get a fire going to warm her.

In the meantime, they'd have to use body heat. He unzipped his jacket, inviting her inside, and she stepped closer, sliding her arms around him. His muscles tightened in awareness of her breasts against his chest. She rested her head on his shoulder. He tugged the jacket around them and listened to the rain.

It was too late to head back to Kaweah. They were going to be in for a cold, wet night. Maybe he could stay awake and avoid another scene like this morning.

She shifted in his arms, pressing her cold nose to his throat. Although the sensation was far from erotic, it affected him on a gut level.

He grasped her shoulders with the intention of pushing her away. Then she glanced up at him and he got distracted. Her eyes were half-lidded, lashes wet. A fine sheen of moisture coated her skin. Her lips were dewy, petal-soft.

She looked…delicious.

If she'd let him touch her after the way he'd behaved, maybe *she* had a few screws loose. But he was dying for another taste of her. Being with Hope made him feel alive; kissing her was the only thing that made him feel *good*.

So instead of putting distance between them, he brought her closer. She tilted her head back in blatant invitation. As he lowered his mouth to hers, he heard the unmistakable sound of pebbles scraping beneath booted feet.

They weren't alone.

CHAPTER EIGHT

JAVIER DIDN'T KNOW what to do with Faith.

His decision to bail overboard and feign injury had been made in haste. He assumed that the authorities were looking for him. They might have been trying to contact Ron with a warning on his radio. Ron probably wouldn't have been stupid enough to confront him, but nervous people did crazy things.

Javier's larger concern was Gonzales. After seeing his boss's helicopter, every instinct told him it was time to run.

What he hadn't anticipated was Faith volunteering to hike with him. He would have preferred Caleb. The guy had proven himself to be less of a *puto* than he appeared, but Javier would've had no problem cracking his skull with a rock.

He couldn't do that to Faith. He was reluctant to pull his gun and scare her off. She might get hurt or lost, alone in the wilderness.

Her sister, the park ranger, complicated matters. He wouldn't shoot a woman by choice, but neither would he surrender without a fight. Being captured meant certain death, whether he was convicted here or deported to a Venezuelan prison. No one who betrayed Gonzales's crew was safe behind bars.

Ahead of him, Faith paused to adjust her pack.

They'd both changed into warmer clothes after the clouds rolled in. Her snug sweatpants had hearts on the back pockets. She was a hot little piece, but being sexy didn't make her dumb. Sooner or later, she'd figure out that he was the man her sister had been tracking.

She was already tired, and they'd only gone five miles. She couldn't hike for a damn. And she was wary of him. Since watching him pop his shoulder back in, she'd cut out all of the cutesy flirting and naughty innuendoes.

They were headed toward Moraine Lake, which was still his best bet for escape, but their progress was slow. His shoulder socket ached. He hadn't dislocated it on purpose since he was a teenager. Right now he was feeling every one of his twenty-nine years.

The helicopter reappeared suddenly. They were walking through a canyon, close to the riverbed, so the sound of the approaching craft was muted. An open meadow stretched out before them, peaceful and deadly.

Javier almost didn't have a chance to stop Faith from running headfirst into danger. He grabbed her by the wrist and pulled her the opposite direction, into the dense forest. Flattening her back against a tree, he trapped her there, pressing his forearm against her collarbone. Before she could speak, he crushed his hand over her mouth.

He didn't expect her to cooperate, so the sharp teeth biting into his palm wasn't a complete surprise. Ignoring the pain, he kept her as still as possible, his heart thumping a wild tattoo against hers.

As soon as the helicopter passed, he relaxed his grip.

"What the hell?" she spat.

He glanced at the crescent mark on his palm. No blood, but it would bruise. "You bite hard."

"Why did you do that?"

"I thought you were going to wave the helicopter down."

"I was, jackass. We need help."

"No, we don't. My shoulder doesn't even hurt that much."

"Great," she said, shrugging out of the heavy backpack. "You can carry this."

He accepted the challenge without complaint, moving the strap gingerly over his left arm. "Those guys might have been drug smugglers."

She studied the empty meadow, a pulse fluttering in her throat.

"I'm sorry I grabbed you like that. I just…had a bad feeling about it."

Her gaze returned to his, quiet and assessing. No, she wasn't dumb. There was a hint of distrust in her eyes. As long as he continued to protect her, she'd probably stick by him. Her only other choice was to hike alone.

Even if she wanted to take off, he couldn't let her wander through the woods by herself. Not when she could be intercepted by the enemy. Gonzales wasn't just looking for the cargo at this point. They were searching for Javier, and they wouldn't hesitate to hurt anyone with him. Gonzales's men weren't as chivalrous with women as Javier. They'd kill a female. They'd done it before.

Javier should have refused to let Faith tag along, but Ron had insisted, and he'd been in a hurry to get away from the rafting group. Now he was stuck with her out in the middle of nowhere.

The afternoon wore on. His wet shoes didn't fit well, and his feet were still raw from his trek down the mountain. His shoulder throbbed dully with every step. Faith was behind him, instead of in front, so he couldn't even enjoy the view.

When it began to rain, he kept trudging forward, aware that every mile they traveled brought her closer to safety. Before they reached Moraine Lake, he'd have to ditch her. If he left her too soon, she might get lost or run into trouble. As they continued through the deluge, a loud crack of thunder gave him pause.

Seconds later, the sky erupted with hail.

Faith cried out in distress, plastering her body against his. He took off the backpack and held it like a shield over their heads. They had to find shelter. Ron's single-man tent wouldn't protect them from the elements, and it might wash away if they set it up in the wrong place. Javier searched the area while she clung to him, shivering.

"There," she said, pointing to a rock outcropping in the distance.

They ran toward it, ducking under the sloped edge. There was enough space to sit down, and it was relatively dry. Without a fire, however, they wouldn't get warm, and twilight was fast approaching.

Faith hugged her knees to her chest, looking bedraggled.

"We should put up the tent," he said.

She seemed relieved by the suggestion, probably because it meant they were done hiking for the day. He removed the tent from his pack, wincing in discomfort, and studied it. There wasn't a label with directions.

"Let me," she said.

He agreed easily, resting his injured arm. While he watched, she scattered the tent poles around and unfolded the tent, trying to make sense of it. He couldn't offer any advice. Caleb and Ted had set theirs up last night with little assistance from him.

"This must go underneath," she said, setting aside a rectangle of nylon. She cleared away some sharp rocks and laid it flat. Then she poked tent poles into various sleeves, twisting and maneuvering until she'd wrestled the thing into submission.

Sort of.

The structure sagged in the middle and looked ready to collapse. She lifted her chin, daring him to criticize.

"Good job," he said, smiling.

She rolled her eyes. "Shut up."

They had beef jerky and dried apricots for dinner. She finished her meal in sullen silence, tearing the tough strips with her teeth like a feral animal. Her hair had leaves in it and there was a smudge of dirt on her cheek. She was adorable.

The storm raged on and the temperature dropped considerably. They were both soaked. In the rain-washed hour before sundown, she began to tremble again. Her skin appeared pale and her lips took on a bluish tone.

"We need to get out of these wet clothes," he said.

She didn't argue when he stripped down to his boxer

briefs. This time, her perusal of his body seemed detached. He climbed into the tent and under the sleeping bag. She joined him a moment later, trembling in her tiny bikini.

He tried to ignore her hard nipples poking against the fabric, and he didn't even glance at the little triangle between her legs. Clearing his throat, he tucked the sleeping bag around them and pulled her close, stomach to stomach, skin on skin.

It was difficult to keep his thoughts pure with a beautiful, near-naked woman in his arms. Memories of the kiss they'd shared sprang to the forefront of his mind. He imagined plumbing the sweet, hot recesses of her mouth. His cold-shrunken package started to warm up and the inevitable unshrinking occurred.

She noticed his erection, of course. Her silky crotch was pressed right up against it. Unlike last night, she didn't seem eager to hop on and go for a ride. She held still, not remarking on his condition. Her attitude toward him had changed since they'd been stranded. She wasn't keen on "taking care of him" anymore, and he didn't blame her. He also respected her for valuing her personal safety. He'd been with a few women who wanted him because they thought he was dangerous. It didn't sit well with him.

She must have trusted him not to press his luck, because she stayed close. He doubted she was waiting for him to make the first move. She hadn't been shy last night. Or sober, he reflected. A shot of whiskey wouldn't be amiss. He didn't want to get her drunk, but he'd like to put her at ease. "I wish I had Caleb's flask."

She lifted her head to look at him, a smile playing on her lips. "You would ply me with alcohol?"

"I'd love to ply you."

Groaning, she pushed away from him and rolled onto her back. The few inches of distance between them didn't ease his arousal. His hungry eyes wandered south.

Coño de la madre, what a body.

"How old are you?" she asked.

He dragged his gaze back to her face. "I'll be thirty next month," he said, wondering if he'd live that long. "How old are you?"

"Twenty-six."

"Perfect."

"For what?"

Oops. He'd been staring at her breasts again.

"Why don't you have a girlfriend?"

"No reason," he said, evasive.

"Come on. I told you about my bad breakup."

He sighed, stretching out on his back beside her. There was barely enough room for them to lie shoulder-to-shoulder. "Were you in love with him, this sports fan?"

"I think so," she said, after a moment.

"And you couldn't accept his hobby?"

"It was more of an obsession, but no. I couldn't."

"Why?"

"I need a lot of attention," she admitted.

He glanced at her, surprised by the bald honesty. And the self-awareness. "The last woman I cared about left me for another man."

Her brows rose. "Ouch."

He'd never talked to anyone about his relationship with Alexia. It was a painful subject, and an awkward one in Gonzales's circles. The boss's closest confidants were aware that he'd stolen Javier's girlfriend.

"She married him," he said.

"Is she happy?"

"No. He has…mistreated her."

She studied him carefully. "Do you still want her?"

He shook his head. Even if a reunion was possible, he wouldn't choose it. His heart had turned cold on the day of the wedding, when she'd suggested that they continue their affair. "I'm not that forgiving."

"You're angry."

He couldn't deny it. He was furious with Gonzales for taking his bride, and with himself for being unable to prevent the abuse she'd suffered. Alexia had been superficial and ambitious, but she didn't deserve to die. "I'm angry with him."

"You were friends?"

"Yes."

"Wow," she said, clutching the sleeping bag to her chest. "Your breakup story is so much deeper than mine. Maybe my sister was right."

He gave her a curious glance.

"Hope says I give up on relationships too easily. She thinks I'm 'flighty.'"

"Are you?"

"Yes," she said, with an impish shrug.

"I like that about you."

"You would."

"Did you tell your boyfriend you were unhappy?"

"Of course. One night I put on sexy lingerie and walked in front of the TV. He didn't even notice."

"Are you sure he was straight?"

She laughed, taking her hair out of the braids. It brushed her shoulders in damp waves. With her warm brown eyes and smoky lashes, she had a sultry look. Sweet, but not so innocent. She sat up and turned toward him, letting the sleeping bag drop to her waist.

He realized that his openness had put her at ease. Either that or she'd decided he was due for a pity fuck. Nibbling on her pouty lower lip, she trailed her gaze down his chest and over his clenched stomach. He sprouted a noticeable tent.

Seeming pleased by the sight, she lifted her arms to the nape of her neck, untying the bikini string. The top fell away, exposing her bare breasts. They were perky and round, with tight little nipples.

Javier almost swallowed his tongue.

HOPE WAITED FOR Sam to kiss her, breathless with anticipation.

She couldn't seem to stop wanting him. Blind lust overrode her logic and emotions. He wasn't good for her. He wasn't good *to* her. Even so, she swayed toward him, begging for more of his bad medicine.

They both heard approaching footsteps at the same time. Sam jerked his head toward the other side of the cavern, where the noise was coming from. Hope grabbed her dry pack, her heart racing. There was a dark passageway directly behind them. She ducked into it, motioning for him to come with her.

He slipped into the hiding place. Following her lead, he flattened his back against the perforated cave wall, among the shadows. She removed her gun from the pack and held it with both hands, pointing down at the ground. Her eyes strained for movement as the sound of footsteps got louder.

Two men emerged from a tunnel into the main cavern. Judging by the lack of stealth, they didn't know Hope and Sam were nearby.

She immediately assessed them as the drug smugglers. They didn't fit the descriptions of Caleb Renfro and Ted Harvey, who were probably miles south, near Mist Falls. One was short and stocky, with dark trousers and a black leather jacket. The other was taller, in jeans and a rain poncho. He had a flashlight. Neither was a typical outdoor type. They'd probably arrived via helicopter rather than hiking in on foot.

Poncho turned off his flashlight and stashed it. Leather reached into his pocket for a pack of cigarettes. They walked right past the passageway where Hope and Sam were hiding, toward the mouth of the cave.

It was still raining heavily, a blessing in disguise. The sound must have washed out their voices.

Hope released a slow breath. Her pulse thundered in her ears and the acrid smell of smoke burned her nostrils. The smugglers were having a cigarette break, not venturing back out into the rain.

Beside her, Sam made an urgent gesture. He pointed at the single dry sack, and then showed her his open hands.

They'd left the other bag near the entrance.

Oh God.

"Now what?" one of the men said.

"We wait."

"Del Norte is long gone. You know he never got over...her."

"How many times have I told you not to talk about that?"

"I didn't say anything."

"Just shut the fuck up."

They continued smoking. Hope couldn't remember the last time she'd been so close to a lit cigarette. No one smoked indoors in California, and the Sierras were full of health nuts. Its residents were more likely to spark up a joint.

"Del Norte isn't the only one who knows where the stuff is," the first man said. Leather, she surmised.

"What do you mean?"

"There's some ranger running around here. She took photos of the stash."

Hope wondered where they got this information. Did they have a mole in park services?

"The next time she checks in on her radio, saying where she is, we'll go get her. She can guide us to the cargo. Problem solved."

She glanced at Sam, who was vibrating with tension beside her. The smugglers had been able to intercept her radio signals.

"Rangers have guns," Poncho said.

They certainly did. She tightened her grip on the weapon, wondering if she should interrupt this conversation right now. These jokers thought they were going to hunt *her* down and push her around?

"So do we," Leather replied.

The fact that they were also armed, and she had no
backup, kept her quiet in the shadows. If they didn't cooperate—and odds were they wouldn't—the risk might
prove fatal. She had to consider Sam's safety, as well
as Faith's and her own. A failed attempt to detain them
could be disastrous for everyone.

Poncho and Leather discussed the plan, still smoking. They knew everything. They knew the suspect was
with a young woman, and that Hope had a male companion. Their priority was to recover the drug stash,
but capturing Del Norte was also essential. Apparently
this guy was persona non grata since he'd gone AWOL.

Sam caught her attention, hooking his thumb toward
the dark recesses. He wanted to creep away, but she
shook her head no. She'd only been in this cave once
before, and she wasn't familiar with its layout. There
was no guarantee of an escape route. They might hit a
wall or a steep drop-off. Any noise they made would
draw attention. It wasn't wise to move out of hiding unless they had no other options.

A moment later, the choice was made for them.

"What the hell is this?" Leather said.

He'd found Sam's pack.

"Go," Sam whispered, grabbing her by the arm and
shoving her in front of him.

It was all wrong. She had the gun, so she should
bring up the rear. But there was no time to argue or
switch places, and they didn't have the luxury of stealth.
Heart pounding, she crept down the dark corridor, praying for a throughway.

If they reached a dead end, they'd be screwed.

Leather and Poncho heard their frantic motions, of

course. The men entered the passage, turning on their flashlight. Its beam illuminated a dip in the cave floor. Hope cried out as she tripped over it and almost lost her footing.

Sam grasped the back of her jacket to jerk her upright.

"Hey!" Leather yelled.

"Go," Sam repeated, pushing her forward but keeping a firm grip on her hood.

She started running, her chest tight with panic. They could hurtle off a sharp precipice or tumble into a well of echoes at any moment. She pictured herself broken and muddy, wrestling skeletons in the muck. The men behind them closed the distance in crashing bounds.

Hope came to a fork in the cavern. She went right, into nothingness, and the path dissolved under her feet. Sam fell with her, unable to fight gravity or forward momentum. Luckily, it was a short drop to the cavern floor. They landed in a jumbled heap. The air whooshed from her lungs and the gun flew out of her hand. While she struggled for oxygen, Sam looked over her shoulder.

"Oh, fuck," he said, staring into the abyss.

She gaped like a fish out of water, her mouth open in a silent scream. Poncho arrived at the entryway, shining a flashlight on the scene. Leather halted beside him, frozen.

Sam heaved her toward a pocket in the cave wall and crammed in next to her. She inhaled a deep breath to clear her head. As the fog lifted, she was struck by a number of disturbing sensory details. The room they'd stumbled into smelled of scat and wet fur. She felt the presence of something…big.

A massive shape lumbered from its depths, emitting a fierce roar.

Bear.

CHAPTER NINE

HOPE CLUNG TO Sam as the bear came closer.

It was immense, at least four hundred pounds, with a thinning summer coat and powerful haunches. While she watched, eyes wide with terror, the bear swiped its claws over the ground and made a loud huffing sound.

She could smell fish on its breath.

The bear was focused on the two men in the passageway. It might have felt challenged because they were standing upright, blocking the path. Maybe it was bothered by the flashlight. Instead of backing away slowly, one of the men drew his gun and fired a warning shot. Not a smart move. The animal went ballistic. In a blur of motion, the bear charged, its roar echoing through the chamber. Both men hollered as they fled down the corridor.

Sam rolled out of his hiding place. "You okay?"

"Yes."

"Let's go."

She didn't need to be asked twice. After finding her gun and stashing it in the dry pack, she scrambled to her feet. Sam grasped her seeking hand. Staying here wasn't a good idea, and she sure as hell wasn't going to follow the bear.

They climbed out of the cavern and headed down the opposite passageway. Hoarse male shouts and low growls reverberated in her ears as they descended into the cave's bowels. She couldn't see her hand in front of her face.

Before they went too far, Sam rigged a simple safety line. Removing the lace from his hiking boot, he tied one end to the front of his belt and attached the other to the racer back of her sports top.

"You think that'll hold?" she whispered.

"It should. It's rappelling cord."

This time, when he insisted that she go first, she didn't mind. She'd rather break a leg than worry about a bear breathing down her neck. Stomach churning, she shuffled through the darkness, arms stretched out before her.

The sounds of bear and man faded. Maybe the smugglers had been mauled and eaten. It was more likely that the bear had scared them off and they'd fled the area. Hope wasn't heading back to find out. They continued down the serpentine passageway. Every few feet, Sam flicked on his lighter, illuminating the space.

After what seemed like hours, they stopped to rest.

Hope's emotions overwhelmed her. She sank to a seated position, her face crumpling. He put his arm around her and drew her head to his chest as she began to cry in ragged sobs. She felt embarrassed by her lack of stoicism. Her tears dried up a few moments later, disappearing as suddenly as they'd struck. He continued to stroke her hair and hold her close.

"Do you want to turn back?" she asked.

"No," he said. "What do you think?"

"I don't know. I'm not familiar with this cave system. We could get lost."

They could get *more* lost, rather. As of now, they'd stuck to the right in hopes of discovering an alternative exit. She wasn't certain she could find her way back to the mouth of the cave, even if she wanted to.

"At least we didn't get shot," she said.

"Or eaten by a bear."

They both burst out laughing, edgy from stress and relief. It was quiet, muffled laughter, impossible to stifle. She clapped a hand over her mouth and rested her forehead on his shoulder, her body quaking with mirth.

"That was close," she said, wiping the tears from her cheeks.

"Yes."

They shared a handful of pistachios and drank half of their water. Sam pressed a tiny rectangle into her palm.

"What is it?" she asked.

"Gum."

"You only have one piece?"

"No, I have a few. I want to save them."

Having lost one of the packs, they didn't have enough food or water. Nodding, she tore the piece in half and searched for his mouth in the dark. As he accepted the gum from her, his tongue touched her fingertips, warm and wet.

She brought the other half to her lips, licking the same fingertips. As if he could see her, or sense the action, she flushed and dropped her hand. "I can't use my radio."

"No," he agreed.

"I'm worried about Faith."

"Do you think she's being held against her will?"

"I don't know," she said, chewing her gum. "According to Ron, she volunteered to hike. That's not like her."

"Why not?"

"She's the indoor type. Shopping is her favorite exercise."

"Has she been whitewater rafting before?"

"No."

"The Kaweah is pretty hard-core," he said. "Some people would rather hike than raft."

She nodded. "Ron also said she was friendly with the suspect. She might have been flirting with him."

"Is that typical?"

"Yes. She's always been boy-crazy."

"How old is she?"

"Twenty-six."

"You mother her," he said.

Although his tone was light, not accusatory, she felt the blood drain from her face. "Do you have sisters?"

"No."

She relaxed a little. He didn't know what he was talking about. "It's not really her fault. Faith is a guy magnet. Everywhere we go, men stare at her."

"The same way they stare at you?"

"Men don't stare at me."

He made a skeptical noise. "Whatever you say."

Hope knew she wasn't as sexy or flamboyant as Faith. In this situation, her sister's popularity was troubling. Hope tried to think on the bright side. Faith had never met a man she couldn't manipulate. Except Tom, perhaps.

"He has a dislocated shoulder," Sam said.

"He's still a killer."

"Maybe he acted in self-defense."

She brought her knees to her chest, shivering. Poncho and Leather were serious criminals. Even if Del Norte wasn't a rapist or a cold-blooded murderer, he was dangerous. Faith could get caught in the cross fire.

"Is your family religious?" he asked.

"No. Why?"

"Hope and Faith."

"Oh. No, my parents are just hippie, free-spirit types. They own an organic plant nursery. We could have easily been Daisy and Meadow."

He laughed softly. "Yours, too? Sam is short for Samson."

"Samson what?"

"Pax Rutherford."

She smiled, thinking it had a nice ring.

"There's no story behind the names?"

"Well, my mother's name is Joy, and my grandmother's name is Charity, so it's kind of a family theme. She also had several miscarriages before we came along. She didn't think she could carry a child to full term. When she got pregnant with me, I was Hope. Two years later, she had Faith."

He didn't respond, and she fell quiet. It was difficult for her to speak about pregnancies and motherhood. Maybe he could hear the yearning in her voice.

"What do your parents think about you working all the way out here?" he asked.

"It's only a few hours from Ojai."

"That's not what I meant."

She was caught off guard by the question. He'd already offered some uncomfortable insights about her relationship with Faith. After a near-death experience, forty-eight hours of stress and two crying jags, she felt intensely vulnerable. "What do your parents think of your free-soloing?"

"They don't care for it."

Of course they didn't. She wished she hadn't asked.

"We should keep going," he said.

She rose to her feet and moved in front of him, taking the lead once again. He couldn't illuminate the path as often because they needed to conserve lighter fluid. If they managed to escape this hellhole, building a fire would be the first priority. Hope was cold and uncomfortable in her wet clothes. Once she stopped moving, the chill would be unbearable.

They fell into a rhythm of shuffling feet and searching hands. Sam had to keep an arm stretched above his head, because his height demanded greater clearance. She continued to worry about Faith and second-guess her exchanges with Sam.

This wasn't her style at all. Like a lovesick schoolgirl, she overanalyzed his contradictory words and actions.

He'd made it clear that he didn't want to sleep with her again. But, before the drug smugglers interrupted, he'd been about to kiss her. He'd scolded her for acting reckless, and seemed critical of her choice to work in a remote area. Was he a hypocrite, or just completely lacking self-awareness?

She was so wrapped up in her own thoughts that she almost didn't notice the change of ambiance. Most of the passageways were cramped, claustrophobic. They had to crouch down in some areas, crawl on their bellies in others. The path suddenly opened up to a larger space, with different sounds and smells.

Hope sensed the emptiness in front of her and stopped, making a squeak of distress. When she shrank back, Sam bumped into her. The combination of her uneasy footing and his forward motion knocked her off balance. She toppled over an unseen precipice.

FAITH DECIDED TO leave her bikini bottoms on.

For now.

She didn't want Jay to get the wrong idea. If he thought she was a sure thing, he might not try hard enough. Some men tried too hard, which was worse. After a bad experience, she'd learned to avoid overeager types.

Jay wasn't like that. He was an excellent kisser, which boded well, but first encounters were unpredictable. Bedroom skills and compatibility varied. Sometimes chemistry fizzled. His injured shoulder could put a damper on their fun.

And…maybe she was a little rusty. She hadn't done this in a while. The last time she'd tried to seduce a man, she'd failed.

Jay wasn't Tom, however. She had his complete attention. His eyes stayed locked on her bare breasts, and his erection tented the sleeping bag.

She arched her back slightly, giving him a show. In addition to being easily aroused—always a turn-on—he was crazy-hot. She liked him in his vintage clothes and nerd glasses. She liked him in his boxer briefs. He had an amazing physique, taut and toned and bronzed all over. With his dark coloring, he might have been

Greek or Italian. She'd always loved foreign men. Even the dyed hair was growing on her.

There was something odd about him, a mysterious edge she found exciting. He hadn't reacted to Caleb's gibes. He seemed impervious to pain. The fact that he responded strongly to *her* made her feel very feminine and powerful.

Her nipples pebbled in the cool air.

"Do you want to touch me?" she asked.

"Yes," he said, his voice hoarse.

When he lifted his hand to her breast, she covered it with hers, encouraging him. As he cradled her soft flesh, teasing her nipple with his thumb, she inhaled a sharp breath. His eyes rose to her face. He cared about pleasing her.

She fell on him with a breathless moan. His erection nudged her belly, hard and hot. Squirming with excitement, she nibbled his lower lip and flicked her tongue against his. He kissed her back in bold strokes, filling her eager mouth. After several steamy seconds, she pulled away, licking the side of his neck.

He let her toy with him. Then again, he didn't have much choice. He couldn't roll on top of her or take control. He was prostrate, sort of…at her mercy.

She liked it.

He'd scared her earlier. When he'd popped his shoulder back into place like an automaton. And later, when he'd hauled her into the woods, crushing his hand over her mouth. Logically, she knew he was still very capable of hurting her.

But he wouldn't.

"How long has it been?" she asked, sliding her palms

down his chest. He felt even better than he looked, all smooth muscle and warm skin.

"Since what?"

"Your breakup."

"Years."

"And there hasn't been anyone since?"

"No one…special."

When she trailed her fingertips over his clenched abdomen, he sucked in a sharp breath. She reached underneath the sleeping bag and curled her hand around his erection. He surged against her palm, raring to go. He wasn't circumcised, which was interesting. She could feel the slight difference as she stroked him. "Perfect," she said.

"Perfect?"

"Not too small. Not too big."

His throat worked in agitation.

Giggling, she pressed a kiss to the center of his chest and ventured lower. He had a sexy whorl of hair around his belly button. Biting him there gently, she tugged down his boxer briefs. He was larger than average, straight and stiff, with a slight ridge around the head of his penis.

She moistened her lips in anticipation.

"Could you pretend…it's too big?"

Ah, men. In this regard, they were all the same. She preferred a happy medium, especially when performing this task. But she humored him, widening her eyes. "Oh my! I don't think I can get my mouth around you."

He laughed at her exaggeration.

She gripped him in her hand and touched her tongue to his taut skin. His amusement cut off like a switch.

But she continued the ruse, feeling mischievous. She licked and nibbled at him, dragging her tongue along his shaft, kissing the ultrasensitive tip. Basically she did everything but take him in her mouth.

He groaned, cupping the back of her head.

She parted her lips, frowning as if he didn't fit. She made another feigned attempt, not opening her mouth wide enough.

"You're too big," she said. "I give up."

"Please," he said, too pained to laugh.

She sat back on her knees to study her work. He was damp from her tongue, throbbing with need. She felt a matching sensation between her legs. Torturing him had gotten her hot. With a glance at his tense face, she untied the strings at her hips. Her bikini bottoms slipped off, baring her lower half.

He stared at her smooth flesh, his eyes dark with lust. "Jesus."

She caressed the slick folds. "I don't think you'll fit here, either. Guess I'll just have to take care of myself."

"No," he said. "I'll fit."

Unable to resist, she widened her thighs and dipped a finger inside. His nostrils flared as he watched her touch herself. She circled her fingers, shuddering with pleasure. With a low growl, he grasped her wrist, bringing her slippery fingertips to his mouth. He sucked them as if she tasted like candy.

Suddenly she was desperate for him. Dropping all pretence, she bent her head and took him deep into her mouth. As she moved up and down, she studied his face, letting him press against the inside of her cheek.

He clenched his teeth, cursing under his breath.

"What did you say?" she asked, lifting her head. "It sounded like Spanish."

Ignoring the question, he threaded his hand through her hair and pulled her close enough to kiss her senseless.

She rubbed her naked belly against his erection. "I want you in me."

"Fuck," he said. "I don't have any condoms."

Rolling off him, she unzipped the front of the tent and reached outside, into her pack. "Good thing one of us is prepared," she said, tossing him the square.

"You're some kind of woman," he said with reverence.

After he suited up for action, she climbed aboard, impaling herself on his length. They both groaned at the sensation. He felt just right, thick and hard. She was dripping wet. It was a perfect fit.

"Touch me," she said, quivering.

His shoulder must not have hurt too much, because he lifted both hands to her breasts, trapping her nipples between his fingers. When she sobbed for more, he increased the pressure, pinching the puckered tips.

She needed to come—now.

Covering his right hand with hers, she pushed it down her belly. He licked his thumb, knowing exactly what she needed. Then he paused, frowning. "Oh, I'm sorry. It's too small. I can't find it."

"What?"

He touched her inner thigh. "Is it over here?"

She was going to kill him. "You know where it is."

He licked the pad of his thumb again, placed it on

one side of her clitoris, and then the other. "Am I getting warmer?"

About to explode, she urged his fingertip to the right spot and held it there. Panting, she moved up and down on him, up and down. Seconds later, she cried out, arching her back. Her head hit the top of the tent. It folded over on her, collapsing at the worst possible moment. She thrashed against the blue nylon, still lost in the throes of orgasm. When she uncovered her face, holding the tent up with her arms, she found Jay sputtering with laughter.

"You did that on purpose!"

"No," he gasped.

"I don't believe you."

"I'll fix it," he said, sobering. She scrambled off him and he freed them from the tent. He rearranged the sleeping bag and they crawled inside together. It was kind of cozy, watching rain cascade off the rock's edge.

He kissed her bare shoulder. "Better?"

She nodded, snuggling against him. His erection prodded her buttocks, indicating that he'd like to finish what they'd started. He stroked her nipples until they jutted forth. Her body tingled with renewed interest.

"Maybe I can make it up to you," he said, moving south. Resting his weight on his good arm, he settled between her parted thighs. Glancing up at her face, he brushed his lips over her unadorned sex.

"Did you lose your place again?"

"I think I remember where I was." He found her clitoris with ease, suckling it gently. His motions were soft and unhurried, bathing her in languid sensation. A second climax rippled through her like warm rain.

She opened her eyes to the sight of his glistening mouth, which struck her as ridiculously sexy.

"Should I stay down here?" he asked, smiling.

She beckoned him up with a crooked finger. He stretched out on his back again and she climbed astride, her slick flesh swallowing his. Feeling deliciously full, she leaned forward to lick her taste from his lips. He groaned, tightening his hands on her waist. She was flush from orgasm, well satiated, so she focused on him. While she worked her hips in sinuous motions, his eyes strayed to the place where their bodies were joined.

Watching his face, she slid down on him slow, slow, slow. He let out a string of guttural curse words and jerked underneath her, his fingertips digging into the soft flesh of her buttocks. She rocked back and forth, squeezing him with her inner muscles, trying to maximize his pleasure as he came. They stayed connected for several long moments, listening to water fall over rocks. Then he lifted her up and went to dispose of the condom. He came back to her, drawing her into his arms.

Before she drifted off, she thought of Tom. If he'd been half as enthusiastic in bed as Jay, she might have accepted his sports obsession.

Sex this good was worth compromising for.

CHAPTER TEN

SAM ALMOST WALKED over the edge with Hope.

If she hadn't halted his forward progress, they both would have fallen. He barely had enough time to grab the safety line and get down on the ground. As the thin cord caught her weight, she let out a sharp cry. He leaned back as far as possible, digging his heels in as she dangled beneath him.

"Hope?"

"My top is ripping," she gasped.

Cursing, he repositioned himself, inching toward her on his belly. He released the cord with one hand and stretched out his arm. "Take my hand."

"I can't reach it!"

He tried again, his fingers splayed wide. She found him by grasping in the dark. Sobbing his name, she grabbed his hand with both of hers. As soon as they connected, her Spandex tore and the line went slack.

She screamed, swinging in space.

"I've got you," he said, reaching down with his other arm. "Try to find a foothold."

While he held on tight, she searched for a convenient grip. Her legs bicycled and came up empty. He could sense the gaping maw around them. She'd fallen off an outcropping with nothingness on all sides.

His palm grew slick with sweat. She was going to slip.

"Stop," he said, nauseous from fear. "I'll pull you up."

She fumbled for a better grip. When his wristband slid off his hand, into the abyss, she nearly went with it. He gritted his teeth and prayed for strength.

"I won't let you go," he said hoarsely.

She curled her fingers around his now-bare left wrist. He did the same, making an interlocking grip. Although he had powerful arms, and she was slender, he wasn't sure it was physically possible to lift her this way. But fuck physics. His blood was pumping with adrenaline and that counted for a lot.

Fueled by fear, he pulled her toward him, his biceps screaming in protest. He thought he might pop an artery in his neck. When she was close enough to grab the collar of his shirt, he fisted a hand in her sports top and yanked her upward. She hooked one knee over the edge and did the rest.

They lay side by side, panting from anxiety and relief. He didn't think his heart could handle any more stress. His nerves were at a breaking point. His brain hadn't been functioning properly since the coma. He was going to need a vacation in the loony bin after this was over. Assuming they survived.

The cavern must have had some ambient light, because he could make out Hope's shadowy figure beside him. Warmth emanated from her body. He was sweating from exertion. At least they weren't cold anymore.

He wallowed in physical sensation, living in the moment. Her rapid breathing was music to his ears. She made noises like that when she came, little gasps of pleasure. His pulse thickened at the memory. There was something intimate about being so close to her in the dark. He felt the primal urge to dominate her.

He still resented her for stirring up his protective instincts, and for bringing unwanted emotions to the surface. Kissing her wasn't the most appropriate punishment he could think of, but the temptation consumed him whenever he was near her. He was keyed up with energy, shaking from the close call.

"Are you hurt?" he asked.

"No. Are you?"

He was pretty sure his elbows were bloody, but it wasn't important.

She reached out to touch his face. "Thank you," she murmured. Leaning over him, she kissed his clenched jaw, his tense mouth.

"Don't," he said.

"Why?"

When he didn't answer, she kissed him again, licking his closed lips.

His control broke. He rolled on top of her and crushed his mouth over hers, forcing his tongue inside. She moaned and kissed him back. Damn her. He shoved her arms above her head, trapping her wrists with one hand. Exerting more pressure with his mouth, he found her torn strap and jerked it down, baring her breasts. When he cupped her roughly, she cried out, her nipple jutting against his sweaty palm.

He stopped kissing her and just hovered near her mouth, brushing his calloused thumb over that pouty nipple. She panted against his lips, little huffs of pleasure. Come noises. Jesus.

His cock swelled at the sound.

He wanted to rip off her clothes and bury himself in her. She'd probably enjoy it. What the hell was wrong with her?

What the hell was wrong with *him?*

He'd been cruel to push her away, but leading her on was worse. They already shared a disturbing connection. If he wasn't careful, his feelings would get involved. Every moment he spent with her, he got more attached.

Maybe, like him, she had deeper reasons for responding to his touch. He'd chosen her that night, but she'd also chosen him. She hadn't let him fuck her because she was drunk and horny. She'd done it because of the dark similarity between them, the buried pain and tendency toward self-isolation.

He released her with regret. "Sorry."

"For what?"

"We have to find a way out of here."

Instead of fishing his lighter out of his pocket, which would be difficult in his current state of arousal, he sat up and studied their surroundings. There was a hole in the ceiling of the cavern that opened directly to the sky. He could hear rain coming through, and see it falling. Maybe the moon would illuminate the interior at some point.

"Down there," Hope said, jostling his shoulder.

He squinted at the cavern floor, which was easier to make out than the ceiling. A small pair of reflective eyes looked up at them. Then the animal turned and scurried through a space that probably led outside.

"Raccoon?" he asked.

"I think so."

"Do they live in caves?"

"No."

Another good sign. It really wasn't that far down, either. He estimated a fifty-foot drop. Sure, they would have broken their necks if they'd fallen. But if he could find some rock features to work with, a safe descent was possible.

"I have twelve feet of cord," he said. "My belt will add another four."

"You'll have to wait until daylight."

"Not necessarily. When the moon rises, that might be enough."

She checked her watch, which glowed in the dark. "It's almost ten o'clock."

They settled in to wait, taking sips of water. Eating would only make them thirstier. He shared another piece of gum with her. It was difficult to sit close to her without imagining a thousand more pleasurable ways to kill time.

"My parents are fine with me working as a park ranger," she said, picking up the thread of their earlier conversation. "They love the outdoors. We visited a lot of national parks when I was a kid."

"Which ones?"

"Yosemite, Joshua Tree, Zion. The Grand Canyon. One year we went to the Washington Monument."

"That old eyesore?"

She laughed in agreement. "They were RV campers."

"My condolences."

"What were your family vacations like?"

His parents were world travelers who did everything

on a grand scale. Their entire life was a vacation. Hope's summer trips actually sounded nice. Normal. "We went far away, to Africa and Australia."

"I'd love to go to exotic places."

"You've never been overseas?"

"Faith and I backpacked through Europe one year. It was amazing."

"What does she think about your job?"

"She thinks I'm a recluse."

He didn't say anything.

"I'm not," she insisted. "I go home on holidays, and I visit her in L.A. I don't close myself off from the outside world."

She hadn't mentioned friends, let alone a boyfriend.

"I might not be partying all night or jet-setting, but I have a life. I stay busy."

"How?"

"I read, hike, ride my bicycle…"

"All solo activities."

"Not necessarily."

"Who do you hike with?"

She was glaring at him. He could tell.

"I'm with Faith," he said. "You're a beautiful woman. There's nothing out here for you but trees and mountains."

"What's wrong with trees and mountains?"

"They aren't human."

"You realize that you also live here, in the sticks?"

"Ah, but I don't deny that I'm a recluse. And I know why I'm isolating myself."

"Why?"

He walked right into that one. "The only single men in the Sierras are tourists. How can you date?"

"I date."

"Who, the park attendants?"

"Maybe."

He made a noise of disbelief. Then he remembered her questions about Owen Jackson and fell silent. He didn't want to picture her with one of his...acquaintances. "When was your last serious relationship?"

"None of your business."

"Exactly," he said, just to make her mad.

"You think you're the only man I've slept with?"

"I know I'm not."

"I dated Doug Dixon," she said.

He gaped at her shadowy outline. "You're kidding."

"No."

"He's married."

"He wasn't at the time."

"How long ago?"

"Two years."

"I can't believe it."

"Why?"

"He's...old."

"He's forty. Not much older than you."

"I'm thirty-two," he reiterated.

"Age doesn't matter to me."

"What about the fact that he's your *boss?*"

"That's why we kept it quiet."

He made a face, shaking his head.

"Are you judging me, really?"

"I'm judging him. A man doesn't date his own employee on the down-low for no reason. He had a perfect excuse not to take you out in public. You're young and pretty. Why would you settle for that?"

"Doug was a perfect gentleman," she said, her voice quavering with anger. "He brought me gifts and served candlelit dinners."

"If he was so great, why did you two break up?"

"Because I wasn't in love with him. When he proposed, I said no."

Sam clenched his hands into fists. Perfect gentleman or not, he hated the idea of Doug touching her.

"You sound kind of jealous."

He couldn't deny it.

"Maybe I have bad luck with men," she said. "Maybe I'm too standoffish or independent. I was definitely lonely, the night I went home with you."

He closed his eyes, wanting to disappear.

"I'm not going to pretend I didn't enjoy it."

"I never said that."

"You look miserable every time you touch me."

"That has nothing to do with you."

"It feels pretty personal."

"Hope, I told you that my brain is fucked up." He rubbed his bare wrist, lamenting the loss of his sweatband. "Christ, I have to read my tattoo every morning just to figure out what's going on."

"What do you mean?"

"I can't remember her death. It happened a few months before the freeway accident. The information is locked away somewhere or lost forever. I wake up, looking for her. I can't believe she's gone."

"Every day?"

"Yes."

"You're not getting better?"

"It's easier to accept now," he said. In the beginning, he'd been confused, half-conscious, inconsolable for weeks. "I can remember what other people have told me, cumulatively. The shock fades faster than it used to."

"So, other than a few minutes in the morning, you're fine. Your brain works normally the rest of the time."

"Being numb isn't normal."

"You're grieving."

"Grieving is a process. This is limbo."

"Maybe you're afraid to let her go."

He frowned into the dark, wishing that was the case. It pained him to admit that he wasn't in love with her anymore. He wanted to let go. His guilt wouldn't let him. "If I knew what happened, I might be able to move on. But no one will tell me."

"Why not?"

"The doctors say I have to remember on my own."

"You don't know how she died?"

"I know it was a fall, and I was with her."

"Oh, Sam."

He gritted his teeth against her sympathy. They said that time healed all wounds, but this one was still raw. "I've imagined a thousand scenarios, from minor negligence to blatant disregard for her safety."

"If you were at fault, could you forgive yourself?"

"I don't know. I can't forgive myself unconditionally. And, no matter what happened, I'll always feel responsible."

"Because you were her partner?"

He hesitated to say more. "We also got engaged the year before. She wanted to start a family. So did I. She had a bucket list of walls to climb before we settled down. Kalymnos was one of them."

"That's where she fell?"

"Yes."

She was quiet for a moment. "What if you never remember?"

"I might not. It usually happens within three years, and two have already passed."

"You don't have a plan?"

"My psychiatrist recommended something called closure therapy. It's for people whose loved ones are lost or missing."

"You agreed to go?"

"No."

"Why not?"

He shrugged, uncomfortable. While he was recovering from the coma, he'd done his share of therapy. He'd seen more doctors than he could count. None of them knew how to bring his memory back. So he'd returned to climbing. The rock face was the only place he'd ever really belonged. Pushing his physical limits had always felt right. And the sport owed him some solace after taking so much away from him. Maybe he was searching for answers he'd never find, punishing himself for things he hadn't done.

Free-soloing wasn't helping any more than therapy had. But he liked it better.

"I haven't decided yet," he said.

"You'd rather stay here and avoid the problem?"

"In this cave?"

"In the Sierras."

"What are *you* avoiding?"

She huffed out a breath. "Not everyone who lives here is running away from their problems. You recommended Owen for a job in the park. Why is it an appropriate place for him to work, but not me?"

"He needed some space."

Sam had thought that mountains and fresh air would be good for Owen. He also knew the kid wouldn't bother him. Unlike Garrett Wright, who called to check up on him every few weeks at the request of his wife, Lauren. The female paramedic had saved Sam's life after the San Diego earthquake. She was relentlessly caring.

Owen kept to himself. He was wary of men, so Sam didn't have to worry about him wanting to be buddies.

"I know about his criminal record," she said.

"Then you can guess what he's running from."

"Do you want him to turn into a hermit?"

"No, but I doubt he'll stay here forever. Some people need time to heal and be alone. Others need to get out and live."

"And others need therapy but are too scared to feel, so they go on suicidal climbs and wallow in self-pity."

He scowled at her frank assessment. He didn't think he was suicidal, and he hated feeling sorry for himself. Survivor's guilt ate at him—he couldn't deny it. The San Diego earthquake had taken thousands of lives. Melissa's nephew had died in a fire, and her family had already suffered so much. It wasn't fair.

Why had Sam been spared, instead of an innocent child?

Hope was right about one thing. He couldn't stand the thought of having an emotional breakdown in front of a group of people. She'd seen him cry yesterday morning. It hadn't felt healthy or cathartic in the least.

He wanted recovery, not closure. Therapy was a last resort. Before now, he'd rejected the idea of saying goodbye to Melissa's memory and leaving his questions unanswered. It sounded like a lot of hard work for little or no payoff. But maybe there were benefits he hadn't considered. He'd like to sleep with Hope again. He missed sex—a lot—and anonymous partners didn't appeal to him.

He ached for another chance to touch her. If he got his head together, maybe they could…date.

Unsettled by the thought, he focused on removing the straps from the dry pack and cutting the waterproof canvas into strips. They tied the strips to the shoelace cord, making knots at regular intervals. His long-sleeved shirt would serve as a harness. Along with the canvas straps, and his belt, they had twenty feet covered.

The rain coming through the sky roof slowed to a drizzle. At about midnight, the moon broke through the clouds, illuminating the space below. The raccoon hole appeared large enough to fit through. He studied the cave wall, planning his descent. There were no reliable-looking handholds, and damp limestone made for a slippery grip. Luckily, a small ledge jutted out, a little more than halfway down. He estimated the drop from there at about fifteen feet.

It was doable, but they had to move fast to take advantage of the meager light.

Working quickly, he wrapped the shirtsleeves around his body, under his arms, and tied a knot over the center of his chest. Then he cinched his belt to the shirt. The cord was already threaded through the last belt hole, and attached to the straps. He looped the end over a stalagmite and tested his weight. The rope held.

"I'm aiming for that ledge," he said, pointing it out to her. "When I get there I'll take off the harness and you can pull up the rope."

"Looks like a steep drop."

"It is. But I'll catch you."

"Who'll catch you?"

"Dharmakaya," he said with a smile, naming a rock spirit some climbers believed in. The sport had never been a religion for Sam, but he was a dedicated athlete. He hadn't made a joke like that since the accident, and it felt good.

It would feel even better to kiss her for good luck. Smothering the urge, he started down the cave wall. The limestone was smooth and damp, not an ideal climbing surface. He made short work of the distance and reached the ledge quickly. Once there, he removed the harness and dropped to his stomach, lowering himself over the side. He gripped the ledge, waiting until his body was fully extended before he let go.

The landing wasn't graceful, but he knew how to fall safely. He hit the ground and tumbled backward, rolling with the force of gravity rather than fighting against it. After taking a moment to gather his wits, he scrambled to his feet and flicked on the lighter to investigate the hole in the cave. It was wide enough for his shoulders, and led directly outside.

"Okay?" she asked.

"Yes," he said, returning to the wall. As long as the

drug smugglers weren't lurking nearby, they could stay in this chamber and try to start a fire.

Watching Hope climb was much more nerve-racking than performing the task himself. He became convinced that the impromptu gear was faulty. His belt could come undone or the cord might snap at any moment. Any number of things could go wrong.

She wasn't as strong as Sam, or as fast. His heart pounded with anxiety as the minutes ticked by. Just when it appeared as though she would arrive at the ledge without incident, he realized his mistake.

She wasn't as tall as him, either.

Her feet dangled six inches above the ledge. She pointed her toes but still couldn't reach.

"Can you get out of the harness?" he asked.

"I think so."

While he waited, his throat dry, she freed her right arm and slid down to the ledge. Then she pulled the loop over her head.

So far, so good.

"Okay, now lower yourself over the side, just like I did."

As she clung to the ledge, the moon went behind the clouds once again and the cavern went dim. He could barely see her.

"I'm afraid to let go," she said.

"Push away from the wall," he ordered. "Come toward me."

"I don't want to fall."

"I'll catch you."

For a minute, he thought she wasn't going to do it. Then he heard her cry out and felt her hurtling toward him. He absorbed the impact with his body and went down to the ground, cushioning her in his embrace. His bones rattled from the hard jolt. Catching her was twice as hard as falling himself.

"Are you all right?" he asked, reluctant to release her.

"Yes." She palpated his rib cage, as if searching for fractures. "Did I...break you?"

"I think you knocked me out. Who are you, again?"

She inhaled a sharp breath.

"Hope. It's a joke."

"Not funny."

"No?" Maybe his sense of humor was rusty. He let her go and dusted himself off, wincing at the pain in his elbows. "We should try to start a fire."

After a short hesitation, she agreed. Even if the smugglers were nearby, the cavern was a good hide-out, easy to defend. Sam crawled out of the raccoon hole and searched for wood. Everything was damp, but he tore some dead branches off a pine tree. He also found a cache of resin inside that would act as an accelerant.

Pleased, he returned to Hope and used his utility knife to strip the damp outer bark from the branches. When he'd gathered enough dry kindling, he sparked it up, adding a chunk of resin. Within minutes, they had a cozy blaze.

He'd like a hot meal to go with it, but they needed water to eat, and they were almost out. After sharing the last bottle with him, she curled up in her safety blanket, clearly exhausted. "Are you going to sleep?"

Not a chance. "I'll keep the first watch."

She closed her eyes, acquiescent.

He meant that he would watch out for the bad guys,

but he studied her while she slept. The sight of her, warmed by his fire, filled an empty place inside him. The space was vast—like this cavern. Mostly cold and dark.

Still, it was a start.

CHAPTER ELEVEN

JAVIER JOLTED AWAKE, tightening his arms around Faith.

He heard the sound of a gun cocking—his gun—and squinted at the flashlight in his face. Two figures loomed at the edge of the sleeping bag, crouched under the rock outcropping. This wasn't good.

"Wake up, motherfucker!"

Relief poured through him. It was Caleb and Ted. He would survive this confrontation. They wouldn't hurt Faith.

She roused, turning her sleepy head toward the light. "What's happening?"

"Get your hands off her," Caleb ordered.

Javier put his right hand up where Caleb could see it, but kept his injured arm at his side. He'd been able to ignore the pain last night, for the most part. Right now it was best to exaggerate his weaknesses.

Faith sat forward, clutching the sleeping bag to her chest. With her shoulders bare, her blond hair mussed and her lips swollen, she looked as if she'd had a wild night. He was acutely aware of their nudity.

"Are you okay, honey?" Caleb asked.

She stared at the barrel of the gun, swallowing. "I'm fine."

"Did he hurt you?"

"No...."

"Don't worry, you're safe now," Caleb said.

"Safe?"

"Get up," he ordered Javier, gesturing with his gun.

The zipper was on Faith's side. He couldn't crawl out of the sleeping bag without exposing her, so he didn't move.

"I said get up!"

Faith lowered the zipper with shaking hands, her face pale. When she was done, Ted grabbed the corner of the sleeping bag and yanked it open. His eyes widened with surprise at what he'd revealed.

"Holy shit," Caleb murmured, ogling her.

Javier wanted to kill them both. It was an opportune time to strike, while they were visually occupied. But Caleb wasn't stupid. After a quick exam of Faith's perfect breasts, he returned his attention to Javier.

He stayed still, fighting the urge to cover himself. His parts didn't draw the same interest as Faith's, but he felt damned vulnerable with his dick out.

"Move," Caleb said.

Javier got up, leaving the sleeping bag to Faith.

She scrambled to hide her naked body. "Why are you doing this? Just leave us alone!"

"He's the killer they're looking for," Caleb said. "He must have faked that shoulder injury yesterday, if he felt good enough to screw you."

"No," she said, her lips trembling.

Javier looked away.

"Tie his wrists," Caleb said to Ted.

"Can I put my clothes on first?"

"Please."

Javier pulled on his jeans in stiff, awkward motions.

When he was decent, he gathered her clothes with his good arm and handed them to her.

"Is it true?" she asked.

"Of course it is," Caleb said. "This is his gun."

Javier donned his shirt and sat down to put on his shoes, his mind reeling. He'd been carrying the 9 mm in his waistband, and had left it wrapped in his jeans. After exhausting himself with Faith, he'd fallen into a deep sleep.

"You bastard," she said, her voice flat.

"I'm sorry."

Caleb stepped forward, landing a swift kick to his ribs. Javier smothered a cry of pain, doubling over. While he struggled for breath, his eyes watering, Ted wrenched his arms behind his back and bound his wrists with rope.

Once Javier was subdued, Caleb became cockier than usual. He watched Faith wrestle into her clothes, licking his lips. She emerged from the sleeping bag in her snug track pants and a thin tank top. Both garments clung to her slender curves, making it clear she hadn't bothered with underwear.

She was the kind of woman men fought over. Like Alexia, she radiated sensuality. He'd known she'd be hot in bed, but he hadn't imagined laughing out loud with her. He'd never had so much fun during sex.

"How was she?" Caleb asked in a stage whisper.

Javier ignored the question, staring straight ahead. It was a mistake to show feelings in front of an enemy. He knew that from experience.

Caleb dragged him upright and sucker-punched him. Javier coughed and stumbled backward, cracking his skull on the side of the rock. Black spots danced in his vision. He barely managed to stay on his feet.

"You want a turn?" Caleb asked her.

When she advanced, Javier forced himself to meet her gaze.

"What's your real name?"

"Javier," he said.

She flinched at his accent, which he laid on thick. He didn't regret sleeping with her, or deceiving her about his ethnicity. But he wondered if she'd have refused him, had she known. "Did you fall overboard on purpose?"

He didn't see any reason to lie. "Yes."

She drew back her arm and let him have it, whaling him across the cheek. Caleb's blows had a lot more power, but this one stung hard. He hated being hit by women. His mother had slapped him the last time he'd visited her.

"Desgraciado," she'd said, throwing his money back in his face.

"I almost jumped in after you," Faith said, her eyes glittering with tears.

He glanced away, his throat tight. If she wanted another shot at him, she was welcome. Although he hadn't meant to hurt her, she had every right to be angry. He'd endure as many blows as she could dish out.

Instead of striking him again, she dropped her hand to her side and clenched it into a fist. Ted packed up camp while the first rays of dawn penetrated the dark, wet woods. Although the rain had abated, the air was still cool and damp.

After breakfast, which wasn't offered to Javier, they

set out toward Moraine Lake. Caleb made Javier walk in front. The thick mud was difficult to slog through. His shoulder throbbed with every step and his ribs ached. Whenever he thought of Faith, something in the center of his chest hurt, too.

In the far distance, a familiar-looking pair of mountains jutted up toward the sky. He recognized one as the plane crash site.

"We should go to Mineral King," Ted said, looking that direction. "The trail won't be as muddy away from the river."

"We're going to Moraine," Caleb said.

"Can we stop for a minute?" Faith asked.

They agreed to a short break. Caleb and Ted walked into the trees to relieve themselves, confident that Javier wasn't going anywhere. If he ran, they could catch him. Faith approached his side warily.

"Who did you kill?" she whispered.

"The pilot I work with."

"Why?"

After the crash, Javier had decided to seize his chance to walk away. When the pilot attempted to notify Gonzales of their location, Javier pulled his gun, and they had exchanged fire. "You know that guy I told you about, the friend?"

"Yes."

"He's my boss. Six months ago, his wife...my ex... disappeared. I think he killed her. I've wanted out ever since."

"And the pilot?"

"He tried to stop me."

She searched his eyes warily. "You can explain it to the police."

"No. That would be a death sentence. My boss pays them off. I think he has someone inside this park, in fact."

"Who?"

"Help me escape," he said, ignoring the question. "I won't kill anyone else."

To his surprise, he wanted to keep that promise. Even after taking a beating from Caleb, he had no interest in revenge. He'd still defeat Gonzales if he got the chance, but he'd lost his taste for senseless violence. Spending time with Faith had brought out his softer side. He'd seen a glimpse of happiness.

Caleb's and Ted's return interrupted their conversation. Faith moved past Javier and ducked into the bushes. He asked for a drink of water and was ignored. As soon as she came back, they started hiking again.

He cooperated, biding his time. When they were in the middle of a thick copse, with no open spaces nearby, he stopped. "I have to take a piss."

"Piss your pants," Caleb said, shoving him forward.

He stumbled and went down hard, choosing his uninjured shoulder to break his fall. Seething with anger, he rolled over in the mud and sat up. Faith stood between Caleb and Ted, her expression troubled.

"Please," he said to Caleb. "I can't hold it."

"You want me to hold it for you?"

Javier gritted his teeth at the indignity. "If you tie my hands in front, I can manage."

With a shrug, Caleb agreed. Taking the gun out of his waistband, he gestured for Ted to do the honors.

"Do you really know how to use that?" Faith asked, moistening her lips.

"Sure." Puffed up with importance, Caleb showed her the gun's safety mechanism. She leaned in to take a closer look, her breasts pressing against his arm.

She was good. Javier held still while Ted untied him, thanking his lucky stars for her effect on men. Her sexuality was a powerful weapon. When his wrists were free, he flexed his fingers, grimacing as the blood rushed back into the tips. Then he brought his hands forward and waited for Ted to retie him.

As the other man reached down, Javier grasped the front of his shirt. He slammed his head into Ted's nose, breaking the fragile cartilage, and yanked him forward. Ted did a somersault over Javier's shoulder and went sprawling.

In the same fluid motion, Javier leaped to his feet. He must have looked scary, because Faith shrank aside with a little shriek. He advanced before Caleb had a chance to release the safety. Hooking his arm around Caleb's, Javier struck his throat with the heel of his hand. The gun flew out of his grip. Any more pressure would have crushed Caleb's windpipe, but Javier wasn't operating at full strength.

Caleb choked and sputtered, gasping for air.

He could feel Ted coming, and Caleb hadn't been incapacitated yet. Keeping Caleb's arm in a tight lock, he kicked out with his right foot, connecting to Ted's stomach. Ted went down again, groaning.

Most inexperienced fighters were easy to catch off guard, but Caleb was young and fit and arrogant. Before he'd even caught his breath, Caleb drew back his left arm and punched Javier in the ear, scoring a direct hit.

Javier released him and stumbled sideways, reeling from the impact. He shook his head, trying not to lose focus. If he didn't move fast, his opponent would regain the upper hand. When Caleb scrambled to pick up the gun, Javier saw his opening. He kicked him under the chin. Caleb flew backward, his eyes rolling up.

He dropped to the ground and stayed there.

Javier glanced at Ted, who didn't rise. They were both conscious, but they'd had enough. He grabbed his gun and tucked it into his waistband, looking for Faith. She was hiding behind a tree, shaking like a leaf.

"Give me your pack," he said.

She shrugged out of it, her lips pale. Even though she'd helped him, she didn't trust him. Not after witnessing the brutality he'd just unleashed. As he donned the backpack, his heart twisted in his chest.

"Your boss works with someone in the park," she said. "Who is it?"

He hesitated, because giving her information about Gonzales would put her in danger. "Why do you ask?"

"I'm worried about Hope."

The park ranger. Faith's fear for her sister was justified—and it touched a sentimental place inside him. "I've never met him. We pick up the cargo at a landing strip in Long Pine. That's all I know."

Her eyes filled with tears. "Promise me you won't hurt her."

"I don't hurt women." Not physically, anyway.

She let out a choked sob, clearly regretting the kindness she'd done him. He was glad he'd been able to break away without using deadly force, because watching Ted and Caleb die would have upset her even more.

"Stay with them," he said, indicating the fallen men. "They'll take care of you."

Ted was using his shirt to stanch his bloody nose. Caleb still looked dazed. Javier thought about warning them not to touch her, but decided against it. They wouldn't be up for any sexual shenanigans.

He examined her one last time, drinking in every detail. There was something he wanted to say to her. Something he wanted to do before he left. *"Eres la única,"* he murmured, pressing his lips to hers. *"Adios, amor."*

FAITH BROUGHT a trembling hand to her mouth as she watched him go.

He walked the opposite direction, as if heading back to Kaweah. She wondered where her sister was, and who she was with. Considering her preoccupation with "park business," Hope was probably right in the middle of the fray.

Damn Caleb and Ted. If they hadn't come to the rescue, she'd be halfway to Moraine Lake with Jay—or Javier—by now. It was all Javier's fault. He'd lied to her and seduced her and *killed* someone. God, she had shit taste in men.

Eres la única.

What did that mean?

Adios, amor. Goodbye, love.

Just love, as in honey or dear. Not *my* love. Unless she was confused about Spanish pronouns and endearments, it sounded like a brush-off. Who the hell did he think he was, anyway?

Bastard. Dirty, sexy, drug-smuggling bastard.

Caleb rose to his feet. He had a nasty lump on his chin where Javier had kicked him. "You let him get away."

"He broke my nose," Ted said, his voice muffled.

"Why didn't you fight back?"

"I tried."

"Well, you *suck*."

"You're the one who lost the gun!"

"You're the one who untied him."

"Because you said to."

"At least I got a punch in."

"Yeah," Ted muttered, taking the T-shirt away from his face and studying the bloodstains. "Way to go, dude."

Caleb scowled, looking around for another scapegoat. "You," he said, pointing at Faith. "You fucking bitch."

"Leave her alone," Ted said.

"She rubbed her tits on me! She distracted me on purpose."

"You're an idiot."

"It's her fault your nose is broken."

"No, it's yours," Ted said, spitting blood. "You wanted to charge in and save the day. Ron told us not to get involved."

"She needed help."

"Didn't look like it to me."

Caleb grunted in response, glancing in Faith's direction.

"We didn't have to bring him along, either. That was dumb. We should have tied him up and left him."

"He'd have escaped."

"He *did* escape. We're lucky he didn't shoot us."

"This is why I can't get laid," Caleb said, bracing his hands on his hips. "Nice guys always finish last."

If she wasn't so exhausted, she'd have laughed at his false estimation of himself.

"It's on you when he kills someone else," he said to Faith.

"Let's keep walking," she said, her stomach churning with anxiety. She had a bad feeling now that Javier had gone. Criminal or not, he'd protected her from the men in the helicopter, and prevented her from falling overboard. Despite Caleb's "good intentions," she knew she couldn't count on him if they ran into trouble.

Cursing, Ted staggered upright. As the trio trudged forward, fat droplets of water fell from the heavy leaves and tree branches, hitting the ground like stealthy footprints. Birds and squirrels rustled in the bushes nearby. The forest sounds seemed magnified in the otherwise silent dawn. She imagined villains lurking around every corner.

They approached a misty meadow that reminded Faith of the one Javier had stopped her from entering. Her pants were already wet and muddy from the knees down. Moisture clung to her skin and eyelashes. Her hair frizzed.

Ugh. She was so tired.

The next thing she knew, two men were hiking toward them. One had on a rain poncho, which seemed appropriate, but the other was wearing a leather jacket. It looked wildly out of place on a nature trail.

"Act cool," Caleb said under his breath. The men were too close to run from, so feigning nonchalance was the only option.

"Hello," the man in leather said. He had a slight accent. Was this Javier's boss, the man who'd stolen his girlfriend? With his broad face and low forehead, he wasn't handsome. "We're looking for our friend."

"We haven't seen anyone. Sorry."

The man nodded. He appeared close to forty, and Hispanic. His companion was a scruffy, dark-haired white guy in his early twenties. "Where are you coming from?"

"Kaweah Camp," Caleb said. "We're going to Moraine Lake."

"And you haven't seen anyone?"

"Not a soul."

The man glanced at Faith, as if she might have a different answer. She pressed her lips together to keep them from trembling. "We heard our friend was with a girl named Faith. A pretty blonde."

Her heart dropped.

Ted and Caleb exchanged a nervous glance.

"This is Katie," Caleb said, clamping his hand around her upper arm. "We have to get a move on. Sorry we can't help you."

She let Caleb guide her past the men, her pulse pounding. Ted brought up the rear. Seconds later, a loud pop split the air. Caleb let go of her arm. Faith glanced over her shoulder as Ted crumpled to the ground. Everything seemed to progress in slow motion after that.

Caleb yelled for Ted, but his voice was muffled. The echo in her ears drowned out all other sounds.

Ted was facedown, unmoving. Behind him, the older man held a gun. While she watched, drawing her breath to scream, he aimed and fired again. Caleb staggered sideways and fell down, clutching his thigh.

She turned to run. Her throat felt raw from the ragged shriek she could barely hear. Saving her breath, she clapped her mouth shut and concentrated on getting away. Her muscles were weak from overexertion, but panic gave her an energy boost. She zipped toward the trees, pumping her legs as hard as she could.

Why hadn't she listened to Hope? If she was in better shape, she could sprint faster, and they'd never catch her.

But she hadn't listened to Hope, and she couldn't keep up the pace. She sensed a presence behind her, heavy footfalls crashing down the trail. He was gaining on her. With a terrified sob, she ducked right, trying to evade him. The underbrush whipped against her shins, and the bumpy ground threatened to trip her up.

He grabbed a handful of her hair, snapping her head back. They went down to the ground in a tangle of arms and legs.

It was the younger man. She tried to kick and claw him, her mind filled with sexual assault memories, but her fingernails found no purchase on his rain poncho. He used his weight to subdue her, shoving her arms over her head. Another man had held her down like this once, overpowering her with his strength, refusing to take no for an answer.

"I'm not raping you," he said. "Calm down!"

She realized that she'd been screaming rape and fell silent, although his words didn't reassure her. His partner had just shot at two men, maybe killed them. Being violated was, perhaps, the least of her worries.

The guy rolled her over and wrenched her arms behind her back. He was so much stronger than she was, she couldn't move an inch. A feeling of helplessness overwhelmed her and she whimpered, her cheek pressed to the muddy earth as he bound her wrists with a hard, thin material that cut into her skin.

He lifted himself off her and dragged her upright. She was breathing hard, her damp shirt plastered to her chest. With her arms tied behind her back and her breasts thrust forward, there was no hiding the fact that she wasn't wearing a bra.

Her captor noticed, but didn't remark on the sight. He gave her body a detached perusal, as if searching for injuries, not places to grab when he had more time. "Let's go," he said, clearing his throat.

Although she didn't want to cooperate, she was afraid not to. Her scalp ached from the hair-pulling. She trudged forward on shaky legs, finding it ironic that Javier had been in this position less than an hour ago. Maybe he was still nearby.

Caleb's blood was all over the trail. He struggled to tie a piece of cord around his thigh. Ted wasn't moving. She assumed he was dead, and her stomach did a sickening roll. The shooter waited for her and his friend to approach, gun pointed down at the ground.

"Where's Del Norte?"

"Del Norte?"

"Javier Del Norte, the man you were with."

Faith had no idea which direction he'd gone. If she led them to him, would they kill him? If she didn't, would they kill *her?*

"I think he went this way," she said, tilting her head north.

CHAPTER TWELVE

WHEN HOPE AWOKE, Sam was watching her.

She sat up with a start. Her right shoulder and hip ached from the prolonged contact with the hard ground. Her entire body was sore, especially her arms. Rock climbing, kayaking and hanging off a ledge had stressed her muscles.

She'd dreamed about falling again. No surprise there. In another disturbing nightmare, she'd been searching the woods for a wailing infant. She followed its cries to the wrecked plane at the top of Angel Wings. When she looked inside, Faith was sitting in the pilot's seat, her hair dark with blood.

She blinked away the image, placing a hand over her pounding heart. She could still hear the baby crying. The plaintive sound echoed in her ears, making her ache with emptiness. Her hand lowered to her flat stomach and then clenched into a tight fist.

Sam's eyes followed the motion.

"What time is it?" she asked, her voice hoarse.

"Six-thirty."

He'd been busy. The fire was still going, and he must have collected water, because a full container sat near her.

"Rainwater?"

"I treated it."

She took a long drink. "Did you sleep?"

"No."

"Why didn't you wake me up?"

He glanced away, rubbing at the tattoo on his wrist. It was now bare of elastic. "I didn't want to disturb you."

Or himself, she figured. He was reluctant to fall asleep near her because of what had happened yesterday morning. Instead of making the same mistake or showing emotion again, he'd avoided sleep altogether.

His retreat felt like another rejection, deeper than the others. He'd shared intimate details with her about Melissa and his head injury. He'd kissed Hope passionately after rescuing her. But he couldn't share her blanket or allow himself to get close to her?

They ate the last two energy bars in silence.

After breakfast, she turned on her radio. Last night, she'd switched it off to preserve the batteries. Revealing her location wasn't an option, because she might be overheard, but she could listen to the other rangers.

The radio had three channels. Channel one dealt with emergencies and law enforcement. It transmitted park-wide to all rangers, and could be used by local police. Channel two, for daily operations, transmitted among coworkers at individual stations. Channel three was reserved for conversations with the park manager. Although those transmissions could also be intercepted, it was less likely.

Hope switched between the first two channels, hearing some discussion from rangers at Moraine Lake and Kaweah Camp. Their efforts sounded disorganized, which was unusual. Ron and the rafting group had checked in. The others, including Faith, were still MIA. Channel three was silent. Where was Dixon?

She returned to the second channel, puzzled.

"Ranger Banning, come in," the dispatcher said.

"I can't answer," she said to Sam.

"Does it have GPS?"

"No, but if someone is listening, they might be able to estimate my distance from the strength of the signal."

He nodded, following her logic. "What about code?"

"Do you know Morse?"

"Just the SOS."

That wasn't much help. She needed to communicate information, not a distress call. "If they were on channel three, I might answer."

"Why?"

"No one but Dixon uses it."

His mouth tightened at the mention of her former boyfriend. "Are you ready to head back?"

"I'd rather keep going south. We're almost halfway to Moraine Lake."

"Where do you think those guys went?"

"I don't know." After a night of rain, there was no use looking for their trail at the main entrance of the cave.

"What about the suspect?"

Hope assumed her sister was still with him. If Del Norte was smart, he wouldn't walk along the river at all. It made more sense for him to head west, toward the Mineral King Station. Angel Wings and Valhalla were visible from the path. An alternative route veered through the glacier-carved gorge, between the rock faces.

"Let's go as far south as the fork," she suggested. "From there, we can turn toward Mineral King."

He agreed, probably because he thought it was the safest choice. Hope didn't tell him that she planned to look for footprints—and follow them, if one set belonged to her sister. Finding Faith was still her top priority.

"I'm not spending another night out in the open."

She didn't blame him. Without food and shelter, they couldn't go far. They had to get supplies or rejoin civilization this evening.

Breaking camp was easy. She folded up the blanket and passed it to Sam. He made a bundle out of his long-sleeved shirt, carrying it like a messenger bag. Her sports top kept falling down on one side, so she tied the torn ends together before they left the cavern. As they entered the forest of trees outside, she glanced around warily. The rain had abated, leaving the earth damp and fragrant.

They found the path and followed it south. She took the lead because she was armed, and a better tracker than Sam. The ground was covered with wet leaves, which made it hard to detect footprints.

She lowered the volume on her radio and kept going, glancing over her shoulder at him. He had dark smudges under his eyes, and his jaw was shadowed by stubble. Last night, he'd asked her what she was avoiding. After everything he'd revealed, she felt as though she owed him an honest answer, but she didn't know how to broach the subject.

She related to Melissa's aspirations for a family, and wondered at the timing of her death. "You said that Melissa had a bucket list. What was on it?"

His brows rose at the question. "Peaks to climb."

"How many?"

"Seven."

"Kalymnos was the last one?"

"No, it was number six. She didn't get to Mount Whitney." His expression grew pained. "I was supposed to go there to spread her ashes."

"When?"

"Before the quake. I went to San Diego to get the urn from her parents. I mean, I think that's what I was doing there. I had a map to Whitney Portal and her ashes with me during the freeway collapse."

Oh God. Her heart broke for him. "Starting a family wasn't on the list?"

"Not this list."

"So you weren't…trying."

He stopped in his tracks. "What are you asking?"

She turned to face him, hearing the outrage in his tone.

"You want to know if she was pregnant," he accused. "You think I took my pregnant fiancée on a climbing trip and let her die."

Her stomach sank. "No."

"Over the past two years, no one's had the nerve to ask me that. Congratulations, Hope. You win the insensitivity award."

"I'm sorry," she said, her mind reeling. "You said you wanted children and I got the impression—"

"That I was a baby killer, in addition to a fiancée killer?"

"No." Melissa's death wasn't his fault. She knew that, even if he didn't.

"She was on birth control. She planned to stop taking it after we climbed Whitney. Not that it's any of your business."

"It's not."

"What if I didn't know for sure? Jesus. If I wanted to jump off a cliff, a question like that would send me right over the edge."

She hadn't anticipated his anger, but of course he was offended. "I didn't mean to upset you. I was just wondering if the reason you…freaked out…after we slept together had something to do with a pregnancy."

He gave her a blank look. "We used condoms that night."

"I'm not explaining this right."

"Yeah, maybe you should just drop it."

"You asked what I was avoiding! I'm trying to tell you."

He fell silent, waiting for it.

"Children and pregnancy are on my mind right now, because of…my past. I thought you might have asked me to leave that night because the marks on my stomach triggered a memory about Melissa."

"Marks?"

"The stretch marks."

"You have stretch marks," he said, his tone disbelieving.

She tugged down the waistband of her pants and pointed to the silvery lines on her lower abdomen.

He squinted in confusion. "I don't get it."

She didn't think he was lying. Either he hadn't noticed her stretch marks that night or he'd forgotten about them. "When I was seventeen, I had a baby."

His gaze jerked up to her face.

"I gave her up for adoption," she said, her voice wavering with emotion. "It was the best choice for both of us, but the experience changed my life forever. I've struggled with moving on. Maybe I have been avoiding relationships, for some of the same reasons you are. I know how hard it is to let go."

Sam shifted his weight from one foot to the other, absorbing her revelation. After a taut moment, his mouth twisted with derision. "You think you know what it's like to be me because you had an unplanned pregnancy ten years ago and *decided* to get rid of the baby? No," he said, rejecting the notion. Rejecting her, as a person. "I'm sorry, Hope. The situations are totally different. My memory was taken from me. Melissa was taken from me. She's dead, gone forever. I didn't have a *choice*."

Hope let her waistband snap into place dully. She turned and stumbled down the trail, blinded by tears. He didn't understand, but that was her fault. She hadn't expressed herself well, and this wasn't the place to discuss it.

His words hurt, though. So much. They soaked into every vulnerable crack within her, expanding her pain. She'd agonized over the decision to give up her daughter. If he thought her grief didn't compare to his, he was wrong.

Her sacrifice had affected everything she'd done over the past ten years. It was why she held herself at a distance from others; she was afraid to love and lose again. The only person she gave her entire heart to was Faith.

They didn't talk for several minutes. The tightness in her chest eased, little by little, and she was able to hold her tears at bay.

She'd break down later. When she was alone.

"Ranger Banning, come in."

Struck by inspiration, she picked up the radio and transmitted three taps. After a short pause, she tapped three more times. Then she clicked over to channel three and waited, hoping the operator would take the hint.

"Ranger Banning, is that you?"

She gripped the radio until her knuckles went white. The transmission wasn't from Dispatch, and the voice sounded very close.

"We have Faith."

"Don't answer," Sam warned.

Worried that he'd try to interfere, she edged away from him as she pressed the button. "This is Ranger Banning."

"Where are you?"

"Let me talk to my sister," she said.

Faith's cry of distress rang out in the background.

A chill traveled up Hope's spine. She had no idea how they'd found a way to communicate with her. Modern scanners could pick up signals, but only employees with programmed radios could respond.

She moistened her lips, glancing at Sam. "What do you want?"

"A guide to the cargo."

"Say no," Sam ordered.

"Come to the waterfall by the moon-shaped meadow. Alone."

Mist Falls. It was only three miles away. "I'll be there in an hour."

The transmission ended.

Sam gaped at her. "You can't go."

"Why?"

"They'll kill you after you help them."

Hope would worry about that when Faith was safe. She'd "gotten rid of" her baby. She wasn't giving up on her sister. "Stay here," she said. "Or head back to Kaweah. It doesn't matter. I'm going to the falls."

"I won't let you."

She pulled the gun from her waistband and pointed it at his chest. "You know that thing you said earlier, about not having a choice?"

His eyes darkened with regret.

"Don't follow me," she said, leaving him there.

JAVIER JOGGED NORTH until he found the trail that led toward the twin peaks.

Heart pumping, he skirted around the fork in the path, not wanting to leave footprints at this critical junction. He continued to walk alongside the trail for several miles until it passed through a copse. At that point, the path was covered with leaves, and crashing through the underbrush would make an obvious disturbance.

He emerged from the trees and climbed uphill, so worried about being followed that he almost forgot to pay attention to what lay ahead. As he reached the top of the slope, the hairs on the back of his neck prickled with awareness. Instead of continuing down the other side, he ducked behind a boulder, his pulse thundering in his ears.

When he looked around the rock, he caught a glimpse of a man in the distance. Cursing, he flattened his belly against the ground and edged forward, studying the approaching threat from a safer position.

The guy was alone and unarmed. Although he wore a park uniform, he probably wasn't a member of law enforcement. He had a radio attached to his belt, along with a flashlight or pepper spray. Javier estimated his height at well over six feet. He had a lean build. He was young. He looked a little green.

Javier could probably take him. Even so, he hesitated, giving the man a closer study. He sized up all of his opponents based on his experience in the boxing ring and his work as an enforcer for Gonzales. There was something different about this guy. Unlike Caleb and Ted, he proceeded with caution, scanning the landscape. He expected trouble. Javier would have a hard time sneaking up on him.

He'd also promised Faith he wouldn't kill anyone else.

Maybe Javier should let the scout pass by. But logic told him he wouldn't get another opportunity to disguise himself.

He scrambled back down the hillside, into the copse. He found a good hiding spot and drew his gun. Normally he'd wait for the mark to walk past him in a situation like this. Worried that the worker would sense his presence, Javier jumped out from behind the tree trunk and rushed at him with a feral yell.

"Turn around," he said, aiming the gun between his startled blue eyes. "Turn around and put your hands up or I'll fucking shoot you!"

The guy was stunned, but he wasn't stupid. Javier was blocking his path. He had no choice but to comply. Hands raised, he turned slowly, getting a good look at Javier as he faced the opposite direction.

"Don't look at me, motherfucker! Take off your backpack."

He shrugged out of the pack and let it drop.

Javier kicked it aside. "Now get down on your knees."

This order was met with some resistance. The park employee stared straight ahead, his shoulders taut with tension.

"Get down on your fucking knees," Javier repeated.

Keeping his hands up, the man lowered himself to the ground.

"Take off your clothes."

The worker glanced over his shoulder at Javier, his expression guarded.

"What the fuck are you looking at? Take off your clothes, bitch."

Moving his gaze forward, the park employee unbuttoned his shirt with shaking hands. His fear wasn't unfounded, but there was an edge to it that Javier didn't understand. He glanced around, keeping his gun trained on the back of the ranger's head. When he refocused on his target, he noticed a scar on the side of his neck.

It looked like a burned-off tattoo.

The worker removed his shirt, revealing more ink on his back. Javier couldn't think of the English word for the symbol, but he knew what it meant. The three-pronged leaf, or *trébol,* was used by an Aryan gang in prison.

This man had been inside. Well, well. No wonder he didn't want to get down on his knees or take off his clothes. Other than the tattoos, he was a real pretty boy, with short blond hair and nice features.

Javier had a soft spot for abused women and children, but his sympathies didn't extend to white supremacists. Behind bars, they'd be enemies. He wouldn't hesitate to beat a guy like him to a pulp.

"Now the pants, *muñeco,*" he said. "Show me that sweet ass."

"Fuck you," the guy said from between clenched teeth. "You'll have to kill me first."

"Just give me your pants," Javier said, impatient. "I don't want anything else from you."

Shoulders trembling, he lowered his hands to his belt. He must have believed Javier wasn't planning a sexual assault, because he unfastened his pants and unzipped the fly. When two shots rang out, the park employee jumped at the sound.

"Who was that?" Javier asked.

"I don't know."

"Are there other officers in the area?"

His hesitation indicated that he was alone.

Javier glanced toward the river, wavering. This worker was his meal ticket. He probably had a set of keys in his pocket, and a vehicle parked at the trailhead. If Javier went back to check on Faith, he'd lose his chance to escape.

He pictured her lovely face. Her lips trembling against his.

"Fuck!"

Abandoning the idea of stealing the man's uniform, Javier tucked the gun into his waistband and took off running. The gunshots sounded as though they'd come from the south, where he'd last seen her.

When he glanced back, Javier saw the park worker jogging after him, his shirt flapping open. The guy had balls. He also had longer legs than Javier. By the time they reached the fork, he'd almost caught up with him.

Javier hooked a right, his lungs burning. It was a short distance to the bloodstained trail. Caleb and Ted were lying in the middle of the path. Haphazardly discarded, rather than hidden. Faith wasn't with them.

When he got closer, Javier realized the men weren't dead. Ted was unconscious. Caleb appeared to have a gunshot wound in his left leg. He'd managed to stop the bleeding, but he was in bad shape.

Javier dragged a hand down his face, shocked by the scene. These guys were harmless. Their only crimes were arrogance, stupidity and marijuana possession. Now they were hurt, maybe dying, and Faith was in danger. This was all Javier's fault.

The ranger stood at a distance, waiting to see what he'd do. Javier examined the ground for footprints, but they went both directions. He didn't know where to go. He had to save Faith, and he needed help.

Setting the gun on the ground, he held his hands up

in the air. The irony of the situation didn't escape him. He was placing himself at another man's mercy, after having threatened and ridiculed him.

The worker approached warily.

"I'm Javier Del Norte," he said.

"Owen Jackson."

"The men who did this…they kidnapped a woman named Faith."

"How do you know?"

"I left her with them an hour ago." He pointed at Caleb and Ted.

Owen used his radio to report the accident, requesting wilderness medics. When Ted regained consciousness, he groaned at the sight of Javier hovering over him.

"I have to go after Faith," Javier said. "I think they're going to kill her."

The young man glanced down the trail. "They went that way," he said, gesturing north. "Three sets of shoes."

"I'm following them."

Owen hesitated, studying the injured men. "Can you hang on until the medics arrive? They should be here soon."

Ted said he'd be okay. Caleb didn't look good, but his bleeding was under control, and there wasn't much they could do for him.

"I'll come with you," Owen said to Javier.

Nodding, he bent to pick up his gun. He thought about apologizing for the ass comment, but perhaps that subject was better left untouched. Owen buttoned up his shirt, covering a bold tattoo over his stomach.

"What were you in for?" Javier asked.

"None of your fucking business."

Fair enough. Javier didn't really care about Owen's past or his future. At present, they were allies. "Let's go, then."

CHAPTER THIRTEEN

HOPE APPROACHED MIST Falls, her stomach churning.

She didn't see anyone. There was a large pool at the base of the waterfall, feeding into the Kaweah. The rushing rapids drowned out all other sounds, and moisture rose like a cloud, coating the rocks nearby with a dewy sheen.

Although the scene was picturesque, she couldn't appreciate its beauty. She glanced around, wondering if she should start climbing. As far as she knew, Sam had listened to her warning and stayed behind. He hadn't tried to stop her.

Her radio beeped. "Throw your gun into the water and come to the top."

She depressed the talk button, her eyes swimming in the harsh sunlight. Over the past hour, the temperature had warmed at least ten degrees. By noon, it would be sizzling hot. "Is my sister up there?"

"You'll see her."

Heart slamming against her ribs, she removed the weapon from her waistband and tossed it into the jade-green pool. She felt naked without it, but the request wasn't unexpected. They wouldn't allow an armed woman to approach. As long as Faith wasn't hurt, Hope would cooperate with these men. There was nothing she wouldn't do for her sister.

The path to the summit was a steep, slippery climb, popular with cliff divers because of the deep water below. Rangers had placed a bolted line along the edge of the falls for safety. She used the rope when she needed to, grasping rock handholds when she didn't.

Near the top, a man emerged from between boulders. It was Leather, although he wasn't wearing his jacket anymore. His black T-shirt was damp and his pants were bloodstained.

"Where's Faith?" she asked.

He glanced across the falls.

Her sister was on the other side with Poncho, who had also discarded his outerwear. Faith's hands and feet were bound. A strip of cloth bisected her mouth. She'd been crying. Her face was streaked with tears and mud.

Hope's chest constricted at the sight. "Let her go."

"After you guide me to the cargo."

"I'll tell you where it is."

"You'll show me," he countered.

"I want to stay with Faith."

"No. You come with me. Your sister stays here."

She moistened her lips, deliberating. They'd asked for a guide, not a map, so she'd anticipated this argument. If she refused, they might kill her and Faith. They might do that anyway. A helicopter flew over the falls, hovering nearby.

"This is our ride," Leather said. "Take it or leave it."

She took it.

Her hair whipped around her neck as she followed him away from the waterfall, into an adjoining meadow. The helicopter set down long enough to allow them to board. Hope climbed in first, prodded by Leather. Her eardrums were about to explode. She wasn't offered any protection. After taking Hope's radio away, Leather signaled the pilot to lift off.

The trip to Angel Wings only took a few minutes, but the pilot couldn't find a suitable place to land. The wind was too high and the terrain too rugged. He finally found a spot near the summit. She hopped out, ducking her head to avoid the propeller. Leather joined her.

Hiking uphill through underbrush was brutal. Hope put one foot in front of the other, ascending as slowly as possible. She didn't have to feign exhaustion. She was tired and hungry and thirsty.

When they arrived at the stash, she pointed it out and sat down, relieved that her duty was done. The pilot flew over, dropping a large net from the helicopter. Leather retrieved the net and spread it out on the ground.

"Go get the bags," he ordered.

"Do it yourself."

He grabbed her wrist and jerked her upright, shoving her toward the boulders.

She stumbled forward, her mind numb. As she got closer to the crevice, she noticed that some of the bags were missing. There was a faint shoe print in the damp, sandy dirt. It left the distinctive zigzag impression of a large hiking boot.

Although the detail struck her as important, she didn't mention it to Leather. He might destroy the boot print or blame Hope for the theft. She grabbed one of the duffel bags and dragged it to the net. Then another, and another. Leather loaded the bags in the center. The process seemed to take an eternity. Hope endured the strain in her shoulders, praying she'd be reunited with Faith when this was over. Imagining another outcome was impossible.

She couldn't think about Sam.

After the last bag was tossed on top of the pile, Leather gave her an expectant look. "Where's the rest?"

"That's all of them."

He counted the bags. "This is eight. There should be ten."

Hope shrugged. "Maybe there's another hiding place."

Leather grabbed her by the arm and jerked her closer, shoving the barrel of his gun against her temple. "There were ten. You photographed them."

"Someone else was here," she cried, her throat raw and her head aching. "There's a boot mark in the dirt."

He went to inspect the ground, pulling her along with him. After a quick search of the area, he returned to the net, cursing in Spanish. He put his gun away, secured the cargo and called the pilot for a pickup.

Hope couldn't quite overhear his conversation, but she guessed he was talking about her. He murmured an affirmative, his eyes guarded.

She knew then that Sam had been right. Leather didn't need her anymore, and she'd seen his face. She'd seen the pilot. She could identify Poncho. They wouldn't let her live. Faith was probably dead already.

Her heart stalled in her chest, and she struggled to hide her panic. Faith couldn't be gone. She'd feel it. Her sister was still alive; she had to be. Hope clung to that belief, and found the strength to keep fighting.

Leather had to attach the net to a line hanging from

the helicopter, and the task required his full attention. While he fumbled with the hook, she took off running. He couldn't follow until he finished, so she had a good head start.

Instead of going downhill, which was tempting, she went up. He might have greater size and strength, but he couldn't outhike her. She raced to the top of Angel Wings, her blood pumping with adrenaline. There was a gun at the plane crash site, sitting on the passenger seat. She'd beat Leather there and give him a nasty surprise.

She heard him coming after her. As she sailed over the surface, weaving back and forth, he lagged behind. He wasn't slow, but he couldn't catch up with her. The uneven terrain worked to her advantage.

She reached the fuselage and dove inside. Crows flew from the cockpit, squawking and flapping their black wings. The smell of death was overwhelming. The pilot's body had swelled and shifted, listing to the right. As she shoved him aside, she caught a glimpse of his empty eye sockets, picked clean by scavengers.

Gagging, she reached for the gun and shrank down, flattening her back against the interior of the plane.

When Leather appeared at the broken front window, she pulled the trigger. He saw the gun and ducked, but nothing happened. She'd left the safety on. Hands shaking, she released the mechanism and waited for him to enter the fuselage.

"Come on," she urged. *Come and get me.*

The seconds ticked by. She wanted to peek out the window to see where he'd gone. Maybe he'd decided she wasn't worth the trouble. Pleased with her quick thinking and fast footwork, she craned her neck to look for him.

Bullets peppered the side of the plane, penetrating the fuselage. She screamed and curled herself into a tight ball.

He fired again, narrowly missing her head.

Holding the gun in a tight grip, she squeezed off a couple of shots, estimating his location. She was afraid to keep firing, because she didn't know how many bullets were in the chamber. For a moment, everything was silent.

Had she hit him?

Something slammed into the fuselage, jolting her sideways. A second later, the plane moved again. Its metal underbelly scraped along the jagged surface of the rock.

She gasped with terror as it dawned on her.

He was pushing her off the cliff.

SAM HAD NO intention of following Hope to Mist Falls.

None whatsoever.

A part of him wanted to go after her just because she'd told him not to. How dare she order him around at gunpoint? Although he knew she wouldn't actually shoot him, he didn't appreciate her intimidation tactics. Staring down the barrel made him feel like a little kid about to piss his pants. It was a hell of a power equalizer.

He should have tackled her when he had the chance. He could have used his superior strength to hold her down, keep her safe. She'd taken away his only opportunity to save her, and he resented her for it.

Seething with frustration, he stared down the path.

He wasn't going to chase her again. He refused to follow her into another ridiculously dangerous scenario. He was going to hike back to Kaweah, retreat from society and…free-solo until he felt numb.

Cursing, he scrubbed a hand down his face. That wasn't healthy. This wasn't healthy. Everything was so fucked up!

He knew he'd overreacted to her question about Melissa. Last night, he'd opened up to her about his head trauma, and she'd listened to him. She'd pointed out that he was running away from his problems, but she hadn't been cold or uncaring. Then she'd shared her darkest secret with him, and he'd brushed it aside. He'd judged her and dismissed her pain.

He hadn't reacted well to the confession about Dixon, either. Every time she gave him a part of herself, physically or emotionally, he shut her out. He thought he was doing it to protect Melissa's memory. In reality, he was protecting himself.

Deep down, he'd always known there was something special about her. He'd recognized it the first time he saw her, but he hadn't wanted a meaningful relationship. He had to heal himself before he could be with anyone else. Hope represented life, and change, and moving forward.

Over the past three days, he'd been in a constant state of anxiety. It finally dawned on him that his fears weren't caused by triggers, or psychosis, or his tragic past. He was paralyzed with worry because he *cared* about her. She mattered more to him than recovery.

He'd sacrifice his last days with Melissa for a future with Hope.

The suspicion that he might never regain his memory had plagued him for two years. At this point, it seemed almost insignificant. If he lost Hope, he'd be devastated. Nothing else mattered.

He went after her.

Although he ran as fast as he could, leaping over boulders in his path, she had a good head start. He never caught up with her. When Mist Falls came into view, he veered off the trail and studied the area. There was a bolted line on the left side of the falls. Skirting around that expected route, he made his way to the other side, walking behind the curtain of water. He'd been cliff-diving here before and knew of an alternate ascent.

He climbed along the slippery rocks, using the cover of trees and shrubs. The crashing falls drowned out all sound. As he got close to the summit, a helicopter flew over. Sam searched the other side of the waterfall and found Hope. She was standing at the top with one of the drug smugglers. The man looked across the falls, directly above Sam. Hope nodded, and they headed toward the meadow beyond.

Sam couldn't do anything to stop them. He hadn't anticipated a helicopter. He'd assumed she would guide the drug smugglers to the stash on foot, and he'd have hours to find an opportunity to rescue her—not seconds.

He clung to a moss-covered wall, his heart hammering against his ribs. There was a clearing above him. Sam could slither back down the falls, take the dizzying jump to the pool below, or keep going up.

He kept going.

A small outcropping offered a number of handholds. He climbed over it and crawled behind a cluster of bushes, staying low. Near the summit, there was a woman sitting on a flat rock, her mouth gagged. She was bound at the wrists and ankles.

Faith.

She looked a lot like Hope. Slender, pretty, curly hair. She was blonde, and on the skinny side, more petite than her sister.

The man with her was the other smuggler from the cave. His clothes were wet. He held a gun in his right hand. Sam guessed he was about Owen's age, but he had dark, shaggy hair and a bulkier frame.

While he watched, Faith made a mewling sound and gazed up at the young man, fluttering her lashes in distress. She tugged at her bonds imploringly, drawing his attention to her outthrust breasts. Clever girl.

Unfortunately, her captor didn't fall for it. Flushing, he glanced away.

Sam's instincts screamed to help Faith, but the drug smuggler was armed and dangerous. Interfering might put Hope at risk, as well. She'd probably agreed to their demands in exchange for her sister's life.

He knew that Hope wouldn't want him to leave Faith. She cared more about her sister's safety than her own. And, once again, he didn't have much choice. Angel Wings wasn't far, but he couldn't outrun a helicopter. Even if he left now, and speed-climbed the wall, he might be too late to reach Hope.

Saving Faith was a better option.

Sam's pulse pounded as he deliberated an approach. The guy was about his size, but Sam had no experience in fisticuffs.

Faith rolled onto her side and arched her back, still

trying to free her wrists. She couldn't budge them, but she managed to jiggle her breasts and strike a provocative pose. Her efforts weren't in vain. The guy was disturbed, and possibly tempted, by her machinations. He moved to the edge of the falls, turning his back on her.

It was now or never.

Sam was a loner, not a fighter, but he had a distinct advantage. He'd cliff-dived from this very spot.

Rising to his feet, he burst from the bushes and ran toward his target. The guy whirled around quickly, hearing him approach. He didn't have time to step away from the falls or aim his weapon. Sam hurdled over Faith and tackled her captor. They sailed through the air in a tangle of arms and legs.

The blind drop was stomach-curling. While the drug smuggler flailed wildly, letting go of his weapon, Sam braced for impact. Seconds later, they hit the water with a cold shock. Their combined weight resulted in a harder slam and a deeper plunge.

Sam had another advantage in the pool. As a former Olympian, he was a strong swimmer, as comfortable in icy water as on dry land. Shoving his opponent down to the bottom, he kicked toward the surface.

Before he got far, a hand snagged his ankle, jerking him backward. Sam's booted foot glanced off his cheek. The guy let go of Sam, releasing a flurry of bubbles. They broke through the water at the same time.

Sam's new friend punched him in the face. Pain exploded in his mouth and hot blood dribbled down his chin.

He ducked and swam away, executing a swift freestyle. If the pool was larger, Sam could have put distance between them quickly. He could have scrambled out, climbed up the safety line and freed Faith.

But the pool wasn't big enough to make a difference. He reached the shore in seconds, and the smuggler was right behind him. Sam tried a second tackle, having exhausted his attack repertoire. Too late, he realized he should have stayed in the water. The younger man boxed as well as Sam swam.

His opponent stayed on his feet, shoving Sam and advancing. Sam staggered backward, absorbing several blows to the face. They were close to the outer edge of the pool, where the flow fed into the river.

He glanced at the rushing water, dizzy. Maybe it was time to take another dive.

The smuggler made the decision for him. He came at Sam with a fist-sized rock, cracking him over the head.

Everything went black.

CHAPTER FOURTEEN

SAM REMEMBERED.

He remembered his last moments with Melissa. He remembered the morning of the climb, and the day before. He remembered the horrible, harrowing weeks after. He remembered the earthquake.

He remembered everything. The memories were no worse or better than he expected, just different. Hollow, in a way.

"Sam."

The voice drifted into his semiconsciousness. Owen's voice. His hand slapped Sam's wet cheek lightly.

Sam groaned as reality crashed down all around him. His head…fucking *hurt*. He didn't want to open his eyes. His clothes were soaked, and he felt…sick. As if he'd swallowed a bellyful of river water.

It came gurgling up, spewing from him in a violent rush. Owen rolled him onto his side and Sam vomited until he had nothing left. The cool liquid felt alien, like a foreign substance purged from his insides. When it was gone, he dry-heaved weakly. Tears rushed into his eyes with every stomach spasm.

He couldn't focus. The world was a blur.

Owen set him on his back and covered his body with a safety blanket. The cold water, inside and out, had lowered his core temperature so much that he was shaking like a leaf, even while lying on a warm rock in direct sunlight.

"Hope," he croaked.

Owen hovered close, his face a Munch painting. "Do you know where she is?"

Sam blinked several times to clear his vision. The bleeding colors rearranged into something that resembled reality. "Angel Wings."

Owen picked up his radio to call it in.

"No," Sam said, reaching out to stop him. His hand brushed Owen's forearm and fell aside, ineffectual.

Owen flinched at the contact. He always did. "Why?"

Sam lifted his throbbing head to study their surroundings. His body had traveled several hundred feet downriver. The man he'd been fighting was gone. "They're listening to the transmissions."

Owen's brows rose with surprise.

"How long was I out?" Sam asked.

"A few minutes, at the most."

"Is anyone else in the area?"

"No. The other rangers got delayed. They're still hours away."

"Faith needs help," Sam said, trying to concentrate on the most important details. His mind was reeling from the rush of memories. He'd waited years for recovery. Getting it now wasn't just inconvenient, it was a damned nuisance.

"Del Norte went after her," Owen said.

"When?"

"Just now. He caught sight of someone climbing up the side of the falls. He ran that way, saying the man would lead him to Faith."

"He wants to rescue her?"

"That's what he said."

"You have to follow him," Sam said.

"Is she over there?"

"Yes."

Owen examined the trail, his gaze sharp. Then he returned his attention to Sam. "You look like hell."

Sam straightened, staving off a wave of dizziness. There was a tender lump on the back of his head. His teeth ached from the punch he'd taken. He felt nauseated, and he probably had a concussion, but his vision had returned to normal. He wasn't throwing up anymore. The uncontrollable shivering had stopped. "I'm fine."

"Right," Owen scoffed.

"I remember the quake."

"What quake?"

"In San Diego," Sam said. "I remember everything. I remember Melissa's death."

Owen appeared stunned. He was one of the few people who knew about Sam's amnesia—because he'd been there during the freeway collapse.

"Do you have a rack?"

"Of climbing gear?"

"Yeah."

"You can't climb."

Sam tossed aside the blanket and staggered to his feet. If he could stand, he could climb. "Give it to me. I'm going after Hope."

Owen rose also. His expression was skeptical, but he shrugged out of his backpack and handed it over.

"Faith is bound and gagged on the right side of the falls."

"I'll look for her."

"Be careful," Sam warned.

Owen promised he would, and Sam felt his throat close up. He realized that he hadn't managed to smother all of his feelings over the past two years. Somehow, he'd grown to like this messed-up kid from prison.

Maybe it was a mistake to leave Faith's life in the hands of a park assistant and a fugitive criminal, but Sam couldn't think of a better option. He was terrified for Hope. For the first time since the accident, he'd woken with a clear head.

He had to go with his gut. He had to save Hope.

The simple hike was grueling. When he tried to sprint, he started dry-heaving again. He was forced to stop and take sips of water until his nausea abated. After he reached the fork, he felt stronger. He found some crackers and an energy drink in Owen's pack. The snack settled his stomach, and he jogged the last two miles to Angel Wings.

At the wall, he dropped his pack and removed the gear. Owen's harness fit him. His ropes were good. Sam didn't have time to mess around with perfect placements and safety measures. More than an hour had passed since he'd left Mist Falls. He had to speed-climb and pray for strength.

It was, without a doubt, the hardest climb of his life. His balance was off, he felt weak and his muscles didn't work right. The bump on his head was like a beating heart, radiating pain throughout his body. He was sweating profusely, his gut churning. He kept the crackers down, but it was a near thing.

At the halfway mark, a high wind tested his resolve. He swayed and clung to the wall, pressing his belly against the warm rock. His hands were trembling. The odds against him seemed insurmountable.

He was going to fail.

Taking a deep breath, he closed his eyes. Memories of Melissa flooded him. He hadn't argued with her that day, or been careless with their gear, or pushed her beyond her limits. What had happened was an accident. Knowing that didn't assuage his guilt. All these months, he'd assumed recovery would bring closure. Instead, he felt empty. He was overwhelmed by loss, not comforted or at peace.

And how cruel was fate, to put him in the same position with Hope. Unable to save her. So close, but so far. Another life, slipping through his fingers.

Gunfire echoed through the canyon, startling him into action. He continued his ascent, aware that the shots were coming from the mountaintop. It sounded like two different weapons firing, but he couldn't be sure.

A moment later, the remains of the plane toppled over the edge of the cliff, coming straight at him.

THE WATERFALL WAS almost as majestic as the ones he'd seen in Costa Rica.

Javier recognized the man climbing up the path as Nick Kruger. He was Martin's little bitch. Martin Hinojosa did most of Gonzales's dirty work. Both men were likely candidates for Alexia's murder.

He couldn't wait to tear Nick apart.

Tucking the gun into his waistband, Javier began his ascent. Nick had already spotted him, so he didn't bother with stealth. He climbed quickly, closing the distance between them. Near the top, he caught a glimpse of tangled blond hair. Faith sat on the opposite side of the falls. She'd been gagged with dirty cloth, her wrists and ankles bound.

Javier would kill Nick for that offense alone. Although he had him in his sights, Javier hesitated to shoot.

He didn't want to do it in front of her.

Instead of pulling his gun, he continued to the summit. Nick waded across the top edge of the falls, almost slipping in his haste. Javier couldn't let him get to Faith. He traversed the space with caution, but he also made a misstep, sinking into waist-deep water. When he regained his footing, he hurried to catch up.

Nick stumbled and fell before they reached the rock outcropping. He pushed himself off the ground, glancing over his shoulder at Javier. There was a nasty scrape on his left cheek. Faith made a whimpering sound in the back of her throat.

Javier reached for his gun and came up empty.

Coño!

He must have lost it in the water.

Nick realized what had happened and assumed a ready position, putting his fists up. He was a scrappy fighter—Gonzales liked to trawl the boxing ring for employees—but Javier had more experience.

"Why don't you just get the fuck out of here?" Javier offered.

"I'm not a deserter."

Javier wasn't impressed by his loyalty. Gonzales would punish Nick for abandoning Faith, so he didn't have much choice. "No, you're a killer. If those guys on the trail don't survive, you'll get the death penalty."

"I didn't kill anyone," he said, breathing hard. He sounded worried.

Javier had helped Owen pull the unconscious man out of the water. He would have died without their intervention. He might be dead now. "What about Alexia?"

Nick's gaze darkened. "No."

Although Javier wanted to press him for more information, he doubted any would be forthcoming. He glanced at Faith, evaluating her condition. Her clothes were dirty and she had some minor scratches. "Did he hit you?"

Eyes wide, she shook her head.

Good to know. Javier wasn't going to take it easy on him, however. He advanced, feinting to the left and following up with a hard right. The first strike connected, but Nick stayed on his feet. Somehow, he also managed to retaliate with a heavy blow to the gut.

Maybe Javier had underestimated him.

Smothering a grunt of surprise, he retreated a few steps. His left side was still sore, and Nick was perceptive enough to recognize the weakness. He pummeled Javier's left shoulder, striking the tender spot.

Pain exploded on impact. Javier swung out wildly and got lucky with an uppercut. Nick staggered backward.

Faith wasn't content to sit and watch. She wiggled toward Nick like a worm, positioning herself behind him. When Javier came forward, swinging again, Nick tripped over her and went down on his ass.

Javier seized the opportunity to leap on top of Nick. Grabbing the front of his shirt, he punched him again and again. He punched for Alexia, and for Faith. He punched for Caleb and Ted and the guy Owen had pulled out of the river.

He had a strong urge to keep hitting him, but he slowed as soon as Nick went limp. There was no sport in beating a semiconscious man to death. His fist hovered in the air, waiting to descend. Beneath him, Nick moaned, his head lolling to the side. Blood dribbled down his brow, into his ear.

Javier glanced at Faith. Tears leaked from her eyes, making tracks on her dirty cheeks. She didn't need to witness any more brutality.

He let Nick go and went to her. Wiping his hand on his jeans, he knelt beside her, reaching out to remove her gag. She made a noise of discomfort as the rough cloth left her tender mouth. He wanted to kiss her, but he drew her into his arms instead. She pressed her face to his chest and wept.

Gonzales stepped into the clearing, his gun poised. "What a touching scene."

Javier's stomach clenched with tension. He thought about diving into the falls, but the drop looked deadly, and Faith was still tied up. She couldn't land safely, or swim. He'd risk his own life to escape, not hers.

He tightened his arm around her protectively.

"Would you care to explain yourself?" Gonzales asked.

Javier expected to be executed on the spot. Gonzales knew that Javier had betrayed him. The proof was right here, in Nick's blood. He'd come back for Faith, and made enemies of his former comrades. It didn't look good. If Gonzales waited, it was only because he wanted to interrogate and torture Javier first.

Although he couldn't change his fate, maybe he could convince Gonzales to spare Faith. "She doesn't know anything," he said, holding her head to his chest. She trembled against him. "Let her go."

"I'd rather let her watch you die."

"Please," he said, reduced to begging.

Gonzales gestured at Nick, who was showing signs of life. "Can you walk, or should I save you the trouble?"

Nick staggered to his feet, wiping his bloody eyebrow.

"Get up," Gonzales said to Javier. "And bring the girl with you."

Once again, he considered taking a leap off the cliff. It was three short steps to the edge, but Gonzales would shoot him in the back before he reached freedom. He rose and lifted Faith into his arms, ignoring the ache in his shoulder.

A helicopter flew overhead and landed in the meadow nearby. At Gonzales's prodding, Javier headed that direction, resigned to cooperate.

For now.

HOPE RELEASED THE clip and checked for bullets.

Two left.

She shoved it back into the chamber, knowing she had to make them both count. While she took aim at his estimated location, ready to squeeze off another shot,

Leather slammed his shoulder against the fuselage a third time. The nose tipped over the edge. She careened sideways into the dead pilot.

Her stomach sank.

There was nothing she could do. Momentum would send the plane hurtling off the cliff, whether she fired or not.

Killing him wouldn't save her now.

If she stayed inside the fuselage, she would die. If she jumped out, she would die. She braced herself for the crash although it wouldn't make any difference. The plane's belly scraped along the rocks with a metallic groan.

Then she was airborne.

Her head hit the roof as the wreckage toppled nose over tail, smashing against the cliff wall.

The stomach-curling descent ended before she expected it. One second, she was flying around the inside of the fuselage. The next, she was plastered to the ceiling, stunned. The plane came to a sudden halt.

Hope felt suspended in time and space. Was she dead or alive, up or down?

The gun in her hand seemed real. She tightened her grip, trying to regain her hold on reality. Taking a deep breath, she glanced past the dead pilot, out the broken window. Terror coursed through her veins as she realized what had happened. The fuselage was perched on a precarious ledge, halfway down the cliff.

It wasn't stable.

Wind whistled through the swaying cabin. Any moment, she could take another plunge. She had to get out—now.

Heart pounding, she tucked the gun into her waistband and crawled along the roof, clawing her way toward the window. The pilot dangled upside down, eyes empty, mouth gaping open. She skirted around him, whimpering with fear. The fuselage shifted, bringing his face closer to hers.

She smothered a shriek and cowered against the ceiling. If she didn't free herself from the wreckage, she was going to die. She knew it, but she couldn't move.

"Hope!"

It was Sam. Although he sounded distant, and distressed, his voice was music to her ears. The fact that she could hear him at all encouraged her. He had to be within a few hundred feet. Maybe he was climbing the wall.

A gunshot followed his anguished cry.

She started moving again, spurred by the danger. Glass cut into her skin and tore her clothes as she maneuvered through the broken window. Leather was standing on the cliff about a hundred feet above her, pointing his gun down.

She followed its trajectory to Sam.

He was several pitches below her, his body pressed flat to the rock. Leather's bullet must not have hit its target, because Sam appeared unharmed. Unfortunately, there were no outcroppings for him to hide behind. He was a sitting duck.

So was she.

Swallowing hard, she studied the wall in front of her. It offered a number of handholds. If the fuselage fell away, she could grab on.

But for how long?

Her anxiety spiked as she looked down. She had no idea what the plane was resting on. The fuselage might break away and take her with it at any moment.

Pulse racing, she reached out to touch the dusty granite with her left hand. When her grip felt solid, she brandished her weapon, braced herself against the rock and waited. The instant Leather leaned over the edge of the cliff to shoot, she squeezed the trigger. His head exploded in a violent red burst.

Hope barely registered the lucky hit, or the fact that his body was tumbling toward her. She wasn't used to firing one-handed, and the gun's kick was strong. Her arm jerked back and the fuselage shuddered, falling out from under her.

Seconds later, it exploded against the ground.

Screaming, she dropped her weapon and clung to the wall with both hands. Leather flew by like a giant black crow, narrowly missing her. She heard a sickening *thunk* as his bones and internal organs were obliterated.

Hope shuddered, picturing the same fate for herself.

She couldn't feel a ledge or any convenient support beneath her feet. The muscles in her arms were already strained, taxed beyond their limits. Trying not to panic, she looked over her shoulder and studied the distance to the ground.

She was doomed.

"Hold on," Sam called.

"I can't," she said, but he couldn't hear her.

"I'm coming for you!"

The fuselage had been resting on something several feet below her. She wanted to drop down to it, but she didn't know what was there.

"Stay where you are," Sam said. "I'm coming."

Her arms shook, threatening to give out, and her hands felt as if they were bleeding. Maybe they were. The glass had left shallow cuts all over her body. "I can't hold on," she said in a hoarse voice.

"There's nothing under you, Hope. The boulder crumbled down the cliff with the fuselage."

She pressed her forehead to the rock and wept. She wasn't ready to die. Faith needed her. But her fingertips were numb, and her strength was sapped.

Sam continued to talk to her in a calm voice. He positioned himself directly under her, and he sounded close. Almost close enough to save her. When her hands unclenched, she cried out for help.

After a nerve-jolting slide, he caught her.

He trapped her between his body and the wall, locking her in a bear hug. Their combined weight sagged against the line, but the gear held tight. Hope dangled there like a rag doll, sobbing hysterically.

"I've got you," he kept saying. "I've got you."

When the feeling returned to her arms, and her hands tingled with sensation, she let him guide her back to the wall. She gripped the rock, blinking the tears from her eyes while he attached her to his harness with extra rope. Using his belay device, he lowered them both down the cliff safely.

The fuselage was still burning, several hundred feet away. Hope wanted to ask about Faith, but she needed a moment to catch her breath.

As soon as Sam removed the gear, she threw her arms around him. She didn't have any more tears, or any words at all, just gratitude. His shoulders trembled beneath her fingertips. Realizing that he was crying, she reached up to touch the wetness on his face.

A second later, his mouth covered hers. She tasted his fear and desperation. Overwhelmed with emotion, she kissed him back hungrily. His chest was solid against her breasts, his hands strong and his body hard-muscled.

He felt like everything she'd ever wanted, raw and pure and real. The swelling against her abdomen was as life-affirming as the ground beneath her feet.

She couldn't forget what he'd said before they'd parted, or all the pain he'd caused her in a short period of time. Her interactions with Sam were fraught with conflict. His capacity for hurting her was vast.

But so was his capacity for pleasuring her.

He made her feel—lust, anger, frustration, sadness. He made her feel alive. So she gripped his damp shirt and kissed him harder, drinking him in. Wanting more of his heat and heart and hurt.

His hands roved down her back, cupping her bottom and lifting her against his erection. He seemed frantic, as if he might devour her whole.

She broke the kiss, panting.

When the wildness in his eyes faded, he let her go, raking a hand through his hair. "Jesus," he said. "I thought you were going to die up there. The fuselage was teetering on a fucking pebble."

She looked over her shoulder at a boulder the size of an armchair. Hardly a pebble, but small, compared to the plane. "You saved me."

"You saved both of us," he countered.

The remains of the man she'd killed were beyond the wreckage. She tore her gaze away. "Where's Faith?"

His throat worked as he swallowed. "I don't know. I...ran into Owen on the trail. He said he'd look for her."

She'd wondered where his climbing gear had come from. As he handed her a bottle of water from his pack, she noticed movement in the distance.

Owen.

He must have witnessed the kiss, because he was just standing there, as if reluctant to interrupt the intimate moment. Hope took a long drink of water and walked toward him, tension humming through her body.

More rangers and sheriff's deputies were coming down the trail. They were specks in the distance, still half a mile away. "Where's my sister?" she asked Owen.

"I'm sorry," he said, his eyes pained. "They took her."

Her stomach dropped. "Who?"

"The men at the top of Mist Falls. Before I could get there, they hauled her off and left in a helicopter."

"What happened to Del Norte?" Sam asked.

"He was the one carrying her. At gunpoint."

Hope collapsed against Sam, distraught. He lowered her to the ground, where she curled up into a tight ball. She couldn't lose her sister. Faith was her entire world. "No!" she screamed, clenching her hands into fists.

CHAPTER FIFTEEN

As soon as Javier set her down inside the helicopter, his boss hit him over the head with the butt of his gun.

Faith was too terrified to scream. Javier slumped forward, unconscious.

His boss stepped around the body and climbed into the passenger seat. "Nick," he said, tossing a rope over his shoulder.

The man Javier had beaten to a pulp picked up the rope, tying Javier's hands and feet. Leaving him on the floor, Nick urged Faith to sit down and took the space next to her. She studied him warily as he reached across her body to secure her safety belt. He smelled like mud and sweat. His chin was scraped raw. Rivulets of blood snaked from his eyebrow down his dirty face. She held her breath until he moved away.

Nick seemed aware of her disgust. Clearing his throat, he lifted the hem of his T-shirt and held it to his brow.

She turned her attention to Javier's boss. Unlike the unwashed cretin beside her, he was handsome and well dressed, his short black hair cut even more expertly than Javier's. He wore a flashy platinum watch on his wrist.

If this man had been standing beside "Jay Norton" in a different setting, she might have noticed him first.

Javier's boss caught her looking and muttered an

order in Spanish. Nick didn't strike her as a native speaker, but he stopped blotting his forehead and leaned toward her. The cut that bisected his eyebrow was still seeping. It needed stitches. When he reached for her gag, she shied away, trying to avoid his bloodstained hands. But she had nowhere to go. He untied the rough cloth and covered her eyes with it, making a tight knot.

She was cast into darkness as the helicopter lifted off.

Javier shifted at her feet, showing signs of regaining consciousness. She didn't know what to think of him, or how to feel. He was responsible for this predicament. He'd lied to her and put her in danger. But he'd also risked his life to come back for her. He'd fought Nick for her, and begged his boss to leave her behind. If nothing else, the protective streak that had drawn her to him was genuine.

After the helicopter landed, Nick left her side. Javier grunted in pain, as if he'd been kicked awake, and she sensed motion all around her. When everything went quiet, she knew she was alone in the cabin.

Faith had never been a patient person. This wait was the most uncomfortable of her life. She was tired and thirsty. Her arms ached from being wrenched behind her back. Dirt covered her from head to toe.

The mosquito bite on her face itched.

After an interminable, torturous period, someone returned for her. He picked her up and carried her away from the helicopter. She knew it wasn't Nick, because she detected a hint of expensive cologne.

The man walked down a set of stairs and maneuvered

her through a narrow space. By the time he tossed her on a mattress, he was breathing heavily.

She realized he'd just exerted himself, but the sinister sound, paired with squeaking bedsprings and her bound, blindfolded state, sent her into a panic. She screamed for help and tried to roll away from him.

He tugged the cloth from her eyes.

Javier's boss loomed over her, giving her an intense study. His interest didn't seem sexual, or particularly aggressive. "Are you hungry?"

She glanced around the room. It looked normal, if colorless. White walls, beige carpet, tan bedspread. There was a small table with a silver food tray and a large bottle of Evian. She swallowed dryly. "I'm thirsty."

He took a pair of clippers from his pocket to cut the tie at her wrists. Then he poured her a cup of water.

She gulped in great swallows, liquid sloshing down her face and neck. He didn't react to the unladylike behavior. Although she wanted to kick him in the nuts, she settled for tossing the rest of the water in his face. He wicked away the moisture with aplomb, his left eye twitching. The response didn't satisfy her, but it was better than nothing. She reached down to tug at the binding around her ankles.

"I need to ask you a few questions."

"Where's my sister?"

"I'll tell you, if you cooperate."

She just stared at him, waiting. He was a few years older than Javier, darker and more refined-looking.

"I know that your name is Faith. Do you know who I am?"

"Javier's boss. His friend, at one time."

"His friend?"

"Until you stole his woman."

His gaze narrowed. "This woman, is he still involved with her?"

"He told me he was single."

"A common lie for men."

Faith agreed that it was.

"Did he say where he was headed?"

She shook her head. "He mentioned that he works in Las Vegas."

"Did he tell you anything else about Alexia?"

"Who's Alexia?"

"My wife."

She remembered Javier saying that the woman had been killed, but she wasn't going to repeat that to her murderer. "No."

He put his hands in his pockets, pensive. "The truth is that Javier stole her from me, not the other way around. They've been having an affair for years. She disappeared six months ago. I think they were planning to run away together."

Faith searched his eyes for a hint of deception and found none. Javier hadn't been honest with her about everything, but she believed what he'd said about Alexia. He wasn't trying to seduce her—she hadn't needed cajoling.

One of the men was lying.

"Javier told me he didn't want her after you'd had her," she said, pursing her lips. "Sloppy seconds and all that."

His jaw clenched with anger. Finally a real reaction. He crossed the room, removing the silver tray cover. Beneath it, there was an assortment of fruits and cheeses. Her stomach growled as he removed a red grape from the bunch and popped it into his mouth. "Then I know how to make him lose interest in you, don't I?"

She glanced away, her pulse racing. The last thing she wanted to do was show fear, but he scared her.

The threat of rape scared her.

When he paused at the edge of the bed, reaching out to touch her face, she forced herself not to flinch. "You're very beautiful," he said, brushing his knuckles down her cheek. "Del Norte has always had excellent taste."

Her body quivered with tension, but she said nothing.

He dropped his hand. "Your sister shot and killed my man on the top of the mountain. She got away."

Faith's heart leaped at the news.

Removing the scissors from his pocket, he cut the bonds at her feet. "Make yourself comfortable. Eat, drink, bathe. Rest."

She rubbed her ankles. "I'd rather rest at home."

"Javier will be more cooperative if he knows you're here. As soon as I get the information I need from him, you're free to go."

She hoped that was true. "I won't thank you for the hospitality."

"It was a pleasure to meet you," he said, bowing.

"All yours."

With a dark smile, he turned and walked out.

IT WAS THE worst day of Hope's life.

Moments after Owen broke the bad news, a swarm of officials descended on the scene. Caleb and Ted were transported to the nearest hospital, in stable condition. Crime scene investigators studied the plane wreckage and photographed the corpses. Another team went to Mist Falls to search for clues. Hope wasn't allowed to go with them.

The physical strain and emotional stress had rendered her almost useless, anyway. She managed the walk to Mineral King, with Sam's help.

They were interviewed on the trail and again at park headquarters. Hope recounted as many details as she could remember. She'd used deadly force in the line of duty, so she understood the necessity of a thorough report.

The sheriff's department focused their efforts on identifying the remains, but both bodies were unrecognizable. They also contacted the DEA for information on Javier Del Norte. As soon as they found out which criminal organization he was affiliated with, they could begin a search for Faith.

There was nothing for Hope to do but wait.

By the time she left headquarters, the sun dipped low in the sky, and she was exhausted. She'd been able to shower and change clothes earlier, but she wasn't looking forward to retiring for the night. The shared housing for park employees made it difficult to keep anything private. Her coworkers would probably try to comfort her or ask questions. She didn't want to go straight to bed, and she didn't want to stay awake.

Sam was waiting for her in the parking lot, leaning against a silver sports car. It was one of several expensive vehicles he owned. He pushed away from the door and approached her, his expression inscrutable.

He'd also cleaned up. His casual jeans and polo shirt were well worn, but high quality, an unconscious display of wealth. A few years ago, he'd sold all of his multimillion-dollar companies, so he was set for life.

She didn't think less of him for choosing not to work, but she wasn't overly impressed by his financial success. There was a saying about people who were born on third base and claimed to have hit a home run. Although the second part might not apply to Sam, because he wasn't boastful, he'd come from a place of privilege.

Her passion for him had drowned in a river of fear for her sister. When they were riding high on adrenaline, kissing Sam had seemed like a great idea. At the end of a harrowing afternoon, she felt more like slapping him.

"Have you had dinner?" he asked.

She shook her head. They'd delivered a late lunch to park headquarters, but she hadn't been able to eat much.

"Can I take you out?"

She glanced down at her old T-shirt and faded jeans. Although their clothes were similar, she was underdressed for a date. More important, she didn't want to be seen in public. Her sister was missing. She couldn't handle the curious stares.

"We can get room service at the lodge."

"You'll pay for a room, just to have dinner?"

"And to talk."

The cost didn't matter to him, of course. Her stomach ached with emptiness, and she welcomed any distraction from Faith's disappearance. She also enjoyed Sam's company, despite his flaws. They'd been through an ordeal together. He understood what she was going through better than anyone else.

If he expected to get lucky, he was a fool.

"I'll meet you there," she said, climbing behind the wheel of her Jeep. Refusing to ride in his car was a small rebellion. This way, she could walk out on him whenever she wanted, without having to wait for a cab.

At Long Pine Lodge, she parked near Sam's car and followed him inside. He must have called ahead for the room, because the concierge greeted him with a key card. They took the elevator to a suite on the top floor.

Hope had been to the lodge many times, for parties and work events, but she'd only stayed overnight once, with Doug. The evening must not have been very memorable, because she couldn't recall any specific details. She glanced around at the sumptuous fabrics and plush furniture, recognizing nothing.

Maybe Doug hadn't splurged on a suite.

Sam pulled out a chair for her in the dining area. A large window offered a spectacular view of Mount Whitney. She didn't need a menu to choose her favorite dish: angel hair pasta. He ordered room service, adding an entrée for himself and a dessert.

Hope wasn't sure she'd have an appetite, but she ate everything, including a slice of wild strawberry pie with ice cream. After the dishes were cleared away, he offered her a drink. She declined, checking her cell phone for news of Faith.

"Any word?"

"No."

He hadn't said much during the meal. Neither had she. They'd moved past the point of filling every silence with polite conversation. Actually, they'd skipped that stage altogether, along with a couple of others. But the shared meal resembled a date, and his considerate treatment an attempt at courtship.

Maybe he just felt sorry for her.

"I wanted to apologize for what I said this morning," he said, clearing his throat. "About you having a choice."

"I did have a choice."

"Yes, but…I judged you, without even listening."

She shrugged, scrolling through her text messages. The last one from Faith said Love u! Cant wait to see you!

"You aren't making this easy for me."

Hope didn't feel obligated to make anything easy for him, but the man had saved her life. He'd also paid for dinner. The quick intimacy between them had its drawbacks. If this was a real first date, she wouldn't be checking her messages at the table.

She turned off the screen and set her phone aside, studying his appearance. He'd shaved off the beard stubble, exposing the hard angles of his face. His tanned neck made a dark contrast to the light-colored shirt. He was like a rock in the wind. All of the soft layers had eroded, leaving only the strongest elements.

"Would you give me another chance?"

"At what?"

"Listening."

Pressure built behind her eyes, and she released a slow breath. He was so stripped-down and appealing, with his scarred past and weathered good looks. Being rich and handsome hadn't insulated him from heartache. She wasn't protected, either. Just because she knew better didn't mean she wouldn't fall in love with him.

"What do you want to know?" she asked.

"Everything."

Hope faltered, unsure where to start.

"How did you get pregnant?"

"The usual way," she said ruefully. "My boyfriend and I weren't always careful. One night he promised he'd…withdraw."

"Famous last words."

"Yes."

"How old were you?"

"I was a senior. Almost eighteen by my due date. We stayed together for a while, and I thought we could make it work. Get married." She shook her head at the unpleasant memory. "I was stupid."

"Why?"

"I had a scholarship that I was willing to give up, but he didn't want to make any sacrifices. The closer to my due date, the more distant he became. I think… he was scared. It was too much responsibility for him." In their final argument, Paul had accused her of trying to ruin his life. "I realized that he wasn't going to support me, and that a baby would put a huge strain on my family. Especially Faith."

"What do you mean?"

"We shared a room, and a car. She also didn't have a chance at getting a scholarship, to be honest. By giving up mine, I was limiting her opportunities, too. My parents couldn't afford to send us both to college."

"Did you talk to her about it?"

"No. I didn't want her to feel guilty."

"So you made the decision alone."

"Pretty much. My parents didn't pressure me one

way or the other, but I knew adoption was the best choice. I was able to keep my scholarship to Arizona State. I think I'm the only student in the history of the school who never went to parties."

"What about Faith?"

"She went to *all* of the parties," Hope said, smiling a little. "Her first semester, she flunked half of her classes, but the important part is that she went. She got the chance to be young and have fun."

"And you didn't?"

"I tried to…but I'd changed. Everything had changed."

"Do you wish you'd made a different choice?"

She rose from the table and walked to the window. In early June, there was still snow on the mountaintops. "Sometimes. When I'm feeling really…empty…I wonder what my life would have been like with her. I wonder if she's happy."

Sam rose, putting his hand on her shoulder. He didn't need a diagram to understand that the night she'd gone home with him had been one of those times.

"I'm sorry," he said, kissing the top of her head.

"I remember the moment they took her out of my arms," she said, her throat tight. "I've been replaying it over and over today. Losing Faith feels the same way. She's my baby sister. She's everything to me. She's all I have left." When she turned toward him, her face crumpling, he wrapped his arms around her. She braced her palms against his chest and pressed her nose to his neck. He smelled clean, like soap and pine. Beneath her fingertips, she felt soft cotton over hard muscle.

"You—you were right about Doug," she said, looking up at him. "I wasn't serious about him, so I didn't mind keeping our relationship a secret. I have a pattern of avoiding commitment. It's like I'm punishing myself, because I don't think I deserve love, or a good man, or a…family."

Her voice broke on the last word, and she glanced away, blinking the tears from her eyes. He lifted a hand to her chin and forced her gaze back to his. "Hope," he said, brushing his thumb over her lips.

"That's why I want you so much. You have 'emotionally unavailable' written all over you. You're bound to hurt me."

His mouth tightened with regret.

Although she hadn't come here for sex, Hope didn't want to cry anymore. She craved human contact. She needed his touch.

"Please, Sam," she said, licking the edge of his thumb. "Hurt me."

CHAPTER SIXTEEN

THIS WASN'T WHAT he wanted from Hope.

She drew his thumb into her mouth and sucked it gently, her eyes locked on his. With her silky dark hair and beautiful face, she was one of the sexiest women he'd ever seen. Her lips were soft and wet, her tongue hot. The sensation went straight to his cock, swelling him to full arousal.

Okay. He wanted it.

Just not this way, when she was vulnerable. He'd brought her here to apologize, and to comfort her, not to take advantage of her.

He'd made an important self-discovery today. When she'd come sliding down the cliff, hundreds of feet off the ground, with no safety gear, nothing between her and a certain death but him, he'd realized how much she meant to him. He didn't want to live without her.

Although he'd like to express these feelings in words, now wasn't an appropriate time. He also didn't know how to break the news about his recovered memories. He couldn't hijack her grief with his own.

"Hurt me," she said.

If he let this go any further, that's what he'd do. She thought he was an emotionally stunted jerk—and he was. But she also thought she didn't deserve better, and he wanted to prove her wrong. He could be a good man to her. He could love her.

What she was asking for wasn't love. With the blood rushing from his head to his groin, he couldn't think of a compelling reason to say no.

He'd be good later.

He took his thumb out of her mouth and replaced it with his tongue, pressing her back against the wall. She sucked his tongue just like she'd sucked his thumb. And his cock, the first night they'd been together.

He groaned at the memory.

She rubbed against him, twining her arms around his neck. He gripped her bottom and ground his erection into the notch of her thighs. His touch wasn't gentle, but neither was her response. She bit at his mouth and dug her fingernails into the nape of his neck. With a low growl, he turned toward the bed and fell on top of her. Thrusting his hands into her hair, he plundered her mouth again and again. She tasted wild and sweet, like the strawberries in the pie. He wanted to eat her, all over.

When she shoved at his chest, he broke the kiss, panting.

"Take off your clothes," she said.

He pulled his shirt over his head, eager to oblige. Her eyes trailed down his bare chest and settled on his distended fly. While he unbuckled his belt slowly, she removed her T-shirt and unfastened her bra.

Her breasts tumbled free, perky and dark-tipped.

His fingers flexed in anticipation. She kicked off her tennis shoes and jeans, revealing a pair of simple white panties. The fabric was thin, hinting at the shadowy triangle between her thighs and outlining the lips of her sex.

"Jesus," he choked.

Abandoning the attempt to undress, he climbed over her and kissed her berry-flavored mouth once more, skimming his hands along her rib cage. His fly was unzipped, allowing the ridge of his erection to slide up and down her cleft. She gasped, wrapping her legs around his hips and arching against him. He cupped her breast, sweeping his thumb over the taut nipple. Her tongue darted in and out of his mouth.

"You're so fucking sexy," he said, rolling over and bringing her on top. He wanted to play with her tits until she begged to come.

She rode him through the layers of cotton, her panties and his boxer shorts. He alternated between sucking her nipples and pinching them. Soon she was breathing hard, her hips working faster, the tips of her breasts swollen and wet. She rubbed herself along the length of his erection, raking a hand through her hair.

He pulled aside the damp crotch of her panties, exposing her. Suddenly he was desperate for a taste.

Lifting her off him, he set her aside and straightened. While she watched, her eyes half-lidded, he unlaced his boots and stood to shuck the rest of his clothes. She stared at his cock, moistening her lips, but he couldn't get distracted. He stripped her panties down her legs, pushed her thighs apart and buried his face in her.

"Oh God," she moaned, gripping his shoulders.

For the next few minutes, he kissed every inch of her, sucking her sweet little clit, plunging his tongue into her opening. He did everything but get her off. When she trembled on the edge of climax, he lifted his head. She was so pretty like this, panting with need, her sex glistening and her nipples tight.

He reached for the condom in his wallet. After suiting up, he stretched out on his back again and held the base of his shaft, inviting her to climb on. She did, with relish. Her body gripped him like a silky fist.

"I'm going to come before you even move," he said through clenched teeth, reveling in the feel of her. He wanted to grasp her hips and work her up and down, but he waited. Buried deep, he watched her rock back and forth, breasts jiggling. He lifted his hand to her mouth and she closed her lips around his thumb again. The dual penetration was dizzyingly erotic. After sliding his thumb in and out of her mouth a few times, he placed it over her clitoris, strumming her in slow circles. She strained toward his touch and screamed his name, her stomach quivering as she climaxed.

He liked that, her coming with his name on her lips.

With a possessive growl, he rolled on top of her and thrust as deep as he could get, burying himself to the hilt. He stopped thinking about her pleasure and took his own, slamming into her, pounding her against the mattress. She twined her arms around his neck and dug her nails into his shoulders, crying out his name again. He was only vaguely aware that he was giving her what she wanted, a hard fuck to drive the pain away.

He let out a hoarse yell, his head thrown back and his legs locked. His orgasm seemed to go on forever, leaving his body sated and his mind blank.

When it was over, he got up to dispose of the condom. She was already dozing by the time he returned.

He pulled her into his arms, her back to his front, and covered their naked bodies with a sheet.

As he drifted off, he acknowledged that he'd just had the best sex of his life. Being inside her fulfilled him like nothing else. But there was unfinished business between them, emotions to sort through. He hadn't told her he'd recovered his memory. He wasn't sure how he felt. He only knew that he wanted more from her than a sexual relationship.

Satisfying her physically wasn't enough.

As soon as Javier's boss was gone, Faith leaped to her feet.

She crossed the room quickly, testing the door. It was locked from the outside.

"Damn it," she muttered, searching the interior. There were no windows, only slim air-conditioning vents.

Hunger drew her to the table. She shoved a handful of cheese and crackers into her mouth, continuing her search. The room yielded no escape routes or impromptu weapons. There wasn't even any silverware with the tray. The only furniture besides the bed and table was a soft-upholstered chair.

She sat down and finished the food, glum. After she'd eaten her fill, she used the bathroom. It was a narrow space with an oval mirror, an empty sink cabinet and a shower stall. A single towel hung on the rack.

Javier's boss had called her beautiful, but she'd never looked so hideous in her life. Her clothes were gross. She had scratches all over her arms, and a few on her face. The mosquito bump was hardly noticeable among the dirt streaks.

With a grimace, she removed her soiled garments, leaving them in a pile on the floor. She turned on the water and stepped into the shower stall. The warm spray soaked her scalp and cascaded down her shoulders, soothing her aching muscles. She scrubbed every inch of her body and shampooed her hair twice.

When she came out, she felt like a new woman. Stronger, more alert. While she was drying her hair, she noticed the toilet tank. She wrapped the damp towel around her body and removed the porcelain cover, setting it on the sink. It was too awkward to be a good bludgeoning tool, but she could break it. She could also break the mirror. Fashioning a weapon didn't appeal to her as much as finding a way out, however.

Inside the tank, there was a float with a metal rod. Jackpot.

She took the mechanism apart, with some difficulty. When she'd separated the rod from the float, she approached the door. Although the thin metal fit in the keyhole, it wasn't very maneuverable. She didn't know how to pick a lock. For the next hour, she tried anyway, poking and prodding until her shoulders sagged with fatigue.

"Fuck," she yelled, tossing the useless rod aside in frustration. Her eyes filled with tears as she stared at it.

She was glad her sister had escaped—assuming that was true—but Faith worried that Hope was still in danger. Javier's boss had someone on his payroll in the park. Her sister might have killed Martin and gotten

away, but she wasn't out of the woods yet. Neither was
Javier, although his welfare concerned her less.

He'd brought this on himself.

Brushing the tears from her cheeks, she picked up
the metal rod and crawled into bed, stashing it under
the pillows. She tucked the blanket around her body and
closed her eyes, trying to get some rest.

She must have drifted off, because the next thing she
knew, a man was in the room, standing beside the bed.

Gasping, she reached under the pillow.

Nick held up the metal rod. "Looking for this?"

Faith swallowed, her heart pounding with panic. The
towel around her body had come loose while she slept.
With the sheet slipping off her shoulder, threatening to
expose her breasts, she felt intensely vulnerable.

Although he had to be aware of her nudity, his gaze
didn't wander south. He set the weapon on the table behind him. His boss must have allowed him to shower
and change clothes. Clean, he looked only slightly more
civilized. His left brow was bandaged, and there was a
disturbing…deadness…in his eyes. His flat expression
reminded her of Javier. Nick resembled the darker side
of him, the robotic fighting machine.

They were both killers.

"I've been told to rape you," he said, matter-of-fact.

She recoiled in horror, clutching the sheet to her
chest.

"This room has video cameras, but no audio, so it
only has to look real. If you put on a good show, I won't
really have to do it. The more you fight, the better." He
paused, studying her. "Do you understand?"

Everything he said after "rape" was lost.

That wasn't going to happen. Never again.

No longer concerned with modesty, she scrambled off the side of the bed and ran toward the bathroom. She planned to pick up the porcelain tank cover and smash him upside the head with it.

She never got there.

He vaulted across the mattress and caught her easily, locking his arm around her waist. "Good," he said in her ear, as if she was doing something right. Then he shoved her face-down on the bed and unfastened his pants.

She screamed, kicking her legs and flailing her arms wildly. Her foot glanced off his upper thigh. Although she doubted she'd hurt him, he doubled over with a low grunt. When she kicked again, he grasped her ankle, holding it prisoner.

She twisted out of his grip and came up swinging. Almost by accident, she punched him in the nose.

That blow connected better than the first, but his surprised laugh wasn't encouraging. "Wildcat," he muttered, tugging off his shirt. He had a lean physique, nothing special, but the sight of his bare chest and open fly terrified her.

She scooted backward, toward the other side of the bed. Sliding off the edge, she grabbed the food tray and chucked it at him like a Frisbee.

He ducked easily.

Out of options, she stared at him, her heart racing. He came forward in slow steps. When his eyes traveled down her body, lingering between her legs, she made a break for it. He grabbed her by the hair and threw her down on the bed again. This time, he climbed on top of her, using his weight to hold her prisoner.

"Scream," he said, tightening his fist in her hair.

She screamed.

He relaxed his grip, allowing her some freedom of movement. She elbowed him in the ribs as hard as she could.

The kick hadn't slowed him down, and he'd laughed at her punch, but this blow actually caused him pain. He fell over on his side, groaning. She grabbed a pillow and went on the offensive, trying to smother him.

He ripped the pillow away from her and tossed it aside. Before she knew it, he'd flipped her onto her back. He seemed impressed by her evasive maneuvers, but not worried that she'd get away. It was almost as if he admired her for giving him trouble.

She slapped his smug face.

With a low growl, he pushed her arms over her head, trapping her wrists with one hand. He was breathing hard now, no longer amused or patronizing. Using his knee, he forced her legs apart.

She screamed again. "No!"

In the back of her mind, she remembered this moment with Brett. This awful, soul-wrenching moment. Reducing her to nothingness.

Nick freed his penis with one hand and positioned it against her. His first thrust didn't find her opening. Neither did the next, or the next. She twisted her arms and bucked her hips, trying to dislodge him. He continued to go at her like a clueless teenager. On some level, she realized that this was his idea of pretending.

Tears leaked from her eyes, and she begged him to stop. Because it felt real.

FOR JAVIER, the night was endless.

He'd been interrogated, beaten, half-drowned and strapped to a chair. One of his eyes was swollen shut. His head ached and his injured shoulder throbbed. Gonzales kept asking him where Alexia was. As if he didn't know.

"Just kill me," he groaned, praying for oblivion.

Finally Gonzales changed tactics. "Let's talk about the girl you came with," he said. "Did the two of you have an arrangement?"

"No."

Javier had already told Gonzales about the plane crash, which had been an accident, and the shoot-out with the pilot, which he took full responsibility for. There was no way he could have enlisted Faith's help beforehand.

"Don't lie to me, *cabrón.* I know you were planning to leave."

He didn't respond.

They were in a basic white room, probably underground. Other than two chairs, a rectangular table and a large flat-screen television, the space was empty. Gonzales picked up a remote control and turned on the screen.

Faith was lying on a bed, her hands and ankles bound. Her gag had become a blindfold. Javier could see the pulse flutter at the base of her throat as a man reached out to her. It was Gonzales.

"This was shot earlier," Gonzales said, fast-forwarding.

She tossed water in his face and they had a rapid conversation. At one point, he touched her cheek. Gonzales paused the video there, glancing at Javier for a reaction. Javier didn't give him the satisfaction.

He skipped through the next few minutes of Faith tearing apart the room. She sat down to eat and then headed to the bathroom, where there was another camera. The angle switched suddenly, and her body was a rainy blur behind a frosted glass shower door. When she stepped out of the stall to dry off, Gonzales reduced the speed to slow motion. The footage left nothing to the imagination.

Javier's muscles tensed with fury. He hadn't thought it was possible to hate Gonzales more than he had before.

Gonzales pressed a button to show a different feed. "This is live."

Faith was sleeping in a bed. The sheets were tucked under her arms, revealing a portion of her slender back. When Nick entered the room, Javier saw red. "I'll fucking kill you," he said, tugging at his tied wrists. The chair scraped across the tile floor, shuddering from the force of his struggle.

"Relax," Gonzales said. "She looks like the type of woman who enjoys rough play. Alexia did."

"Hijo de puta," he growled, unable to take his eyes off Faith. As soon as she woke up, she tried to flee. Nick chased her across the room and threw her down on the bed. He got right to business, unfastening his pants.

Javier had been at his breaking point since Gonzales killed Alexia. Witnessing Faith's attack pushed him right over the edge. Although Alexia hadn't deserved to die, she was far from innocent. She'd sought out dangerous, powerful men and slept her way to the top. Her family had cartel connections. She'd known what kind of monster she was marrying.

Faith's situation was different. She hadn't courted danger. Javier had brought this violence to her, and he was devastated by the result. He might as well be in the room instead of Nick, because he'd set these events in motion.

"Let her go," he said through clenched teeth. "I'll do whatever you want!"

Gonzales continued to watch the scene unfold. Faith managed to hit Nick a few times, but only because he let her. If anyone enjoyed rough play, it was him.

"I'll talk," he promised.

Nick stopped toying with Faith and held her trapped underneath him. He shoved her legs apart and positioned himself against her.

"Please," he roared, tears of rage filling his eyes.

Gonzales took a cell phone out of his pocket and pressed a button. *"Ya,"* he said.

Enough.

Nick removed himself from her at once. While he stood by the bed, zipping up his fly, Faith curled up into a little ball, sobbing.

Javier was going to kill him. He was going to kill Gonzales, too. Tamping down his bloodlust, for now, he pulled his watery gaze from the screen. "I wasn't sleeping with Alexia. She approached me once. I refused her."

"When?"

He paused, reluctant to go into detail. "On your wedding day."

Gonzales must have already known that, because his reaction was sedate. "I was told otherwise."

"By who?"

"Martin. He said you were meeting her in private."

"He's a fucking liar."

"So are you."

"Where's his proof?"

Gonzales didn't have any. If he'd seen photographic evidence of this alleged affair, Javier would've been dead six months ago. "There are pictures of her going into a motel room, but none of the man inside."

"Bring Martin in here."

"I can't. One of the park rangers killed him."

"Ask Nick. He knows something."

Gonzales spoke into the phone again. *"Ven."*

When Nick joined them, his neck was flushed. He had a flesh-colored bandage on his eyebrow and Faith's slap mark on his face. It turned Javier's stomach just to look at him. "Did you ever see me with Alexia?"

He hesitated, but only for a second. "No."

"Martin was the one sleeping with her," Javier said, making an educated guess. "You ordered him to follow her, or maybe you ordered him to kill her."

Gonzales didn't confirm or deny the charge.

"She seduced him to survive."

"Is that true?" Gonzales asked Nick.

"I have no idea," Nick said, dumbfounded. "He didn't confide in me. I would have come straight to you with information like that."

"Where is she?" Gonzales yelled, clenching his hands into fists.

"I don't know," Javier said.

"Why did you shoot my pilot and run, if not to re-unite with her?"

"I ran because I wanted out, and I shot the pilot because he got in the way." Javier realized that they'd both been wrong. Gonzales hadn't killed Alexia. He'd tried to, and she'd escaped. "This whole time, I thought she was dead. You let everyone believe that because you were too proud to admit she left you."

And now the only man who knew the truth was gone.

"Cara de mierda," Gonzales roared, upending the table. He grabbed the only empty chair and threw it across the room. Alexia had cheated on him and lived, robbing him of the satisfaction of punishing her.

After a few moments of cursing and kicking the chair around, Gonzales quieted. There was nothing left to say.

"What should I do with the girl?" Nick asked.

Gonzales studied Javier, his nostrils flaring. He couldn't reach Alexia or Martin, but he wanted to make someone pay. "Get rid of her."

CHAPTER SEVENTEEN

HOPE WOKE AT dawn.

Her muscles were stiff, but she felt alert and well rested. Despite her fears about Faith, she'd fallen asleep easily. Sam had screwed her into oblivion.

He was good at that.

She sat up, raking a hand through her mussed hair. He was sprawled out on his back beside her, eyes closed, chest rising and falling with deep breaths. The sight of his peaceful slumber made her heart swell with emotion. With his mouth relaxed, and his forehead smooth of worry lines, he looked younger.

The sheet rode low at his waist, tangling around one leg. His other leg was bent at the knee, naked and exposed. He had plenty of muscle, but not quite enough fat. His body was sharp-edged and rawboned, all cord and sinew.

Her eyes wandered south, between his legs, to the only soft place on him. The only hint of vulnerability, other than his face. Most of his pubic hair was showing above the thin sheet. She could see his size and shape beneath it.

She thought about tugging the expensive cotton down and rousing him with her mouth. The idea made her pulse throb and her sex tingle with anticipation. She moistened her lips, fantasizing about pressing kisses along his flat stomach and delineated hip.

He'd groan and lace his hand through her hair, murmuring…

Another woman's name.

Hope pulled her gaze away from him, her throat tight. She slid off the edge of the bed and gathered her clothes, tiptoeing into the bathroom. As soon as she was dressed, she snuck out into the hall, careful not to wake him.

She couldn't make the mistake of sleeping with him again. It hurt too much. If she didn't break the cycle of getting involved with the wrong men, she'd never find happiness. She'd never start a family.

Her cell phone showed a few messages, but no news about Faith. She'd called her parents yesterday evening to explain the situation to them. They'd wanted to start driving from Ojai last night, but she convinced them to wait until morning. Although she appreciated their support, there was nothing they could do to help.

After grabbing a pastry and a coffee in the lobby, she climbed into her Jeep. Faith's disappearance had sunk in. Hope was clearheaded now, and more determined to find her sister. Yesterday, she'd been a mess. The interrogation had gone on for hours, giving her no opportunity to form her own questions.

Hope wasn't familiar with large-scale investigations, but the entire process had seemed arduous and chaotic. Dixon had barely made an appearance.

What had Owen been doing alone on the trail, anyway? All of the other rangers had been working with teams of sheriff's deputies.

She took a sip of coffee, pondering. Although she wasn't supposed to be on duty, it couldn't hurt to poke around. Owen was probably in park housing, asleep. As she drove toward the employee cabins, her mind raced with possibilities. The drug smugglers had been able to respond to her radio transmissions. Maybe they had a partner in local law enforcement or among Long Pine's residents.

She parked outside the men's housing facility and glanced at the mailboxes. Owen Jackson lived in complex eight with half a dozen other workers. A sleepy young man answered the door in his underwear.

He seemed confused by her casual clothes and unannounced visit. "Ranger Banning?"

"I need to speak with Owen."

Pointing down the hall, he beat a hasty retreat to his own quarters. She headed the direction he'd indicated, pausing at a bedroom door. It was ajar, so she peeked in, asking for Owen. None of the men in the bunks were him.

"Storage room," one of them mumbled, rolling over.

Frowning, she continued to a door at the end of the hall. After her hesitant knock, Owen opened the door. Like everyone else in the house, he'd been asleep. He was bare-chested, wearing a pair of unbuttoned jeans.

Hope did a double take. Maybe she was still riding high on sex endorphins, because the first thing she noticed was his physique. Then the disturbing tattoos registered, including one of a burning cross over his heart.

"Sorry," he said, stepping away from the door. Leaving it open for her, he grabbed a shirt and covered up. "I didn't know it was you."

She entered his room, curious. It was more of a big closet, with wooden cubbies for miscellaneous items and sports equipment. The narrow cot he'd been sleeping on took up most of the floor space. In the mornings, he probably folded it away.

He sat down on the cot, gesturing for her to join him.

"Do they make you sleep in here?" she asked.

"No."

She wondered if the other guys gave him guff about his tattoos. If they did, that was his cross to bear. So to speak.

"I have a few questions about yesterday."

His eyes were wary. "Okay."

"Why were you on the trail alone?"

"I came from Mineral King."

She understood what he meant. The station was manned by a single employee, and located in such a remote area that it didn't always make sense to wait for a partner. "On whose order?"

"No one's."

"You made the decision to start hiking by yourself?"

"Yes."

"Why?"

"The teams were taking too long to get organized. It seemed like the different law enforcement agencies were…tripping all over each other."

Hope agreed with this frank assessment, although she knew better than to voice it aloud. The National Park Service often collaborated with sheriff's deputies, but murder was a state crime, and the FBI investigated kidnapping cases. Drug trafficking fell under the DEA umbrella. It was a multijurisdictional nightmare. Many mistakes had been made, starting with Meeks's failure to retrieve the cargo.

"Mineral King is the closest station to Crystal Cave," he added. "I thought you might have taken shelter there."

"Did you ask permission?"

"No. They wouldn't have given it."

She rubbed her forehead, where a tension headache was forming. "Have you been reprimanded?"

"Not yet."

NPS didn't always reward employees for taking initiative. "Tell me everything that happened yesterday."

He began with his run-in with Javier Del Norte, flushing as he recounted the order to take off his clothes. Apparently Del Norte had intended to steal his uniform, but changed his mind when they heard gunshots.

"He wanted to help Faith?" she asked.

"That's what he said."

Owen also claimed that Del Norte had assisted him in fishing an unconscious Sam out of the river. Hope hadn't known this detail, either. She couldn't believe Sam had climbed up Angel Wings with a concussion.

"He didn't tell you," Owen guessed.

"No."

With a slight shake of his head, he continued the story. Owen had seen the men take Faith aboard a helicopter, but he didn't get a good look at their faces.

"Describe the helicopter."

"It was black, and seemed too small for the number of people inside."

"How many?"

"Four. Maybe five, with the pilot."

She wondered how far an overloaded helicopter could travel, and where it might have landed. Even a small aircraft would require a large, flat area on a remote property. There were a number of options close by.

"You gave this information to the FBI?" she asked.

"Yes."

Hope stood, pacing the narrow space. She felt as though she was missing something obvious, like a word on the tip of her tongue, or an important detail slipping through her fingers. "What did you think of Del Norte?"

"I thought he was…scary."

"But you ran after him anyway."

He just shrugged, as if he'd done nothing special.

She marveled at how easily Del Norte could have killed Owen and kept going. The forest worker had shown remarkable courage in the face of danger. He'd set out on his own, saved Sam's life and tried to help Faith. If Owen hadn't come along to rescue Sam from drowning, Hope would be dead right now.

She owed her life to Owen, and to Del Norte, in a strange way. "Thank you," she said, touching his shoulder.

He froze at the contact. "You're welcome."

She dropped her hand, aware that he was uneasy. "Have you thought about training for one of the law enforcement positions?"

"No."

"Why not?"

"I have a criminal record."

"It doesn't necessarily disqualify you." Bill Kruger had been in trouble with the law a few times for domestic violence, and he was a head ranger. "I can put in a good word for you with Dixon."

Instead of accepting the offer, he changed the subject. "I hope you find your sister."

"So do I," she said.

He stood and walked her to the door. She promised to keep him updated before she left, squinting in the bright sunshine. It wasn't even seven o'clock yet, but the sun had already burned through the morning clouds.

She climbed behind the steering wheel again, reaching into the glove compartment for her sunglasses. Her fingers closed around Faith's instead. She took them out, examining the sparkly frames.

The sight brought tears to her eyes.

Just three days ago, she'd hugged Faith goodbye, promising everything would be fine. She'd left her sister scared and alone. Hope wished she could go back in time and make a different choice.

Story of her life.

JAVIER ROCKED HIS chair back and forth until it tipped over.

He landed hard on his injured shoulder. The wooden chair broke under the strain, but he couldn't free his wrists or ankles. Pain reverberated down the length of his arm, tingling in his fingertips, making him nauseated.

Gonzales came forward and kicked him in the stomach.

Javier gritted his teeth, his muscles quivering. Nick was killing Faith right now and he couldn't do anything about it. He couldn't beg, or plead, or retaliate. Gonzales turned on the live feed again, seeming bored.

Faith was still lying on the bed, sobbing. Nick didn't enter the picture. On the contrary, he reappeared in the doorway, startling Gonzales.

"Did you forget something?"

"This." Nick raised a handgun and shot Gonzales in the chest.

He stumbled to his knees, a stunned expression on his darkly handsome face. Blood blossomed across the front of his rumpled white dress shirt. He careened forward, collapsing on a woven rug.

Dead.

It was a perfect kill shot. Almost no mess.

Nick tucked his gun away and stepped into the room. After checking Gonzales's pulse, he removed the boss's weapons and his money clip. Then he rolled the oval floor rug around his body, wrapping him up like a burrito.

"Who do you work for?" Javier rasped.

"Somebody else," Nick replied.

Javier didn't consider this new development a personal boon. He expected to be executed in short order. "I'll pay for the girl."

"With what?"

Unlike Gonzales, Javier wasn't rich. He hadn't been able to amass millions before his escape attempt. There was twenty grand waiting for him in a locker at LAX. It was the most he could save without attracting attention. "Fifty thousand."

"I don't want your money," Nick said, leaving the room.

Javier lay there, staring at the bundle of Hector Gonzales. His nemesis was dead, and he felt nothing. On the screen, Faith sat up in bed, clutching the sheet to her chest. When Nick walked in, she tried to get away. He grabbed her ankle.

"No," Javier shouted, horrified.

Nick held a syringe in his hand. He stabbed her in the thigh, holding down the plunger. After a short struggle, she went quiet.

Javier squeezed his eyes shut, crying silently, his shoulders .racked with sobs. *"Perdóname, Padre, porque he pecado,"* he repeated, over and over again. He was praying for her life, his death. Any salvation.

When Nick reentered the room, he crouched down next to Javier. "A cleanup crew is coming over. We need to leave."

"We?"

"If I untie you, can you carry the girl? She's drugged. Sorry, I can't have her recognizing this place."

"I'll carry her," Javier said, although he wasn't sure he could even stand.

"Good. I'm going to drop you off in the woods."

"Why?"

Nick answered the broader question. "You could've killed me at the falls, but you didn't. Now we're square."

Javier couldn't agree. They'd never be square.

"I didn't rape her," Nick said, taking a knife from his pocket.

"I saw you."

"I was faking." Before he cut Javier's bonds, he squinted at him. "You're dispensable. I've been instructed to spare the girl, not you. Do you understand?"

"I'll do whatever you say."

Nick freed him.

"Help me with this piece of shit," he said, gesturing at Gonzales.

Javier staggered to his feet and grabbed one end of the rug. They heaved the body up a set of stairs and loaded it in the back of a white van. When that was finished, Nick showed him to Faith's room. He rushed to her side, almost weeping with relief. She really was alive. Her chest rose and fell with steady breaths.

Keeping the sheet tucked around her, he lifted her into his arms and carried her to the garage. He set her down next to Gonzales and climbed in, lying flat next to her. Nick drove for about five minutes before he parked behind a group of trees along a deserted road. He opened the back of the van, letting them out. "I don't want to see you around."

The feeling was mutual. Javier moved Faith to a bed of pine needles.

"If I were you, I'd take off now," Nick said.

"I want to talk to her first."

Faith moaned, her eyelashes fluttering.

Nick studied her for a moment. Rape or no rape, he'd terrorized her, and his expression showed a hint of remorse.

"Why didn't you kill Gonzales sooner?" Javier asked.

"I had to wait for the order." He pulled his gaze from Faith to Javier. "Maybe I'll see you in the ring someday."

Javier wasn't interested in another matchup. It wouldn't settle the score between them. "I'd rather hold you down and let her beat you."

"I might enjoy that," Nick mused.

Javier clenched his hand into a fist.

"Adios, amigo."

Javier watched his "friend" get into the van and drive away. The irony of the situation wasn't lost on him. If he'd killed Nick at the falls, he wouldn't have attacked Faith, but they'd all be dead right now.

They were alive. This was a better outcome than he'd dreamed of. Javier was grateful to God, if not to Nick. But he also knew what he had to do. Staying with Faith was impossible. The police would question him, he'd get arrested and one of Gonzales's relatives would shank him in jail. He had to disappear, like Alexia.

Javier didn't have any desire to reunite with his ex-girlfriend. The only one he wanted was Faith. And he couldn't have her.

He sat down beside her, smoothing the pine needles from her hair. His throat closed up with the realization that he'd never see her again. He had to leave in the next few minutes to avoid the authorities.

"Jay?" she murmured.

"Javier."

"Javier." She opened her eyes, but the sun was too bright. Groaning, she closed them. "Where am I?"

"You're safe."

"I need my sister."

"She'll be with you soon."

"That guy—" She winced, touching her temple.

"Did he hurt you?"

"He…scared me."

Javier smothered a fresh wave of fury. "He's gone."

"You killed him?"

"No. But I will, if you want me to."

She moistened her lips. "You said you were done with all that."

"I can make an exception."

"Don't."

Javier murmured an agreement. "He won't bother you again. My boss won't, either. You don't have to worry."

"Will you stay with me?"

He glanced around, struggling to control his emotions. "I wish I could, but I've put you in enough danger already." His voice broke on the last word, but he forced himself to continue. "I'm so sorry, Faith. It was all my fault. They used you to get to me."

Tears leaked from the corners of her eyes.

He took a deep breath. "When you feel well enough, walk alongside the road. Wave down a passing car, or knock on someone's door."

Her face crumpled. "Don't leave."

"I have to," he said, hating himself for hurting her. He wished things could be different, but he couldn't ask her to wait for him. It might be years before he came out of hiding and got his life together. Chest aching with regret, he pressed a kiss to her forehead. *"Ojalá que nos encontremos otra vez."*

Javier got up before he could change his mind. He stumbled into the brush, his throat burning and his heart numb.

CHAPTER EIGHTEEN

AT MIDMORNING, Hope got a text from Dispatch.

Faith had been admitted to the E.R. She was groggy, but in good condition. She'd refused to talk to anyone except Hope.

After reading the message, Hope collapsed on her bed and wept for several minutes, overwhelmed with relief. Then she pulled herself together and drove to the hospital in Visalia. On the way there, her phone chirped again. It was Sam. She'd been avoiding his calls. He'd invited her to come back to the lodge for breakfast, and he actually seemed upset with her for sneaking out on him. His "attentive boyfriend" routine confused her; he'd fought their attraction every step of the way. Maybe he was willing to share his body with her, but his heart still belonged to a dead woman.

He wasn't a good candidate for a relationship.

"Hi," she answered.

"Any news?"

"She's at the hospital, supposedly okay."

"Thank God."

"Yes."

"Do you want me to come?"

"Let me see how she's doing first."

When Hope arrived at the hospital, she parked in the closest available space and rushed to the lobby, only to be told to wait in the lounge. After a few minutes, a slender woman in scrubs came out with a clipboard.

"Miss Banning?"

"Yes."

"I'm Nurse Parker," she said, leading Hope to a small consultation area. "Your sister was brought in by a local woman who found her wandering by the side of the road, wearing nothing but a bedsheet."

Hope clapped a hand over her mouth, distraught.

"We ran a blood test, because she seems to have been drugged, but she wouldn't consent to a vaginal swab."

"Can I see her?"

"Right this way."

The nurse showed her to a bed in the E.R. It wasn't a private room, but there were no other patients nearby, and it had curtain partitions. Faith looked thin and pale in a faded hospital gown, her pretty face marked with scratches. Hope let out a strangled sob, embracing her sister. She was overjoyed and devastated at the same time.

"What happened?" she asked, smoothing Faith's hair away from her forehead.

Her sister's pupils were dilated, her brown eyes dull. The drugs might have taken the edge off, but she wasn't blissfully unaware. "Get me out of here," she said, her voice quavering with emotion.

Hope nodded. She'd provide Faith with comfort, solace or whatever else she needed. Anything her sister asked for, she'd deliver.

"We're waiting for the results of the toxicology," the nurse said. "I'll check on that."

They watched her go.

"Do you have any idea what they gave you?" Hope asked, lowering her voice.

"An injection."

"Why didn't you consent to the swab?"

"Because I consented to the *sex*," Faith snapped.

Hope couldn't hide her dismay.

Faith made a hurt face, hitting her fist against the mattress in a halfhearted punch. "He used a condom, anyway."

"Who did?"

"Javier."

"No one else touched you?"

She stared up at Hope, forlorn. "Not…inside."

"Oh, Faith," she said, aching for her.

"I don't want to talk about it."

"You have to tell."

"Why? They won't get in trouble for groping me."

"They kidnapped you."

"I don't care."

As much as Hope wanted the men who'd abused her sister to pay for their actions, they were connected criminals. Talking to the police might put Faith in more danger. "What if they come after you again?"

"Javier said they wouldn't."

Hope fell silent. Although she was unsettled by Faith's trust in a drug smuggler, she tried not to judge her. "Mom and Dad are on the way."

Faith made a warbled protest. The plaintive sound was so identifiably *hers,* and Hope recognized all of the nuances in it. "Take me back to the woods. No, feed me to a bear. Anything but the 'rents."

Hope bit her tongue to keep from laughing, but it was

no use. She snorted, and that always set Faith off. They both dissolved in a mixture of giggles and tears. That's how Special Agent Sharon Ling found them.

Ling had glossy black hair, sharp eyes and a sturdy figure in unflattering clothes. After introducing herself, she asked Faith a number of questions, but she didn't get much information out of her. Faith couldn't offer any specific details about her kidnappers or the location where she'd been held. Her responses became shorter and less helpful as the interview wore on. She looked and sounded exhausted.

"My sister is very tired," Hope said.

Ling took a few photos from her briefcase and handed them to Hope. "This is Javier Del Norte, the man who infiltrated the rafting trip."

The first image was grainy, showing a handsome, dark-haired man in sunglasses. He appeared to be boarding a private plane.

"He works for Hector Gonzales, the head of one of Las Vegas's top cartels."

Hope studied Gonzales, committing him to memory.

"The next photo is of Martin Hinojosa, now deceased."

"I recognize him," Hope said.

"Both Ted Harvey and Caleb Renfro identified him as the shooter."

"How are they?" Faith asked.

"Lucky to be alive, like you. Renfro's leg was broken in two places. They think he'll walk with a limp."

Faith closed her eyes, seeming both relieved and disturbed by this news. Hope came to the last picture. It featured a young man with shaggy brown hair. He might have been Poncho, but she wasn't sure.

"We think this was Hinojosa's companion."

Hope returned the photos without further comment. Ling passed them to Faith, who examined each face. After pointing out Hinojosa as the man who shot Caleb Renfro, she paused on Del Norte. "Can I keep this?"

Special Agent Ling exchanged a glance with Hope. She probably thought Faith had Stockholm syndrome. "Keep them all," she said, giving Faith a manila envelope. "My contact information is inside."

Ling pulled Hope aside for a private conversation. "We can't protect her unless she cooperates."

"I'll protect her," Hope said.

"Who will protect you?"

"What do you mean?"

"Just that you should lie low for a while. You shot a connected criminal, and they know who you are."

"You think they'll come after me?"

"No. I'm warning you not to go after *them*."

Hope didn't plan to. While she was on administrative leave, her weeks would be filled with counseling sessions and psychological evaluations, not vigilante justice. For the next few days, she wasn't going to leave Faith's side. Anyone who wanted to mess with her sister had to get through Hope first.

After the FBI agent left, Faith gazed at Javier's picture for several moments. Then she put it away with the others. Nurse Parker reappeared, reporting that the sedative in Faith's bloodstream should wear off soon.

"I want to go home," Faith said. "My sister can drive me."

The nurse agreed to start the discharge paperwork.

Hope's cell phone vibrated with missed calls from their mother. She had to answer before her mother freaked out. "I'll be right back," Hope promised, returning to the lobby. As she made her way to the glass doors, someone said her name. She turned to see Doug Dixon rising from a chair in the waiting room. He was a handsome man, stocky and strong, his brown hair starting to gray. Maybe Sam's criticisms of him were fresh in her mind, because he looked older than she remembered—and she'd just seen him last week.

Had Doug taken advantage of his power by pursuing a relationship with her? She'd never felt coerced. Their breakup had been amiable. He'd promoted her after their relationship was over, so she didn't think he held a grudge.

"I came as soon as I heard," he said.

Hope crossed her arms over her chest, unsure what to say.

"She's okay, right?"

"I guess so."

"Where was she?"

"She doesn't know. She was blindfolded the whole time." The exaggeration sprang to her lips with ease. Although Hope wasn't a practiced liar, she was more interested in protecting Faith than telling the truth, even to her boss.

"Is there anything I can do?"

"You can catch the bastards who took her."

"I'm working on it," he said, his gaze narrow. "They've got some balls, kidnapping a woman in my park and shooting at one of my rangers."

She was surprised by his language. He rarely cursed

or became irate. "I tried to contact you on channel three."

"When?"

"Before the shooting."

He made an apologetic face. "I had no idea. I've been juggling a dozen different things. The sheriff, local media, NPS." His cell phone rang, giving credence to the claim. "Sorry, Hope. I have to get back to the park now."

She said goodbye and watched Doug stride away. He seemed like a different man. Maybe he'd changed. Maybe she had. She couldn't remember why she'd been drawn to him. He was polite and attractive, but sort of bland.

Frowning, she stepped out of the E.R. to use her cell phone. Her parents were just outside town, so she couldn't dissuade them from coming to the hospital. While she rubbed the tight muscles in her neck, trying to answer her mother's frantic questions, she noticed Sam walking through the parking lot.

"Shit," she muttered.

"What's wrong, dear?"

"Nothing, Mom. I'll see you soon."

He was wearing the same clothes from last night, loose-fitting jeans and a polo shirt. His short, dark hair capped his head so closely it almost wasn't there. It was spare, bare minimum, like the rest of him.

Her heart skipped a beat at the sight. She'd never reacted this way to Doug.

"How is she?" he asked.

"Okay," she said, nibbling her lower lip. Sam wasn't as easy to lie to. He looked closer. "She's not…injured."

Curiosity flickered in his eyes. He picked up on the nuances in her body language better than Doug had. Hope didn't want to tell him that Faith might have been sexually assaulted. She felt sick about it. She should have been thinking about her sister last night, instead of begging Sam to "hurt" her.

God.

Between her and Faith, she didn't know who had worse taste in men. Her sister had become infatuated with a drug smuggler. Hope was falling for a risk-addicted amnesiac. They were both crazy.

"Someone drugged her and dumped her by the side of the road."

He swore under his breath. "Have they made any arrests?"

"Not that I know of."

"What can I do?"

She sighed, shaking her head. Now that he was here, she felt an overwhelming urge to lean on him. "Come with me to the gift shop?"

He followed her inside, watching while she chose a pair of slippers, a soft T-shirt and some drawstring pants for Faith. When he put the charges on his credit card, she thanked him. He just shrugged, as if he'd bought her a cup of coffee.

Her parents were in the lobby. Her mother's eyes lit up at the sight of her with a man. Even during a family crisis, Joy Banning could find a bright side.

Hope gave her parents a hug before introducing them.

Sam's social skills weren't as rusty as he let on. He shook her father's hand with deference and smiled at her mother. They both radiated approval. Maybe they knew he was a former Olympian.

"We can't thank you enough for saving Hope," Joy said.

Sam acknowledged their appreciation with a nod, clearing his throat. His awkward sidelong glance plucked at Hope's heartstrings. He stayed in the lounge while she took her parents to visit Faith. Her sister downplayed the incident, insisting that she was fine.

The hospital discharged her shortly after. Hope expected more interviews from different law enforcement agencies, but the sheriff's department said she was free to go. They couldn't prosecute her kidnappers if she never identified them. Faith didn't know anything, so the chances of retaliation were slim.

Hope accompanied Faith to the restroom on the way out. "Sam is here," she said while Faith changed into the gift shop clothes.

"Sam Rutherford?"

"Yes."

"Why?"

"It's a long story," Hope said, studying her reflection in the mirror. She looked as if she hadn't brushed her hair for a week. "He bought you those clothes."

"They're hideous."

"Do you want me to get rid of him?"

"Not until I check him out."

Hope knew she couldn't have a future with Sam, but she cared what Faith thought of him. Unlike her parents, Faith had an unfavorable opinion based on Hope's miserable account of their one-night stand. The sisters rejoined their parents and they all walked to the lounge. Sam rose from a chair as soon as he saw them.

"This is Faith," Hope said.

When Faith didn't offer her hand, he dropped his own. His gaze moved back and forth between them, as if noting their similarities. "I'm glad you're okay," he said to Faith. "Hope has told me a lot about you."

"She told me a few things about you also."

He had the grace to flush. Of course, he knew what Faith was alluding to. "It was nice to meet you," he said, including her parents in the statement. After promising to call Hope later, he left.

Faith agreed to a meal in the cafeteria to placate their worried mother. The circles under her eyes stood out in stark relief under the harsh fluorescent lights. She picked at her food, taking a few bites of custard.

Joy suggested a hotel room for the night. "You can relax in the Jacuzzi."

"I just want to go home," Faith said.

"To Ojai?"

"To L.A.," she clarified.

It was late afternoon when the Bannings finally bade them tearful goodbyes. As Hope climbed behind the wheel, she said, "Are you sure you want to go home?"

Faith found her sunglasses and put them on. "Yes, Mom."

"I'm not trying to mother you."

"I just want to feel normal again," Faith said, looking out the window. "I want my makeup, and my shoes. I want smog, and traffic, and tall buildings."

"Okay," Hope said. "I don't have to be back until Monday."

"You can spend a long weekend with me. We'll see art shows."

She understood that Faith took comfort in fashion and city culture. Hope would drive her sister all the way to New York, if necessary. She stopped at Starbucks, ordering Faith's favorite iced drink.

"He's hot," she said, taking a contemplative sip.

"Who?"

"Your rock climber."

Hope didn't say anything.

"I embarrassed him."

"He deserved it."

She reached across the console, taking Hope's hand.

CHAPTER NINETEEN

FAITH AWOKE with a start.

Late afternoon sunlight poured through the cracks in the window blinds, making tiger stripes across her body. Her pulse was racing, her skin damp with perspiration. She sat up in bed, lifting the hair off the back of her neck.

Hope stood at the doorway.

Faith had slept for most of the past two days while her sister puttered around the apartment, double-checking locks and monitoring foot traffic on the sidewalk below. She lived on a busy street, so Hope could profile strangers to her heart's content.

"A nightmare?"

Faith nodded, reaching for the water by her bedside. She drank thirstily and padded to the bathroom. She looked awful.

"That's it," she said to her pale, scared-rabbit reflection.

"What?" Hope asked.

"We're going out tonight."

Faith turned on the water and stepped in the shower stall, wallowing in the comfort of the pulsing spray. She'd taken several long showers since she got home, but she hadn't managed to regain her sense of calm.

She told herself that anyone in her position would be

jumpy. She'd been kidnapped and assaulted. It would take time before she felt relaxed again.

Some of the memories were sharper than others, like fragments of glass in her psyche. Caleb's shooting. Nick, chasing her through the woods. Javier's boss, rubbing his knuckles against her cheek.

She sympathized with Caleb and Ted. Their attempt to rescue her had been a quest for thrills and personal glory, but neither deserved to be attacked. Nick's personal assault disturbed her more than the brutal violence she'd witnessed on the hiking trail, however. She couldn't wash away his touch.

When Faith got out of the shower, she took pains with her appearance. Her hair was blow-dried, straightened and curled under like a '40s pinup. She put on a vampy dress and slick heels. Full makeup with red lips completed the look.

After primping herself, she turned her attention to Hope. Her sister had borrowed a navy shirtwaist dress, one of the plainest items in Faith's closet. The fabric hugged her curvier figure, emphasizing her bust and hips.

"This doesn't fit," Hope said.

Faith disagreed. "It's perfect."

They wore the same size shoes, and Hope humored her by donning a pair of wedge sandals that did great things for her legs. She also let Faith doll her up with mascara, eye shadow and lip gloss.

"You should keep that dress," Faith said. On impulse, she picked up her cell phone to capture the moment. Smiling, she held her arm out straight and leaned in close to Hope as she snapped a photo.

"Don't post this on Facebook. It's too...celebratory."

Faith studied the image, puzzled. Although she looked confident and stylish, she didn't feel that way.

They walked to her favorite sushi restaurant. A couple of guys checked them out as they passed the bar. Usually, Faith enjoyed this type of attention. Tonight, it made her skin crawl. Instead of flashing a flirtatious smile, she avoided eye contact.

She'd told her sister everything about the kidnapping, including the quasi rape. Hope had also shared her side of the story. When she admitted to sleeping with Sam, Faith didn't judge; she pressed for details.

As soon as they were seated, Hope glanced at her cell phone screen. With a small frown, she turned it off.

"Is that him again?"

"Yes."

"Why don't you answer?"

"I'm spending time with you."

"You're ignoring him."

The waiter appeared to take their drink order. Faith requested an appletini. Hope asked for white wine.

They'd discussed the sequence of events, but they hadn't talked much about feelings. Faith understood that Sam Rutherford had some issues. So did Hope. "Are you going to go out with him again?"

"No."

"Why not? You said he was good in bed."

"That's not everything."

"Being rich doesn't hurt."

"Being a jerk does."

Although Faith agreed, her attitude toward Sam had

changed. He'd saved her sister's life repeatedly. She was willing to forgive his other flaws.

"Would you see Javier again?" Hope asked.

"I don't have that option."

"What if you did?"

"I'd see him."

Hope's brown eyes softened with sympathy.

Faith knew there was no chance for her to reunite with Javier, but…she missed him. Even though he was guilty of shocking criminal acts, and responsible for a situation that had gone violently wrong, she still wanted him. She wasn't sure what depressed her more: the post-traumatic stress, or her broken heart.

The waiter arrived with their drinks. After taking a sip of her crisp appletini, Faith ordered a plate of California-roll sushi for them to share. The appetizer came quickly. She selected one of the colorful shapes, adding a tiny dollop of wasabi.

"I think he's in love with you," Faith mused.

Hope almost choked on her sushi. When she recovered, she said, "You saw him for two seconds."

"Yeah, but he looked suitably ashamed after I was rude to him. He bought me that awful gift store outfit, and he was nice to the 'rents. If he didn't care about you, he wouldn't have come to the hospital at all."

"He's in love with his ex," she said dismissively.

"Then why's he chasing you?"

"Because he can't have her. I'm his do-over. Melissa 2.0."

Faith popped another bite into her mouth, wondering if Hope was right. Sam had called her another woman's name once. Minus points for that.

"He also avoids reality, and he's a loner who won't face his past. There's no way he can move on until he deals with his problems."

Faith chuckled at the criticisms, shaking her head. The ironic part was that Hope had just described herself.

"Why is that funny?"

"I'll tell you later."

Hope turned the tables on her. "Are you in love with Javier?"

Although Faith should have anticipated this question, it caught her off guard. She took another sip of her drink. "How could I be in love with him? We just met."

"I've spent the same amount of time with Sam."

"Your affair started months ago," she said.

"We didn't have an affair. He screwed me three times and threw me out."

"Three times, really?"

Her cheeks flushed pink. "What difference does it make?"

"None, if he's the only one who came."

Hope glanced around, as if worried someone could overhear their conversation.

"I have this theory about female orgasms," Faith continued, arching a brow. "You get closer to a man every time he gets you off."

"The important part is that he threw me out, not that he got me off," Hope said in an embarrassed whisper.

"He didn't want you to see him in the morning."

Hope's lips parted with surprise. She'd told Faith about Sam's memory problems and his emotional breakdown after he'd mistaken her for Melissa. But she hadn't been able to put two and two together. For an intelligent,

intuitive woman, Hope really sucked at analyzing her
own relationships.

"We were talking about Javier, not Sam," her sister
said. "Are you planning to stay in contact with him?"

"No. I'm not stupid."

"I never said you were."

"Just 'flighty' and 'free-spirited'?"

Hope flinched at her tone. "Faith…"

"Not all of us want to be perfect ladies."

"I'm not perfect," Hope sputtered, holding a hand
to her chest.

"You're not a wild slut, either."

"Yes, I am! I practically begged Sam to fuck me."

Faith exploded with laughter. She didn't know what
was funnier: the fact that Hope considered this behavior forward, or her frank language in public. "You've
come a long way, sis. Pun intended."

"I can't believe you're encouraging me to date someone so…"

"Risky?"

"I was going to say unbalanced."

"Safe choices aren't challenging, Hope. He might
be good for you."

She looked away, pensive. Faith knew her sister well
enough to guess that she was twisting her hands in her
lap. Hope wanted to play caregiver and counselor to
Faith, even though her experiences over the past two
days had been just as traumatic, if not more so. She'd
come to L.A. to run from trouble—and Sam.

They finished their drinks and the hearty appetizer.
Neither felt like ordering an entrée. The waiter returned
to ask if they wanted a refill, courtesy of two men at

the bar. Faith didn't even glance over there. Hope shook her head.

"We're taken," Faith said, declining the offer.

They left the restaurant, arm in arm. The feminist art exhibit Faith wanted to see was only a few blocks away. She relished the pinch of her stilettos on the way there, finding comfort in the familiar sensation.

"I was date-raped in college," she said.

Hope, whose wedge heels were much easier to navigate, stumbled nevertheless. "What?"

"I was raped. Freshman year."

Hope's eyes darkened with pain. They were like twins. When Faith hurt, Hope felt it. "You never told me that."

Faith swallowed, continuing their stroll. "I never told anyone. I think I blocked it out, even from myself."

"What happened?"

"I was drunk at a frat party. The guy's name was Brett. I'd actually been dating him for several weeks, and we'd had consensual sex before. That night, I was mad at him for flirting with another girl. I decided to get revenge by teasing him and leaving him unsatisfied. He got mad and…threw me down."

"Did he hit you?"

"No. I was too wasted to fight. But he knew I didn't want it. He apologized after."

Hope stopped to give her a hug. "What did you do?"

"Nothing. I didn't even break up with him right away."

"You're kidding."

She shook her head, sighing. "The next time he took me to his room, I felt sick. I couldn't be alone with him anymore. He promised to be gentle, but I didn't want him kissing me or touching me again. I told him it was over."

"Oh, Faith. I'm so sorry."

"I know it wasn't my fault."

"Of course it wasn't," Hope said, her nostrils flaring with rage. "What happened to him? Where is he?"

Great White Hope. She probably wanted to arrest him. "He got in a car accident a few years later. Drunk driving."

"He's dead?"

"Yes."

Hope relaxed a little, her anger shifting back into concern.

Faith wasn't sure why she'd started this conversation. Nick's attack had brought back latent memories of Brett. "I thought I could just go on as if it never happened. I didn't want the experience to drag me down. I vowed to keep flirting with men and having fun. Maybe I went too far in my quest to be carefree."

"This is my fault," Hope said. "I should have known."

"Don't be ridiculous."

"If I hadn't been so wrapped up in my own issues, I could have guessed that you were hurting."

"I wasn't hurting. I was partying."

"As a coping mechanism."

Faith waved a hand in the air, dismissive.

"I always thought you were living it up because you didn't want to be like me. All work and no play."

"That might have been part of it," Faith admitted. "You weren't the only one who felt sad, you know. She was my niece. You're my sister. I was grieving, too. It was hard for me to watch you suffer."

Hope glanced away, blinking tears from her eyes.

Faith knew it was time to confront Hope about the past. They had to deal with this now, not keep it buried, like a shameful secret.

"Do you want to go to the gallery?" Hope asked.

Although they'd arrived at the exhibit, Faith steered her sister back home. "I have something else to show you."

HOPE CHECKED THE locks on the windows and the dead bolt on the door in Faith's apartment.

Nothing had been tampered with. The space was free of intruders.

"Is it all clear, Ranger Banning?"

She frowned at her sister's tone. Faith never took anything seriously. She'd acted more subdued since the kidnapping, but she seemed determined to get back to her regular routine. Hope worried that her sister would be careless with her personal safety. Who would watch over Faith after Hope went back to the Sierras?

She couldn't believe Faith had never told her about the date rape. No wonder the recent attack had traumatized her. Hope was enraged at the thought of anyone hurting her sister. She'd go to the ends of the earth to protect Faith.

Their conversation about Sam had unsettled her further. He knew she was in L.A., and he kept trying to call her. She was afraid to answer. She could forgive his bad behavior and overlook his "brain damage." The real obstacle was her fear of falling in love with him. One nudge, and she'd topple over the edge.

Faith brought a shoe box out of her bedroom. It looked worn at the corners, as if she'd been keeping it a long time. She sat down on the herringbone couch in the living room, holding the box in her lap.

"What is that?" Hope asked, taking the seat next to her.

"I was surprised you'd told Sam about the baby," she said, keeping her fingers closed around the lid. "You don't even talk to me about it."

"You already know."

"I know what happened. Not how you feel."

Hope didn't discuss the experience because it was too painful. She'd assumed her sister understood that. It was the same reason Faith had kept quiet about the date rape. But if she could open up, so could Hope. "I feel bad."

"Why?"

"Because I couldn't keep her."

"Is that so wrong?"

"Yes, Faith. I brought a child into the world that I couldn't take care of. It's a pretty big deal to me."

"I know it's a big deal. What I'm saying is that it's nothing to be ashamed of."

Hope agreed, in theory. She shouldn't feel ashamed, but she *did*. The unplanned pregnancy and subsequent adoption represented her lowest point, her darkest secret. "I can't pretend it didn't happen."

"No. You can stop beating yourself up about it. You can give yourself some credit for making a mature decision."

She knew she had a problem letting go. She'd always felt that she deserved the guilt and melancholy. It was her way of acknowledging her mistakes. Forgetting all that—or forgiving herself—seemed dismissive. What Hope wanted most in life was a second chance at motherhood, but she didn't consider herself worthy. She'd lost the right to be a parent. It wasn't fair to have another baby, after giving up her firstborn.

"What's in the box?" she asked.

Faith smoothed her palms over the surface, seeming nervous. "You don't have to look, if you don't want to."

"What is it?"

"Yearly photos."

Hope was stunned. "From who?"

"The adoptive parents."

"You talk to them?"

"No. I go through the adoption agent."

The agreement Hope had signed was open on the side of the adoptive parents. They could contact her, through the intermediary, for medical information or anything else they needed. Hope hadn't wanted the same option for herself. She'd chosen not to attempt any communication. It seemed easier for everyone.

"Mom went to the office to get the photos the first few years. When they offered email, I became the recipient."

"Why didn't you tell me?"

"I thought it would be too hard for you. I know you didn't want to give her up."

Tears flooded Hope's eyes, overflowing and spilling down her cheeks. She resented Faith for confronting her with this. Why now, when she was vulnerable?

She already felt needy and scared. She couldn't handle another emotional roller coaster.

"Would you like to see the photos?"

Hope nodded, wiping the tears from her face. Curiosity trumped her trepidation. She'd always wondered what her daughter looked like.

Faith opened the box and drew out a stack of photos, tied with a lacy ribbon. "I'll start with the first birthday."

Hope accepted the stack of about ten photos. Her mother had taken some snapshots at the hospital, so Hope had seen pictures of the baby as a newborn. She'd been squalling and wrinkly, with a tiny little tuft of hair.

The first photo made Hope sob out loud. Her daughter looked so different at six months! She was lying on her back in a crib, wearing a frilly outfit, holding a baby rattle. She was adorable and bright-eyed. The wall beside the crib was painted with butterflies. Everything in the room appeared comfortable and high quality.

Hope couldn't have afforded such finery.

She studied each of the first-year pictures in detail, memorizing the images. The last one featured a party dress and a birthday cake. On the back, there was an inscription: Grace, Age 1. "Her name is Grace?"

Faith grabbed a tissue to blot her eyes. "They thought… it was fitting."

She was touched by the gesture from the adoptive parents. It connected Grace to her birth family, and made Hope feel valued.

The next stack of photos showed a vibrant toddler. Her hair was already a riot of curls. "Oh my God," Hope said. "She looks just like you."

Faith laughed, shaking her head. "She looks like *you*."

One of the photos included the adoptive parents. They were a fit couple in their late thirties, both smiling. Their devotion to Grace was evident. Hope could see that her daughter had been placed in a loving home. These people had given Grace the best of everything. In addition to feeling relieved and grateful, she was wildly jealous.

Hope examined the years of her daughter's life, tears sliding down her face. There were photos of Grace running through the grass on chubby legs, blowing bubbles. Jumping into a sparkling swimming pool, taking a trip to the zoo, making a snowman. Her first day of school, her first bicycle, her first lost tooth.

The most recent photos made Hope's heart ache. Grace was so beautiful. She had mischievous brown eyes, like Faith. Something about her smile reminded Hope of Paul. They hadn't spoken since he'd signed away his rights.

She gazed at the last picture for a long time, wondering what her voice sounded like. How it would feel to hug her.

"She knows she's adopted," Faith said. "They've been open about it."

Hope's pulse kicked up. "Does she ask about me?"

"I don't know."

She gave the photo back, her mind reeling. What if Grace thought Hope didn't want her? What if her daughter hated her?

For the first time, Hope reconsidered the terms of the agreement she'd signed. She didn't want to interfere with Grace's life, but she'd like to let her know she cared. That she hadn't made the decision lightly.

Faith closed the box. "She can request your information when she turns eighteen, but her parents have considered letting her contact you sooner."

"Really?"

"Would you be interested?"

Hope didn't even have to think about it. "Yes!"

Faith smiled, grabbing another tissue. "I think they're going to wait until she's twelve or thirteen to give her the option."

Grace was eleven now, so a possible meeting was right around the corner.

"It's her choice, you understand."

"Of course," Hope said. The idea of seeing her daughter, or just speaking to her, filled her with an inexpressible joy. If Grace didn't want to take that step, Hope would respect her wishes. Either way, she felt as though a weight had been lifted off her shoulders. Her daughter was safe, healthy and adored. "I'm glad she's happy."

"She'd have been happy with you, too."

Her throat closed up. "Do you think I made a mistake?"

"No. I think you made a sacrifice." When Faith put her arms around her, Hope's face crumpled with sorrow and she started to weep uncontrollably. "You did what was best for everyone but you."

Hope wasn't sure how long she cried. She felt as if eleven years' worth of pain and regret came pouring out of her. Her sister had known, all this time, that she'd factored into Hope's decision to give up the baby.

"I thought it was what I wanted," she said, sniffling. "I thought we'd have fun in college."

"I had fun," Faith said, petting her hair. "Even after Brett."

"I wish I'd been there for you."

"You're here now."

Hope lifted her head from Faith's shoulder, where she'd left a smudge of eye makeup. "I've ruined your dress."

"I can get it cleaned."

"When did you turn into the mature, reasonable sister?"

She offered Hope a tissue. "Get ready for more of my sage advice."

"Uh-oh."

"I know I can't see Javier again. He's too dangerous. I'm sad, because I really liked him, but it's not the end of the world."

Hope blew her nose, nodding.

"I don't want you to make another sacrifice for me. We didn't party together in college, and we don't have to be lonely singles together. If you think Sam is the right guy for you, stop running away from him. Let him catch you."

Hope blinked her teary eyes. "You think he's the right guy?"

"Maybe. He cares about you, fucks like a champ and tries to apologize for bad behavior. That last quality is pretty rare."

"He needs therapy."

"Everyone does."

Hope rested her cheek on Faith's shoulder again. She

didn't know what to do about Sam, but she appreciated her sister's support. "I love you, Faithie."

"I love you, too."

CHAPTER TWENTY

HOPE DROVE BACK to the Sierras on Sunday afternoon, her mind in turmoil.

Faith was staying with her friend and coworker Charlie. She'd promised not to go anywhere without the male hairdresser as her bodyguard. Hope was glad her sister had someone strong to protect her.

She hadn't returned any of Sam's calls over the weekend. Every time she glanced at his text messages, she felt overwhelmed. Her emotions were too complicated to sort through. She had a dozen other things to worry about.

According to Faith, Javier Del Norte's boss had bribed members of local law enforcement. The product they smuggled was grown here. They picked it up at a landing strip in Long Pine.

Hope wondered if there were any rangers on Gonzales's payroll. She'd notified the sheriff's department about the radio communications with Faith's kidnappers. Anyone with a similar device, or even a cell phone app, could eavesdrop on their channels, but only those within the network could respond. Either the computer system had been hacked or the smugglers had a programmed radio, provided by a staff member.

She hadn't heard of anyone losing a radio lately. The head rangers of each region were responsible for the devices. If she wasn't on administrative leave, she could make inquiries. She was supposed to be resting, not investigating.

Deputy Meeks's failed attempt to retrieve the cargo also struck her as suspicious. His team should have been able to camp and reach the summit. Maybe he'd forgotten the equipment on purpose.

She didn't know much about the young deputy. He was a war veteran, and a bit of a ladies' man. He'd offered to buy her a drink the same night she'd gone home with Sam. Although Meeks wasn't bad-looking, she'd declined. He was in his early twenties, on the too-young side, and he'd been sitting with someone she disliked at the bar. Who was it?

Her stomach dropped as she remembered: Bill Kruger.

That's why she hadn't stayed to chat with Meeks. She'd gone to the other side of the bar to avoid Kruger. A few minutes later, she met Sam.

And the rest was history.

Bill Kruger was a head ranger, so he had access to radios. He was also from Las Vegas. He'd moved to the Sierras after his younger sister, Kim, married Doug Dixon. He lived in a cabin that Doug owned. It was in a remote area on the outskirts of town. Next to a flat, empty field where a helicopter could land.

Not far from the place Faith had been found.

"Oh my God," she breathed, slapping a hand over her forehead. This was the missing piece of information she'd been racking her brain for. Why hadn't she thought of it sooner? Kruger was the mole. He had to be.

Another disturbing idea occurred to her. Kruger

might have double-crossed the drug smugglers by stealing part of the stash. Had he left the boot print at Angel Wings?

She tightened her hands around the steering wheel, her heart racing. Maybe Meeks and Kruger were both dirty. There could be widespread corruption in park services and the sheriff's department. What if Dixon was in on it?

Although Hope's heart wanted to reject the notion on the basis of their past relationship, she forced herself to consider it. With his powerful connections and cool head, Doug had the means to pull the puppet strings. Meeks was a rookie deputy, Kruger a washed-up drunk. They weren't criminal masterminds. And Doug wasn't a poor manager, despite the chaos of the past few days. He'd never been distracted or incompetent before. It was possible that Doug had overlooked "mistakes" in the investigation to cover their tracks.

This new suspicion totally changed the game. Doug had a spotless reputation. He was a respected member of the community. No one would believe her.

She didn't know who to call.

Her safest bet would be to contact the FBI, but she hesitated. She was familiar with agency procedure. Special Agent Ling would demand to talk to Faith again, maybe even charge her with obstructing justice. Getting a warrant to search the cabin would be difficult. Any investigation would proceed at a snail's pace.

In the meantime, Faith would be in danger. She admitted to Hope that she'd seen the faces of her captors. She could identify the inside of the cabin. If Hope brought forth her suspicions, they might try to eliminate Faith as a witness. These were hardened criminals. They could come after Hope, too.

She needed proof before she called the FBI. If she went in empty-handed and no evidence turned up, she'd be putting her job *and* her sister at risk.

That was unacceptable.

Instead of driving to her shared unit in park housing, she turned on the deserted road that led to the ranger station at Mineral King. Owen Jackson had been filling in for her again. When she arrived, he was locking up for the day.

"Ranger Banning," he said, nodding hello.

"Hope."

"Hope," he repeated dutifully. "How's your sister?"

"She's better."

"That's good to hear."

She studied him for a moment, disconcerted by his serious blue eyes. Even though she'd seen him shirtless, with ugly tattoos marring his lovely chest, she was the one who felt naked. "I need to get something inside my office."

"Sure," he said, opening the door for her.

She went straight to her desk and pulled out the top drawer. Her trembling fingers closed around a key, which she used to unlock a metal box she kept stashed in the utility closet. It housed a Glock 9 mm handgun. Her backup weapon.

A girl had to be prepared.

Hope tucked the gun into the waistband of her jeans, letting her jacket hide the telltale bulge.

"Where are you going with that?"

She turned to see him standing in the doorway. "Home."

He just stared at her. His mother must have taught him not to argue with women, because he didn't say anything. There was a distinct possibility he'd call Sam, however. They were friends, and Owen had seen her kissing him.

"Okay," she said, as if he was badgering her. "I want to search Kruger's cabin."

"Bill Kruger?"

After a short hesitation, she decided to divulge all. The fact that Owen was an outsider made him more trustworthy. His brave, independent actions had won her over. "I think Kruger was involved in my sister's kidnapping."

"Why?"

Hope explained how she'd come to the conclusion. It was really just a hunch, and she doubted the FBI would be convinced by her reasoning. Owen had no trouble believing her. He'd worked with Kruger on forest maintenance, and probably had better insight about criminal behavior than most young men.

"He always seemed shady to me," Owen said.

"I can't go to Dixon with this."

"No," he agreed.

"Do you know anything about Meeks?"

"Just that he's drinking buddies with Kruger."

"Maybe I should drive by the lodge first."

"How are you going to get in the cabin?"

"Dixon owns the place. He used to keep a key by the back door."

"How do you know that?"

"We went there several times when we were dating."

His brows shot up. "You dated Dixon?"

She squinted, daring him to criticize.

He didn't. "What if the key isn't there?"

"I'll have to break in."

Hope acknowledged that her proposal was unorthodox—and illegal. But she couldn't continue to work in a dangerous, corrupt environment. If Kruger was caught up in a drug smuggling ring, she wanted to see him nailed to the wall. Any evidence they found could be rediscovered through an authorized search warrant. She wasn't the first ranger to bend the rules, and she wouldn't be the last.

"I'll come with you," Owen said.

Although she could use a lookout, she was reluctant to involve him. "Aren't you on probation?"

"Prison inmates get parole, not probation."

"You're on parole, then?"

"No. I just got off."

After a short pause, she accepted. If she had to smash a window, she'd make sure he stayed outside. At any rate, she didn't plan on getting caught.

By the time Owen dropped off his service vehicle at headquarters, it was early evening. He climbed into the passenger seat of Hope's Jeep, and she cruised by the bar. Sure enough, Kruger's black pickup truck was in the parking lot.

They went to the cabin next. The windows were dark and quiet. "Okay," she said, glancing at her navigation system. "I'll park on Whispering Rock Avenue. We can approach from the back. It's not fenced."

Owen nodded, tugging a beanie over his light hair.

After she hid her Jeep behind some bushes at the side of the road, she pulled up the hood of her sweatshirt, covering most of her face. Then she pocketed a flashlight from the glove compartment.

"Ready?" she whispered.

"Ready."

They trudged through a copse of pines. A sliver of moonlight illuminated the path. When the back of the log cabin came into view, they stopped to study it. She noticed one new addition to the property. A pointy-eared shape was curled up in the corner of a chain-link enclosure.

"There's a dog," he said.

"It's locked up."

"What do you think we'll find in there?"

"The drugs he stole, hopefully. Or some proof that my sister was there. Her clothes, hair, something."

"Her clothes?"

"She was wrapped in a sheet when they found her."

Owen understood the implications of her nudity, and his mouth made a thin line of anger. He seemed as eager as Hope to bust Kruger. She wondered if he had some kind of personal vendetta against men who abused women.

They crept forward. The dog began to bark furiously as she approached. Hope kept moving, disturbed by the sight of the Doberman's glistening teeth, gnashing at the gate. A light came on when she reached the back door.

She smothered a scream.

Owen grasped her upper arm, ready to run.

"It's a motion detector," she whispered.

His grip relaxed, but his face stayed tense.

She didn't want to trigger an alarm by breaking in, so she prayed the key was still there. As she stepped closer, she noticed a pair of muddy hiking boots by the back door. They were about a size twelve. Kruger was a big man. Years of dissolute living had put some extra weight around his middle.

Blood pounding in her ears, she picked up the boot and glanced at the tread. The zigzag pattern was unmistakable. She took a photo of it with her cell phone. After replacing the boot, she found the key under a skull-sized rock. She straightened, inserting the key and turning the knob. The door swung open with a faint creak. No sirens blared and no masked men rushed at them as they entered the residence.

The interior looked the same. It was a cozy space with exposed ceiling beams. She'd spent several weekends here with Doug. His company had been pleasant. He wasn't a challenge, like Sam. He hadn't made her tremble with excitement, or feel half as vulnerable.

Had their entire relationship been a lie? She couldn't imagine him taking bribes from drug smugglers, but she also couldn't imagine him being unaware of Kruger's illegal activities, some of which were perpetrated in his own cabin.

She headed to the basement first. Faith told her that she'd been kept in a room without windows.

With Owen following close behind, she descended a dark stairwell, drawing the flashlight from her pocket. There were two doors to choose from. She opened the one on the left and glanced inside. Other than a rectangular table and a few chairs, the space was bare. It wasn't the bedroom Faith had described.

Moving on, she studied the second door. It appeared to lock from the outside. She passed the flashlight to Owen and brought out her phone. While he waited, his eyes darting toward the stairs, she snapped a photograph. Then she entered the room, taking more pictures of the interior. It was spotless, the bed stripped bare and the table wiped clean. She searched the corners for video equipment. Nothing.

Her stomach twisted with distress as she pictured Faith here with her attacker. She looked under the bed and inside the bathroom. There were no dirty clothes on the floor, no blond hair in the drain. Every surface was immaculate.

Hope's spirits plummeted. A reverse lock wasn't the smoking gun she needed. She had to find some concrete evidence.

Owen glanced toward the exit, seeming agitated.

She motioned for him to wait. Returning to the bathroom, she glanced at the toilet tank, struck by a sudden inspiration. Sticking her phone in her pocket, she lifted the porcelain tank cover and looked inside.

Bingo.

The bulb was floating loose, unattached. Parts were missing. Faith had used the rod to try to jimmy open the door!

Heart racing, she set aside the cover and took photos of the toilet tank. This was too much of a coincidence to ignore. It might not convince anyone else, but Hope knew with complete certainty that her sister had been here.

Before she had a chance to replace the tank cover, a

mechanical hum started. It took her several seconds to place the sound as an automatic garage door.

She pocketed her phone and fumbled with the tank cover. It was still askew when Owen grabbed her wrist, urging her out the door. As she raced down the hall, she could hear Kruger's truck pull into the garage.

What now?

She looked at Owen, unsure if they should hide or flee.

"Go," he ordered, shoving her up the stairs. She took two at a time, trying not to trip, her adrenaline pumping. As they burst onto the main floor, Kruger entered the house from the garage. Instead of moving through the kitchen, he stopped to listen.

Caught.

She ran toward the back door with Owen on her heels.

"Hey!"

She prayed for a clean escape as they sailed outside. The Doberman snarled at the gate, thirsty for blood. Hope sprinted for the trees as fast as her legs could carry her. Owen kept pace beside her. They were lucky Kruger didn't open fire. He could probably get away with shooting intruders on his property.

As they darted across the short expanse, Kruger shouted obscenities. She knew they could outdistance a hard drinker. When they reached the copse of pines, she thought they were home free.

She was wrong.

Kruger released his hound.

Hope ran faster, her lungs burning. She heard the Doberman gaining on them, its paws thundering against the ground. Owen stumbled over a root and lost his balance. He went down hard on his hands and knees.

Skidding to a halt, she turned back to help him, but the dog was already there. In a blur of sharp teeth and glistening saliva, it attacked, tearing at his ankle. She pulled the 9 mm from her waistband, her chest tight with panic.

She didn't know where to shoot. The dog was all over the place, biting Owen's thrashing arms and legs.

"No," she shouted, trying to dislodge the Doberman with a kick. "Bad dog!"

Owen and the dog rolled across the pine-needle-strewn ground. For a moment, she thought he'd break free. Then Owen was underneath and the dog was on top, growling and snapping, its muzzle inches from his throat.

Hope didn't have a choice. She raised her gun, aimed for the animal's barrel chest and squeezed off a shot. The boom thundered in her ears as the weapon jerked in her hands, filling the air with residue.

With a sharp yip, the dog collapsed.

She sobbed out loud as Owen shoved the animal's body aside and scrambled to his feet. They started running again, worried that Kruger was closing in. Tears streamed down her face as she stumbled through the woods. When they arrived at her Jeep, she gestured for Owen to climb in first, pointing her weapon at the trees.

Kruger didn't emerge.

Keeping her eyes peeled, she went around to the driver's seat and got in, placing her weapon on the console. She fumbled for the keys and started the engine. Her tires kicked up dirt as she stepped on the gas.

"Are you hurt?" she asked Owen.

"I think I'm okay," he said, but he sounded shaky. His jeans were ripped and blood snaked down his left forearm.

"Put pressure on the wound."

"Let's get out of here."

He didn't have to say it twice. She drove away from the scene like a stuntwoman, barely breaking for curves. They both managed to secure their seat belts on a straight stretch of road. "I'm going to the hospital."

Owen pulled a ringing cell phone out of his pocket. "It's Sam."

"Shit."

"Should I answer?"

"Yes," she said, distracted. "We're lucky Kruger didn't try to…"

Headlights penetrated the rear window, illuminating the interior of the vehicle. The words *follow us* died in her throat.

Kruger was coming after them.

CHAPTER TWENTY-ONE

Hope put her foot on the gas, increasing her speed.

The pickup truck's front grill kissed her back bumper, causing the Jeep to lurch sideways, zigzagging across the road. With a cry of distress, she straightened the wheel, trying to regain control of the vehicle.

"He's coming again," Owen warned.

She drove faster, determined to put distance between them. The next thing she knew, the rear window shattered, sending safety glass flying through the cab. She screamed, ducking her head to avoid another bullet.

Owen twisted in his seat, looking back. "Swerve! He's got us in his sights."

Gritting her teeth, she cranked the wheel to the right. Her gun tumbled over the console, into Owen's lap. Kruger's next shot missed by a wide margin. They came upon a series of hairpin turns that required both drivers to focus on the terrain.

"Just a second," Owen said into the phone. Setting it aside, he picked up her gun.

"You know how to use that?" she asked.

"Yeah."

"Return fire."

"What should I go for, his tires?"

"Hell no," she said. Vehicle tires were difficult to hit in any situation. Unless he was a crack shot, which she doubted, he needed to pick an easier target. "Aim at his head. Shoot through the front windshield. Anything."

Face pale, he trained the gun on Kruger.

Hope realized she was asking a lot from a convicted felon, but this was a clear case of self-defense. She jerked her attention forward, narrowly avoiding a collision with a parked car. She did her best to weave around. It was a difficult task at top speed on a lonely mountain road. Owen crouched in the passenger seat, ready to fire.

Another bullet slammed into the tailgate.

"Fuck!"

Owen squeezed off several shots. She glanced in her rearview mirror, gasping as the truck's front window exploded. Kruger slowed down, and Owen fired twice more. The noise was deafening. It ricocheted inside her ears, drowning out all other sound.

"Did you hit him?" she asked.

"I don't think so."

She slammed on the brakes and hooked a right, heading away from town. Kruger might gather a posse from the sheriff's department. Meeks could sic every patrol car in the area on them. They weren't safe in the Sierras, and there was only one escape route. She had to take the twisty 198. It was a dangerous road on a good day. At night, with a madman trying to run them down in a high-speed chase, the chances of a serious accident were high.

She put the pedal to the metal, punching it on a straightaway. Owen tried, and failed, to incapacitate the pickup with her gunfire.

Tires squealing, she merged onto the 198 northbound. The highway flanked the mighty Kern River, and rose several thousand feet in elevation before falling again. She wanted to lose the tail on the way up, rather than continuing the chase downhill.

"Wait until he gets close again," she said.

Letting his gun arm drop, he picked up the phone again, shouting their location at Sam. "We just passed Cold Springs Road."

The hairpin turns made her stomach clench with fear, and the heights were dizzying. She anticipated death around every corner. The truck inched closer again. As they entered a tunnel, she could see Kruger's deranged face in the rearview mirror.

"Now!" she ordered.

The last bullet connected. Kruger's shoulder jerked from the impact, and he let go of the wheel. His passenger door scraped the tunnel wall, sending sparks into the air. He steered the truck back toward the center of the lane, but he couldn't continue to shoot. The only weapon he had left was his vehicle.

"He's going to try to run me off the road," she said, driving faster.

She couldn't believe the numbers on the speedometer. They were already traveling at a breakneck pace. Kruger rammed her bumper in a bone-jolting crash. She sideswiped the guardrail as they exited the tunnel. He struck again, tapping her bumper at an angle. The Jeep went into a sickening spin.

She held her breath, expecting to fly over the cliff. Instead, she came to a grinding halt on the opposite side of the road, facing the other direction.

"Go!" Owen shouted.

Heart pounding, she stepped on the gas. Kruger turned around to continue his pursuit. She realized that she couldn't outmaneuver him. Her vehicle was built for off-road treks and smooth freeway trips. The pickup could go faster and hit harder. But Kruger was injured, and he'd probably been drinking. She could outthink him.

As they neared a sharp curve at the side of the cliff, she slowed down, glancing in the rearview mirror. Kruger took the bait. He advanced, ready to slam her bumper. A second later, she cranked the wheel to the left.

Kruger didn't have time to slow down. His truck hit the guardrail at full speed and launched off the edge.

It was a very steep drop to the river below. She doubted he'd survive the fall.

Unfortunately, Hope couldn't avoid her own disaster. When she swerved onto the gravel embankment on the opposite side of the road, she was going way too fast to correct her mistake. The wheel jerked out of her hands. She slammed on her brakes, but her tires found no purchase on the loose gravel. The Jeep skidded across the road, careening toward the guardrail in a shuddering slide.

Like Kruger, they went over.

SAM HAD WAITED all weekend for Hope to call.

On Sunday afternoon, she'd sent one short text about driving back from L.A. He texted back immediately: Come over. Even though she didn't respond, he tidied up his house, washed the sheets, and stocked the fridge with groceries. Now it was late, and he still hadn't heard back. Had she made it home okay?

After burning off some energy in the climbing gym, he checked his messages again. There was a strange text from Owen:

Hope is searching cabin owned by Dixon, 443 White Pine Ave

What the hell?

He tried to call a dozen times before Owen finally picked up. And then he didn't even talk. Sam could hear Hope shouting in the background. It sounded like a car chase. When gunshots erupted, Sam's knees started shaking. The term he'd heard climbers use for this re-action was "Elvis legs" or "sewing-machine legs." It was a normal side effect of fear and physical exertion. Sam hadn't felt it until now.

He didn't know if he should hang up and call 911, or stay on the line. Forcing his wobbly legs to move, he stumbled toward the house phone. The problem with calling the police was that he didn't know what to tell them.

"Where are you?" he repeated several times.

Owen shouted something about Cold Springs Road and hung up. Instead of using the landline, Sam grabbed his keys and ran outside, getting behind the wheel of his Range Rover. Cold Springs was off the 198, less than ten minutes away.

He drove like a madman to get there, taking a series of twisty mountain back roads. With his free hand, he dialed 911 to report gunshots and a vehicle accident on the 198. The operator kept asking questions he couldn't answer. Making a sound of frustration, he ended the call and tried Owen again.

No response.

Cursing, he went north on the highway, searching for headlights. He passed Cold Springs and kept going. To his dismay, he saw a vehicle fly off the side of the cliff, near the tunnel. Tires squealing, he pulled over on the shoulder to take a better look. While he watched, horrified, a second vehicle followed the first.

It looked like Hope's Jeep.

"No," he croaked in disbelief. "No!"

Heart pounding, he leaped out of his SUV and ran toward the guardrail. One vehicle had plummeted several hundred feet and burst into flames. The other took a slower tumble down an angled slope. It landed in the ravine, out of his line of sight.

Into the middle of the river.

"Shit," he said, jumping behind the wheel. He couldn't get to them from here. He'd break his leg scrambling down the steep hill. Backing up, he turned around and headed the opposite direction. Kern Road was only a few hundred yards away. Its scenic bridge offered easy access to the riverbed. He squealed to a stop by the bridge and got out, hitting the ground running.

Sam knew he had to reach them in minutes. Occupants of a submerged vehicle were likely to become drowning victims. Assuming Hope and Owen had survived the plunge, they might still be trapped inside.

Please, God. Let them be alive.

He raced along the river's edge, scrambling over rocks and skirting between trees. There was no path, and the ground was uneven. It was dark. Branches whipped across his face and tugged at his clothes.

When he finally reached the wreckage, he knew it was too late. Too much time had elapsed. The Jeep was upside down in the river, its back bumper almost invisible. The front end was completely under water.

He stared at the still, wet tires, his blood turned to ice.

This couldn't be happening. Not again. He felt like screaming at the sky, bellowing until his voice went hoarse. If Hope was dead, he didn't want to go on.

He pushed the thought out of his mind, baring his teeth. Fuck death. He'd defeat death with his bare hands. With grim determination, he shrugged out of his jacket and waded into the water, ignoring the cold bite. When it was waist-deep, he dove in, swimming the short distance to the vehicle. He took a deep breath and went under.

Sam was trained in swift-water rescue, as well as high-angle, so he understood the danger of approaching a vehicle in a river. It could shift and roll at any moment, trapping him below the surface.

But he was also well versed in taking extreme risks. If all of those free-solo climbs had prepared him for this task, he didn't regret a single second on the rock face. He entered through the open front window, swimming around the cab. The passenger seat was empty. So was the driver's seat.

He needed more air, so he exited the way he came and broke through the surface. After a quick gasp, he went down again. This time, he searched the backseats and the cab space, running his hands along twisted edges.

Nothing.

They weren't here.

Sam knew what that meant. Some accident victims were thrown clear of the wreckage. Maybe Hope and Owen had been tossed from the Jeep as it fell. If they'd landed at the bottom of the cliff, their chances of survival were slim. If they'd ended up in the river, the bodies had already been swept away.

He swam back to shore, shuddering from the cold. Like a zombie, he trudged along the riverbed for another quarter mile. He didn't see any broken remains, but he found the crash site where the Jeep had entered the river.

If they'd managed to get out, they'd be here.

Sam collapsed on the bank, numb. His chest ached with sadness. It felt as if there were a vise wrapped around his torso, crushing his internal organs. He was vaguely aware of a dull throb in his palm and blood dripping down his fingers.

It was nothing compared to the emotional pain. His heart was bleeding. He hadn't been able to save Melissa, and he'd failed again with Hope. He hadn't defeated death. Death had defeated *him*.

The hot sting of tears burned his eyes. He gave in to it, letting sorrow take him. Shoulders shaking, he hung his head and cried.

HOPE BRACED HERSELF for the crash, expecting to die in a burst of flames.

A couple of images danced in her mind in the seconds they were airborne. Her baby's pink, wrinkled face as she let out her first cry. Faith on her birthday, blowing out the candles. Sam, asleep in the hotel bed.

How could her life flash by? It hadn't even started yet.

Although they'd gone off the same cliff as Kruger, they didn't take the same trip. Instead of flying into space like the General Lee, the Jeep tumbled end over end. Her seat belt caught hard across her chest, almost knocking the wind from her lungs. Twin airbags deployed. She couldn't count the number of times the vehicle rolled. Her knees and elbows banged against the interior with every stomach-jolting impact.

When it finally came to a stop, they were both alive. She had about two seconds to count her blessings. Because the Jeep landed upside down in the Kern River.

The icy current rushed in the broken windows, hitting her like a slap in the face. Murky water filled her mouth and nostrils. She sputtered and choked, trying to avoid the deluge, but it was no use. The Jeep was fully submerged before the airbag had even deflated.

Her first instinct was to right herself, but she was dizzy and disoriented. She couldn't breathe. The front end of the vehicle sank to the river bottom and scraped along the rocks, groaning from the pressure.

She had to get out.

Pushing the airbag away from her face, she attempted a swimming motion. Her seat belt pulled tight, trapping her in place. Hope's lungs burned from lack of oxygen. The extreme cold had stolen her motor skills and robbed her ability to think. She tugged on the seat belt in confusion. It wouldn't budge.

Another pair of hands slapped hers away and released her seat belt. Her body floated up. Owen tucked a forearm under her chin and pulled her backward, out the broken rear window. They surfaced together, gasping.

He had saved her.

The tail of the Jeep was sticking out of the water, but it was hardly stable. Any minute, the current could sweep them downriver. As oxygen bubbled back into her brain, she realized they were in serious danger. The Kern was wider and deeper than the Kaweah. It claimed drowning victims on a regular basis. The longer they stayed in the water, the colder they'd get. They'd lose simple functioning.

"Can you swim?" he asked, shouting to be heard above the roar.

She didn't have a choice. It was swim or die. "Yes."

"Let's go," he said.

As they kicked away from the Jeep, it shifted, dislodging the rocks on the river bottom. Hope swam with all her might, fighting a current that threatened to suck her down, carry her away or trap her underneath the vehicle. Although it was a short distance to the bank, her arms grew heavy and her legs sluggish. She had to fight to keep her eyes open. The combination of shock and cold created a dangerous lassitude, inviting her to sleep.

When her foot glanced off the side of the Jeep, she realized it was gaining on her. A surge of panic gave her the strength to fight her way to the shore. She climbed out of the water on her hands and knees. Coughing and shivering, she collapsed next to Owen.

They watched the Jeep sail downriver, into the darkness.

"Wow," he said, staring after it. "That was intense."

Hope shrugged out of her soaked sweatshirt and took stock of her injuries. There weren't any bones sticking out of her skin. She was cold, and she might freeze to death if she spent the night in wet clothes. But she wasn't injured, by some miracle.

"Are you okay?" she asked.

"I don't know."

Her cell phone was gone. So much for the photographic evidence she'd collected. "Where's your phone?"

"In the river, I guess."

Owen still had the flashlight in his pocket. After he gave it to her, she turned on the beam and evaluated his condition. The bite wound on his forearm looked awful. There was a jagged laceration and several deep punctures. He needed stitches.

She used her sweatshirt to make a sling for his arm. Once it was immobilized, he could walk comfortably. Their best bet was to travel downriver, rather than attempting to ascend the steep cliff. Before they headed that direction, Hope caught sight of flickering flames. She was curious about the wreckage.

"You think he's alive?" Owen asked.

"No."

"Should we check?"

"Might be wise."

By tacit agreement, they started hiking toward the burning truck. It was less than a quarter of a mile away, on the other side of the river. When they got close enough to see the mangled truck parts, Kruger's fate became clear. A blackened corpse sat behind the wheel of a twisted frame. The smell of charred flesh hung in the air.

"This didn't end well," Owen said.

"Not for him."

He seemed surprised by her glib comment. She'd never thought of herself as hardened, but after the events she'd lived through, she felt a little disconnected from reality. She'd shot a man at Angel Wings. Now she had another death on her hands, and she hadn't yet processed the first one.

She stared across the river, realizing that she regretted killing the dog more than the humans. Did that make her cold?

Faith was right. Hope had been isolated in the Sierras, insulated from loss and heartbreak. She had to stop distancing herself from others. Embrace her feelings.

A searchlight stabbed down the cliff, illuminating the macabre scene. Kruger's face was scorched beyond recognition. The skin around his mouth had burned away, exposing his teeth in a chilling grin.

She grabbed Owen by the good arm and pulled him behind a pine tree. Flattening her back against the bark, she waited for the light to pass by.

CHAPTER TWENTY-TWO

WHEN THE COAST was clear, Hope and Owen weaved back through the trees along the riverbank, sticking close to the shore.

There was a bridge about a mile away on Kern Road. They could climb out of the ravine and walk to safety. As they neared the area where her Jeep had entered the river, Hope noticed a shadowy figure sitting on the bank. She froze in her tracks.

The man must have sensed her presence, because he lifted his head. "Hope?"

It was Sam.

He lumbered to his feet and strode forward, wiping his eyes. His clothes were soaked, like theirs. Looking back and forth between them, he blinked several times, as if he couldn't believe they were real. "You're alive," he said, gripping her upper arms. With a strangled laugh, he embraced her, and then Owen. "You're both alive!"

She realized that his clothes were wet because he'd searched the wreckage. Her Jeep must have been visible downriver. As she pictured him diving beneath the surface and swimming through the empty cab, she started to shiver uncontrollably. He'd risked his life to attempt a rescue that would never have been successful.

Had he been…crying?

He's in love with you, Faith had said. Hope still wasn't convinced, but his repeated, superhuman efforts to save her felt good.

"I thought the river had swept you away," he said, his voice hoarse. "I thought you were dead."

With a sudden rush of clarity, she understood why she'd been avoiding his calls. It wasn't her fear of falling in love with him. That was a fait accompli. She was afraid of *losing* him. She hadn't allowed herself to get attached to a man since she'd given up Grace.

"I'm fine," she said, her heart racing. "Owen needs to get to a hospital."

"What happened?"

She gave Sam the abbreviated version, glancing toward the top of the cliff. There were multiple flashing lights now, indicating that patrol cars had descended on the scene. The trees and shrubs along the riverbank made excellent cover, but they couldn't linger here for long without being discovered.

Sam's euphoria at finding her in one piece disappeared. Anger flared in his eyes, masking his other emotions. "You broke into Kruger's cabin?"

"I used a key," she mumbled.

"What did you find?"

She told him.

"You took photos of a toilet and muddy boots," he said in a flat tone. "That's the evidence you almost died for?"

Hope fell silent, not bothering to mention the photos were gone.

He turned his wrath on Owen. "You thought this was a good idea?"

"Not…really," Owen said, wincing.

"Why did you call him instead of me?"

"I didn't call him," she said. "And you wouldn't have gone along with it."

"Exactly!"

Hope stomped past him. "Let's continue this conversation at the hospital. I don't know about you, but I'm freezing my ass off."

"You're lucky your ass isn't scattered across the cliff," he said, following her. "What if you'd been killed? What if Owen had been killed?"

She clamped her mouth shut, skirting around a tree. His free-solo habit was more dangerous than anything she'd ever done, but they'd discussed that already. She didn't think it was fair for him to criticize.

Before they reached the bridge, Hope paused, seeing more lights in the distance. "Did you call 911?"

"Of course."

"They're here."

"Good."

For once, she wasn't glad help had arrived. Ambulances came with squad cars, and she didn't trust anyone in law enforcement. Meeks could be waiting, ready to take her for a ride. She moistened her lips, glancing across the river. There was a forest service road on the other side of the Kern. Maybe they should make a quick escape.

"Sam," a man shouted in the distance. "Sam, are you there?"

It was Dixon.

Although they were in the sheriff's jurisdiction, it wasn't unusual for NPS to respond to the scene. Rangers often took emergency calls outside park limits, and the accident involved three of its employees.

Dixon's presence wasn't suspicious, but she didn't trust him. He had ties to the drug smugglers. They'd held Faith in his cabin. Kruger was his brother-in-law. The facts added up, and not in his favor.

She started to backtrack, her pulse racing. Her shoulders met the hard wall of Sam's chest.

"What should we do?" he asked in a whisper.

"Go on. Tell him you couldn't find us."

He shook his head fiercely. "We stay together."

There was no time to argue, so she took him by the hand and went the opposite direction. His reluctance to leave them made her heart swell with emotion. She didn't know if his feelings were real, or fueled by adrenaline. They'd battled several life-or-death situations together. Would he lose interest once the smoke cleared?

Hope didn't want to think about that—and they had to survive first. Avoiding Dixon and the rescue crew meant crossing the river again.

None of them wanted to take another swim, but they didn't have much choice. Teeth chattering, she waded into the current with Sam and Owen. When they reached the other side, she was chilled to the bone. Dripping wet, they climbed the embankment to the dark, deserted forest service road.

"Where does this go?" Sam asked, glancing to the right.

"Terminus Dam. It follows the river for a stretch and then winds around uphill."

They started walking. Going the other way would take them right back to Dixon.

At least the hike would keep their blood pumping and prevent hypothermia.

After about a mile, they stopped to rest at a lookout point. Sam's cell phone wasn't working. Hope couldn't see much through the trees lining the ravine, but lights from emergency vehicles were still visible near the bridge on Kern Road. An accident crew was working the scene at the top of the cliff. They'd need a crane to bring up the remains of Kruger's truck.

Her sweatshirt made a wet, uncomfortable sling for Owen. She took it off and Sam used his utility knife to cut the fabric into long strips. As she bandaged the wound, she noticed a cut on Sam's hand.

"Let me see that," she said, grasping his wrist.

He turned his palm up, showing a deep laceration. "Your Jeep bit me."

When she was done fixing up Owen, she wrapped a strip of fabric around Sam's hand, tying it over his knuckles.

"How's your sister?"

"Better," she said, glancing up at him. "She rested most of the weekend. Had a few nightmares."

His eyes glinted in the dark. "You avoided my calls."

"I didn't know what to say," she admitted. The thought of confessing her feelings to him scared her more than their current predicament. Maybe they could keep running away from their troubles…together.

While she pondered that, a vehicle turned on the forest service road and started heading uphill. "Hide!"

They scurried behind some prickly manzanita bushes and crouched down, waiting for the vehicle to pass.

"Your sweatshirt," Sam whispered.

They'd left the torn remains on the side of the road, and there was no time to retrieve it. She stayed put, praying the mistake would go unnoticed. An old Chevy pickup chugged around the corner, going slow. Searching.

"It's Morgenstern," she said.

"Should we run?"

She hesitated. The park volunteer might spot the motion and call for reinforcements. Maybe if they stayed still he wouldn't see them.

The pickup rolled past the sweatshirt and stopped, shifting into Reverse. So much for not getting caught. He took out a flashlight and pointed it at the wet bundle. She had to take action before he communicated this find to NPS. Morgenstern was a loose cannon, but he hated Kruger and Dixon. He might help them just to be contrary.

She scrambled out from behind the bushes. "Over here!"

Morgenstern moved the beam of light to her face. "Banning?"

She squinted, shielding her eyes with one hand. Sam and Owen rose up behind her. "We need a ride to the hospital."

"They're dredging the river for your Jeep."

"Can you help us?"

He harrumphed an agreement, motioning with the flashlight. "Get in."

There wasn't room in the front seat for all of them, so Sam climbed into the bed of the pickup. Hope sat in the middle, between Morgenstern and Owen. The truck smelled like sweat and menthol cream.

"Take the long way," she said.

He stepped on the gas, heading uphill. The road passed by Terminus Dam and circled back toward Visalia, where the nearest hospital was located. Morgenstern didn't argue with her about the route or ask any questions. Although he was a brooding, taciturn sort of fellow, his lack of curiosity struck her as…curious.

"How did you know we were out here?"

"I didn't," he said.

"You were just driving by?"

Morgenstern frowned, his uneven mustache covering his entire upper lip. "No. I heard about the accident on my radio."

As a volunteer, he wasn't supposed to have a radio among his personal belongings. She didn't see one inside the truck, either. While she looked around for it, puzzled, he picked up speed, traveling a little too fast around the curves.

Something wasn't right.

She glanced at Owen, who appeared tense and pale beside her. Morgenstern gripped the wheel with hairy knuckles. For a man in his sixties, he was in pretty good shape. He was tall and knobby, carrying no extra weight.

"Where's your radio?" she asked.

"I must have left it in the trailer."

"Do you have a cell phone?"

"Nope. Things cause cancer."

Although it sounded like a typical Morgenstern state-ment, cranky and cynical, she knew he was lying. She'd seen a cell phone in his trailer just a few days ago. He'd put his bologna sandwich right next to it.

Why would he tell her he didn't have any commu-nication devices? There was only one reason she could think of.

He didn't want her to call for help.

Judging by his increasingly reckless driving, Mor-genstern was aware of her suspicions. He took the turns at full speed, his tires kicking up gravel, slipping on the soft shoulder. Sam was getting the ride of his life in the back. He banged on the rear window in an unsuccessful attempt to get Morgenstern to slow down.

"You couldn't leave well enough alone," he growled. "You had to poke around in everybody's business."

Hope gripped the dash with one hand, bracing herself for a crash. Owen also assumed a defensive posture. He looked ready to protect her from Morgenstern's blows. "You were in on it with Kruger?"

"Your whore sister wasn't even hurt."

She wanted to punch him for badmouthing Faith. "Why would you get involved in this? You hated Kru-ger."

"I hate Dixon more. We had that in common."

Morgenstern's animosity wasn't difficult to under-stand. Dixon had been in the unenviable position of laying off the "less productive" employees when the recession hit. Morgenstern and his wife were among the first to go.

She didn't know why Kruger resented his brother-in-law. Dixon had given him an honest job and a decent home. Instead of appreciating those generous gifts, Kruger found a way to exploit the situation further.

One thing was clear: these men had conspired *against* Dixon, not with him. Hope had run away from the wrong man—and jumped right into the enemy's truck.

"It's over now," she said, her stomach clenched. "They'll investigate and connect you to Kruger. The evidence at the cabin…" She trailed off, aware that Kruger's boots and toilet tank wouldn't raise any eyebrows. Not without a statement from her or Faith.

Morgenstern concentrated on the road, his face a cold mask. They'd arrive at the dam in moments.

Terminus Dam was on the opposite side of Moraine Lake, built along the edge of a very sheer cliff. It was a long way down to the bottom. Hope's breath quickened as she pictured their bloody corpses at the base of the spillway. When the river water poured in, which happened at regular intervals, their bodies would be swept clear.

She turned to Owen, her pulse racing. "Jump out on the next turn," she said in his ear. "I'll be right behind you."

He nodded in agreement.

Morgenstern put the pedal to the metal, as if anticipating their actions. When they spun around the curve, Owen opened the door and tumbled out. He timed the escape perfectly, rolling clear of the tires. Hope scooted across the seat, eager to follow. Morgenstern grabbed her by the hair and yanked her back. Pain seared her scalp.

She balled her hand into a fist, blinking the tears from her eyes.

CHAPTER TWENTY-THREE

SAM KNEW THEY were in trouble when Morgenstern's driving became erratic.

One minute he was sitting in the back of the pickup, cold and uncomfortable, teeth rattling with every bump in the road. The next he was flying across the rusted metal flatbed, slamming into the wheel well.

When he regained his bearings, he crawled toward the rear window and pounded on it. He wanted Hope to slide the divider open, but she didn't even glance over her shoulder. She kept her attention on Morgenstern, her lips moving as she spoke. They appeared to be having a serious conversation.

For the next few minutes, Sam concentrated on staying in the back of the truck. He was thrown up in the air, jolted sideways and almost knocked out. After he found a haul hook to grab on to, he gripped it like a pommel and held tight.

Owen fell out of the passenger side and rolled down a gravel embankment, landing free of the spinning tires.

Holy shit!

Sam searched the interior for Hope. It was hard to see clearly while the truck was bouncing up and down on the dirt road. When he caught sight of Morgenstern's fist in her hair, Sam's vision went red.

Mother. *Fucker.*

Hope was under attack, and he couldn't help her. The passenger door was still open, banging in the wind as the truck flew around corners. It didn't seem possible to climb into the cab that way. Sam wanted to bust through the rear window, but he didn't have a blunt object. Morgenstern's window was closed.

While he watched, powerless, Hope fought like a wildcat. She punched Morgenstern in the nose and clawed his face. He hollered a protest and extended his arm, holding her at a distance. She continued to struggle, pummeling his shoulder.

Sam had to get inside the vehicle through the open passenger door. It was his only option. The road straightened, making it easier for him to stay upright in the back of the truck. His stomach plummeted as he looked ahead. They were almost at the top of the dam. Morgenstern might drive the truck right over the edge.

At this speed, the guardrail wouldn't stop them.

He gripped the doorjamb with one hand and climbed over the side, stretching out his right leg until his foot touched the passenger seat. Swallowing hard, he glanced at the road again, judging the number of seconds before they were airborne.

Less than ten.

No time to hesitate. He lifted his other foot from the bed of the truck and shifted his weight forward, straining toward the interior. Morgenstern swerved back and forth, trying to shake him off. Sam almost couldn't hang on. The open door banged against his ribs, causing a sharp pain. He clung to the jamb, half in, half out.

Morgenstern's attempt to dislodge him didn't work, but he'd robbed Sam of any opportunity to get inside and take control of the vehicle. They'd be sailing into space in five seconds.

Four.

Three.

Hope reached for the transmission lever, her fingers splayed wide. At the last possible moment, she gripped the lever and dropped the truck into Neutral. Morgenstern cranked the wheel to the left and slammed on the brakes, cursing. The truck came to a hard stop against the guardrail, its passenger side parallel with the edge. Sam flew backward, into the precipice. He collided with the hanging passenger door and managed to hook his arm through the open window. That arm saved him.

His legs dangled above a deadly drop. A piece of groaning metal was the only thing between him and the spillway several hundred feet below.

"Sam!"

Forcing his legs not to scissor wildly, he glanced at Hope. Morgenstern was dragging her out the driver's-side door. While Sam fought for his life, she fought for hers. Punching and kicking, she made a valiant effort to break free.

The door wouldn't hold forever. A pin popped loose from the hinge, dropping him down a few inches. His stomach plunged all the way to the bottom. Taking a deep breath, he swung his legs toward the guardrail, hooking one foot under the lip. The climbing maneuver worked. Once braced, he pulled his body closer to the truck, stretching out his arm to reach the doorjamb. He hauled himself upward, into the cab.

Sam scrambled across the seat and stumbled out the

other side, looking for Hope. Morgenstern was standing at the edge of the dam.

With a gun to her head.

Although he was on terra firma now, Sam felt dizzy. He'd reached his breaking point. If they survived this, he'd never court death again. He'd never free-solo. He wanted a different life. A quiet life. Any kind of life, as long as it involved Hope.

He was in love with her.

Jesus.

What a moment to realize the extent of his feelings. He was paralyzed with the fear that he wouldn't get the chance to tell her. She might die here, on this very spot, never knowing how much he cared.

Trying not to panic, he inched closer. "What do you want?"

Morgenstern ground the barrel of the gun against Hope's temple until a whimper escaped her lips.

Sam forced himself not to react. "If it's money, I have millions."

The offer seemed to enrage Morgenstern. He tightened his grip on Hope's hair, his eyes burning with fury. Sam didn't know if he planned to kill them and himself, or just them. He'd almost driven off the cliff.

He was clearly capable of pulling the trigger.

Morgenstern kept his gaze on Sam. "When I was young, all of the rangers were men. Then bitches like this one came along to ruin everything." He shook Hope for emphasis. "Demanding equal pay. Taking jobs they couldn't handle."

Sam thought Hope handled herself as well as, if not

better than, her male counterparts. She was brave and dedicated to a fault.

"My wife worked as a park secretary for twenty-seven years," he continued. "She never complained, never showed up late, never called in sick a single day. She got cancer the year she was laid off. Six months later, I was forced into early retirement because of a bad knee. We couldn't afford treatment."

"I'm sorry," Hope said. "Please, don't—"

"Hush up," he said. "I needed thirty thousand dollars for Maureen's chemotherapy. Insurance wouldn't cover the costs. It might as well have been thirty million. When I asked Dixon for my job back, he refused."

"Why not shoot him, then?" Sam asked.

"If he was here, I would."

"Hurting an innocent woman won't change anything."

"It'll get his attention. Maybe get him fired. Kruger and I were running marijuana right under his nose. He's a disgrace."

"If you really want attention, shoot me," Sam said. "I'm a fucking icon around here. Nobody cares about Hope."

"Don't shoot him," Hope said shrilly. "He's suicidal. He'll enjoy it!"

"I'm not suicidal. She's lying."

"I'll shoot you both," Morgenstern warned.

"I liked Maureen," Hope said.

"You're not fit to say her name!"

"She supported the female rangers, Alan. She was a good person. Don't sully her memory this way."

"Let Hope go," Sam begged. "Take me."

Hope's face crumpled with sadness. Sam felt a matching pressure behind his eyes. He didn't want to die. Not anymore. He wanted to grow old with Hope, but he'd give his life for her in a heartbeat.

Morgenstern wavered, looking back and forth between them. He might be a sexist, disgruntled madman, but he'd loved his wife. Her death had driven him crazy. Sam knew how that felt.

"Don't kill an innocent woman," Sam said. "Think of your wife."

The volunteer glanced over the edge of the dam, considering. Lights flashed across the wide expanse. Two squad cars were approaching from the opposite side. They'd arrive on the scene in minutes.

Sam exchanged a glance with Hope, his body humming with tension. More deputies might cause Morgenstern to do something rash. Sam stepped forward with caution, praying he could save Hope.

"Stay back!" Morgenstern shouted.

Sam went still.

"I only wanted justice for Maureen," he said in a strangled voice. "I only wanted my due for a lifetime of service."

Hope stared at Sam, her expression taut. If Morgenstern was going to shoot, he had to shoot now. The squad cars were almost upon them.

Making a tortured sound, Morgenstern shoved Hope forward and leaped over the guardrail. He fired three times in rapid succession, aiming at the sky. It was a startling rebellion, cut short when his body hit the ground below.

Sam rushed toward Hope, drawing her slack form

into his arms. She was in shock, her shoulders trembling.

"Are you hurt?" he asked, studying her face.

"No."

He cupped his hand around her neck and brought her head to his chest, tears of relief spilling from his eyes. Even if she had cuts and bruises and broken bones, he was overwhelmed with happiness.

Because she was alive.

HOPE DIDN'T STOP shaking until they got to the hospital.

The heater in the squad car was on full blast, and she had a safety blanket wrapped around her, but she couldn't seem to get warm. When they arrived at the emergency room, she was treated for mild hypothermia. A nurse gave her a gown to wear while her clothes were laundered. As soon as she was dry, she felt better.

Sam needed five stitches in his palm. Hope returned to his side during the procedure, offering her emotional support.

"Looks like you've got a new lifeline," the doctor joked.

Hope met Sam's gaze, startled by the words. "I think you're right," he said, squeezing her hand.

After a few hours, their clothes were returned and they were free to go. They went to check on Owen, who was being prepped for surgery.

His injuries were more extensive than she'd realized. The dive he'd taken out of Morgenstern's truck hadn't helped. His bite wounds went down to the bone, and he had a torn ligament in his elbow. An orthopedist had been called in to repair it.

Hope had spoken to Dixon and the sheriff at the top of the dam. She'd explained her impulsive search of the cabin and the resulting car chase. Dixon had seemed insulted that she'd suspected him of drug smuggling, but he didn't scold her. The fact that he'd been oblivious of his brother-in-law's criminal activities wouldn't sit well with the park superintendent. Instead of riding her ass, Dixon needed to cover his own. Special Agent Ling was coming in tomorrow to oversee a park-wide investigation.

They found Owen in a bed near the operating room. He looked a bit woozy, as if he'd been given morphine. Sam reached across to shake his good hand, holding it for a moment. "Playing the hero again, I see."

Owen glanced at Hope questioningly.

"Hope told me you pulled her out of the Jeep," Sam said. "Pretty hard to do with a messed-up arm."

"It didn't hurt at the time. Adrenaline kicked in."

"I'm sure it hurts now."

"It's not that bad," Owen said.

Hope leaned over to kiss his forehead. "Thank you, all the same."

Flushing, he mumbled an acceptance.

"Is there anyone you want me to call?" Sam asked.

"No."

"What about your mom?"

"She'll just worry."

Sam frowned in concern. "Have you talked to Penny?"

"Not since the wedding."

"I bet she'd like to hear from you."

His scowl wasn't difficult to interpret. He wanted Sam to drop the subject.

"Who's going to take care of you after the surgery?" Hope asked. "You can't recover in that closet."

"He can stay with us," Sam said.

"With us?"

"At my house."

Although it was a good idea for safety reasons, she hadn't made any arrangements to go home with him. It was sneaky of him to secure her agreement this way. "We'll be here when you wake up from the anesthesia," she promised Owen.

After he was wheeled away by a nurse, Hope and Sam had breakfast in the cafeteria. "Who's Penny?" she asked, spreading jam on an English muffin.

Sam took out his cell phone, which had gotten wet earlier. He'd dismantled it to dry the components and now it was working again. After scrolling through a collection of photos, he handed the phone to her. "This is Penny."

Hope saw a beautiful young woman with long, dark hair and a dazzling smile. Her simple flowered dress might have looked demure on a less spectacular figure. There was an adorable toddler in her arms. "Wow."

Sam smiled, sipping his coffee.

"Is that her son?"

"Yes."

"Where was this taken?"

"At a wedding."

"Whose wedding?"

"Lauren and Garrett's. We all met during the San Diego earthquake."

Hope scrolled down to a picture of Owen standing beside them, tall and handsome in an ill-fitting suit.

Borrowed from Sam, perhaps. She studied the little boy with interest. He had dark eyes like his mother, but his hair was tawny brown. "Is Owen the father?"

Sam almost choked on his coffee. "No."

"They look like a family."

He nodded thoughtfully. "He saved them."

"Is she single?"

"I think so."

"And he likes her?"

"Sure."

"Does she like him?"

"As friends, yes."

"Nothing more?"

"I don't know," he said, shrugging. "She might go out with him. I doubt he'd ask her."

"Why not?"

"He...doesn't have a very high opinion of himself."

Hope wondered how a boy who'd been in prison, and was covered in racist tattoos, could drum up the nerve to ask any girl on a date. "What if she said yes?"

"Her father is Jorge Sandoval. Former mayor of L.A. Current governor of California."

"No," she breathed.

"He'd disown her."

She glanced through the set of photos, troubled. The bride and groom made a very attractive couple. Sam wasn't in any of the pictures. Most were taken from a distance. "When was the wedding?"

"Six months ago. Just before Christmas."

With a frown, she closed the images. "Do you mind if I call my sister?"

"Go right ahead."

She sent Faith a quick text and handed the phone back to him. Suddenly her raspberry jam looked unappetizing. Disturbing thoughts floated through her mind. Owen's mangled arm, the dog's pitiful yelp, Kruger's death grimace.

"You should eat," Sam said, putting his phone in his pocket.

"I can't."

He took her plate away and came back with plain yogurt. She managed to eat a little, and drink some tea. Although he prompted gently, she didn't want more. They returned to the lobby after breakfast. When he put his arm around her, she curled up beside him.

"I shot a dog," she said.

"You did?"

She told him a longer version of the story, letting it pour out of her like a sickness. "If I hadn't gone to search the cabin, Kruger and Morgenstern would still be alive."

"Don't think that way," he said, kissing the top of her head. "Your intentions were good. Theirs weren't."

As she snuggled closer, it occurred to her that they'd hooked up a week before Christmas, around the same time as the wedding he'd attended. "The night we met... was that before or after the wedding?"

"Directly after. I flew in from San Diego and went straight to the bar."

"Why?"

"The ceremony reminded me of Melissa."

No wonder he'd been drowning his sorrows. "Did you anticipate that?"

"Of course. I didn't even want to go, but it meant a lot to Lauren. She took care of me when I was in a coma."

"Do I look like her?" she asked, her throat tight.

"Melissa, you mean?"

She nodded against his chest.

"No."

"That's not the reason…"

He framed her face with one hand, meeting her eyes. "The first time I saw you, I felt this shift inside me, like a crack in ice. Being with you chipped away at the misery I'd built up, and that scared me. I was afraid I'd have nothing left without it."

Hope couldn't hold her emotions inside any longer. Instead of trying, she clung to his neck and cried.

CHAPTER TWENTY-FOUR

THE EARLY MORNING hours passed in a blur.

Special Agent Ling stopped by the hospital to interview Hope and give her an update on the investigation.

Deputy Phillip Meeks had disappeared in the middle of his shift. The sheriff went to question Meeks about his possible involvement, and caught him in the process of transporting a quarter million dollars' worth of stolen drugs from his apartment to his car. The deputy confessed to everything.

Meeks and Kruger had been working with a local grower. During the summer months they distributed large amounts of marijuana to a member of the Gonzales cartel, who flew it to Las Vegas. According to Meeks, it was Kruger's idea to go after the stash. Meeks had taken the investigators on a wild-goose chase to buy time, and his actions served a dual purpose of leading Gonzales's men off track.

Meeks claimed that he didn't know about Faith's kidnapping. He said he'd never met the grower or worked with any cartel members. Kruger handled both ends of the business. Meeks was just a hired badge, paid to keep the heat off.

Rescue workers had found Hector Gonzales's body in the Kern River last night, wrapped up with a rug Dixon recognized from his cabin. It was suspected that Bill

Kruger had killed him. With both Kruger and Morgenstern gone, they might never know.

Hope was confident that Special Agent Ling would weed out any remaining corruption in the park. Ling vowed to put the staff under a microscope. She wasn't going to let anyone sweep this scandal under the rug.

Owen's surgery had gone off without a hitch. When he was a little more alert, they could take him home.

Hope learned that Owen's surgeon had also worked on Caleb Renfro, the whitewater rafter who'd been shot twice in a valiant attempt to rescue Faith. While they waited for Owen, she decided to say hello. Sam accompanied her.

Caleb was lounging in a narrow bed, his cast elevated. He looked like many of the young men she saw in the park, long-haired and handsome in a surfer-dude kind of way. A friend of his, probably Ted Harvey, sat in a chair at his bedside. They were watching a crocodile eat a zebra on *Animal Planet.*

"Holy shit," Caleb said, turning off the television. "You're Sam Rutherford."

With a tight smile, Sam came forward and shook his hand.

"I'm Ted," his friend said, equally excited. "Stoked to meet you."

After a moment of gazing at Sam in adoration, Caleb finally noticed Hope. "You must be Faith's sister."

"How did you know?"

"You look alike."

They exchanged a few words about Faith, and Caleb launched into a graphic description of the bolts and pins in his broken leg. The doctor said he'd run again, but with a slight limp. He gushed about rock climbing and whitewater kayaking for the next twenty minutes. Caleb's voice was animated, his gestures wild.

When Sam gave Hope a pointed glance, she stepped in to save him. "Thank you both so much for helping Faith. I don't know what I can do to repay you."

The young men puffed up at the praise.

"If there's anything you need, let me know."

"I need something," Caleb said.

"What?"

"A date with your sister."

Hope rubbed her eyes, trying not to laugh at the request. Faith broke all the boys' hearts. "I'll put in a good word for you."

"Is she on Facebook?"

"Yes."

"Are you?"

She didn't know what to say. Maybe Caleb considered her an acceptable alternative. She had to admire the audacity of a college kid with a broken leg trying to hook up with two sisters at the same time.

"She's with me," Sam said, touching the small of her back. "Take care, you guys."

As soon as they left the hospital room, Hope started giggling. She wasn't sure if it was brought on by stress, or relief, but Sam joined in, laughing along with her. The humor had a hysterical edge. Soon she was close to tears again.

She took a deep breath to calm down. "Were you like that at his age?"

"Cocky, you mean? Only on the rock face."

"Not with girls?"

"No."

"I suppose they chased after you."

He shrugged, putting his hands in his pockets. Despite his status as a local icon, he wasn't comfortable with fan worship. He hadn't talked about himself much the night they met. She couldn't imagine him using his celebrity status to pick up women.

Owen was released from the hospital at midmorning, his legs a bit wobbly and his arm in a sling. He was instructed to rest for the remainder of the day. Sam said he could stay at his house while his arm healed.

She still hadn't agreed to Sam's plan, whatever it was. Did he expect her to spend a few nights with him, or move in? They needed to talk, and Hope wasn't sure their fledgling relationship would survive a heart-to-heart. They had passion and chemistry and near-death experiences in common, but did they have staying power?

Faith told her to stop running away from her emotions and let Sam catch her. Although she longed to take that advice, her feelings for Sam didn't change the fact that he wasn't good boyfriend material. She wanted to settle down. She wanted a family. Only a fool would choose a free-solo climber with amnesia to father a child.

As Sam drove home, her anxiety grew and grew. Maybe she'd made an epic mistake by falling in love with him. Sam was a man on the edge. His touch thrilled her, and she'd never be bored with him, but he wasn't a steady guy.

Owen dozed off during the trip, and he was kind of loopy from pain medication. Sam helped him inside the house. He stretched out on the living room couch, eyes closed. When Sam brought him a pillow and a blanket, he murmured thanks.

"Let me know if you need anything else," Sam said, giving him an affectionate cuff on the neck.

"I'm glad you got your memory back."

Hope glanced at Sam, startled. Why would Owen say that?

"Me, too," Sam said, clearing his throat. When he met her gaze, her stomach fluttered with trepidation.

He had some explaining to do.

Sam didn't want to talk about his amnesia.

He hadn't been able to find the right moment to explain it, and now he was in a predicament. Hope looked upset, as if she might bolt at any moment. He felt her slipping away from him, and he was desperate to hold on.

"Let's go in the kitchen."

She followed him, crossing her arms over her chest. "You recovered your memory?"

"Yes."

"When?"

"The day I followed you to Mist Falls. I got hit in the head with a rock. I must have been unconscious for a few minutes before Owen pulled me out of the river. When I came to, my memory was back."

"Why didn't you tell me?"

"I haven't had the opportunity," he said, incredulous. "You wouldn't return my calls, remember?"

"What about the other night?"

"Your sister was missing, and you were exhausted."

"Not that exhausted."

He felt a twinge of guilt, as if he'd taken advantage of her. Faith's kidnapping had left her in a vulnerable state. Maybe he'd been a little too eager, or a little too rough. He probably shouldn't have touched her at all.

She placed a hand over the center of her chest, her eyes flashing with hurt. "I can't believe you kept this from me. I opened up to you about my daughter, but you couldn't tell me you'd recovered your memory?"

"You were upset. I was trying to comfort you."

"You comforted me, all right."

He didn't like the insinuation that he'd used her for sex. "I think you're forgetting something important."

"What?"

"I gave you exactly what you asked for in that hotel room. You didn't want to talk. You begged me to touch you."

She flushed, glancing away.

"It also wasn't the right time," he said, softening his tone. "You were hurting. I just wanted to be there for you."

"Don't pretend the choice wasn't self-serving," she said. "It's easier for you to express yourself physically than emotionally."

He was stunned by her insight. "You're right," he said, nodding. And getting defensive about it wouldn't help win her over. "That night, I asked you to give me another chance to listen. Do you remember?"

Her mouth twisted. "Yes."

"I'm not as good at talking, but if you'll give me another chance at that, I'll try." He sat down at the kitchen table, his heart pounding.

She took a seat across from him, ready to hear him out.

"We've been on shaky ground since the beginning, and that's my fault. I wanted to make it up to you, to show you I could be good to you. I probably would have told you in the morning, but you left without saying goodbye."

"Don't you know why?"

He swallowed hard. "No."

"I thought you'd mistake me for Melissa again."

Sam groaned at the realization that he'd been a fool. He'd screwed everything up—again. His deplorable behavior had doomed their relationship from the start. "I'm sorry," he said.

She nodded, seeming to accept his apology.

"For the past two years, I've been obsessed with recovering my memory. I was desperate to know how she'd died. But as soon as I remembered, it didn't seem important anymore. The only thing I cared about was you."

Her brows drew together. "Will you tell me what happened?"

He took a deep breath, unsure where to begin. "The months leading up to the accident were good. We didn't fight any more or less than usual. She was planning the wedding without much input from me. We were... happy."

She waited for him to continue.

"The morning of the climb was the same as any other. I didn't have nightmares or feelings of foreboding. Our gear was in excellent condition. The weather was perfect." He stared at the surface of the table, unable to come up with a single incongruent detail. "There are times when I've had misgivings, but kept climbing anyway. This wasn't one of them. I had no indication that anything would go wrong."

"What did?"

"We were almost to the summit when a rock fell. I don't know what dislodged it, because there weren't any climbers above us. I heard it coming and shouted a warning to Melissa. She couldn't get out of the way."

"Was she wearing a helmet?"

"Yes. She always did. In this case, it didn't matter. The impact broke her neck."

Her eyes filled with tears. "Oh, Sam."

He glanced away, struggling with his own emotions. "She fell about twenty feet before her rope caught. I was in the lead, so I rappelled down to her. I couldn't accept the fact that she was dead."

"What did you do?"

"I put her on my back, as if she was just injured, and continued up."

She covered her mouth with one hand, her face crumpling. He'd been a madman that day. Instead of belaying Melissa's body to the ground, he'd taken her to the summit. The "rescue" had required superhuman effort.

"When I reached the top, I was delirious. I found some other climbers and demanded an emergency helicopter. They didn't speak English, and I was out of my mind. Two men had to hold me down while medics examined her body. Of course they didn't call for a helicopter. They lowered her to the ground like a haul sack."

"I'm so sorry," she choked.

He fell silent until he trusted his voice again. "The good news is that I remember the grieving process. I'm going through it all over again, but it's easier now. I have a foundation to build on, instead of a black hole."

She wiped her cheeks, sniffling. He didn't have any tissues handy, so he offered her a paper towel. "Thanks," she said.

He shifted in his seat, uncomfortable. Melissa's story wasn't easy to tell, and sharing it hadn't made him feel better. But he recognized the importance of communicating with Hope, even when it hurt.

"Have you spoken to a doctor?" she asked.

"Yes. The neurologist wants me to get another CT scan. He said a second blow to the head was more likely to kill me than cure me."

"What about the psychologist?"

"I need to make an appointment with him, too." The idea of returning to therapy didn't terrify him as much as it used to. "There's something else I should tell you."

She twisted the paper towel in her hands. "What?"

"I have a theory about my amnesia. Maybe I had an emotional block that prevented me from recovering sooner. I wasn't ready to deal with it. Before you came along, that memory of Melissa would have destroyed me. It still hurts, but I'm stronger now. I have a reason to live, a reason to get better."

Her eyes filled with tears again.

"The reason is you, Hope. I'm in love with you."

She rose from the table and crossed the kitchen, putting distance between them. He wasn't the only one who avoided deep, unsettling emotions. Hope also had the habit of running away from her issues. This confession might scare her off for good, but he had to put himself out there and take that risk. He'd do anything to win her heart. If he failed, it wouldn't be because he hadn't tried hard enough.

He was willing to grovel.

"You're in love with danger," she said.

"No. That's never been true. I've always enjoyed a challenge, but risking my life isn't part of the draw."

"No one who free-solos can say that with a straight face."

"I'm done with free-soloing."

"You have a head injury."

"I'm thinking clearly."

"We almost died a bunch of times. It's only natural that you'd mistake relief and excitement for…stronger feelings."

He didn't know how to convince her that his love was real. She made a reasonable argument. Before she'd walked into his life, he hadn't given a damn about anything. He'd buried his emotions for too long. She'd been his catalyst for change, but he couldn't blame her for doubting him. More important, he couldn't expect her to love him back. She might not feel the same connection he did. Ever.

He stood, trying not to panic. "I understand if you're not ready to get serious. We can take things slow."

"How slow?"

"I want you to be my girlfriend, but I'd settle for going out on a date."

She hesitated, her fingertips sliding along the edge of the countertop. "Are you still interested in having children?"

"Yes."

"When?"

"Anytime."

Her gaze met his, searching. "Faith's been keeping a box of pictures of my daughter. They named her Grace."

His throat tightened. "That's…pretty."

"She knows she's adopted. Her parents are going to let her contact me, maybe next year, if she wants to."

He stepped closer, cupping his hand around her chin.

"I'm worried that she'll hate me," she said, her mouth trembling.

"She won't hate you."

"How can I start a family, after giving her up? She'll think I didn't love her enough."

"You were seventeen. She'll understand."

"I'm so jealous of her adoptive parents, I could die."

Sam slipped his arms around her, and she rested her head on his shoulder for a few minutes, crying softly. The fact that she accepted his comfort was encouraging. Little by little, she was letting him in.

When her tears quieted, she moved away from him, wiping her cheeks. "You're really done with free-soloing?"

"Yes."

"Why?"

"I want to grow old with you."

She laughed, as if he was joking. "What will you do for a living?"

The question took him by surprise. He'd been free-loading off his own wealth for the past two years, and he could do that indefinitely. "I've been invited to develop another video game. Rock climbing for Wii."

"Is that fun?"

"Yes, actually. It's creative, and the pay is unreal. I

could feed a third-world country with the money they throw at me."

"Where would you work?"

"From home."

Her mouth pursed in contemplation. He doubted she was worried about his finances. She was skeptical about his life skills, which had been sorely lacking. In order to earn her trust, he had to prove he could be stable.

Sam realized that the transition from brain-damaged nomad to caring boyfriend wouldn't be easy. He had to put effort into building a relationship with Hope. Recovering his memory hadn't solved anything. Clarity wasn't a miracle cure or a magic panacea. It was a starting point. He felt as though he'd been trapped in a fog on a mountaintop. He'd already reached the summit, and now he had to find his way back.

But, as all climbers knew, the descent could be treacherous. It offered infinite opportunities to stumble.

"Will you quit climbing, if the doctors tell you to?"

Sam couldn't imagine leaving the sport. Not at his age. Another bump on the head might do him in, but as long as he had the mental and physical strength, he'd climb. It was who he was. "No. I won't quit."

The look in her eyes said that he was an idiot. An honest idiot, though. Her idiot. "What am I going to do with you?" she asked, lifting her hand to his cheek.

He could think of a few things.

But she looked troubled, and exhausted. He'd like to comfort her and help her sleep, but he didn't want to rush anything. This time, he wouldn't make the mistake of pouncing on her when she was vulnerable. She hadn't even agreed to a date. He could keep his hands to himself while she made up her mind.

"I should call my sister," she said.

He found his backup cell phone in a kitchen drawer and passed it to her. "You don't have to return it."

"Thanks."

She appeared to want some privacy, or maybe just an escape. "There's an extra bedroom upstairs. You can rest, take a shower, whatever."

"I could use a nap," she said, hesitant.

Instead of wrapping his arms around her and pulling her close, he stood still, leaving the decision up to her.

After a short pause, she slipped away.

CHAPTER TWENTY-FIVE

FAITH WENT BACK to work on Tuesday.

She was tired of moping around Charlie's apartment, feeling like a third wheel. He had a new boyfriend and they were all over each other. Normally she'd have found their antics adorable—or hot. But she was nursing a broken heart, wavering between paranoia and depression.

To be fair, Charlie had no idea she'd been kidnapped or assaulted, so he didn't realize she was traumatized. She couldn't bear to retell the painful story, so she said her apartment had been broken into. She'd asked to stay at his place while her security system was being installed. Shacking up with a female friend might have been a better choice, in hindsight. Charlie was fit and strong, and they worked at the same salon, so he made a convenient bodyguard. He was also one of her best friends. But he was a man, and she didn't think he'd understand what she was going through.

The day dragged on.

Late in the afternoon, a new customer walked in for a quick cleanup cut. Although Faith was available, she asked Charlie to take him.

Charlie pulled her aside. "What's wrong?"

"Nothing," she lied.

"That guy is straight."

"So what?" Faith knew as well as Charlie did that hetero men were often more comfortable with female stylists. She usually jumped at the chance to service them. "If he's homophobic he can fuck off."

"We need to talk," Charlie said, shaking his head.

Faith cleaned up her station while he did a short consultation. The client didn't seem uneasy, and Charlie handled him like a pro. When the guy gave Faith a curious glance, she flushed, embarrassed by her skittishness.

He was just a walk-in. Not an assassin.

After Charlie was finished with the cut, he returned to Faith's side. "He'd have given you a better tip."

"Maybe I should have taken him to the back room for a happy ending."

"That's not what I meant," Charlie said, frowning.

Tears pricked at her eyes. She blinked them away, frustrated. "I know. I'm just—upset. I left my round brush in my apartment."

"Do you want to go get it?"

"Yes."

"Okay. I'll take you over there after work."

Faith nodded, trying to pull herself together. Charlie was a good friend to put up with her psychotic behavior.

Minutes before closing time, another stranger walked in, and Faith couldn't foist this one off on any of her coworkers. It was Special Agent Ling. Hope had called to update her on the latest news, so Ling's appearance wasn't unexpected.

Just unwelcome.

Faith studied the woman's boxy trousers and uninspired ponytail. Her fingers itched to take down her glossy black hair and work some magic on it. Ling probably wouldn't appreciate the style suggestions. She seemed like a no-nonsense type, sort of militant-looking. Not an ideal candidate for a makeover.

"Can we speak privately?"

"Sure," she said, leading the agent to the esthetician's room. Ling skirted around the waxing pots, declining the invitation to sit. Her brows needed refining. Faith smothered the urge to offer her a Brazilian. "What's up?"

"Your sister told me you'd been in contact with Javier Del Norte."

"That's a lie," Faith said, rolling her eyes.

"He didn't speak to you the morning you were admitted to the hospital?"

She looked away, refusing to answer. In a moment of weakness, she'd searched translations online for the Spanish phrases he'd used.

Eres la única: you're the one.

Ojalá que nos econtremos otra vez: I hope we meet again.

Faith wouldn't share those private exchanges with Ling. Her last moments with Javier were special, and she didn't want to be pitied or criticized for cherishing them. She already knew she was a fool for falling for him.

The agent removed a few photos from her portfolio and passed them to her. "Do you recognize this man?"

It was Nick. They'd found some better shots of him. In one, he even looked handsome. Her stomach turned at the sight of his youthful smile. He'd stolen her peace of mind, and he was barely old enough to drink.

"We found video footage of him assaulting you."

She gave the photos back, her hands shaking. The thought of a group of federal agents watching those terrible moments, studying her like an insect, made her ill.

"If he raped you, why wouldn't you agree to a swab?"

"He didn't rape me, and a swab wouldn't have proven anything."

"It might have proved you had sexual contact with Del Norte."

She moistened her lips, nervous. "Who told you that?"

"Caleb Renfro. Evidence to corroborate his story was found at the campsite where you and Del Norte stayed overnight."

Faith couldn't deny it. She lifted her chin, refusing to be shamed.

"You're a beautiful woman, Miss Banning. Men like you. You like them."

Her eyes narrowed. "What are you saying, that I deserved it?"

"Maybe you consented to both encounters."

"No," she said with vehemence, insulted by the accusation. "I slept with Javier by choice. I didn't want what Nick did to me."

"What did he do?"

Faith realized she'd fallen into a trap, revealing the name of her attacker and confirming that he'd touched her against her will. "Nothing," she said, her throat closing up. "He did nothing."

"Did he penetrate you?"

"No. He just held me down and thrust against me."

Ling's expression softened. She believed her. "We can still prosecute him."

"For what?"

"Sexual assault and kidnapping."

Faith gave her a brittle smile. "I'm not willing to testify."

"If you're subpoenaed, you won't have a choice."

She prayed that Ling was bluffing. Surely the FBI had better cases to pursue. Nick had been acting on Gonzales's orders, not terrorizing her for kicks. He deserved to be locked up, but she didn't think he was a danger to other women. Javier said he wouldn't bother her again. Ling could find another victim to exploit.

Ling put the photos away. "We've identified him as Nick Kruger, son of Bill Kruger, the ranger your sister tangled with over the weekend. He worked for Hector Gonzales, former leader of a Las Vegas cartel."

"Former leader?"

"His body surfaced in the Kern River. He'd been shot."

Faith wasn't sorry to hear it.

"There's a rumor going around that Gonzales wanted to get rid of Del Norte. According to our informant, Gonzales thought Del Norte was sleeping with his wife. She was actually having an affair with Nick Kruger."

"Maybe Nick killed Gonzales," Faith said.

"Did you witness that?"

"No. It's just a guess."

"You could be right."

"Will he go after my sister?"

"I doubt it. His relationship with his father was strained, though they worked together. Bill Kruger was arrested for spousal abuse several times. Until recently, Nick lived with his mother in Las Vegas."

"What about Javier?"

Ling brought out several more photos from her portfolio. The first depicted a charred corpse in a plane. The second was Gonzales, his face swollen. Faith wrinkled her nose at the macabre shots.

"Your boyfriend is a killer."

"He's not my boyfriend," she said.

"There's no reason to lie for him. The pilot was burned beyond recognition. We don't know who shot Gonzales. Even if Del Norte murdered these men in cold blood, we can't prosecute with little or no evidence."

"Then why are you looking for him?"

"To offer our protection."

In exchange for information, Faith interpreted. They wanted to take down every man connected to the cartel.

"If he's still alive, he's in danger."

"You think he's dead?"

"It's only a matter of time. Gonzales's relatives will be gunning for him. Either I'll find him or they will, Miss Banning. Odds are on them, because Del Norte isn't my priority. He's a Venezuelan national. He'd probably be deported, rather than standing trial for drug trafficking."

Faith was chilled by her reasoning.

"Will you let me know if he tries to contact you again?"

She accepted another business card that she had no intention of using. "Where do you get your hair cut?"

"My aunt does it."

"The color and texture are great, but I know a style that would suit your face better."

Ling gave her an icy stare. "Maybe some other time."

After she left, Faith cleaned the mirror at her station, feeling surly. She worked in a salon because she enjoyed making women feel good. Sparring with Ling hadn't improved her day. She wasn't usually so sensitive about her fun-loving reputation.

Men liked her. Big deal.

Faith had never cared what anyone thought. That hadn't changed, but she saw *herself* differently now. The assault had stripped away her easy confidence and flirty style. Although Nick hadn't even penetrated her, he'd gotten inside.

She'd always been a social butterfly. Dressing up, going out and getting noticed were her favorite activities. She wasn't like Hope, who preferred trees and animals to human interactions. Faith thrived on male attention. It soothed and satisfied her.

She realized that the date rape had changed the way she related to men. Maybe she'd ramped up her sexuality as a defense mechanism, but she hadn't let the experience break her. She'd overcome this, too.

Faith knew what she needed to erase Nick's touch: another man. A positive sexual experience, chosen and controlled by her, would fix her right up. If she couldn't have Javier, she'd find someone else.

Charlie put his hand on her shoulder, startling her. "Are you ready?"

"Yes," she said, grabbing her purse. "Let's go out tonight."

JAVIER FOLLOWED FAITH home from the club.

Since he'd crawled out of the woods, and hitched a ride to L.A. in the back of a semi, he'd been keeping an eye on her. A cursory internet search at the local library had brought up her Facebook page and place of work. From there he'd found a copy of her hairdresser's license, which listed her home address.

If he could find her this easily, so could anyone else.

She'd been staying with a friend, and lying low, but tonight she'd gone out. Javier didn't enjoy watching her flirt with other men. He hadn't felt this jealous since Alexia's wedding. Actually, those circumstances didn't compare. By the time his ex married Gonzales, Javier had been over her.

He still wanted Faith. Desperately. But while she sipped her drink and cock-teased a stranger in an expensive suit, he stood on the street corner like a bum, his eye still black from the beating he'd taken.

He couldn't blame her for moving on. He was a fugitive. They had no future together. Even so, it hurt to see her smile at another man, days after she'd smiled at him. When she touched her breasts to his arm, Javier's blood boiled. He fought the impulse to charge in and drag her away. A few minutes later, her hairstylist friend had stepped between them, encouraging her to leave the club. She stumbled out the door in her high heels, giggling and tipsy. Her friend held on to her arm to steady her.

It was clear that their relationship was platonic, but Javier was jealous of him, too. He longed to be the one she laughed with, the man she leaned on.

Faith got into a car with her friend while Javier hopped on the bicycle he'd bought at a thrift shop. He wouldn't be able to retrieve his money from the storage locker until the heat died down, and he was already running low on cash. Luckily, he could pass for Mexican as easily as Californian. With his baseball cap and old clothes, he looked like an undocumented immigrant. He could work like one, too. He'd survive.

Instead of going to her coworker's apartment, they drove to Faith's. Her friend took her inside and came out a few minutes later, whistling.

Javier regretted telling her that she'd be safe as long as he kept his distance. He didn't think Nick would bother her, but he couldn't be sure. He had no idea who Kruger worked for, or why he'd spared her. What if someone decided Faith was a liability?

He'd assigned himself as her secret bodyguard for the next few weeks, and he vowed not to invade her privacy. She'd never need to know he was there. Even if she paraded boyfriends in and out of her bedroom, or performed sexual favors by the pool, he wouldn't give away his location. He owed her his protection. Her personal life was none of his business.

Parking his bike in the alley, he set up camp behind some bushes across the street from her apartment. She lived on the second floor in a building with minimal security. The front entrance was open; anyone could walk in. Out back, the pool area was surrounded by a tall fence with a locked gate.

He'd already scoped out the complex and memorized its floor plan. There were laundry facilities and a storage room. Each section of the building had a different staircase, offering a number of dark corners to crouch behind.

On the plus side, it was a quiet, artsy neighborhood, not gang-infested. It wasn't near the freeway or any of the major colleges. If Faith could afford to live here, she was doing well for herself. Perhaps hairstyling paid more than he thought, because she seemed to have an array of designer purses and shoes.

Maybe she'd been pampered by rich boyfriends.

He squashed the thought in annoyance. Faith wasn't Alexia. She might be flighty, but she liked sex for its own sake. He could tell. A gold digger wouldn't have been interested in scruffy Jay Norton. A coldhearted opportunist wouldn't have helped him escape, or slapped him for deceiving her, or cried when he left.

It didn't matter, anyway. He wasn't here to judge her character, and compared to him, everyone was a saint. As long as no one tried to attack her, he'd move on.

Hasta la vista, baby.

While he sulked in the dark, hungry and unwashed and alone, he catalogued all the cars on the street. He couldn't identify any suspicious vehicles or people. Traffic lulled. After about an hour, his eyelids started to droop.

Then a figure crept out of nowhere.

Javier snapped to attention, his pulse jackknifing. A man approached Faith's apartment complex on foot. He wore a jean jacket and motorcycle boots. His hair was cut military-style. He hurried up the sidewalk, casting a nervous glance over his shoulder. If he'd looked a little less conspicuous, Javier might have assumed he lived there. He reached for something underneath his jacket as he entered the stairway.

Hijo de puta.

There was no time for stealth, so Javier burst from the bushes and ran across the street. His only weapon was a bike chain wrapped around his fist. He clenched his fingers around the skin-warmed metal, his teeth gritted.

The instant Javier came through the entrance, he realized his mistake. The guy was lying in wait *for him*. He punched Javier in the face, hard. Javier reeled sideways from the impact, but he didn't let it knock him off balance. Instead of fighting against the momentum, he used it to spin around and strike back.

His chain-heavy fist slammed into the other guy's midsection, making him grunt in pain. The man was quick to retaliate with a brutal uppercut.

Javier staggered backward.

His opponent scrambled up the stairs, disappearing around the corner. Javier wiped the blood from his mouth, surprised he was still alive. This dumb-ass had gotten the drop on him, but he'd wasted his advantage.

If he had a gun, why hadn't he used it?

Unraveling the chain from his throbbing fist, he ascended the stairwell. This was Faith's section. At the corner, Javier hesitated, listening for movement. Sure enough, his attacker was right there. When the barrel of a pistol came into view, Javier swung his chain. The weapon discharged as the metal struck, burying a bullet in the stucco. Neither of them could hang on. As the chain flew out of his stinging hands, the gun clattered down the stairs.

Now Javier was going to make him pay.

Leaping up the last step, he advanced. Grabbing his opponent by the back of his jacket, he drove his head into the rough-textured wall. The man struggled to break free, so Javier body-checked him again.

When he was sufficiently stunned, Javier wrenched his arm behind his back. "You came here to hurt an innocent woman?"

"I came for you," he panted.

"Who sent you?"

He didn't answer. Javier doubted the Gonzales family had hired him, because he wasn't ruthless enough. Maybe he worked for the same boss as Nick. Before Javier could squeeze him for information, a woman appeared at the top of the stairway, her gun drawn.

"We're FBI," she shouted. "Drop your weapon!"

She didn't know he was unarmed. He glanced to his right, toward a railing that overlooked the pool. Fuck it. He shoved his attacker at the female agent and launched over it, dropping twenty feet before he hit the cool blue water. His elbow brushed the coping, narrowly missing a bone-shattering impact.

He sank all the way to the bottom and used his feet to push up, bubbles floating from his nostrils. When he surfaced, he felt as if he were swimming in slow motion. His clothes hampered his efforts and his shoes grew heavy. Gasping for breath, he found the edge and climbed over it, sloshing water as he lunged toward the gate.

"Jay!"

It was Faith. She called him by the wrong name. Maybe she preferred Jay, the nice guy, to Javier, the low-

life. But he couldn't resist one last look, so he glanced
up. The female agent was running down the steps with
his opponent. Faith stood on the terrace, leaning against
the railing as if she wanted to jump.

His heart lodged in his throat.

"Que...que nos encontramos otra vez!"

Her Spanish wasn't perfect, but she was.

"Ojalá," he said, kissing his fingertips.

God willing.

And he escaped through the gate, into the dark night.

CHAPTER TWENTY-SIX

HOPE WOKE to a phone call from Faith.

She said that Special Agent Ling had almost caught Javier Del Norte at her apartment. The FBI had set up a sting that didn't quite work. Javier had thwarted Faith's would-be attacker and jumped off the balcony to get away.

"Why weren't you at Charlie's?" Hope asked.

"I'm going there now."

She furrowed a hand through her hair, sighing.

"I think it's over," Faith said, sounding melancholy.

"What is?"

"Everything."

After making sure her sister was safe, Hope hung up the phone, promising to call her in the morning.

Was it really over? Gonzales was dead. Kruger and Morgenstern were dead. Meeks was in custody. The main players in the organization had been taken down, and the worst of the danger had passed. She'd rest easier when Dixon was cleared, but she felt reassured by the progress in the investigation.

She rose from the guest bed, her stomach growling. It was past midnight, and she'd skipped dinner.

Downstairs, Owen was awake, raiding the fridge. He gathered the ingredients to make a sandwich and carried them to the granite countertop, wincing in discomfort. His pain medication must have worn off.

"Let me," she said, taking the loaf of bread from his hand.

He probably wanted to do it himself, but her proximity made him uncomfortable. Muttering an agreement, he shuffled away and sat down at a barstool.

"How are you feeling?"

"Not bad."

"You slept for a long time."

"I had a nightmare," he said, frowning.

"About what?"

"I can't remember."

"You called out for Penny."

He rubbed a hand over his face, seeming embarrassed. "I still dream about the earthquake sometimes."

She started building the sandwiches, not wanting to disturb him with nosy questions. When she lifted the mustard jar questioningly, he nodded. "And this?" she asked, noticing the ketchup container.

"My mom makes them that way."

Hope added ketchup to his sandwich and sliced it down the middle, putting some potato chips on the side of the plate.

"Thanks," he said, digging in.

"Where is your mom?"

"Salton City."

"You're from there?"

"Yep."

Hope didn't ask if he planned to go back. Salton was a dead-end desert town a few hours east of San Diego.

She imagined that most young men wouldn't return by choice. "That's a rough place to grow up."

He shrugged, taking another bite.

She finished making her own sandwich and sat down next to him. They ate in companionable silence. "Sam showed me a picture of Penny."

"Yeah?"

"She's lovely."

A flush crept up his neck. He couldn't deny this.

"I asked him if her son was yours."

His eyes widened. "Why would you think that?"

"His coloring, I guess. And the way you looked together in the picture."

Owen didn't respond for several minutes. Finally he said, "If he was mine, I'd live closer and take care of him."

"Where do they live?"

"Los Angeles."

She heard the yearning in his voice, the dull ache. It gnawed her insides, too, whenever she thought of Grace.

"I like Sam with you," he said, changing the subject.

"What do you mean?"

"I've never seen him act this way." He wiped his mouth with a napkin. "Before you, he had two moods. Pissed off and indifferent."

Her lips quirked into a reluctant smile. "How many does he have now?"

"Three, at least."

She finished her last bite of sandwich, considering.

"Are you going to give him a chance?"

"I don't know," she said, pushing her plate away. "It's great that he got his memory back. He claims I had

something to do with his recovery. I wonder if he's…
overstimulated. Hopped up on adrenaline."

"You think he *enjoyed* getting hit over the head, or
searching the river for you?"

"No," she said. "I'm just not sure his feelings are
real."

He pondered her words carefully. "You're right about
one thing. A life-or-death situation can bring people together who might not normally…get along. It's a bond-
ing experience. But that doesn't mean the relationships
won't work out. Lauren and Garrett are a good example.
They just got married."

"They met during the earthquake?"

"Yes, and I know they're for real."

His affection for Penny and her son seemed genuine,
as well. She murmured good-night to him and wandered
back upstairs, uncertain.

Taking a shower always helped her think, so she
climbed into the stall in the guest bath and let the
pounding water soothe her. When she came out, the
answer was clear. She had to take Faith's advice and
start living.

Sam might hurt her. She might hurt him. Whatever
happened would be a move forward, which they both
desperately needed.

She didn't have any clean clothes to wear, so she
wrapped a towel around her body and glanced in the
closet. He had an expensive set of golf clubs that looked
unused. There were a couple of dry suits and wetsuits,
as well as a somber three-piece. She fingered the cloth,
wondering why he kept this garment here with his

sporting equipment. When a flash of gold in the back of the closet caught her eye, she pushed the suits aside.

It was an urn. Melissa's ashes. Apparently Sam had never gone to the summit at Mount Whitney to distribute them.

She closed the door quietly, her pulse racing. Was he ready to move on, or just using Hope as a temporary replacement? He said he was in love with her. Although she returned his feelings, she was nervous about taking the plunge.

Sam was a good man. Not a perfect man. He'd been honest with her about his plans to continue climbing. She felt reassured, if a bit exasperated, by his dedication. He wouldn't be an easy person to live with, but there was something comforting about that. She needed a strong partner, and so did he. They could challenge each other.

Clutching the towel to prevent it from slipping, she tiptoed to his bedroom. It was dark, but the door was ajar. When she knocked, it swung open.

He sat up in bed. "Hope?"

"Were you asleep?"

"Not really," he said, reaching out to turn on a bedside lamp. He was shirtless, a sheet tangled around his waist.

She closed the door behind her, trying not to stare at his beautifully sculpted physique. She'd seen it all and more. "I need to borrow some clothes."

He pointed at a chest of drawers on the other side of the room. It was a spare, masculine space, devoid of personal touches. She padded across the hardwood floor, glancing at her reflection in the rectangular mirror on the wall. Her eyes were wide with trepidation, her hair a disarray of damp curls.

What a temptress. Not.

"There should be some T-shirts on top," he said, watching her.

She opened the first drawer, selecting a soft gray V-neck and a pair of striped cotton boxer shorts.

"I'll take you by your place tomorrow to pick up a few things."

Setting the clothes on top of the dresser, she turned to face him. "I have an appointment with a therapist at ten o'clock."

"I'll drive you."

"Okay," she said, smiling. "It's a date."

He smiled back at her. Attending each other's doctor visits might become a regular activity for them. Then her choice of words sank in, and his expression changed. He jumped up from the bed in his underwear. "A date?"

She nodded.

His throat worked in agitation as he approached her. He seemed eager, but uncertain about where this was going. His utter lack of confidence was endearing, and kind of a turn-on. She suddenly felt very pleased with her decision.

"Are you sure?" he asked.

She let her towel drop to indicate that she was. His eyes darkened, traveling from her face to her breasts. Her nipples tightened from the visual caress. He continued south, lingering on the abbreviated triangle at the apex of her thighs.

Instead of touching her, he stood motionless, seeming sort of lust-struck. That suited her fine. She'd been fantasizing about exploring his lovely muscles, rousing him with her mouth. When she stepped forward, smoothing her palms over his pecs, his erection bumped her middle. She let out a huff of laughter.

"What?"

"You're already hard," she said, pressing her lips to the base of his throat. She squeezed his biceps, her nipples brushing his chest. When she slid her hand down his corrugated stomach, into the waistband of his boxer shorts, he sucked in a sharp breath.

"I can't help it."

She noticed his gaze drift over her shoulder. She followed it, seeing their reflection in the mirror. They made an erotic picture, with her naked back and his mostly naked front. Her fingers wrapped around him beneath the cotton.

She sank to her knees, offering him another view. His cock sprang free as she pushed his shorts down. He wasn't just hard; he was passion-flushed, painfully erect. She curled her hand around him and brought the tip to her lips, licking delicately.

He groaned, cupping the nape of her neck. She watched him watch her in the mirror. It was incredibly hot. She took him into her mouth, her eyes half-lidded.

This couldn't last. He was too aroused, and she was right there with him. She closed her eyes and sucked him deep, letting him guide her head up and down. Her nipples felt tight, her sex swollen. Making a humming sound at the base of her throat, she clenched her thighs together to assuage the ache.

"Wait," he rasped, stilling her movements.

She wanted him to come, but he eased out of her

mouth, removing himself from temptation. She stared up at him, her pulse pounding. He pulled her to her feet and brushed his thumb over her tingling lips. His erection jutted against her belly, thick and hard. A few strokes would probably get him off.

He kissed her desperately, plundering her mouth with his tongue. To finish this, he needed only to lift her up against the dresser and enter her. But instead of rushing things, he continued kissing her, tasting her parted lips.

"Turn around," he said, his voice hoarse.

When she didn't move, he took her by the shoulders, spinning her to face the drawers. She shivered with pleasure as he pushed aside her hair and kissed the back of her neck. God yes. He remembered what she liked.

Keeping his mouth locked on the nape of her neck, he cupped her breasts, kneading the soft flesh. She moaned for more, arching her back. He toyed with her nipples, pinching the distended tips. His hand skimmed down her belly to cover her mound. She gasped as his calloused fingertips found her, hot and wet.

He bit her neck gently, growling an order to spread her legs. She widened her stance, breathless with anticipation. He traced her slippery cleft and dipped a finger inside.

"Fuck," he groaned, removing his hand.

"Please."

He took a condom out of the drawer and put it on. Pressing against the small of her back, he urged her to lean forward. She braced her hands on the surface of the dresser, her heart pounding. He positioned himself against her. Hissing out a breath, he slid the blunt head of his penis into her slick opening.

Hope tried to take more of him, but he wouldn't let her. Trapping her against the drawers, he teased her with shallow strokes, barely penetrating her. She couldn't move, but she could see their reflection in the mirror. She watched, moaning with frustration, as his thick cock inched back and forth.

"Please," she repeated, begging for completion.

"Please what?"

"Come…inside me."

He gripped her hips, moving her body from the dresser to the floor in front of the mirror. He sank to his knees behind her and buried himself in her with one smooth thrust. She reveled in the sensation, gripping the soft woven rug beneath her fingertips. When he remained motionless, as if fighting for control, she straightened until her shoulders touched his well-muscled chest.

His eyes met hers in the mirror. Her cheeks were flushed, her nipples tight. Her sex stretched around him in a tight fit. He reached down to where their bodies were joined, strumming her clitoris in slow circles.

"Oh God," she panted, gripping his wrist.

"Like that?"

"Just like that."

He licked his fingertips and did it again, driving her crazy. She slid along his length, arching her spine and straining toward orgasm. When he bit down on her shoulder, she cried out his name, exploding in ecstasy.

Sam didn't wait for her to recover. Urging her onto her hands and knees, he surged forward, driving all the way to the hilt. She shuddered in delight, her inner muscles clenching around him. He drove into her again and again, thrusting as deep as he could get, penetrating the core of her being.

When she climaxed a second time, he followed her with a hoarse yell, his hips jerking violently. He stayed buried inside her for several moments, his heartbeat thundering against her back, his breath hot against her neck. Then he rose to discard the condom. He carried her to bed, wrapping his arms around her.

She drifted in and out of dreams, some about falling.

"Don't let go," she murmured.

"Never," he said, kissing the nape of her neck.

CHAPTER TWENTY-SEVEN

THE NEXT TWO weeks were the best of his life.

Sam spent as much time with Hope as possible while she was on leave. He drove to her psychologist appointments, and she attended his. Owen recovered well enough to return to park housing, but Hope stayed with Sam.

The drug smuggling scandal made national news. Phillip Meeks claimed to have been acting on Bill Kruger's instructions. He was trying to plead guilty to a lesser crime. Law enforcement hadn't caught up with Nick Kruger or Javier Del Norte, who'd been named as "persons of interest" in the investigation. Doug Dixon had been cleared of wrongdoing but demoted from his leadership position.

Hope seemed to be taking the upheaval in stride. There was some scrambling within NPS for a new manager. A district ranger from Yosemite had stepped in as Dixon's replacement. Hope would be transferred to Giant Forest, the most popular area of the park. Cordova had taken over Kruger's position at Kaweah.

As always, Hope's main concern was Faith. During another short visit to L.A., Hope told Sam she was worried about her sister's flighty behavior. Faith had been going out to clubs and seeing an ex-boyfriend.

Sam tried to offer Hope comfort and support without

judging Faith. He knew how difficult it was to make safe, healthy decisions when you were hurting.

"Give her time," he'd said.

Hope needed time, too. She'd let him in physically, holding nothing back in bed. He was always hungry for her, so he had no complaints on that front. They'd also grown closer emotionally, talking and laughing together. He cherished the playful moments with her as much as the quiet ones. But he wanted more.

He wanted her love.

The most difficult conversation they'd had was about Melissa. Sam still wanted to distribute her ashes at Mount Whitney, but he balked at the idea of Hope coming with him. It was a hard climb, and reaching the summit had been Melissa's dream. He didn't think Hope should feel obligated to fulfill it.

"I don't feel obligated," she'd said. "I have some goodbyes of my own to say."

They finally agreed to make the trip on the last weekend of her administrative leave. Melissa had planned to hike the High Sierra Trail, a strenuous seventy-mile trek that approached the mountain from the west side. Sam and Hope would drive around to the east face instead, which offered easier access. From that route, known as Whitney Portal, they could ascend the highest point in hours.

On the morning of the climb, they rose well before dawn. When they reached Iceberg Lake, the sun had risen, bathing the east-facing wall in brilliant white light. The upper section of the mountain was much like Angel Wings, Valhalla and the other sharp peaks in the area. It reached an altitude known as alpine climate, treeless and bare.

The east slope was in the rain shadow, as well. Most of the precipitation fell on the lush green blanket of the Sequoia National Forest. On the opposite side of the High Sierras, the landscape was barren. The desolate flat stretched out for hundreds of miles, into the sun-baked crags of Death Valley.

Sam's unease didn't dissipate until they reached the summit. He needed time to adjust, like everyone else. He might never completely overcome his fear that she would be killed or injured in an accident. With time and practice, he could be a more relaxed partner, better equipped to handle the emotional stress.

At the zenith, they stood side by side, awed by the view. Iceberg Lake resembled a pupilless blue eye in the valley below. It was humbling to know that the granite peaks surrounding them had been here, unchanged, for thousands of years.

After lunch, he took the ashes out of his pack and moved to the cliff's edge. It still hurt to think of Melissa's death, but he could face the memory of the accident without breaking down. He could also move beyond it, and focus on the good times. He could acknowledge her many strengths and flaws.

Tears burned in his eyes as he released the ashes. "Goodbye," he murmured, picturing her pretty face.

He said goodbye to her boundless ambition and unswerving confidence. Her kind heart and easy athleticism. Her passion and impatience, her quick mind and sharp tongue. To the wedding they'd never have; to their life together.

Although he was ready to let go, he'd loved her deeply, and no amount of time or healing would take all of the pain away.

When his emotions were under control again, he glanced at Hope. She grasped his hand, smiling at his sentimentalism. He wished he wasn't embarrassed about the tears, but he was, and probably always would be.

She had her own set of ashes to distribute. Last night, she'd made a list of the things she wanted to say goodbye to. When she was finished, she crumpled the paper into a ball and set it on fire inside a glass jar.

"Goodbye, Paul," she said, naming her high school sweetheart. "Goodbye to my feelings of resentment. Goodbye to my teenage dreams." Her voice trembled, but she soldiered on. "Goodbye to martyrdom. Goodbye to my jealousy of Grace's parents. Goodbye to guilt, and secrecy, and shame."

She let the ashes spill from the container, her eyes shining.

They lingered at the summit for another hour, exploring the area with other climbers. He enjoyed the air of exaltation among them, the grinning camaraderie and triumphant faces. This was why he climbed. Not for fame and glory and adrenaline, but for the simple satisfaction of setting a goal and achieving it.

Their plan for the afternoon was to hike down the east slope. Of the three trails available, they chose the one less traveled. It was more of a scramble than the others, with steeper drops and sharper switchbacks, but it was scenic and secluded.

A few miles down the path, a sturdy rope bridge stretched across a deep gorge. After they reached the other side, Hope paused to take in the majestic view. Glacier water rushed over boulders and fallen logs in a cool white cascade, feeding into a stream more than two hundred feet below.

"Beautiful," he said, wrapping his arms around her.

She rested her back against his chest, sighing with contentment. At least, he hoped it was. That's what he felt. Pure peace.

Her fingertips wandered a lazy path from his elbow to his hand. She touched the square bandage on the inside of his wrist. "What's this?"

Sam's pulse kicked up at the question. Since recovering his memory, he'd considered getting his tattoo removed. He didn't bother to cover it anymore, and he didn't need the visual reminder. But the tattoo was part of him and he wanted to keep it. Instead of discarding one memento, he'd added another on the opposite wrist.

He hesitated to reveal his new tattoo. Although his skin was healed well enough, he didn't know if she'd like the message. They hadn't exchanged any promises or made plans for the future. He hadn't even told her he loved her again. She seemed uncomfortable with romantic declarations, and he didn't want her to feel pressured.

He'd learned from his mistakes, however. He couldn't hide anything from her. So he peeled away the bandage, baring all.

Her mouth went slack as she read the script: *Hope Forever.* "When did you get that?"

"When you were in L.A. I thought about covering up the other one with a set of wings." He wasn't sure how she felt about him having another woman's name on his body. "I could still do that, I guess."

"No," she said, brushing her thumb over the new tattoo.

"You don't mind?"

"I know how much you loved her," she said, lifting her gaze to his face. "I'd never try to...replace her."

His chest tightened with emotion. He couldn't say he loved Hope more than he'd loved Melissa, but he was a different man with her. A better man, in many ways. For years, he'd chased thrill after thrill, always looking for a new adventure. After Melissa's accident, he'd actively courted death. Now he appreciated life. He cherished every moment.

"I don't want a replacement," he said. "I love *you*."

She stared up at him, her lips trembling. He thought about kissing her to save her from having to respond.

Then she took a deep breath. "I love you, too."

His heart lodged in his throat. For several seconds, he couldn't form any response. When he'd recovered enough to speak, he said, "Okay."

"Okay," she repeated, sputtering. "That's it?"

He took her by the hand, smiling at her incredulous expression. "When I thought you'd drowned in the river with Owen, I wanted to die. I'd never felt so low. Then I saw you alive, and I was overwhelmed with relief. That moment would have sustained me for the rest of my life. This one tops it. Hearing you say you love me back is beyond the limit. It's like...climbing above the sky."

Her eyes filled with tears. "Really?"

"Yes."

She wrapped her arms around his neck. "Who are you, and what have you done with Sam Rutherford?"

He laughed, hugging her back with pleasure. She'd

given him new hope, a new chance, a new life. Their bond felt strong and real and unbreakable. Together, they'd face the inevitable ups and downs, incredible highs and lows. Sam planned to live each moment to the fullest, embracing challenges and enjoying the climb.

He looked forward to every step.

CHAPTER TWENTY-EIGHT

Six months later

FAITH USUALLY LOOKED forward to the holidays.

She liked the music, the parties, the shopping sprees. December's cooler weather finally gave way to a short season of winter fashions. L.A.'s sun-drenched darlings brought out their high-heeled boots, designer jeans and fuzzy sweaters. The salon bustled with last-minute hair and nail appointments. Tips were good. There was an air of gaiety.

Not this year.

Business was great, and she enjoyed wearing her warmer clothes, but that was about it. The festive mood hadn't grabbed her, and it was ten days to Christmas. Charlie must have felt sorry for her, because he took her on a lunch date. They walked from the salon to an Italian restaurant, where Faith declined a glass of wine.

"You've really got it bad," Charlie said.

She sighed, shaking her head. After the skirmish at her apartment, she'd told Charlie about the sexual assault and kidnapping. He'd understood better than she'd anticipated, and she appreciated his support.

"Are you going home for Christmas?" he asked.

"Yes," she said dully. "My sister is bringing her boyfriend."

"What's wrong with that?"

"Nothing. He's hot and rich and my parents love him."

"He sounds like an asshole."

She laughed. "He's actually not. I'm the asshole."

"Why?"

"Because I should be happy for her. Instead, I'm wallowing."

"Wallowing is underrated," he said, lifting his wine glass in a toast. He'd broken up with his boyfriend a few weeks ago. "You can come to Aspen with me, if you'd like. Plenty of rich, hot assholes there."

Her mouth twisted into a rueful smile. She'd tried using other men to forget Javier. It hadn't worked so far. "Thanks for the invite, but I can't." Her mother would be upset if Faith blew off the holidays. She'd been a little extra attentive since the…incident, calling more often to check up on her. "You should come to Ojai."

"Do you have any brothers?"

"You know I don't."

They finished the meal and visited a nearby fountain, wallowing together. Charlie did a double take over Faith's shoulder. "Maybe we don't have to go all the way to Aspen," he said. "A hot guy is checking you out."

She didn't care.

"Faith…he's coming this way."

With reluctance, she glanced across the courtyard. The man walking toward them was Javier Del Norte. Her lips parted with surprise and she took a step back, almost stumbling into the fountain. "Oh my God."

"That's him, isn't it?"

She couldn't answer. Javier didn't look like himself.

Or he didn't look exactly the way she remembered him. His hair was pitch-black, and cropped short. His clothes might be vintage, but they weren't quirky or ironic. The worn Levi's jeans and the basic button-down shirt, not tucked in, were nondescript, at best.

Javier closed the distance between them, his expression cautious. "Hello," he said, nodding to Faith and Charlie.

Faith was at a loss. Was she supposed to introduce him? "Charlie, this is…"

"Jay," he supplied, shaking Charlie's hand.

Charlie returned the handshake warily.

"Do you have a minute?" Javier asked Faith.

"Sure," she said. Aware that he wanted to speak to her alone, she gestured to an empty bench on the other side of the courtyard.

"I'll wait right here," Charlie said.

Javier gave him a courteous nod. "Thank you for taking care of her."

Although his words sounded sincere, Charlie narrowed his eyes with suspicion. He considered Javier a dangerous criminal, and a threat to Faith's safety. His body language was protective, his muscles tense.

Faith stepped in and hugged her friend. "I'll be fine," she murmured in his ear. "You don't have to stay."

But he did, lingering at the fountain as they walked away.

"Is he your boyfriend?" Javier asked.

"What do you think?"

He shrugged. It was fairly obvious that Charlie was gay. "Stranger things have happened."

"Yes." Like their hookup.

She sat down on the bench next to him. It overlooked a tree-lined sidewalk that was popular with joggers and strollers. In the middle of downtown, the touch of greenery was refreshing. Not that she missed the woods.

"How have you been?" he asked.

"I've been better."

His eyes wandered over her face. "You look beautiful."

She still took pains with her appearance, but derived little satisfaction from it. This was partly his fault. A strange mix of joy and resentment warred within her. She was glad to see him. Glad to see him alive.

He'd seemed encouraged by her willingness to speak with him. At her apartment all those months ago, she'd called out drunkenly to him in Spanish: I hope we meet again. The time had dragged on since then with no word from him, and her feelings had changed. She'd begun to hope they wouldn't meet again.

Now she just wanted to forget him. If he thought she'd welcome him back into her life with open arms, he was wrong.

He lowered his voice. "The FBI caught up with me at a storage locker where I'd stashed some money. They gave me a new identity, and a green card, in exchange for consulting with them about the cartel."

"You're a legal citizen?"

He took a card out of his wallet to show her. It was white, not green.

"José Duran," she read.

"I've been going by Jay."

She handed it back, frowning. This wasn't what she'd expected.

"The agents don't think anyone from my old crew is looking for me, but they said it would be safer to change my name. I wasn't allowed to contact you before now. They just gave me clearance to meet you in a neutral location."

"Where do you live?"

"East L.A. I have an apartment. It's tiny, and the furniture is awful, but it's mine."

"And you get paid to do consulting?"

"No," he said, glancing back at the fountain. Charlie was watching. "They don't pay me. They confiscated the cash from my locker, too. I put in real hours at a real job."

"Doing what?"

"Trash collecting."

She tried not to grimace. "How do you like it?"

"Compared to jail or deportation, it's great," he said with a rueful smile. "The FBI placed me there, so I'm required to stay for two years."

"What will you do after that?"

"I don't know. I might go back to Venezuela."

"You want to go back?"

"No. I want to live here, with you."

She wasn't ready to hear that. For the past few months, she'd been trying to harden her heart against him. In some ways, she'd succeeded.

"Are you seeing anyone?" he asked.

"Have you been spying on me?"

"Not since…that night."

She remembered drinking too much and flirting with strangers before Charlie dragged her home from the bar. It wasn't the only time she'd sought out male attention.

She'd looked for comfort in all the wrong places. "I've been with other men."

His jaw tightened with displeasure. "I understand."

"No, you don't."

"Then tell me."

She gazed at the tall buildings in the distance, catching sight of a billboard advertisement for dental veneers. "During the first few weeks, I kept having nightmares about Nick. I was afraid of strange men, jumping out of my own skin. I thought sleeping with someone else would…cure my phobia."

"Did it?"

"Not really. I went back with Tom, my ex-boyfriend. He was safe. After the kidnapping, he finally saw me as a person, instead of a plaything he'd grown bored with. But my feelings for him weren't there anymore."

He said nothing. Feelings or no feelings, it was clear that he didn't want other men touching her.

This next part would probably enrage him.

"I liked myself the way I was," she said. "I liked… owning my sexuality. When Nick held me down against my will, he took that from me, and I wanted it back. So I went out with someone not quite as safe."

"Who?"

"Caleb."

He stared at her in dismay, stricken by the confession. "You did this to hurt me, not to heal yourself."

"Maybe."

"Was it good?"

"Yes."

Too agitated to sit there, he rose to his feet and stepped forward, putting some space between them.

Faith felt a twinge of regret. The sex with Caleb hadn't been special. His leg was in a brace, and he'd been "horny as hell" after getting the cast off. It was safe, because he had limited mobility, and not safe, because she didn't know him very well.

She stood to defend herself. "It wasn't *that* good."

"Did you see him more than once?"

"No. He's a jerk. I have no interest in seeing him again."

He let out a harsh laugh. Though humorless, it made her feel just a little bit like her former self. She moved closer, curling her hand around his upper arm. Lifting trash cans hadn't weakened his muscles any. Her tummy fluttered in awareness. The thrill of female admiration was pure Old Faith.

"It meant nothing," she continued, encouraged when he didn't pull away. "I didn't know where you were, or even if you were alive."

"You thought I was dead?"

She swallowed hard. "I considered it a distinct possibility. Hope told me that the FBI was no longer pursuing you."

"They already had me."

"Yes, well, I didn't know that. I couldn't stop worrying about you. I was…traumatized. I'm still not the same."

He looked down at her, weighing those words. He seemed reassured by the fact that her encounter with Caleb hadn't fixed any problems. "You need someone who cares about you *and* makes you feel sexy."

Tears pressed behind her eyes, because he was right. "Are you applying for the position?"

"You know I am."

She smiled and squeezed his arm, blinking the moisture from her eyes. She'd been wondering how to get her mojo back for six months. He'd thought of a reasonable solution in six minutes.

"What are you doing tomorrow night? I'll take you out on a date."

"Okay," she said, playing it cool. On the inside, she was squealing with glee. "I should get back to Charlie."

They said goodbye and made arrangements to meet at the fountain again. She rose on tiptoe to kiss his cheek, very close to his lips, before she walked away. In true Faith style, she left him staring after her, wanting more.

CHAPTER TWENTY-NINE

HOPE DIDN'T USUALLY look forward to Christmas.

During the holidays, she felt lonely and restless. She was more aware of the empty place inside her. The Sierras were quiet and still, the mountain peaks softened by a blanket of snow. It was a season of long, cold nights.

Not this year. With Sam, everything was different.

They were going to Ojai in a few days to visit her family. She couldn't wait to see Faith, who'd recently reunited with Javier. According to her sister, they were "taking things slow." Hope had laughed at Faith's coy tone, delighted for her. She sounded like herself, with a hint of new maturity. Her baby sister was All Grown Up.

She wasn't the only one. There was another reason this holiday season was extra special: Hope got her first letter from Grace.

Sam had pointed it out to her as soon as she came home from work. She'd been living with him for several months, so all of her mail got forwarded to his address. Heart racing, she tore the envelope open.

It was a basic Christmas card with a pair of red mittens on the front. Inside, there was a warm holiday greeting, signed by her adoptive parents. Hope was more interested in the folded, handwritten note. Her hands shook as she read it:

Hello.

My name is Grace. My mom says your name is Hope. I will call you by your first name if that's okay.

My parents said I could email you from their account. I don't have my own email or Facebook page yet, so I decided to write a real letter. They said they wouldn't read it if I didn't want them to.

I am eleven years old. You know that, I guess. I'm in the fifth grade. We have a dog named Buster. I like gymnastics and volleyball. My dad coaches my volleyball team. What I like most is reading. My favorite book is *Vampire Academy*. I wonder what you liked to do when you were eleven.

My parents said you were in high school when you had me. I think that would be hard. I watch the show *Teen Mom* sometimes. I wonder what you look like. I will send you a picture. Can you send me one?

I'm not sure what else to say. I want to know everything about you. I worry that my mom might be sad to read that. I love my mom a lot. She says we can meet in person this summer. I would like to see you.

Your daughter

Grace

P.S. Do you have any other kids? I've always wanted a brother or sister.

Hope read the letter five times, tears pouring down her face. When she handed it to Sam, he accepted with reverence, smiling at her sentimental reaction.

They spent the next hour going through her digital photos. Hope wanted to print and send the perfect one. She also planned to raid the box of extra pictures at her parents' house. Maybe Grace would enjoy some shots of her and Faith as kids.

She decided to wait until the following day to pen her response. There were so many ideas and stories bouncing around in her head. She didn't want to overwhelm Grace with too much information.

Instead of rushing ahead or worrying about the future, she settled in next to Sam on the couch in front of the fire. Enjoying the moment.

"Cheers," he said, touching his glass to hers.

She sipped her white wine while he enjoyed a whiskey on the rocks. The days were short, but they'd been taking advantage of the long, cold nights. Spending cozy evenings with him was no hardship.

"It's our anniversary," he announced.

"It is?"

"We met a year ago tonight."

Smiling, she set her wineglass aside. "I know how I'd like to celebrate," she said, snuggling closer. She dipped her finger into his tumbler and touched it to her lips, flavoring her mouth with whiskey.

"How?" he asked, tasting her with a light kiss.

"By taking off your clothes," she said, nibbling her way down his neck, "licking every inch of your body..." She reached into his tumbler again. Distracting him with kisses, she slipped an ice cube down the back of his shirt. "And locking you outside, naked!"

He jumped off the couch in surprise, shaking the ice free.

Hope laughed at his disgruntled expression. She never played pranks on him, but she was in high spirits. Everything seemed hilarious. When she stopped giggling, she noticed that he was just staring at her.

She wiped the tears from her eyes, taking a calming breath. "It was a joke."

"I know."

"You didn't think it was funny."

"I'm sorry," he said, raking a hand through his hair. He looked nervous, as if he had some bad news to share.

Her stomach sank. She'd felt so blessed lately, so ecstatic. Faith's phone call, and the letter from Grace, had pushed her into the stratosphere. But life couldn't be an embarrassment of riches for long. "What is it?"

"I have something to ask you. I've been planning it all week, and I wanted the moment to be perfect. Now I feel like I already screwed it up by mentioning our anniversary. You'd probably rather forget that night."

She didn't know what he was agonizing over, but he sounded so forlorn that she stood, lifting her hand to his cheek. "No."

"Are you sure?"

"Of course. I wouldn't make light of it if I was still upset."

Some of the tension in his face eased. "I'll stand outside naked anytime you like."

"Tell me something I don't know."

His lips curved into a smile. They'd stripped off their clothes in a number of remote settings. "Okay," he said, going down on one knee. While her heart fluttered with a pleasant sort of unease, he removed a black box from his pocket. "I want to be with you for the rest of my life. Will you marry me?"

Hope snatched the box from his upturned palm and opened it, her pulse racing. "What an obscene diamond," she gasped.

"I can buy a smaller one."

She tried the ring on for size. The slim white gold band fit her finger, and the diamond was beautifully clear. It wasn't quite a doorknob. "Yes."

"Yes, to a smaller stone?"

"Yes, I'll marry you."

He leaped up, wrapping her in a tight embrace and lifting her off her feet. She'd never thought she could be this happy, not in a million years. Not in her wildest dreams. "I love you so much," he said against her hair, his voice hoarse.

"I love you, too." The words came easy now, floating right off her tongue.

She was his. He was hers. Forever.

* * * * *

Don't miss Jill Sorenson's
next exciting romantic suspense,
BADLANDS.
Available January 2014!

There is a fine line between peril and passion

JILL SORENSON

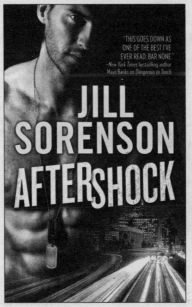

"THIS GOES DOWN AS
ONE OF THE BEST I'VE
EVER READ, BAR NONE."
—*New York Times* bestselling author
Maya Banks on *Dangerous to Touch*

JILL
SORENSON
AFTERSHOCK

As an emergency paramedic, Lauren Boyer is dedicated and highly capable. Until an earthquake strikes, trapping her beneath the freeway with a group of strangers—including Iraq war veteran Garrett Wright....

Available wherever books are sold!

REQUEST YOUR FREE BOOKS!

2 FREE NOVELS
FROM THE SUSPENSE COLLECTION
PLUS 2 FREE GIFTS!

YES! Please send me 2 FREE novels from the Suspense Collection and my 2 FREE gifts (gifts are worth about $10). After receiving them, if I don't wish to receive any more books, I can return the shipping statement marked "cancel." If I don't cancel, I will receive 4 brand-new novels every month and be billed just $6.24 per book in the U.S. or $6.74 per book in Canada. That's a savings of at least 22% off the cover price. It's quite a bargain! Shipping and handling is just 50¢ per book in the U.S. and 75¢ per book in Canada.* I understand that accepting the 2 free books and gifts places me under no obligation to buy anything. I can always return a shipment and cancel at any time. Even if I never buy another book, the two free books and gifts are mine to keep forever.

191/391 MDN F4XN

Name	(PLEASE PRINT)	
Address		Apt. #
City	State/Prov.	Zip/Postal Code

Signature (if under 18, a parent or guardian must sign)

Mail to the **Harlequin® Reader Service:**
IN U.S.A.: P.O. Box 1867, Buffalo, NY 14240-1867
IN CANADA: P.O. Box 609, Fort Erie, Ontario L2A 5X3

Want to try two free books from another line?
Call 1-800-873-8635 or visit www.ReaderService.com.

* Terms and prices subject to change without notice. Prices do not include applicable taxes. Sales tax applicable in N.Y. Canadian residents will be charged applicable taxes. Offer not valid in Quebec. This offer is limited to one order per household. Not valid for current subscribers to the Suspense Collection or the Romance/Suspense Collection. All orders subject to credit approval. Credit or debit balances in a customer's account(s) may be offset by any other outstanding balance owed by or to the customer. Please allow 4 to 6 weeks for delivery. Offer available while quantities last.

Your Privacy—The Harlequin® Reader Service is committed to protecting your privacy. Our Privacy Policy is available online at www.ReaderService.com or upon request from the Harlequin Reader Service.

We make a portion of our mailing list available to reputable third parties that offer products we believe may interest you. If you prefer that we not exchange your name with third parties, or if you wish to clarify or modify your communication preferences, please visit us at www.ReaderService.com/consumerchoice or write to us at Harlequin Reader Service Preference Service, P.O. Box 9062, Buffalo, NY 14269. Include your complete name and address.

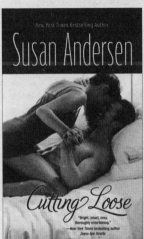

PORTIA DA COSTA

When it comes to diamonds—like their men—some women prefer them rough

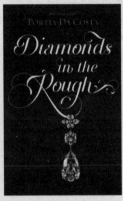

Thanks to her grandfather's complicated will, Miss Adela Ruffington, along with her mother and sisters, is about lose her home and income to a distant cousin, the closest male heir to the Millingford title. For Adela, nothing could be more insulting—being denied her rightful inheritance for a randy scoundrel like Wilson, the very man who broke her heart following a lusty youthful dalliance years ago.

Still smarting from the betrayal of his latest paramour, Wilson Ruffington never anticipates the intense desire Adela again stirs within him. Despite his wicked tongue and her haughty pride, their long-ago passion instantly reignites at a summer house party, the experience they've gained as adults only adding fuel to the flames.

Wilson and Adela are insatiable, but civility outside of the bedroom proves impossible. Determined to keep Adela in his bed, Wilson devises a ruse—a marriage of convenience that will provide her family with a generous settlement, as well as prevent scandalous whispers. Their plan works perfectly until family rivalries and intrigue threaten to destroy their arrangement...and the unspoken love blooming beneath it.

Available wherever books are sold!

Be sure to connect with us at:
Harlequin.com/Newsletters
Facebook.com/HarlequinBooks
Twitter.com/HarlequinBooks

www.Harlequin.com

PHPDC811

Sophie Littlefield

Of living things there were few, but they carried on

"Evocative, sensual, harrowing."
—*Publishers Weekly* on *Aftertime*, starred review

Cass Dollar is a survivor. She's overcome the meltdown of civilization, humans turned mindless cannibals and the many evils of man.

But from beneath the devastated California landscape emerges a tendril of hope. A mysterious traveler arrives at New Eden with knowledge of a passageway North—a final escape from the increasingly cunning Beaters. Clutching this dream, Cass and many others follow him into the unknown.

Journeying down valleys and over barren hills, Cass remains torn between two men. One—her beloved Smoke—is not so innocent as he once was. The other keeps a primal hold on her that feels like Fate itself. And beneath it all, Cass must confront the worst of what's inside her—dark memories from when she was a Beater herself. But she, and all of the other survivors, will fight to the death for the promise of a new horizon....

Available wherever books are sold!

Be sure to connect with us at:

Harlequin.com/Newsletters

Facebook.com/HarlequinBooks

Twitter.com/HarlequinBooks

HARLEQUIN® LUNA™

™ www.Harlequin.com

LSL354